WELCOME TO
DESOLATION ROAD

DR. ALIMANTANDO—The town's founder and resident genius, he perfects his homemade time machine and vanishes forever. Sort of.

PERSIS TATTERDEMALION—An ace flier grounded forever in Desolation Road, she tends bar at the Bethlehem Ares Railroad/Hotel and waits for the chance to reclaim her dream.

RAJANDRA DAS—The railroad hobo who has a mystical way with machines—there isn't a mechanical object on Mars that doesn't love him.

THE BABOOSHKA—A barren, feisty grandmother, she wants nothing more than to settle down with a good farming man and grow herself a child—in a fruit jar.

PATERNOSTER JERICHO—Overthrown crime lord of the Exalted Families, he says he's "just passing through" Desolation Road, but twenty years later he still says the same thing.

THE GALLACELLI BROTHERS—Ed, Louie, and Umberto. Identical triplets, so identical they each fell in love with—and married—the same woman . . .

These are just a few of the inhabitants of Desolation Road. They and their children shaped a town, a planet, and a history. And the only thing they had in common was their belief that destiny had passed them by . . .

Other Bantam Spectra books of interest.
Ask your bookseller for titles you may have missed

RUMORS OF SPRING
BY RICHARD GRANT

MEMORY WIRE
BY ROBERT CHARLES WILSON

THE YEARWOOD TRILOGY
BY PAUL HAZEL

A MASK FOR THE GENERAL
BY LISA GOLDSTEIN

DOVER BEACH
BY RICHARD BOWKER

DESOLATION ROAD

IAN McDONALD

BANTAM BOOKS
TORONTO • NEW YORK • LONDON • SYDNEY • AUCKLAND

DESOLATION ROAD
A Bantam Spectra Book / February 1988

ISBN 0-553-27057-5

Published simultaneously in the United States and Canada

Bantam Books are published by Bantam Books, Inc. Its trademark, consisting of the words "Bantam Books" and the portrayal
of a rooster, is Registered in U.S. Patent and Trademark Office
and in other countries. Marca Registrada. Bantam Books, Inc.,
666 Fifth Avenue, New York, New York 10103.

PRINTED IN THE UNITED STATES OF AMERICA

O   0 9 8 7 6 5 4 3 2 1

To all the numerous people who helped raise Desolation Road from the dust, and especially to Patricia—architect, constant supporter, and First Lady of the town

DESOLATION
ROAD

1

For three days Dr. Alimantando had followed the green-person across the desert. Beckoned by a finger made from articulated runner beans, he had sailed over the desert of red grit, the desert of red stone, and the desert of red sand in pursuit of it. And each night, as he sat by his fire built from scraps of mummified wood, writing in his journals, the moonring would rise, that tumbling jewel-stream of artificial satellites, and it would draw the greenperson out of the deep places of the desert.

On the first night the meteors were flickering high in the stratosphere when the greenperson came to Dr. Alimantando.

"Let me near your fire, friend, let me have warmth, give me shelter, for I am of a warmer age than this." Dr. Alimantando gestured for the greenperson to draw closer. Observing the strange, naked figure, Dr. Alimantando was moved to ask, "What manner of a creature are you?"

"I am a man," said the greenperson. His mouth, his lips, his tongue, showed leaf-green as he spoke. His teeth were small and yellow like nibs of maize. "What are you?"

"I also am a man."

"Then we are the same. Stoke up the fire, friend, let me feel the blaze." Dr. Alimantando kicked a knot of gray wood and sparks fled upward into the night. After a time the greenperson said, "Have you water, friend?"

"I have, but I want to be careful with it. I don't know how long I will be crossing this desert, or if I will find any water on my journey."

"I will lead you to water tomorrow, friend, if you will give me your flask tonight."

Dr. Alimantando was still for a long time beneath the tumbling lights of the moonring. Then he unhooked one of his flasks from his pack and passed it over the flames to the greenperson. The greenperson drained the flask dry. The air about him sparkled with an aroma of verdure, like forests after spring rain. Then Dr. Alimantando slept and did not dream at all.

The next morning there was only a red rock by the embers of the fire where the greenperson had sat.

On the second night Dr. Alimantando made camp and ate and wrote in his journal. Then he sat, just sat, made vast with the exhilaration of the desert of stone. He had sailed and sailed and sailed, away from the hills of Deuteronomy, away from the desert of red grit, through the desert of red stone, across a land of chasms and fissures, like a petrified brain, over polished stone pavements, between eroded pinnacles of dark volcanic glass, through forests petrified for a billion years, down water-courses dry a billion years, through wind-sculpted palisades of ancient red sandstones, over haunted mesas, plunging over thin granite lips into infinite echoing canyons, gripping wide-eyed with terror to every handhold as the windboard's pro-magnetic levitators fought to hold it aloft. He had run before the long wind, he had sailed and sailed and sailed until the first pinpricks of the evening stars pierced the sky.

As he sat thus, bluehot lasers flickered fitfully across the vault above him, and the greenperson came to him again.

"Where is the water you promised?" asked Dr. Alimantando.

"Everywhere was water once and will be water again," said the greenperson. "This stone was sand once and will be sand again on a beach a million years from here."

"Where is the water you promised?" cried Dr. Alimantando.

"Come with me, friend." The greenperson led him to a notch in the red cliff and there, in the deeper darkness, was the chuckling of lonely, clear water, trickling from a crack in the rock and dropping into a small dark pool. Dr. Alimantando filled his water flasks but did not drink. He was afraid of defiling the ancient lonely water. Where the greenperson had stood, pale green shoots now pushed through the damp imprints of his feet. Then Dr. Alimantando slept and did not dream that night at all.

The next morning there was a withered gray tree by the embers of the fire where the greenperson had sat.

Upon the third night after the third day, when he had sailed the desert of red sand, Dr. Alimantando built his fire and made his camp and wrote his observations and speculations into his leather-bound journals in his fine, delicate hand, all loops and curlicues. He was weary that night; the passage of the desert of sand had drained him dry. At first he had tingled with exhilaration and wind-driven sand as he rode the wind-board up and over, up and over, up and over the ever-breaking waves of sand. He had ridden the red sand and the blue sand, the yellow sand and the green sand, the white sand and the black sand, wave after wave after wave until the waves broke him and left him drained dry, exhausted to face the desert of soda and the desert of salt and the desert of acid. And beyond those deserts, in the place beyond exhaustion, was the desert of stillness, where could be heard the ringing of distant bells, as if from the campaniles of cities buried a billion years beneath the sand, or from the campaniles of cities a billion years yet unborn that would stand there. There, at the heart of the desert, Dr. Alimantando stopped, and beneath a sky huge with the riding lights of a SailShip arriving at the edge of the world, the greenperson came a third time to him. He squatted upon his heels beyond the edge of the firelight, drawing figures in the dust with his forefinger.

"Who are you?" asked Dr. Alimantando. "Why do you haunt my nights?"

"Though we journey through different dimensions, like you I am a traveler across this dry and waterless place," said the greenperson.

"Explain these 'different dimensions.'"

"Time and space. You space, I time."

"How can this be?" exclaimed Dr. Alimantando, who was passionately interested in time and temporality. Because of time he had been driven out of his home in the green hills of Deuteronomy, labeled "demon" and "wizard" and "eater of children" by neighbors who could not accommodate his harmless and creative eccentricity within their tightly defined world of cows, clapboard houses, sheep, silage, and white picket fences. "How can you travel in time, something I have sought to accomplish for years?"

"Time is a part of me," said the greenperson, standing tall and brushing his body with his fingertips. "So I have learned to control it as I have learned to control any other part of my body."

"Can this skill be taught?"

"To you? No. You are the wrong color. But one day you will learn a different way, I think."

Dr. Alimantando's heart leaped.

"How do you mean?"

"That's for you to decide. I am here only because the future demands it."

"You riddle much too well for me. Say what you mean. I can't abide obtuseness."

"I am here to lead you to your destiny."

"Oh? So?"

"Unless I am here, certain trains of events will not come to pass; this my fellows have decided, for all time and space is theirs to manipulate, and they have sent me to guide you to your destiny."

"Be more explicit, man!" cried Dr. Alimantando, his quick temper flaring. But the firelight flickered and the sky-filling sails of the Praesidium vessel twinkled in the light of the vanished sun, and the greenperson was gone. Dr. Alimantando waited in the lee of his wind-board, waited until his fire died to red-glowing embers. Then, when he knew the greenperson would not be returning that night, he slept, and dreamed a steel dream. In this dream titanic machines the color of rust peeled back the skin of the desert and laid iron eggs in its tender flesh. The eggs hatched into squirming metal larvae, hungry for hematite, magnetite, and kidney ore. The steel maggots built for themselves a towering nest of chimneys and furnaces, a city of belching smoke and hissing steam, of ringing hammers and flying sparks, of rivers of white molten steel and pulpy white worker drones who served the maggots.

The next morning Dr. Alimantando woke to find the wind had risen in the night and covered the wind-board with sand. Where the greenperson had squatted at the edge of the firelight was a cracked boulder of green malachite.

The breeze strengthened and carried Dr. Alimantando

away from the heart of the desert. He breathed in the wine-sharp air and listened to the crack of the wind in the sails and the whisper of windblown sand streaming away before him. He felt the sweat dry on his skin and the salt-burn etch into his face and hands. He sailed and he sailed and he sailed, all morning. The sun had just reached its zenith when Dr. Alimantando saw his first and last mirage. A line of pure, shining silver ran straight through his musings on time and its travelers: purest, bright-shining silver, running east-west above a line of low bluffs which seemed to mark the end of the desert of sand. Drawing nearer, Dr. Alimantando discerned dark shadows in the silver glare and a reflected green glow, as if from green things that might be growing there.

Trick of a dry mind, he told himself, portaging the floating wind-board up a faint track through the cave-riddled bluffs, but on reaching the top of the rise he saw that it was not a trick of a dry mind, nor any mirage. The glow of greenness was indeed the glow of green growing things, the shadow the dark silhouette of a peculiar outcropping of rock which bore on its summit an antennae-feathery microwave relay tower, and the line of silver was precisely that, two sets of parallel steel standard-gauge railroad tracks catching the sun.

Dr. Alimantando walked a little while in the green oasis remembering what green smelled like, what green looked like, how green felt under his feet. He sat listening to the chuckling of water running through the cascading system of little irrigation ditches and the patient chunk, creak of the wind-pumps drawing it up from some stratum of subterranean aquifer. Dr. Alimandanto helped himself to bananas, figs, and pomegranates and ate a moody lunch in the shade of a cottonwood tree. He was glad to be at the end of the stern desert lands, yet the spiritual wind that had carried him through that separate landscape had died out of him. The sun beamed down on the bee-buzzy oasis and Dr. Alimantando slipped into a lazy, comfortable siesta.

An indefinite time later he was woken by a sting of grit on his cheek. For a closed-eyed, lazy moment the significance escaped him. Then realization struck him like a nail hammered between his eyes. He sat bolt upright, shivered to the pith by a bolt of pure horror.

In his haste he had forgotten to tether the wind-board.

Carried off by the rising wind, the loose wind-board bobbed and swooped across the dry flats. Helpless, Dr. Alimantando watched his only means of deliverance sail away from him across the High Plains. He watched the bright green sail until it vanished into a speck of color blindness on the horizon. Then for a long and stupid time he stood trying to think what to do, but he could not think of anything but that mocking, bobbing wind-board. He had lost his destiny, he had let it sail away from him on the wind. That night the greenperson would step out of time to talk with him but he would not be there because he had missed his destiny and all those trains of events that the great minds of the greenpersons had foreseen would never come to be. All gone. Sick with stupidity and disgust, Dr. Alimantando set down his pack and hoped for rescue. Perhaps a train might come up the line. Perhaps he might tinker with some mechanism in the relay tower to signal his distress through the airwaves. Perhaps the owner of this fertile, green, deceptively soft place might help him. Perhaps . . . perhaps. Perhaps this was all just a siesta dream from which he might waken to find his battered wind-board floating beside him.

Perhapses led to if-onlys. If only he had not fallen asleep, if only he had tied that rope . . . if only.

A molar-grating subsonic rumble shook the oasis. The air shivered. Water trembled in drops from the leaves of the plants. The metal relay tower shuddered and Dr. Alimantando leaped to his feet in consternation. There seemed to be some disturbance beneath the desert for the surface boiled and moiled as if some huge object was tumbling and turning deep below. The sand blistered into a great red boil and burst, shedding torrents of sliding grit, to reveal an enormous boxlike thing, bright orange, with soft rounded edges, emerging from under the Great Desert. Its mountainous flanks bore the word **ROTECH** lettered in black. Drawn by his fatal curiosity, Dr. Alimantando crept nearer to the edge of the bluffs. The orange box-thing, big as a house, sat on the desert floor, humming potently.

"An orph," whispered Dr. Alimantando, heart pounding in awe.

—Good afternoon, man! said a sudden voice inside Dr. Alimantando's head.

"What?" yelped Dr. Alimantando.

—Good afternoon, man. I apologize for not greeting you more readily, but you see, I am dying, and I am finding the process most troublesome.

"Pardon?"

—I am dying; my systems are failing, snapping like threads, my once-titanic intellect is plunging toward idiothood. Look at me, man, my beautiful body is scarred, blistered, and stained. I am dying, abandoned by my sisters, who have left me to die in this dreadful desert rather than on the edge of the sky as an orph should, shields down and blazing to brief stellar glory in the upper atmosphere. A curse upon those faithless sisters! I tell you, man, if this is what the younger generation has come to, then I am glad to be leaving this existence. If only it weren't so undignified. Perhaps you can help me to die with dignity.

"Help you? You? You're an orph, a servant of the Blessed Lady; you should help me! Like you, I am abandoned here, and if I am not aided, my demise will shortly follow your own. I have been abandoned here by capricious fate, my means of transport has failed me."

—You have feet.

"Surely you're joking."

—Man, do not trouble me with your petty needs. I am past aiding you. I cannot transport you away from this place; I cannot transport myself even. Both you and I will remain here, in the place I have created. Admittedly, your presence here is unscheduled, much less official; the Five Hundred Year Plan does not allow settlement in this micro-environment for another six years, but you may stay here until a train comes past to take you somewhere.

"And how long will that be?"

—Twenty-eight months.

"Twenty-eight months?"

—I am sorry, but that is the forecast of the Five Hundred Year Plan. The environment I have prepared is admittedly rough and ready, but it will support and sustain you and after my death you will have access to all the equipment within me. Now, if you have quite finished troubling me with your woes, may I address myself to mine?

"But you must take me away from here! It is not my destiny to be . . . whatever it is you want for me. . . ."

—Communications systems warden.

"A communications systems warden: there are great events I must set in motion elsewhere!"

—Whatever your destiny, it must be worked out here from now on. Now, kindly spare me your whinings, man, and let me die with a little dignity.

"Die? Die? How can a machine, a ROTECH environmental engineering module, an orph, die?"

—I will answer this one question, and then I will answer no more. The life of an orph is long, I myself am almost seven hundred years old, but we are no less mortal than you, man. Now, give me peace and commit my soul to the care of Our Lady of Tharsis.

The pervasive hum ceased abruptly. Dr. Alimantando held his breath in anticipation until it was uncomfortable, but the orph sat unchanging and unchanged on the red sand. In reverent silence Dr. Alimantando explored the little handmade kingdom the orph had bequeathed to him. He found particularly fine caves threading the outcrop of rock which bore the microwave relay; these Dr. Alimantando chose for his home. His few possessions seemed trivial in the large round caverns. He unrolled his quilt bag to air and went to pick dinner.

Darkness was falling. The first jewels of the moon-ring were shining in the sky. Up there the unfeeling orphs were rolling and tumbling, forever caught in the act of falling. Trapped by soil and gravity, their moribund sister cast giant purple shadows across the sand. Dr. Alimandando ate a spiritless supper and went to sleep. At two minutes of two a great voice woke him up.

—God rot ROTECH! it cried. Dr. Alimantando hurried through the pitch-black caves to see what was happening. The night air hummed with power, searchlight beams lanced the darkness, and sections of the orph's mighty body slid in and out, open and shut. The orph sensed Dr. Alimandando shivering in his nightshirt, and transfixed him like a martyred saint with its searchlights.

—Help me, man! This dying thing is not as easy as I had imagined.

"That's because you are a machine and not a human,"

shouted Dr. Alimantando, shielding his eyes against the searchlights' glare. "Humans die very easily indeed."

—Why can one not die when one wants to? Help me, man, help me, come down to me and I will show you how you can be merciful to me, for this creeping debility, this mechanical incontinence, is intolerable. Come down to me, man. Help me!

So Dr. Alimantando scrambled barefoot down the rough trail up which he had portaged that morning. He realized that he must have sailed over the buried orph without ever knowing. Strange things, strange things. He hurried over the yet-warm sand to the humming face of the behemoth. A dark spot appeared on the smooth metal about the size of a twenty centavo piece.

—This is my systems termination activator. Touch it and I will cease to be. All my systems will shut down, all my circuits will fuse and I will die. Do it, man.

"I don't know . . ."

—Man, I am seven hundred years old, as old as this earth that you walk upon; does old age no longer command respect among you humans in these degenerate days? Respect my wishes, I desire nothing more than to be gone. Touch the spot. Do it, man. Help me.

Dr. Alimantando touched the dark spot and at once it faded into the warm orange metal. Then very slowly, very gradually, the life-hum of the orph dwindled and faded and died and was gone into the silence of the Great Desert. As the great machine relaxed into death, its multitudinous panels, hatches, and sections opened, revealing the marvelous mechanisms of its interior. When he was quite sure that the orph was dead, Dr. Alimantando crept back to his bed, troubled and guilty over what he had done.

In the morning he went to pick the body of the orph he had killed. From it he built, over five days of furious, driving, and utterly enjoyable labor, a lozenge-shaped solar collector five times as tall as himself and mounted it, with some difficulty, on a wind-pump gantry. Energy and hot water secured, he went on to knock windows in the walls of his caves and glazed the unparalleled view of the Great Desert with plastic from the orph's polymerization plant. He dismembered the corpse and carried it piece by piece up the bluffs to his new home. He rooted through the bowels of the machine to carve out chunks of machinery that might make good automatic cultivators, irrigation pumps, electrical heating plates, lighting panels, methane digesters, sprinkler systems, all with just a little bit of work and inventiveness. Dr. Alimantando worshipped inventiveness, particularly his own. Every new improved device delighted him for days on end until he built the next one. Day by day the orph was reduced to a pitiful shell, and then to sections as Dr. Alimantando built new solar-collectors, then to plates, and then one night the storm wind blew really hard, so hard that Dr. Alimantando, upon his homemade bed, shivered and curled up inside his quilt bag. In the morning the bones of the dead machine had vanished like an ancient city beneath the drifting sands.

But through its death Dr. Alimantando had transformed the waiting oasis into an actual, comfortable, technological hermitage, a private world unknown even to those who had built the world, where a man might ponder long and deep upon destiny, and density, time, space, and the meaning of life. All this Dr. Alimantando did, and paper being scarce, he wrote his speculations on the walls of his caves in black charcoal. For a year and a day he covered his walls with algebraic expressions and theorems in symbolic logic, and then one afternoon he saw the steam of a train plume on the western horizon and knew that the orph's promise had come true, and all of seven months early. He waited until the train was close enough for him to read the name Bethlehem Ares Railroads, and then went up the topmost chamber in his house, his weather-room, and sat looking out at the great desert until the train had passed over the eastern horizon. For he realized that destiny is a numinous, quicksilver thing; from his studies he knew that it took many paths through the landscapes of time and paradox to reach its destination, for were not destiny and destination the same word spelled with different letters? This was his destiny, to live a life of fruitful solitude atop a desert pinnacle. He could think of worse things. So one morning, shortly after the first train in history passed through Dr. Alimantando's universe, he took himself and a bottle of peapod wine to the weather-room. The topmost cave, with its four windows pointing out in each direction of the compass, was of such fascination to him that he visited it only rarely, so that it would remain special. He looked out upon each preview for a long time. Then he poured a glass of peapod wine, and another, and another, and another, and with the last drop from the bottle he raised his glass and gave a name to everything he could see.

"Desolation Road," he slurred, drinking down the final glass of peapod wine. "You are Desolation Road." And Desolation Road it remained, even though Dr. Alimantando realized when he sobered up that he had not meant Desolation Road at all, but Destination Road.

2

Mr. Jericho had pumped the rail-bogie through forests and plains. He had it through meadows and metropolises. He had pumped it through paddy-fields and orchards, marshes and mountains. Now he was pumping it through the Great Desert. He was patient. He was obdurate. He was a small gnarled man, tough and black as the polished root of some desert tree, ageless and adamant. He would pump that hand-crank off the edge of the world if it would hide him from the men who wanted to kill him. They had found him in Telpherson, they had found him in Namanga Loop, they had found him in Xipotle and even he had had difficulty in finding Xipotle. For five days he had looked over his shoulder and then on the sixth day it was no longer necessary, for the city-dressed killers had stepped off the train, drawing every eye to them, and Mr. Jericho left that same hour.

It had been a move of desperation, striking out across the Great Desert, but desperation and desert were all that was left to Mr. Jericho. There were blisters on his hands from the hot thrust-bar and his water was running low, but he kept pumping pumping pumping that ridiculous hand-crank rail-bogie across kilometers and kilometers and kilometers of stone and blazing red sand. He did not relish dying in the stone and blazing red sand. It was no way for a Paternoster of the Exalted Families to die. So said Jim Jericho. So said the collected wisdom of his Exalted Ancestors tumbling in the limbochip embedded in his hypothalamus. Perhaps an assassin's needle was preferable. And perhaps not. Mr. Jericho grasped the thrust-bar once more and slowly, painfully, creaked the bogie into motion.

He had been the youngest Paternoster to accede to the Exalted Lines and had needed all the stored wisdom of his forefathers, including his lamented immediate predecessor, Paternoster Willem, to survive his first few months in office. It was the Exalted Ancestors who had prompted his move from Metropolis to the New World.

—A growing economy, they'd said, a thousand and one operational niches for us to exploit. And exploit them he had, for exploitation was the purpose of the Exalted Families: crime, vice, blackmail, extortion, corruption, narcotics, gambling, computer fraud, slavery: a thousand and one economic niches. Mr. Jericho had not been the first but he had been the best. The audacity of his criminal daring may have taken the collective public breath away in gasps of outraged admiration, but it also provoked his rivals into forsaking their petty divisions and allying to destroy him and his Family. Peace restored, they could resume their internecine strife.

Mr. Jericho paused to wipe salt sweat from his brow. Even aided by the Damantine Disciplines, his strength was nearing its end. He closed his eyes to the sun-sand glare and concentrated, trying to squeeze his adrenal gland into triggering the noradrenaline surge that would power him onward. The voices of the Exalted Ancestors clamored inside him like crows in a cathedral; words of advice, words of encouragement, words of admonition, words of contempt.

"Shut up!" he roared at the ion-blue sky. And it was quiet. Strengthened by his denial, Mr. Jericho seized the push-bar once more. The bar went down. The bar went up. The bogie creaked into motion. The bar went down. The bar went up. As it came up Mr. Jericho caught a glimpse of a green shimmer on the close horizon. He blinked, wiped stinging sweat out of his eyes, looked harder. Green. Complimentary green on red. He disciplined his vision as he had been taught by Paternoster Augustine, focusing on the boundaries between objects where differences became apparent. Thus aided, he could distinguish tiny pinpricks of light: sunlight glinting from solar panels, deduced the massed wisdoms of the Exalted Ancestors. Green on red and solar panels. Habitation. Mr. Jericho seized the thrust-bar with renewed vigor.

Between his feet were two items. One was a silk paisley-pattern scarf. Wrapped in it was a manbone-handled needle-pistol, traditional weapon-of-honor among the Exalted Families. The other was a deceptively small leather bag, of the type once called Gladstone. It held three and a quarter million New Dollars in United Bank of Solstice Landing bills of large denomination. These two items, along with the clothes on his back and the shoes on his feet, were the only things Mr. Jericho had been able to take with him on the Eve of Destruction.

His enemies had struck all at once, everywhere. Even as his empire collapsed around him in an orgy of bombings, burnings, and murder, Mr. Jericho had paused for a moment to admire his adversaries' efficiency. Such was the path of honor. He had sadly underestimated them, they were not the bumpkins and petty parochial war lords he had mistaken them for. He would know better next time. And they in their turn had underestimated Jameson Jericho if they thought that he would fall to them. His staff was dying around him: very well, he would work alone then. He activated his escape contingency. In the fractional instant before the virus programs dissolved his data-net into protein soup Jameson Jericho had a new identity. In the split-split-split-second before the government audit programs battered into his credit-matrix, Jameson Jericho funneled seven million dollars into false company deposit accounts in bank branches in fifty small towns across the northern hemisphere of the planet. He had debited only what lay in his black Gladstone bag by the time the Paternosters penetrated his falsified death (poor dupe of a doppelganger, but business was business) and sent assassins and tracer programs out after him. Jameson Jericho left behind him home, wife, children, everything he had ever loved and everything he had ever created. Now he was running across the Great Desert on a stolen Bethlehem Ares Railroad's pump-bogie in search of the last place in the world anyone would think of looking for him.

It was drawing on evening when Mr. Jericho arrived at the settlement. It was not impressive, least of all to a man accustomed to the grand architectural vistas of the ancient cities of the Grand Valley, who grew up on Metropolis, the ring city, the mightiest city of all. There was one house, a rough adobe shack propped against an outcrop of window-pocked red rock, one microwave relay tower, a handful of solar-collectors and wind-pumps, and a lot of slightly unkempt green garden. Yet the very isolation of this place impressed Mr. Jericho greatly. No one would ever look for him here. He climbed down from the creaking bogie to soak his blisters in the water-butt beside the house. He dampened his red handkerchief and dabbed the base of his neck with the warm water while mentally cataloging the market garden. Corn, beans, matoke, onions, carrots, potatoes, white and sweet; yams, spinach, various herbs. Water trickled redly through irrigation channels between allotments.

"Should do nicely," said Mr. Jericho to himself. The Exalted Ancestors agreed. A desert hawk croaked from the top of the microwave tower.

"Hello!" shouted Mr. Jericho at the top of his voice. "Helloooooooo . . ." There was no echo. There was nothing for his voice to echo from, save the red hills on the southern horizon. "Hellooooo . . ." After a time a figure emerged from the low adobe shack; a tall, thin man, very brown, like leather. He had long twirling moustachioes.

"Jericho's the name," said Mr. Jericho, eager to gain the advantage.

"Alimantando," said the tall, thin leatherman. He had a doubtful look. "Doctor." The two men bowed to each other rather stiffly, rather uncertainly.

"Pleased to meet you," said Mr. Jericho. Alimantando was a Deuteronomy name: touchy people, the folk from Deuteronomy. Among the very first settlers, they tended to think the whole planet was theirs and were rather intolerant of newcomers. "Listen, I'm just passing through, but I need a place for the night: some water, some food, a roof over my head. Can you help me?"

Dr. Alimantando studied the uninvited guest. He shrugged.

"Look, I'm a very busy man, I'm in the middle of important research and I do appreciate not having my peace of mind disturbed."

"What is it you're researching?"

"Compiling a compendium of chronodynamic theories."

The Exalted Ancestors threw the appropriate response to the surface of Mr. Jericho's mind.

"Ah, like Webener's Synchronicity Postulates and the Chen Tsu Triple-Paradox."

Dr. Alimantando's suspicious glance held a twinkle of respect.

"How long are you staying?"

"Just one night."

"Sure?"

"Pretty sure. I'm only passing through. Just one night."

And Mr. Jericho stayed just one night, but it lasted for twenty years.

The storm was close now and the rail-schooner ran before it full-sailed to steal every kilometer of distance from the boiling brown dust-cloud. For three days it had run before the storm, three days since the morning Grandfather Haran turned his left eye, his weather-eye, to the western horizon and noticed the dirty ochre rim to the sky. "Dirty weather coming," he had said, and dirty weather came and was coming closer all the time, now so close upon the pioneers that even Rael

Mandella, cursed with the gift of pragmatism, realized there was no outrunning it and that his family's only hope lay in finding some place of refuge before they were engulfed in dust.

"More speed, more speed!" he cried, and Grandfather Haran and dear, beautiful Eva Mandella, mystical wife, heavily pregnant, hung out every last handkerchief of sail until the rail-schooner hummed and sang along the straight steel tracks. Spars creaked, hawsers twanged and shrieked, the wind-bogie rocked and swayed. In the equipment trailer the goats and llamas bleated fearfully and the pigs scrabbled at the bars of their cages. Behind, rollers of brown dust spilled across the land in ever-closing pursuit.

Again Rael Mandella lashed himself for the rash decision to bring wife, father, and unborn child across the Great Desert. Four days ago, at Murcheson Flats, the choice had been simple. Throwing the points lever one way would send his family south into the settled lands of Deuteronomy and the Great Oxus, throwing it the other would send them out across the Great Desert to the empty places of Northern Argyre and Transpolaris. He had not hesitated them. It had pleased him to think of himself as a bold pioneer breaking new ground, building his own land with his own hands. He had been proud. This then was the punishment for it. His charts and maps were relentless, the ROTECH surveyors marked no habitation for a thousand kilometers along this line.

A crack of wind caught the mainsail and ripped it down the middle. Rael Mandella stared dumbfounded at the flapping rags of sailcloth. Then he gave the order to close-haul. Even as he did so, three more sails split with cracks like gunshots. The rail-schooner shuddered and lost some of its headlong momentum. Then Eva Mandella stood up, swaying, clutching a humming hawser. Her belly heaved in imminent labor, but her eyes had the far look and her nostrils were wide as a startled deer's.

"There's something out there," she said in a voice that slipped under the shriek of the wind and the wires. "I can smell it; something's green and growing out there. Haran, you've got the eye for it, what can you see?" Grandfather Haran pointed his weather-eye down the geometrically perfect line and in the swirling dust and haze that presaged the storm he saw what Eva Mandella had smelled: a blob of green growingness, and more besides; a tall metal tower and some lozenge-shaped solar collectors.

"Habitation!" he cried. "A settlement! We're saved."

"More sail!" roared Rael Mandella, the shreds of sailcloth flapping around his ears. "More sail!" Grandfather Haran sacrificed the ancient family banner of finest New Merionedd silk, with which he would have proudly proclaimed his son's kingdom in the land beyond the desert, and Eva Mandella her cream organdy wedding dress and finest petticoats. Rael Mandella sacrificed six sheets of irreplacable plastic solar sheeting, and together they were all hoisted up the mast. The wind caught the rail-schooner and it gave a little shudder and a little jump, and looking more like a traveling carnival caught up in a waterspout than pioneers intent on the new lands, the frontier-family Mandella spun down the line to sanctuary.

Dr. Alimantando and Mr. Jericho had seen the rail-schooner while still far off, a scrap of many-colored cloth flying before the front of the storm. They had braved the first tugs and gusts of the dust-devils to fold up the delicate petals of the solar collectors into tight buds and retract the feathery antennae and dish aerials into the relay tower. While they worked, heads and hands wrapped in thick turbans of cloth, the wind rose to a shout-defying shriek and filled the air with flying needles of dust. As the rail-schooner braked furiously in a shower of shrieks, screeches, and sparks, Dr. Alimandanto and Mr. Jericho ran up to help unload the caboose. They worked with the silent, selfless synchronization of men who have known only each other for a long and solitary time. Eva Mandella found their tireless, mechanical lifting and carrying rather frightening: livestock, rootstock, seedstock, tools, machinery, materials, fabrics, domestic items, nails, screws, pins, and paints; carry and set, carry and set, all without a word being spoken.

"Where can we put them?" screamed Rael Mandella. Dr. Alimantando beckoned with a cloth-wrapped finger and led them to a warm dry cave.

"This for you, the one connecting there for your equipment."

At seventeen minutes of seventeen the dust storm struck. The same moment, Eva Mandella went into labor. As her wedding dress, her petticoats, the family banner, and six sheets of valuable solar sheeting were whirled up into the atmosphere on winds that might shred a man's flesh from his bones, she squeezed and squeezed and moaned and gasped and squeezed and squeezed in the warm dry cave by the light of tallow candles; squeezed and squeezed and squeezed and squeezed until she squeezed two squawling infants into the world. Their advent wails were lost beneath the greater wailing of the storm. A little red sand trickled into the mouth of the cave. In the yellow flickering candlelight Rael Mandella picked up his son and daughter.

"Limaal," he said to the child in his right hand. "Taasmin," he said to the child in his left, and in doing so he cursed them with his curse, so that his right-handed rationalism passed into his son and his wife's left-handed mysticism passed into his daughter. They were the first natural citizens of Desolation Road, and their citizenship bestowed citizenship upon their parents and grandparent, for they could not press on to the land beyond the desert while there were still infants at the teat. So they stayed forever and never found the land beyond the mountains for which all Mandellas have been searching ever since, for they know that Desolation Road is always one step short of Paradise and they are not content with that.

4

Rajandra Das lived in a hole under Platform 19 of Meridian Main Station. He shared this hole with a lot of other people, and there were a lot of holes under Meridian Main Station, so there were a lot of people. They called themselves gentlemen of leisure, connoisseurs of freedom, scholars in the Universuum of Life, Blythe Spirits. The railroad managers called them gutter boys, tramps, beggars, freebooters, goondahs, and bums. The passengers called them distressed gentlefolk, unfortunates, fallen souls, and knights of misfortune and opened their purses to them as they squatted on the station steps, hands outstretched to receive showers of centavos, their eyes gazing milky-blind courtesy of special cataract contact lenses manufactured by the Eastern Light Spectacle and Optics Company on East Bread Street. Rajandra Das, however, was above the largesse of the train-traveling people of Meridian. He existed wholly within the subterranean community of Main Station and lived on what the beggars could afford to pay for his services. He enjoyed a certain measure of respectability, (though what respectability might amount to in a kingdom of tramps was questionable), because he had a talent.

Rajandra Das had been given the power of charming machinery. There was nothing mechanical, electrical, electronic, or submolecular that would not work for Rajandra Das. He loved machines, he loved to take them apart, tinker with them, put them back together again, and make them better than before, and the machines loved the feel of his long, dextrous fingers stroking their insides and tweaking their sensitive components. Machines would sing for him, machines would purr for him, machines would do anything for him. Machines loved him madly. Whenever any device went wrong in the holes under Meridian Main Station, it went straight to Rajandra Das, who would hum and haw and stroke his neat brown beard. Then he would produce screwdrivers from his jacket of many pockets, take the device apart, and within five minutes have it fixed and running better than before. He could coax two years out of four-month light bulbs. He could tune wirelesses so fine they could pick up the cosmic chitchat between ROTECH habitats in high orbit. He could rewire prosthetic arms and legs (of which there were no shortage in Meridian Main Station) to be faster and stronger than the fleshly parts they replaced.

Such abilities did not go unnoticed by the station authorities, and when on occasion there was a pre-fusion percolator that just wasn't settling right or a persistent kink in the number three pinch bottle that had the engineers slamming their E-M field-inducer wrenches to the concrete in frustration, then the most junior subapprentice would be sent into the feces-redolent warren of runways and tunnels to get Rajandra Das. And Rajandra Das would straighten the kink and adjust the faulty percolator and everything would be right as ninepence again, if not righter.

So Rajandra Das led a charmed life; immune to the periodic transport police purges of the tunnels, respected and liked and comfortably off. Then one day Rajandra Das won the Great Railroad Lotto.

This was a cunning piece of social engineering devised by a legendary bum known only as the Old Wise Fellow, and this was how it worked. Once a month the name of every subterranean beneath Meridian Main Station went into a big tombola. A name was drawn and the winner invited to leave Meridian Main Station that same night on any train of his choice. For the Old Wise Fellow had recognized Meridian Main Station for the trap it was; a comfortable, warm, dry hole, an invitation to an eternity of contented beggarhood and self-mortification. It was the denial of everything potential in a human. It was a gentle jail. Because he was Old and Wise, (old as the world, the legend went) the Old Wise Fellow made two laws to govern his game. The first was that every name without exception must go into the tombola. The second was that no winner could ever refuse his prize.

And then the tombola in the little room with picture postcards from past winners on the walls gave a little whirr and a little cough and coughed up Rajandra Das's name. It may have been pure luck. Then again, it may have been sheer eagerness to please on the part of the tombola machine. Either way, Rajandra Das won and while he packed his few possessions into a canvas bag word spread across Meridian Main Station, both above and below ground, from the Esterhazie Avenue Freight Siding to the office of Mr. Populescu, the station master: "Rajandra Das has won the lotto . . . have you heard? Rajandra Das has won the lotto . . . he's leaving tonight . . . really? Yes, he won the lotto," so by the time midnight came and Rajandra Das was crouching in an inspection pit beside Number Two Main Downline waiting for the signal light to change, there were over a hundred people lining the track to see him off.

"Where you heading for?" asked Djong Pot Huahn, holemate and faithful provider.

"Don't know. Wisdom eventually, I think. I've always wanted to see Wisdom."

"But that's right on the other side of the world, R.D."

"Makes it all the more worth reaching."

Then the signal light did turn green and down the line in the bright glow of Meridian Main Station there came a puffing and panting of fusion-heated steam. Out of the glare and the steam came the train, a thousand and a half tons of clunking clanking Bethlehem Ares steel. The box cars rolled ponderously past Rajandra Das's covert, crushingly slow and heavy. Rajandra Das counted twelve, his lucky number, and made his jump. As he ran along between the train and the rows of well-wishers, hands reached out to slap him on the back and voices called out shouts of encouragement. Rajandra Das smiled and waved to them as he jogged along. The train slowly gathered speed. Rajandra Das picked his car and hopped onto the coupling. Shouts, whoops, and applause came out of the dark at him. He edged along the side of the car and tried the door. His charm had not failed him. It was unlocked. Rajandra Das slid the door open and rolled inside. He made himself comfortable on a pile of boxed mangos. The train rumbled into the night. In his fitful, fretful sleep, it seemed to Rajandra Das that the train stopped for long times at anonymous junctions while brighter, faster trains screamed past. At dawn he woke and breakfasted on mango. He slid the door open and sat with his legs dangling over the track, watching the sun rise beyond a vast red desert, eating slices of mango which he cut with his multibladed Defense Forces knife, stolen from Krishnamurthi Specialty Hardware on Water Street. There being nothing to look at except a lot of red desert, he went back to sleep again and dreamed of the towers of Wisdom glistening in the dawn light as the sun rose beyond the Syrtic Sea.

At twelve minutes of twelve Rajandra Das was awakened by a small explosion at the base of his spine. Stars blazed before his eyes, he gasped and gasped for breath, winded, agonized. There was another explosion, and another. Rajandra Das was now sufficiently awake to recognize them as kicks to his kidneys. Too winded even to howl, he rolled over and a bristling, sweaty face breathed a foul miasma over him.

"No good goddamn freeloading lazy bum of a tramp," growled the greasy face. A foot drew back for another kick.

"No no no no no no no no no, no no don't kick," wailed Rajandra Das, finding the air in some pocket of his lungs to plead, hands raised up in futile defense.

"No good goddamn freeloading lazy bum of a tramp," said bristle-breath again, for emphasis, and kicked the wind out of Rajandra Das. A hand grabbed Rajandra Das's threadbare coat and lifted him.

"Off you go," said the face, dragging Rjandra Das to the open door. Red desert sped by beneath the wheels.

"No no no no no," pleaded Rajandra Das. "Not here, not in the desert. It's murder!"

" What do I care?" grumbled the sweaty face, but some vestige of decency untouched by Bethlehem Ares Railroads must have been stroked, for he set Rajandra Das down on a heap of mango boxes and sat down to watch him, tapping his nightstick against his thigh. "Next place we so much as slow down, you going off." Rajandra Das said nothing. He was feeling his bruises turn purple up and down his back.

After half an hour the car jolted. Rajandra Das could tell from the pressure on his purple bruises that the train was slowing.

"Where are we, hey? Someplace civilized?"

The guard smiled, showing a wicket of rotting teeth. The train slowed. With a gritty grinding of brakes, the train stopped. The guard slid the door open, admitting a blaze of brilliant sunshine.

"Hey hey hey, what is this?" said Rajandra Das, blinking and blinded. Then he found himself lying on hard dirt with the wind knocked out of him again. His canvas bag thumped painfully onto his chest. Whistles blew, steam hissed, pistons churned. A trickle of burning hot liquid ran down Rajandra Das's face. Blood! he thought, then blinked, spat, sat up. The guard was urinating on him, laughing uproariously as he tucked his warty member back into his rancid pants. The train blew and moved off.

"Bastards," said Rajandra Das to the railroad company in general. He wiped his face clean with his sleeve. The urine formed a dark red stain in the dust. It might well have been blood. Rajandra Das took a long look from the sitting position at the place he had landed in. Low adobe houses, a white wall or two, some greenery, some trees, some wind-pumps, a handful of large lozenge-shaped solar-collectors, and a stubby microwave relay tower on top of a pile of rocks that looked as if someone lived in them.

"It'll do," said Rajandra Das, beloved of tombolas and trains and boxcars but not guards, never guards of the Bethlehem Ares Railroad Company. Figures were approaching, indistinct in the noontime heat-haze. Rajandra Das picked himself up and went to meet his new hosts.

"Hey," he said, "there wouldn't be any picture postcards of this place, would there?"

5

The Babooshka did not like trains. Their bulk intimidated her. Their weight crushed her. Their speed alarmed her and the sound of their wheels was that of doomsday approaching. She feared their steam and their spoutings and the possibility of their fusion tokamaks exploding and blasting her to loose atoms in the upper atmosphere. She hated trains. Especially trains that had to cross dreadful red deserts. Trains, they were largely indifferent to the Babooshka. Even this one that was crossing a dreadful red desert.

"Misha, Misha, how much longer until we can get off this horrid engine?"

Mikal Margolis, mineralogist, industrial chemist, dutiful son, and young pioneer, looked away from the hypnotic red desert; clean, spare, and beautiful in its geological potential, and said to his little old mother, "We shall be through it when we're through it, and then we shall be in Paradise Valley, where it rains only at two o'clock in the morning, where when you plant a seed you have to stand back because it will shoot up and hit you on the chin, where tame songbirds come and sing on your finger and where you and I, Mother, will make our fortunes and see our days out in wealth, health, and happiness."

The Babooshka was pleased by her son's simple tale of wonder. She liked the bit about tame songbirds sitting on her fingers. The only birds in New Cosmobad had been raucous black crows.

"But how much longer, Misha?"

"Next stop, Mother. No towns in this desert, so we don't

stop until we are there. Next stop, then we change to the mountain railroad that will take us to Paradise Valley."

"Oh, changing trains, I do not like it. I do not like trains, Misha, I do not like them at all."

"Never worry, Mother. I'm here. Now, would you like some mint tea to soothe your nerves?"

"That would be very nice indeed, Misha. Thank you."

Mikal Margolis rang for the steward, who brought mint tea in a smart pot decorated with the black and gold Bethlehem Ares Railroads livery. The Babooshka sipped her tea and smiled at her son between sips. Mikal Margolis smiled back and wondered what he was going to tell his mother when they got to Paradise Valley, for the only Paradise it was was an industrial chemist's one; where the rain fell at two o'clock in the morning because that was when the refineries vented their tail-gasses into the atmosphere, where it was ethylene in the soil that made the plants shoot up overnight, then wither, then die, and where all the birds had succumbed long ago to toxic fumes and the ones that sat upon fingers were cunning mechanical duplicates, all part of the Company's public relations program.

He would worry about that nearer the time. Outside the polarized window was the thrilling red desert, a man's landscape, a gritty wonderland of raw rocks and minerals. He imagined himself riding across it on horseback, wrapped in serape and headcloths, his leather specimens case slapping against his back. Caught up in such reverie, it was not long before the gentle rocking of the train sent him off to sleep.

He woke in pandemonium. Not the pandemonium that was the name of the interchange for Paradise Valley, but the other, more dreadful sort. Valves were hissing, voices shouting, metal clanking against metal, and someone was shaking him by the shoulder, calling, "Sir, your mother, sir, wake up, sir, your mother, sir, sir, sir." He focused on the pale face of the steward. "Sir, your mother, sir." The Babooshka was not in her seat. All the luggage was gone. Mikal Margolis dashed to the window to see his mother gliding happily down the side of the track, waving along a slender young man with a beard grinning under a pile of parcels and cases.

"Mother!" he roared. "Mother!"

The Babooshka looked up and waved, a tiny, happy china doll of a woman. Her voice was tiny as a doll's.

"Misha! Come on! Can't waste time. Have to find the other station."

"Mother!" bellowed Mikal Margolis. "This is not the right stop!" But his words were lost in a billow of steam and the thunder of fusion engines powering up. Creakingly, agedly, the train began to roll. "Sir, sir!" cried the flapping steward. Mikal Margolis straight-armed him into an empty seat and dashed for the door. He jumped as the carriage passed the end of the makeshift platform.

The Babooshka swirled up the platform in a storm of small indignation.

"Misha, the shock you are giving me, your poor dear mother! Falling asleep on the train, no less. Come, we shall miss the mountain railroad."

The cheeky porter-type had to put the bags down, he was laughing so hard.

"Mother, where are the mountains?"

"Behind the buildings."

"Mother, you can see right over the buildings, they are so low. Mother, this is not the right station."

"Oh, no? Then where is this your poor dear mother has put you?"

Mikal Margolis pointed to some words laid out in pretty white pebbles by the edge of the track.

"Desolation Road, Mother."

"And this is the next stop, no?"

"We were meant to get off at Pandemonium. The train was not supposed to stop here. This town is not supposed to be here."

Then blame the railroad company, blame the town, but not your poor dear mother!" fumed the Babooshka, and lambasted, lampooned, be-jasused, and generally cursed the railroad company, their trains, their tracks, their signals, their rolling stock, their drivers, their engineers, their guards, and anyone even remotely connected with Bethleham Ares Railroads down to the meanest lavatory attendant, third-class, for approximately twenty minutes.

Finally Dr. Alimantando, nominal head of Desolation Road, pop. 7, elev. 1250 m., "One step short of Paradise," arrived to settle the altercation so he could return to his chronokinetic studies in peace. Only the day before he had commissioned Rajandra Das, general factotum, sorcerer's apprentice, odd-job man, and station porter, to spell out the name of the town in proud white pebbles so that any train that might pass would know that the people of Desolation Road had pride in their town. As if lured by a malicious sympathetic magic, the train bearing the Babooshka and Mikal Margolis pulled over the horizon and stopped to take a look. Rajandra Das's charm over machines was powerful, but surely not that powerful. Nevertheless, he had charmed the Babooshka and her son into being, and now Dr. Alimantando had to decide what to do with them. He offered them refuge in one of the warm dry caves that riddled the bluffs until such time as they chose to leave or had a more permanent residence constructed. Stiff with indignation, the Babooshka refused the offer of sanctuary. She would not sleep in a dirty cave with bat droppings on the floor and lizards for company; no, nor would she share it with a son who was a faithless wastrel and did not know how to treat an old lady who was his poor dear mother. Dr. Alimantando listened with what little grace he would muster and then prevailed upon the Mandellas, whose house was built with family in mind, to take in the waif. Mikal Margolis took the cave. There were bat droppings and there were lizards, but there was no mother so it was not that bad.

In the Mandella household the Babooshka found a contemporary in Grandfather Haran, who entertained her with peapod wine and honey-tongued flatteries and asked his son to build an extra room onto the already rambling Mandella home especially for the Babooshka. Every night they would sip wine, reminisce on the days when both they and the world were young, and play the word games the Babooshka loved so much. On one such night, in early autumn, as Grandfather Haran was putting the word *bauxite* down on a double-word triple-letter, the Babooshka noticed for the first time his distinguished gray hair and fine upright body, chipped by time like a china god, but strong and uneroded. She let her eyes rest upon the iron-stiff beard and the lovely little shiny button-eyes, and she let out a quiet sigh and fell in love with him.

"Haran Mandella, as we say in Old New Cosmobad, you are much much gentleman," she said.

"Anastasia Tyurischeva Margolis, as we say in Desolation Road, you are much much lady," said Grandfather Haran.

The wedding was set for the following spring.

Mikal Margolis dreamed in his cave of the mineral springs of Paradise Valley. He would never find his fortune lying around in the rocks of Desolation Road, but he did find crystals of sulphate of dilemma. With time it refined into a pure form: to find his fortune he must leave Desolation Road and his mother; to leave her would mean leaving on his own and he did not have the courage for that. Such was the essence of Mikal Margolis's purified dilemma. The resolution of it into useful compounds, and his quest for personal anti-maternal courage was to lead him through adultery, murder, and exile to the destruction of Desolation Road. But not yet.

6

One afternoon, shortly after the official end of the siesta, while people were still unofficially blinking, stretching, and yawning out of sweaty sleep, a noise was heard in Desolation Road like none that had ever been heard before.

"Sounds like a big bee," said the Babooshka.

"Or a swarm of bees," said Grandfather Haran.

"Or a big swarm of big bees," said Rajandra Das.

"Killer bees?" asked Eva Mandella.

"No such things," said Rael Mandella.

The twins made gurgling sounds. They were toddling now, at the age of perpetually falling forward. No door in town could be closed to them, they were intrepid, fearless adventurers. Killer bees would not have fazed them.

"More like an aircraft engine," said Mikal Margolis.

"Single engine?" ventured Dr. Alimantando. "Single engine, one seater crop-sprayer?" Such things had been a familiar sight in Deuteronomy.

"More like twin engine," said Mr. Jericho, straining his tuned hearing. "Twin-engined, two seats, but not a crop-sprayer, a stunter, Yamaguchi and Jones, with two Maybach/ Wurtel engines in pull-push configuration, if I'm not mistaken."

Whatever its source, the noise grew louder and louder. Then Mr. Jericho spied a fleck of black on the face of the sun.

"There it is, look!"

With a howl like a big swarm of killer bees, the airplane dived out of the sun and thundered over Desolation Road. Everybody ducked save Limaal and Taasmin, who followed it with their heads and fell over, unbalanced.

"What was that?"

"Look . . . he's turning, he's coming back."

At the apex of its turn everyone caught full sight of the airplane that had buzzed them. It was a sleek, shark-shaped thing with two propellors nose and tail, angled wings, and a downraked tail. Nobody failed to notice the bright tiger stripes painted on its fuselage and the snarling, toothy grin on its nose. The airplane swooped over Desolation Road once more, barely skimming the top of the relay tower. Heads ducked again. The airplane hung at the point of its bank and afternoon sunlight blazed off polished metal. The people of Desolation Road waved. The airplane bore down upon the town again.

"Look, the pilot's waving back!"

The people waved all the more.

A third time the airplane swept over the adobe homes of Desolation Road. A third time it pulled into a tight bank.

"I do believe he's coming down!" shouted Mr. Jericho. "He's coming down!" Landing gear was unfolding from the wingtips, the nose, and the downswept tail. The airplane made a final pass, almost at head height, and dropped toward the empty place on the far side of the railroad tracks.

"He'll never do it!" said Dr. Alimantando, but nevertheless he ran with the rest of his people toward the great cloud of dust pluming up beyond the line. They met the airplane coming nose on toward them. The people scattered, the airplane swerved, snapped a wing wheel on a rock, and crashed onto its side, plowing a huge slewing furrow in the dust. The good citizens of Desolation Road hastened to the aid of pilot and passenger, but the pilot was free and, sliding back the canopy, stood up and screamed, "You dumb bastards! You dumb, stupid bastards! What you want to go and do that for? Eh? She's ruined, ruined, never fly again, all because you dumb bastards are too dumb to know to keep out of the way of airplanes! Look what you've done, just look!"

And the pilot burst into tears.

Her name was Persis Tatterdemalion.

She was born with wings, there was aviation grade liquid hydrogen in her veins and wind in her wires. On her father's side were three generations of Rockette Morgan's Flying Circus, on her mother's a genealogy of crop-sprayers, commercial pilots, charter flyers, and daredevils back to great-great-grandmother Indhira, who reputedly piloted Praesidium SailShips while the world was being invented. Persis Tatterdemalion was born to fly. She was a great soaring, roaring bird. To her the loss of her airplane was no less a matter than the loss of a limb, or a loved one, or a life.

All her time, money, energy, and love had, since the age of ten, been poured into the Astounding Tatterdemalion Air Bazaar, a one-woman, one-ring flying circus, a chautauqua of the skies that not only thrilled gaping audiences with death-defying aerobatics and stunting, but also educated them by providing those who paid her modest fee with aerial views of their farms, close-ups of the weather and sight-seeing jaunts to places of local interest. Thus employed, she had moved eastward across the top half of the world until she reached the plains town of Wollamurra Station. "See the Great Desert," she sang to the sheep farmers of Wollamurra Station, "marvel at the dizzying depths of the mighty canyons, wonder at the forces of Nature that have sculpted stupendous natural arches and towering stone pillars. The whole history of the earth laid out in stone beneath you: I guarantee for one dollar fifty centavos, this is a trip you will never forget."

For Junius Lambe, dazedly furious in the tail seat, the sales pitch was quite true. Twenty minutes out from Wollamurra Station, with not a canyon, stupendous arch, or towering pillar within a hundred kilometers, Persis Tatterdemalion noticed that the fuel gauge had not moved. She tapped it. The red display indicators flickered and plummeted to the empty mark. She tapped it again. The indicators sat where they were.

"Oh, shit," she said. She plugged in a taped commentary on the wonders of the Great Desert to keep Junius Lambe quiet and checked her charts for a close-by settlement where she could make a forced landing. She could not return to Wollamurra Station, that was obvious, but the ROTECH maps gave no comfort. She checked the radio location equipment. It indicated a leak of microwave radiation not twenty kilometers distant, of the type associated with the relays in the planetary communications net.

"Check it out, I suppose," she said to herself, and committed herself, her airplane, and her passenger to her decision.

She found a tiny settlement where no settlement should have been. There were neat squares of green, and light flashed from solar-collectors and irrigation channels. She could make out the red tile roofs of houses. And there were people.

"Hold tight," she said to Junius Lambe, for whom this was his first inkling that anything might be wrong. "We're going in."

With her last teardrop of fuel she had brought her beloved bird down, and then what had happened? So deep was her disgust that she refused to leave Desolation Road with Junius Lambe on the 14:14 Llangonedd-Rejoice Ares Express.

"I flew in, I'll fly out," she declared. "The only way I'm going out of here is on a pair of wings."

Rajandra Das tried to charm the wheel back onto the wingtip, but it was beyond his power or even the power of Rael Mandella's welding torch to make the airplane airworthy again. What was most galling of all to the sole survivor of the Astounding Tatterdemalion Air Bazaar was that Rael Mandella's welding torch ran on nothing less than hundred percent, pure, unadulterated aviation-grade liquid hydrogen.

So Dr. Alimantando found Persis Tatterdemalion a home and a garden so that she would not starve, but she could not be happy because the sky was in her eyes. She saw the lean desert birds gather on the aerials of the relay tower and grew bitter because her wings had been broken by foolish people. She stood on the edge of the bluffs and watched the birds ride the thermals up the evening and wondered how wide she would have to spread her arms to rise like them and be drawn up the spiral of air until she vanished from view.

One night Mikal Margolis made her two propositions and because she knew that only by losing herself in them could she forget the sky, she accepted them both. That night, and for twenty successive nights, the peace of the citizens was disturbed by strange noises from the Margolis dwelling. Some of them were the howls and mauls of intercourse. The others sounded like interior decoration.

When the sign appeared, everything became obvious. It read:

BETHLEHEM ARES RAILROAD/HOTEL
EATS * DRINKS * SLEEPS
PROPRIETORS: M. MARGOLIS, P. TATTERDEMALION

"Is no son of mine," declared the outraged Babooshka. "Ignoring his dear mother to take up with some cheap, foreign woman, and filling the peaceful nights with sounds the like of which I will not describe; such shame he is bringing! And now, this den of sin and sodomy! B.A.R./Hotel, hah! As if his dear mother does not know what it meant! Thinking his dear mother cannot spell, eh? Haran," she said to her husband-to-be, "not one foot will I ever set in that place. From now on, he is no son of mine. I disown him." She spat demurely on the ground before the Bethlehem Ares Railroad/Hotel. That night Persis Tatterdemalion and Mikal Margolis threw a grand opening party, with as much maize beer as anyone could drink, which was not very much, as there were only five guests. Even Dr. Alimantando was persuaded to leave his studies for an evening to celebrate. Grandfather Haran and the Babooshka remained to mind little Limaal and Taasmin. Grandfather Haran would have loved to have gone and earned himself reproaching glances every time the Babooshka caught him glancing wistfully out toward the light and the noise. Her total ban on crossing the B.A.R.'s threshold necessarily extended to her husband.

The day after the party Persis Tatterdemalion took Rajandra Das, Mr. Jericho, and Rael Mandella over the railroad lines and the three men dismantled the sand-scarred stunt plane and packed it into fifteen tea chests. Persis Tatterdemalion said nothing during the dismantling operation. She locked the pieces of her airplane in the deepest darkest cave in the B.A.R./Hotel and put the key in a jar. She could never quite bring herself to forget where that jar was.

One morning at two minutes of two she rolled on top of Mikal Margolis and whispered into his ear, "Do you know what we need, darling? What we really need to make everything perfect?" Mikal Margolis held his breath, expecting wedding rings, children, little perversions with leather and rubber.

"A snooker table."

7

There were three Gallacelli brothers: Ed, Louie, and Umberto. No one knew which was Ed, which was Louie, and which was Umberto, because they were triplets and as mutually indistinguishable as peas in a pod or days in a prison. They grew up in the farming community of Burma Shave, where the citizens held three common opinions about them. The first was that they had been found abandoned in a cardboard box on the edge of Giovann' Gallacelli's maize field. The second was that they were something more than triplets, though what that something might be no one was prepared to say for fear of offending the saintly Mrs. Gallacelli. The third was that the Gallacelli boys had swapped identity at least once since infancy so that Louie had grown up to be either Ed or Umberto, Umberto Louie or Ed, and Ed Umberto or Louie, and all possible successive permutations of further swaps. Not even the boys themselves were certain which was Ed, which was Louie, which was Umberto, but it was certain among the folk of Burma Shave that they had never seen such identical triplets ("clones," oh, dear, that's it said, it just popped out, you know, that word you're not meant to mention in front of their parents): or such devilishly handsome ones.

Agneta Gallacelli was a squat toad of a woman with a heart of warm milk chocolate. Giovann' Gallacelli was tall, thin, and spare as a rake. Ed, Louie, and Umberto were dark-eyed, curly-haired laughing love gods. And knew it. And so did every girl in Burma Shave. Which was how the Gallacelli brothers came to depart from Burma Shave in the small hours of a Tuesday morning on a motorized railcar they had adapted themselves from a farm delivery truck.

There was this girl. She was called Magdala, Mags for short. There is always a girl like her, the kind who flirts and plays and messes around and leaves no doubt that she is one of the boys until the boys are boys, when they, and she, realize that she isn't one of the boys at all, not at all. For Mags her moment of realization came two weeks after her trip round the more out-of-the-way fields in the back of the Gallacellis' delivery truck. For Ed, Louie, and Umberto it came when the truck was peppered with bird shot as they drew up outside the Mayaguez homestead to inquire why Mags hadn't been to see them for so long.

Fraternal solidarity was the pole star of the Gallacelli brothers' lives. It did not waver when confronted by a resigned father and a furious neighbor. They refused to say which of them had impregnated Magdala Mayaguez. It was entirely possible they did not know themselves.

"Either one of youse says, or ye all marry," said Sonny Mayaguez. His wife gave weight to his demands with a shotgun. "Well, what'll it be? Talk, or marry."

The Gallacelli brothers chose neither.

Anywhere else in the world no one would have lost one wink of sleep over a silly little girl like Mags Mayaguez. In nearby Belladonna there were counted on Tombolova Street alone eighty-five abortion parlors and twelve transplant-fostering bureaus for silly little girls in just her situation. Belladonna, however, was Belladonna, and Burma Shave was Burma Shave, which was why the Gallacelli brothers chose Belladonna over Burma Shave. There they earned ten-dollar diplomas in farm science, law, and mechanical engineering from a hole-in-the-wall universuum. They would have lived there contentedly for the rest of their lives but for a sad misunderstanding with a knife, a drunk shuttle loader, and a girl in a bar on Primavera Street. So they ran away again, for there was still some law in Belladonna where the next best thing to a totally honest police force is a totally corrupt one.

They were drawn down the network of shining steel rails that covered the world like a spider's web: the farmer, the lawyer, the mechanic. Ed was the mechanic, Louie the lawyer, Umberto the farmer. With such qualifications they could have made it anywhere in the world because the world was still young enough for there to be more than enough work for every hand. But the place they actually made it to was Desolation Road.

They bounced off their railcar grim, sweaty but still devilishly handsome and swung into the Bethlehem Ares Railroad/Hotel. They banged on the service bell one after the other. Heads turned to look at them. The Gallacelli brothers smiled and waved.

"Ed, Louis, and Umberto," one of them introduced themselves.

"Looking for a place for the night," explained another.

"Clean beds, hot baths, and hot dinners," said the third.

Persis Tatterdemalion emerged from the beer cellar, where she had been fitting a fresh barrel.

"Yes?" she said.

"Ed, Louis, and . . ." said Ed.

"Looking for . . ." said Louie.

"Clean beds, hot . . ." said Umberto, and all at once, all at the same instant, they fell dreadfully, desperately passionately in love with her. There is a theory, you see, that states that for everyone there is one person who will fulfill their love perfectly and absolutely. The Gallacelli brothers, being the same person multiplied three times, of course shared that common, unique love, and the absolute fulfillment of that common love was Persis Tatterdemalion.

The next morning the Gallacelli brothers went to see Dr. Alimantando about becoming permanent residents. He gave Umberto a large patch of land, he gave Ed a shed where he could fix machines, and because he could not give Louie an office or a district court or even a corner of the bar to practice his art, he gave him a piece of land almost as big as Umberto's and advised him to take up animal husbandry, that being the closest thing Desolation Road could offer to jurisprudence.

8

Mikal Margolis had a problem. He was painfully in love with the lady veterinarian across the road in House Twelve. But the object and satisfaction of his lust was Persis Tatterdemalion, his bed-and-business partner. The lady veterinarian in House Twelve, whose name was Marya Quinsana, had a problem too. It was that she was the object of lust of her brother Morton. But she did not love him, even fraternally, nor did she love Mikal Margolis. The only person she loved was herself. But that self-love was cut like a diamond with many shining facets so that beams of that self-love reflected off Marya Quinsana onto those about her and deceived them into thinking that she loved them, and they her.

One such was her brother Morton Quinsana, a dentist of strange obsessions whose possessiveness of his sister fooled no one. Everyone knew he secretly desired her, and she knew he secretly desired her, so it was no secret desire with so many people knowing. But such was Morton Quinsana's respect and possessiveness that he could not bring himself to lay so much as one finger upon his sister. So he burned an arm's length away in a hell of frustration. And the longer he burned the hotter grew the fires of obsession. One evening he caught his sister flirting with the Gallacelli brothers, laughing at their coarse farmyard humor, drinking their drinks, touching their rough and ugly hands. He swore then and there that he would never ever treat any of the Gallacelli brothers, not even when they came to him screaming and begging with toothaches, not even when the agony of rotting dentine loosed the animal inside them and set them beating their heads against walls; no, he would turn them away, turn them away without another thought, banish them to moaning and suffering and gnashing of teeth for having cast the net of their prurient desires at his sister Marya.

Another such fool was Mikal Margolis. Because of his mother, he had never been happy in love. Once his mother announced her engagement, he became happy in love, happy with enthusiastic, vivacious, voracious Persis Tatterdemalion. Then Morton and Marya Quinsana stepped down from the weekly supply train from Meridian. Mikal Margolis had been collecting beer barrels and crates of spirits from the station, when he noticed the tall, strong woman walking down the platform with the natural grace and implied power of a hunting cat. Their eyes had met and then passed on, but in the flicker of contact Mikal Margolis felt a shock of spinal electricity fuse the base of his heart, where all decency and honesty lay, into thick black glass. He loved her. He could not think of anything else but that he loved her.

When Dr. Alimantando gave the Quinsanas a cave, he had rushed to help build them a home. "Hey, what about the polishing, what about cleaning some glasses?" Persis Tatterdemalion had demanded. Mikal Margolis waved and went. When Dr. Alimantando gave the Quinsanas an allotment, Mikal Margolis came and ditched, diked, and dammed until the moonring sparkled like diamonds. "How about serving a few drinks?" said Persis Tatterdemalion. "How about making some dinner for these hungry people?" And when Morton Quinsana and his sister came to the Bethlehem Ares Railroad/Hotel, he gave them each a bowl of hot lamb pilaf and as much complimentary beer as they could drink, then joked and chattered with them until closing time. When a chicken fell sick in the hotel even though it was destined for that night's pot, it was taken all the same to Marya Quinsana, who poked it and probed it with her skilled fingers while Mikal Margolis fantasized about her fingers doing the same thing to him. A lot of Margolis's and Tatterdemalion's animals fell ill that autumn.

Yet Mikal Margolis was not happy. He oscillated between the love of a good woman and the love of a bad woman, like a little quartz crystal ticking away time. Persis Tatterdemalion, worldly and innocent as an eagle upon the sky, asked him if he was sick. Mikal Margolis groaned a groan of pure frustrated lust.

"Maybe you should go and see someone, love, your mind hasn't been on your work these past few days. What about that lady vet, eh? I mean, humans are just another kind of animal, aren't they? She might be able to help."

Mikal Margolis turned to look at Persis Tatterdemalion.

"You're kidding, aren't you?"

"No. Straight up."

Mikal Margolis groaned all the louder.

As for Marya Quinsana, she did not care. Exactly that, she did not care, she had nothing but contempt for anyone weak enough to love her. She despised her fool of a brother, she despised that silly boy who ran the bar. Yet she could not resist a challenge. She would win that silly boy away from the doting simpleton he lived and loved with. It was the game, the game; the pieces don't matter in the game, the mind that moves them is what is important; that and the winning, for in winning she came to despise the losers all the more. With one inspired gambit she could triumph over both Mikal Margolis and her damned brother. Then she could at last break away from him and let the world hear her name. "Look after Morton" had been the dying words of her iron mother; "look after him, take care of him, let him think he's making all the decisions but ensure he makes none. Marya, I command it."

Take care of Morton, take care of Morton; yes, she had been faithful to her mother's will for five years now. She had followed him out into the desert after that affair with the little girl in the park, but the time must come, Mother, when Morton stands alone, and on that morning she would be on the first train to Wisdom.

That was why there were the games. They amused her, they kept her sane through the five years of Morton's growing infatuation, they gave her hope that through them she would be strong enough to step on that morning train to Wisdom. Oh, yes, the games kept her sane. So she contrived to be out feeding her chickens at the same time every day as Mikal Margolis across the alley in the backyard of the B.A.R./Hotel was feeding his. It was the game that made her ask him to come and look at her methane digester to see why it wasn't working properly, though Rajandra Das would have done the job better. "Chemical problems, miss," said Mikal Margolis, "someone's dumped a load of used sterilant into it and inhibited the bacteriophages." Marya Quinsana smiled. She had poured three bottles of surgery sterilizing fluid into the tank just that morning. The game was going well. Out of gratitude she invited him in for drinks, then conversation, then bed (all the while Mikal Margolis trembled like a reed), then sex.

And in that bed were the seeds of Desolation Road's destruction spilled.

9

The trouble between Stalins and Tenebraes began when they discovered that they had been sold the same piece of land in the idyllic, paradise town of Desolation Road by Mr. E. P. Vencatatchalum, formerly land agent of the Vencatatchalum Immigration and Settlement Bureau, currently sitting in a white room facing questions on complicity to defraud from Inspector Djien Xhao-Pin of the Bleriot Constabulary. Not only had Stalins and Tenebraes been sold the same piece of land (which was not Mr. E. P. Vencatatchalum's to sell in the first place), they had also been double-booked for the same sleeping compartment on the 19:19 Solstice Landing Night Service, calling at North Ben'stown, Annency, Murchesonville, New Enterprise, Wollamurra Station and Desolation Road. Neither family would give way to the other. The sleeping car attendant locked himself in his cabin and turned his wireless up loud. They could settle their own disputes. No one got much sleep in car 36 of the Solstice Landing Night Service. Five people, with five people's luggage, were trying to live in a sleeping compartment for three, with three people's luggage. The first night only little Johnny Stalin, aged 3 ¾, had a bed to himself. That was because he was a highly strung fat little bulb of a boy who would have screamed and screamed and screamed himself sick if he had not gotten a bed to himself. His mother acquiesced and popped him three or four adult-dosage sleeping pills to keep him quiet and docile. Johnny Stalin was a spoiled, junkie, highly strung fat little bulb of a boy.

The next day passed in brittle silence until Gaston Tenebrae cleared his throat at fourteen o'clock precisely and suggested it might be a good idea if everyone slept shifts. He and his wife, Genevieve, would sit up all night and sleep all day if the Stalins would sit up all day and sleep all night.

The arrangement seemed equable at first. Then the simple, unkind logistics of the sleeping compartment took command. One bed would have to be folded down to form seats for the two to sit upon, which left three bodies in two beds. Then there would be three sitting and two sleeping in comfort. Mr. and Mrs. Stalin thrashed and grumbled in their tightly constricted bed, little Johnny snored asthmatically, and Gaston and Genevieve Tenebrae held little private, loving arguments, with much whispered fury and small, aggressive hand gestures as the train clashed and clanked and reversed and split to form new trains and by such fits and starts drew ever nearer to Desolation Road.

The scrambled changeover from seat to bed on the morning of the third day saw the formal commencement of hostilities. Genevieve Tenebrae accused young Johnny Stalin of trying to peer up her skirt as she climbed the steps to the upper berth. Mr. Stalin accused Gaston Tenebrae of rifling his luggage while his family were supposedly asleep. Gaston Tenebrae accused Mr. Stalin of making improper advances to his pretty wife in the line for the second-class washroom. Mrs. Stalin accused Mrs. Tenebrae of cheating at bezique. Flurries of bickering broke out, like the flurries of snow that precede the big winter; and it was the fourth day and fourth night.

"Desolation Road!" called the cabin attendant, come out of hiding and tapping on the door with a silver pencil. Tap tap tap. "Desolation Road! Three minutes!" Tap tap tap.

Anarchy paradoxically reigned for two minutes thirty seconds as Stalins and Tenebraes got up got washed got dressed collected bags books valuables, bulbous sons and crammed slammed jammed down the narrow corridors and out through the narrow door into the thin wide sunshine of seven o'clock in the morning. All this without once looking out the windows to see where they were, which was a pity, because if they had, then they might not have gotten off the train. But when they did look, they saw, "Green meadows . . ." said Mr. Stalin.

"Rich farmlands, ripe for the plow," said Gaston Tenebrae.

"The air soft with the perfume of a million blossoms," said Mrs. Stalin.

"A serene, tranquil heaven on earth," said Genevieve Tenebrae.

Johnny Stalin looked at the glaring white adobe and the baked red earth, the sun-bright flickers of the solar-collectors and the stark skeletons of the pump gantries. Then he screwed up his face like a wet sponge about to be wrung dry and prepared for a screaming tantrum.

"Ma!" he wailed. "I don't . . ." Mrs. Stalin fetched him a stunning crack across the left ear. He wailed all the more furiously and that was the cue for Stalins and Tenebraes to release upon each other a barrage of blistering invective which left scorch marks on close-by walls. Johnny Stalin waddled away to be alone with his misery, unheeded and therefore unloved. Limaal and Taasmin Mandella found him sitting huffily beside the main methane digester as they scampered on their way to find something new to play on a new day.

"Hello," said Limaal. "You're new."

"What's your name?" said Taasmin, forty-eight seconds older than her brother.

"Johnny Stalin," said Johnny Stalin.

"You going to be here a long time?"

"Think so."

"Then we'll show you where there is to play here," said Taasmin, and the two quick, lithe children took pale and blubbery Johnny Stalin by the hand and showed him the wonderful hog-wallow, the water pumps, the irrigation channels where you could sail toy boats, the pens where Rael Mandella kept the baby animals born from his germ-kit, and the berry bushes, where you could eat until you were sick and nobody would mind, not one bit. They showed him Dr. Alimantando's house, and Dr. Alimantando, who was very tall and very old and very nice in a rather scary way, and Dr. Alimantando took the mud-shit-water-and-berry stained boy back to his still squabbling parents and made them permanent residents of Desolation Road. The first two nights they spent in the Bethlehem Ares Railroad/Hotel while Dr. Alimantando pondered what to do with them. Finally he summoned his most trusted friends and advisors: Mr. Jericho, Rael Mandella, and Rajandra Das, and together, aided by Mr. Jericho's Exalted Ancestors, reached a decision of stunning simplicity.

Desolation Road was too small to afford big-city luxuries like warring families. Stalins and Tenebraes must learn to live together. Therefore Dr. Alimantando gave them houses next door to each other and allotments with a long common border and only one wind-pump. Pleased with his Solomonic wisdom, Dr. Alimantando returned to his weather-room and his studies of time, space, and everything.

10

"Tell me again, Father, why are we going to this place?"

"To get away from the unkind people who say bad things about you and about me, away from the people who want to take me away from you."

"Tell me again, Father, why these people want to take you away from me."

"Because you are my daughter. Because they say you are unnatural, a freak, an engineered experiment, my little singing bird. Because they say you were born contrary to the law, and because of that I must be punished."

"But tell me again, Father, why should they punish you? Amn't I your daughter, your little singing bird?"

"You are my little singing bird and you are my daughter, but they would say that you are nothing more than . . . a doll, or a machine, or any other made thing, and it is against such people's law for a man to have such a daughter, a daughter he has made for himself, even though he loves her more than life itself."

"And do you love me more than life itself, Father?"

"I do, my little cherry pip, and that is why we are running away from these unkind people, because they would take me away from you and I could not bear that."

"Nor could I, Father, I couldn't not have you."

"So we will be together, eh? Always."

"Yes, Father. But tell me again, what is this place we are going to?"

"It is called Desolation Road, and it is so tiny and far away that it is known only because of the stories that have been told about it."

"And that is where we are going?"

"Yes, kitten-bone, to the last place in the world. To this Desolation Road."

Meredith Blue Mountain and his daughter, Ruthie, were quiet people. They were plain people, unremarkable people, unnoticeable people. In the third-class compartment of the slow Meridian-Belladonna cross-desert stopper they were invisible under piles of other peoples' luggage, other peoples' chickens, other peoples' children, and other people. No one talked to them, no one asked if they could sit beside them or pile their luggage chickens children selves on top of them. When they got off at the tiny desert station, no one noticed for well over an hour that they were gone, and even then they could not remember what their traveling companions had looked like.

No one noticed them step off the train, no one saw them arrive in Desolation Road, not even Rajandra Das, the self-appointed station master who greeted every train that arrived in his ramshackle station, no one noticed them enter the Bethlehem Ares Railroad/Hotel at twenty minutes of twenty. Then something very much like a sustained explosion of light filled the hotel and there, at the epicenter of the glare, was the most beautiful woman anyone had ever seen. Every man in the room had to swallow hard. Every woman fought an inexpressible need to sigh. A dozen hearts cracked down the middle and all the love flew out like larks and circled round the incredible being. It was as if God Himself had walked into the room.

Then the God-light went out and there was a blinking, eye-rubbing darkness. When vision was restored, everyone saw before them a small, very ordinary man and a young girl of about eight who was quite the plainest, drabbest creature anyone had ever seen. For it was the nature of Ruthie Blue Mountain, a girl of stunning ordinariness, to absorb like sunlight the beauty of everything around her and store it until she chose to release it, all at once, like a flashbulb of intense beauty. Then she would return again to dowdy anonymity, leaving behind her an afterimage in the heart of unutterable loss. This was Ruthie Blue Mountain's first secret. Her second was that this was the way her father had created her in his genesis-bottle.

The remarkable goings-on in the B.A.R. were still talk as Meredith Blue Mountain and his daughter went up to see Dr. Alimantando. The great man was at work in his weather-room, filling the walls with illegible algebraic symbols in black charcoal.

"I am Meredith Blue Mountain and this is Ruthie, my daughter" (here Ruthie bobbed and smiled the way her father had patiently rehearsed her in their hotel room). "I am a livestock breeder from Marsaryt sadly misunderstood by his community. My daughter, she means more to me than anything but she needs shelter, she needs protection from cruel and hurtful people, for my daughter is alas a poor and simple creature, arrested at the mental age of five. So I am asking for shelter for myself and my poor daughter." So pleaded Meredith Blue Mountain.

Dr. Alimantando wiped his glasses.

"My dear sir, I understand perfectly what it is to be misunderstood by one's community and I can assure you that no one is ever turned away from Desolation Road. Poor, needy, persecuted, despairing, hungry, homeless, loveless, guilty, consumed by the past, there is a place for everyone here." He consulted the master Five Hundred Year Plan on the weather-room wall, threatened by encroaching mathematics. "And your place is Plot 17, Cave 9. See Rael Mandella about tools for farming and Mr. Jericho about building a house. Until it's built you can stay free of charge at the town hotel." He handed Meredith Blue Mountain a scroll. "Documents of citizenship. Fill them out in your own time and return them to me or Persis Tatterdemalion. Now, don't forget the two rules. Rule one is knock before you enter. Rule two is no shouting during the siesta. Keep those rules and you'll be happy here."

So Meredith Blue Mountain took his daughter and went to see Mr. Jericho, who promised a house in one week, with water, gas from the community methane plant, and electricity from the community solar plant; and Rael Mandella, who lent them a hoe, a spade, a mattock, an autoplanter, and assorted seeds, tubers, rhizomes, cuttings, and rootstocks. He also gave them some accelerated-growth cultures for pigs, goats, chickens, and llamas from his stock of cells.

"Father, tell me, is this the place where we are going to stay forever?"

"It is, my little kitten-bone, it is."

"It's nice, but it's a bit dry, isn't it?"

"It is indeed."

Ruthie did say some dumb and obvious things, but what could Meredith Blue Mountain expect from a girl with the mental age of a five-year-old? Anyway, he loved her dumb questions. He loved her devoted dependence and utter adoration, but sometimes he wished he had designed her with a higher I.Q.

11

On the first day of spring in the year Two, the Babooshka and Grandfather Haran were married under a cottonwood tree in Dr. Alimantando's garden. The day was clear and crisp and blue, as befitted the first day of spring. But most days were clear and crisp and blue in Desolation Road. Dr. Alimantando officiated, Rael Mandella was best man, Eva Mandella and little Taasmin were attendants-of-honor, and Mikal Margolis willingly gave the bride away.

"You must give your dear mother away," twittered the Babooshka on their only meeting since their arrival in Desolation Road.

"Me, Mother? Surely you could have found someone better?"

"I tried, Mishka, I tried, but it would not have been honorable for anyone but a son to give his dear, worn-out mother to be married. So you must give me away."

Mikal Margolis had never been able to say no to his mother. He consented, despite Persis Tatterdemalion's scorn at his weakness and his mother's parting words to him.

"Oh, and don't forget, Mishka, this is your mother's special day and I don't want it spoiled by having that cheap woman of easy virtue around, do you understand?"

So Persis Tatterdemalion was kept well to the back as Dr. Alimantando read the service. He had written it himself. He thought it sounded very well. Dr. Alimantando liked to think he had a good reading voice. After all the reading and the signing, the exchanging of rings and the crowning of the heads, there was the party.

It was the first party in the history of Desolation Road, and because of that, it was to be the best. Whole lambs were roasted over pits of glowing charcoal, trays of luocoum and stuffed dates circulated for the nibblesome, great vats of matoke and couscous steamed, and glasses of cool fruit punch eased the revellers' throats. Sweets were tied with ribbons to the branches of the cottonwood tree, and the children jumped up and pulled them down. Limaal and Taasmin, little lithe monkeys of children, soon ate themselves sick on milk-candy angels. Blubbery Johnny Stalin, despite an advantage of age, pulled down none and whined disgustingly under a table for the rest of the afternoon.

When the first stars penetrated the dome of night, paper lanterns were lit in the trees and little cages containing live glow-beetles suspended from the branches. The children poked the beetles into activity with long straws, and it was as if a galaxy of soft green stars had fallen out of the moonring and caught in the branches of the trees. Then came the most wonderful event of the evening. Rajandra Das and Ed Gallacelli wheeled in the big wireless they had secretly built for the wedding out of one of Rael Mandella's packing cases. Rajandra Das bowed lavishly and announced, "Ladies and gentlemen, happy couple, dear friends, let the dancing begin! Let the music play!"

Ed Gallacelli twiddled the tuning knob and there was music—scratchy, distant, poorly tuned, but music. The revellers held their breath in expectation. Rajandra Das touched his charmed fingers to the tuning knob, the wireless gave an audible sigh of ecstasy, and the music flooded out;

strong, insistent, foot-itchy music. There were cheers. There was applause.

"Shall we dance?" said Grandfather Haran to his bride. The Babooshka dimpled and curtsied. Then Grandfather Haran seized her up and in a moment they were whirling in a bluster of petticoats and hand-sewn silk across the foot-pounded earth. Inspired by the example, everyone found partners and danced danced danced to the earthy, gutsy music of Western Solstice Landing. Dr. Alimantando led Eva Mandella in a ponderous, stately folk dance from his home land of Deuteronomy. Ever fearful of his mother's censure, Mikal Margolis danced with Marya Quinsana, who smiled and moved her body against his in such a way that he danced the rest of the night with a painful erection. The Stalins and the Tenebraes danced with their appropriate partners and commented on the ungainliness and clumsiness of their enemies, though Genevieve Tenebrae had one quick swirl with Mr. Jericho, who she thought was wonderfully quick on his feet. Jilted for the night, Persis Tatterdemalion danced with each of the Gallacelli brothers in turn and saw the same face so many times that she felt she had been dancing with the same man all night. Limaal and Taasmin Mandella pranced about with each other with unflagging energy and Johnny Stalin sneaked about, helping himself to leftovers.

They danced and they danced and they danced under the hasty moons until the radio announcer said that the station was going off the air now and he wished everyone a good night.

"Good night!" said everyone.

"Peeeeeeeeeeeeeeeeee," said the wireless.

And everyone had had a good night.

"The best night," said Rajandra Das to Mr. Jericho as they stumbled drunkenly toward their respective beds. And all the Exalted Ancestors agreed.

Marriage was beautiful for the Babooshka and Grandfather Haran, and all who saw them felt the aura of love that surrounded them when they were together and were made joyful. Yet the couple's joy was not full, for there was a shadow in the heart of it. That shadow had been spoken into the world by the Babooshka one night, wrapped up against the chill evening in her scarlet flannel pajamas.

"Haran, I wish to have a child."

Grandfather Haran choked on his hot chocolate.

"What?"

"Why can't we have a child, dear husband? A little, perfect child."

"Woman, be serious. We are too old for children."

"But Haran, this is the Twelfth Decade, miracles are happening every day. This is the age of the possible, so we are told, so it is possible for us, not so? Tell me, my man, do you want a child?"

"Well . . . it would be lovely, but . . ."

"Husband, it is what I am living for! Ah, to be a wife is wonderful, but to be a mother too! Haran, tell me, if I can find a way for us to bear children, will you agree to us having a child? Will you?"

Thinking this wrongly to be a passing whim of a recently wed wife, Grandfather Haran set down his mug, rolled over in his bed, and growled, "Of course, dearest, of course." He was soon asleep. The Babooshka sat up in bed until the dawn came. Her eyes were bright and twinkling as garnets.

12

There was very little in Desolation Road that missed the attention of Limaal and Taasmin Mandella. Even before Dr. Alimantando, besieged by algebra in his weatherroom, had turned his opticon upon it, the twins had spotted the plume of dust on the edge of the other half of the world beyond the tracks. They rushed to tell Dr. Alimantando. Since their true grandfather's marriage, Dr. Alimantando had become a much more satisfactory grandfather figure, a grandfather with a touch of the wizard in him, kindly, but a little awesome. Dr. Alimantando heard Limaal and Taasmin clattering up the winding staircase and was happy. He rather enjoyed being a grandfather.

Through the opticon the plume of dust took on the shape of a paisley-patterned caterpillar, which under increased magnification was seen to be a truck and two trailers, advancing at great speed across the dry plains.

"Look," said Dr. Alimantando, pointing at the display screen. "What does that say?"

"ROTECH," said Limaal, in whom the seeds of rationalism were germinating.

"Heart of Lothian: Genetic Education," said Taasmin, similarly cursed with mystery.

"Let's go and meet this Heart of Lothian, shall we?" suggested Dr. Alimantando. The children took his hands, Limaal right, Taasmin left, and dragged him down the steep, winding stairs and out into the scalding sunlight of fourteen minutes of fourteen. The rest of the population had preceded them but lacking their titular head they did not know what to do and stood about uncertainly, slightly in awe of the word ROTECH on the front of the paisley-patterned tractor. A huge round woman with a face like a potato was handing out business cards.

"Welcome to Desolation Road," said Dr. Alimantando, bowing correctly. The children aped his actions. "Alimantando."

"Pleased to meet you," said the big big woman. She spoke with a curious accent that nobody would quite place. "Heart of Lothian: genetic engineer, hybridization consultant, eugenic education officer for ROTECH. Thank you." She bowed her ponderous bulk to Dr. Alimandando, Limaal, and Taasmin in turn. "One thing," she said, "this place doesn't show up on any of the maps . . . you sure you're registered with the Bureau of Development?"

"Well," said Dr. Alimantando, "er . . ."

"Doesn't matter," boomed Heart of Lothian. "Run into them all the time. I'll sort it out with the boys in China Mountain when I get back. Happens all the time, but it's no skin off my nose. Here . . ." She handed them each a business card and shouted in a voice like a thunderstorm, "The cards you're holding entitle you to one free admission, with a glass of wine, to Heart of Lothian's Traveling Genetic Education Show: all the wonders of today's biotechnology made available to you, at no cost, through the generosity of ROTECH's regional development council. Roll up, roll up, bring the family, old and young, man and boy, come one, come all and see how ROTECH can help your plantation, your garden, your orchard, your pastureland, your livestock, your fatstock, your birds beasts and bushes, all at the Great Paisley-Pattern Biotechnology Show. Doors open twenty o'clock. First ten get free ROTECH badges, stickers, and posters. Hats for the kiddies and everyone gets a free glass of wine. Then," she added with a twinkle in her eye, "I'll show you how I make it."

At twenty hours every man, woman, and child in Desolation Road was standing in line outside Heart of Lothian's traveling show. It had somehow unfolded from a tractor and two trailers into a blossom of paisley-patterned canvas and flashing neon lights. A tethered helium balloon hovered a hundred meters overhead, trailing a long banner proclaiming the glories of Heart of Lothian's Traveling Genetic Education Show. Loudspeakers poured out fast foot-twitching dance music. Everyone was very excited, not on account of the benefits their smallholdings might reap (though Rael Mandella was growing increasingly worried at the depletion of his germ bank and the resulting inbreeding of the town's livestock), but because in a place of ten houses, where even the arrival of the weekly train was an event, the advent of a traveling show was only a little less awesome than if the Panarch and all the hosts of the Five Heavens had marched over Desolation Road to the sound of flutes and drums.

At twenty minutes of twenty Heart of Lothian threw the doors open and the people streamed in in a jostling, elbowing mass. Everyone got a bag of mixed ROTECH goodies: given Desolation Road's tiny population, to limit the largesse to the first ten would have been unjust. Glasses of wine in hand, the people beheld the wonders of ROTECH's genetic science. They were amazed by the fertility hormones that enabled a goat to give birth to as many as eight kids at one time; they marveled at the clone-kits that could grow live chickens out of nothing but eggshells and feathers; they oohed and ahhed at the growth accelerators that could bring any living thing, vegetable or animal (even human, said Heart of Lothian), to full maturity in a couple of days; they wondered at the engineered bacteria which could eat rock, make plastic, cure plant diseases, generate methane gas, and produce iron from sand; they goggled at Heart of Lothian's fermentory, a great bag of blue artificial flesh that digested any form of household waste and bled red, white, or rosé wine on demand from its nipples; and they crept timorously into the darkened room marked *Monster Mash* and pretended to be offended by the genetic mish-mashes that lurked, roared, or slithered within their protective environments. Decked out in orange paper caps printed with the word ROTECH and the nine-spoked Catherine wheel symbol in black, Limaal, Taasmin, and Johnny Stalin stayed there for hours, taunting the agapanthas to snap their meter-wide jaws and the dragons to puff little balls of witch-fire. Finally Heart of Lothian herself had to throw them out when she found Limaal and Taasmin trying to force Johnny Stalin through the gas lock into the piranha bats' low temperature cage.

The people stayed late, very late for farming folk who rose and set with the sun. They asked questions, placed orders, lifted armfuls of the abundant free literature, and drank down glass after glass of Heart of Lothian's excellent red, white, or rosé. Rael Mandella bought a job lot of germ plasm ("guaranteed stronger and healthier," said Heart of Lothian) to replenish his failing stock. The Gallacelli brothers, too much red, white, and rosé in them, asked Heart of Lothian if she could engineer for each of them the same wife, perfect in every physical detail. Heart of Lothian laughed them out of her office but told them to come back after the show was folded up if they wanted to sample the perfection of her own ample flesh. Mr. Jericho and his Exalted Ancestors engaged her in stimulating and high-flown conversation for over an hour, Meredith Blue Mountain bought some bacterial treatment for his potatoes, Tenebraes and Stalins obtained various breeds of huge and disgusting slugs to use against each other's gardens, Persis Tetterdemalion put down an order for a garbage-eating home winery (even though the Great Paisley-Pattern Biotech Show had reminded her sadly of the lamented Astounding

Tatterdemalion Air Bazaar), and last of all came the Babooshka.

The neons had all flickered out, the awnings and paisley-patterned tents were folding back into the trailers, the Gallacelli brothers lurking unnecessarily under a wind-pump, and the stars shining bright when the Babooshka came to Heart of Lothian.

"Madam, I have seen your wonders and your marvels, and yes, they are indeed wonderful and marvelous, the things that can be done these days, but I am wondering, madam, if it is possible for all this science and technology to give me what I want most in all the world, and that is a child."

Heart of Lothian, great earth-mother of a woman, studied the Babooshka, small, tough as a desert sparrow.

"Lady, there is no way you can bear a child. No way at all. But that doesn't mean you can't *have* one. It would have to be gestated out of the body, and I could do that by adapting one of my stock placentories, a bovine one, probably, cows used to commonly be used for surrogating human babies, did you know that? I could fertilize the egg *in vitro*, elementary stuff, you could even do it yourself; I should be able to find an egg in you somewhere; failing that, I could splice up some cell samples . . . your husband, is he still potent?"

"Pardon?"

"Could I get a sperm sample off him, lady?"

"That is for him to say. But tell me, it is possible to give me a child?"

"Entirely so. Genetically, it will be yours, even though it will be impossible for you to bear it within you. If you want to go ahead with it, come and see me tomorrow, at nineteen, with your husband."

"Madam, you are a treasure."

"Just doing my job."

The Babooshka crept away into the night and the Gallacelli brothers crept in out of the night. No one saw either the goings or the comings.

Likewise, no one saw the Babooshka three days later carrying home the placentory in a Belden jar.

"Husband Haran, we have our child!" she sighed, and swept off the discreet covering cloth to reveal the pulpy red pulsing thing in its glass jar.

"That, that, that . . . abortion, is our child?" roared Haran Mandella, reaching for a stout stick to smash the unclean thing. The Babooshka interposed herself between the outraged husband and the wet, sucking artificial womb.

"Haran Mandella, husband, that is my child, more dear to me than anything in this world, and if you so much as lay one finger upon this jar without my consent, I will walk away and never come back."

Grandfather Haran's resolve wavered. The stick quivered in his hand. The Babooshka stood before him, small and defiant as a blackbird. She sang him down.

"She will be beautiful, our child, she will dance, she will sing, she will make the world bright with her beauty, our child; the child of Haran and Anastasia Tyurischeva Mandella." Grandfather Haran put the stick back in its stand and went to bed. In the window, where the dawning light could nourish it, the placentory belched and pulsed.

But the Babooshka's midnight skulkings had not gone entirely unnoticed. Since they had heard that the Stalins were taking delivery of an order of huge and disgusting slugs from Heart of Lothian, the Tenebraes had been on constant guard against slug forays by their enemies. On the night the Babooshka took possession of the blastocyte, Genevieve had been on slug watch. She had seen the old woman and the bundle in her arms and she had known with a sure and certain insight the exact nature of the Babooshka's business with Heart of Lothian. And her own heart had crazed and cracked with envy.

Genevieve Tenebrae did not trust her husband. She did not trust him because he refused to give her a child, the child which would have bound her family into a tight Gordian knot of coziness, the child which would have made her the equal of those damned snobbish Stalins, and what had they to be so damn proud of anyway when their only son was a fat tub of lard, precocious, bad-tempered, and spoiled to the point of ruination. A child would give Genevieve Tenebrae everything she wanted, but a child Gaston Tenebrae would never give her.

"A child, a child, all I want is a child, why will you not give me one?" she would nag every day and every day Gaston Tenebrae would proffer some flimsy excuse, some thin tissue of fabrications that reduced down to selfishness, yes selfishness, pure and simple, and now here was this crone, this hag, this womb-withered Mandella-by-marriage who had a child she was physically incapable of bearing and here was she with a womb as fertile as Oxus Blacksoil, but no seed to sprout in it; it wasn't fair; no, not at all, and then the idea came to her as she hid in a clump of dwarf matoke bushes on slug watch, the idea, the terrible wonderful idea.

The next morning while the whole settlement was waving off Heart of Lothian, waving her back to China Mountain, and the official blessing of ROTECH upon their town, Genevieve slipped into the annex to the Mandella house that the Babooshka and Grandfather Haran inhabited. The placentory quivered and pulsed on the window ledge. She approached it with distaste and determination. From out of her bag she drew a biological support jar given to her husband by Rael Mandella. A few minutes messy, fish-smelly work and she was gone again in a cloud of dust and guilt, the jar pressed close to her heart, the tiny blastocyte turning pale, blind cartwheels within. So that the absence of the fetus might not be noticed, she had slipped an underripe mango into the artificial womb.

As soon as the dust of Heart of Lothian's leavetaking had settled, Genevieve Tenebrae knocked on Marya Quinsana's door.

"Good morning, Mrs. Tenebrae," said Marya Quinsana, sharp and professional in green plastic overalls. "Business or pleasure?"

"Business," said Genevieve Tenebrae. She placed the support jar on the surgery table. "This is the child Heart of Lothian made for me. She didn't have time to implant it herself, but said you would be able to do it."

The operation took ten minutes. When tea and caramels were done, Genevieve Tenebrae slipped home to her vain and petty husband. All guilt was gone, excised by Marya Quinsana's clever instruments. In her skirt pocket rattled a jar of immuno-suppressives so that she might not reject the fetus; in her womb she imagined she could feel the stolen child already kicking and flexing. She hoped it would be a girl. She wondered how she was going to tell her husband. His expression would be interesting to see.

13

Rael Mandella feared his children were growing up to be savages. For three years they had run innocent and ignorant as chickens round and round the tiny town of Desolation Road. It was the only world they knew, wide as all the sky yet so tightly described that a hyperactive three-year-old could run all the way around it in less than ten minutes. That there was a world and a sky and even a world beyond the sky, all of them full of people and history, never occurred to the twins. The trains that steamed in and out at peculiar intervals came from somewhere and went to somewhere, but thinking about that somewhere made the children edgy and uncomfortable. They liked their world to be small and cozy as a bed quilt. Yet Rael Mandella insisted that they learn about those other worlds. "Education," this process was called, and it involved the sacrifice of whole mornings which could be so much more profitably utilized listening to Dr. Alimantando, who was nice but not a great communicator, or Mr. Jericho, who knew so much about the world it was frightening, or learning to read from their mother's beautifully illustrated picture books which told the stories of days when ROTECH and St. Catherine built the world.

Limaal and Taasmin remained enthusiastic savages. They greatly preferred to spend their days making fat Johnny Stalin's life a misery with mud, water, feces, and inimitable feats of acrobatic skill on the water pump gantries. Yet Rael Mandella was adamant that his children would not grow into stoop-backed slaves of the shovel, dull as old boots. They would have the things that he could not. The world would be their toy. He tried to instill the excitement of learning in them, but even

Heart of Lothian's Genetic Education Show had left them cold. Until, that is, the day Adam Black's Traveling Chautauqua and Educational 'Stravaganza came to town.

The night before the great showman's arrival the eastern horizon had popped and sparkled silver and gold with fireworks. Desolation Road was left in no doubt that an event of great moment was due to descend upon it. Next morning an unscheduled train drew into Desolation Road's makeshift station and was waved into a siding by Rajandra Das, unofficial station master. It stood there billowing steam and blaring stirring music from loudspeakers mounted on the locomotive while the people gathered to see what had come now.

"Adam Black's Traveling Chautauqua and Educational 'Stravaganza," read Rajandra Das from the brash playbill script painted in red and gold on the rolling stock. He spat in the dust. The music played on. Time passed. The air grew hot. The people grew tired of waiting in the heat. Genevieve Tenebrae almost fainted.

Suddenly there was a simultaneous fanfare and blast of steam that made everybody jump.

"Ladies and gentlemen, boys and girls, the one and only . . . Adam Black!" bawled a curiously mechanical-sounding voice. Stairs unfolded from the carriages. A tall, thin elegant man stepped forward. He wore a dark long-tailed coat, and pants with a real gold stripe. There was a black bootlace tie around his neck, and on his head a huge cartwheel hat. He carried a gold-topped cane and his eyes twinkled like jet. And of course he had a thin pencil-line moustache. Anyone more like an Adam Black it was difficult to imagine. He made sure everyone had taken a good long look at him. Then he shouted, "Ladies and gentlemen, you see before you the ultimate repository of human knowledge: Adam Black's Traveling Chautauqua and Educational 'Stravaganza. History, art, science, nature, wonders of earth and sky, marvels of science and technology, tales of strange places and faraway lands, where the miraculous is workaday, all are within. *See* the mighty works of ROTECH at first hand through the Adam Black Patent Opticon; *hear* Adam Black's tales of mystery and imagination from the four quarters of the globe; *marvel* at the latest developments in science and technology; *wonder* at the train, yes, this very train, which drives itself with a mind of its own; *goggle in amazement* at the Dumbletonians, half man, half machine; *learn* of the mysteries of physics, of chemistry, of philosophy, of theology, art, and nature: all this can be yours, ladies and gentlemen, this cornucopia of ancient wisdom; yours for only fifty centavos, yes, fifty centavos, or equivalent value in whatever commodity you choose: yes, ladies and gentlemen, boys and girls, Adam Black presents his Traveling Chautauqua and Educational 'Stravaganza!" The prancing dandy rapped his cane smartly on the side of the red, gold, and green carriage and the locomtive blew five steam rings, one inside the other, and played march music at an ear-shattering volume.

Adam Black opened the doors to his wonderland of learning and was almost swept aside as Rael Mandella and his mulish children led the rush to education. The mysteries of physics, chemistry, philosophy, art, and nature did not excite Limaal and Taasmin Mandella. They yawned at the Dumbletonians, half man, half machine, they fidgeted in boredom when the computerized train with a mind of its own tried to engage them in conversation, they talked and giggled through Adam Black's illustrated talk on the natural wonders of the world. But the mighty works of ROTECH, viewed through Adam Black's Patent Opticon, made their eyes pop.

They sat in a carriage on hard plastic chairs. Limaal found that the chairs squeaked if he rocked back and forward, and this is what he was doing when the room was suddenly plunged into darkness as black as death. Screams came from the back, where the Gallacelli brothers were sitting behind Persis Tatterdemalion. Then a voice said, "Space: the final frontier," and all of a sudden the carriage was full of drifting sparks of light. The twins tried to catch them and hold them in their hands but the bright motes passed through their fingers. A swirling spiral nebula passed straight through Limaal's chest. He snatched at it but it had flown out through the back of the carriage. A star detached itself from the glowing galactic web and grew in size and luminosity until it threw definite shadows on the walls of the carriage.

"Our sun," said Adam Black. "We are approaching our solar system at a simulated speed of twenty thousand times the speed of light. As we enter the system of worlds, we will slow to enable you to view the glories of the planets." The star was now a distinct sun. Planets waltzed past in a stately procession of orbs and rings. "We are passing the outer worlds; the cloud of comets that envelops our system, there you see distant Nemesis, our sun's far, faint companion, here is Avernus, here Charon; Poseidon, that is ringed Uranus, and Chronos with its rings also . . . here is Jove, mightiest of all worlds, if our world, which you see now, beyond the jumble of rocky asteroids, were peeled like an orange and placed on mighty Jove's surface, it would seem no larger than a fifty centavo piece . . . this is our world, our home, we shall return to it in one moment, but first we must pay a fleeting visit to shining Aphrodite, and tiny Hermes, closest to the sun, before turning our attention to the Motherworld from which the peoples of our earth sprang."

A spot of light at the edge of the room exploded into a system of two great worlds, one a dull white lifeless skull, the other an opal-blue orb, milk-mottled like a marble. The dead white skull-world rushed past the spectators into the stellar distance and the twins found themselves hovering over the blue womb-world like two dirty-faced seraphs of the Panarch. They saw that this busy blue world was girdled by a silver hoop, the dimensions of which beggared their imaginations. Again the holographic focus shifted and the thin spokes, like the spokes of a bicycle wheel, which bound the hoop-world to the sphere world were clearly visible to all.

The small dark room was dense with awe. The twins sat silent and still. The terrifying things in the sky had shaken all movement out of them. Adam Black continued his lecture. "You see before you the Motherworld, the planet from which our race sprang. It is a very old world, unbelievably old. There have been people on our world for only seven hundred years, most have come since the manforming was completed less than a century ago, but upon the Motherworld there are civilizations thousands upon thousands of years old." The blue Motherworld turned beneath the twins' omniscient gaze. As its cloud-shrouded landscapes passed into night, they sprang to life with the ten million million lights of continent-spanning cities. "An old, old world," sang Adam Black, mesmerizing his audience with his dancing words, "old and used up. And crowded. Very crowded. You can't imagine how crowded."

Limaal Mandella clung to his father in fear, for he could

imagine it only too well. He could see all the naked, bald people jammed shoulder to shoulder; a living, breathing carpet of flesh draped over hill and dale and mountain and plain until it reached the edge of the sea. Here the people had been pushed waist-deep into the oily water, pushed deeper and deeper by the ever-growing Malthusian mass until the water closed over their heads. He imagined that ponderous globe of exploding flesh falling from the sky by its sheer weight and crushing him with its masses.

"So great is the population that the land masses have long ago been filled up, and even the great cities that sail the oceans of the world cannot hold any more. So the people have been forced up these spokes, these orbital elevators, to live in the ring city they have built in the space around their world, where energy and resources are abundant."

The projection focus closed in upon the silver hoop and resolved it into a disturbing jumble of geometric shapes growing out of each other like crystals. Closer yet and the details of the geometric shapes, huge as whole towns, became apparent; tubes, spheres, fanlike formations and odd protuberances, cubes and skewed trapezoids. Closest of all, the transparent roofs could be clearly seen, and beneath them bacteria-small figures bustled and hustled.

Taasmin Mandella's eyes were tightly shut and hidden behind her closed fingers. On the other side of her father Limaal Mandella sat with mouth wide open, annihilated by knowledge.

"The name of this city is Metropolis," said Adam Black. Mr. Jericho had mouthed the name "Metropolis" in simultaneous silence. He had half-feared that he might have seen himself beneath that great transparent roof, sitting at the feet of Paternoster Augustine. "Despite its great size, its population is growing so fast that the machines that are adding to it every hour of every day still cannot match the pace of expansion. Now we say farewell to the Motherworld," and the blue opal-world, its hoop, its skull-satellite, and its pressing trillions dwindled to a distant dot, "and turn our attention closer to home."

Now the earth swelled before the twins and they beheld its atlas-familiar snowy poles, its blue land-locked seas, its green forests and yellow plains and wide red deserts. They looked down upon Mount Olympus, so tall her summit rose above the highest snows, and the bustling lands of the Grand Valley, thick with cities and towns. As their earth loomed closer, they saw the glittering moonring and here the oracle-eye rested, filling the room with incomprehensible drifting shapes. Some were so huge they took minutes to cross the room, some were tiny and tumbling, some were busy as insects, flitting through the spectators intent upon their small errands; all of them bore the name ROTECH somewhere upon them.

"Behold, the forces that shaped our world and made it a place fit for man to live. A thousand years ago certain wise men, holy sages all, I do not doubt, foresaw what you have just seen, that the Motherworld could not hold all the people who would come to be. Other worlds must be found, but all the worlds within reach were dead and lifeless, even this one. Yes, our earth was as dead and lifeless as that white skull of a world you saw but minutes ago. Yet these wise men knew that it could be made to bear life. Approaching the various governments of the nations of the Motherworld, they founded ROTECH, the Remote Orbital Terraforming and Environmental Control Headquarters, and armed with all that age's science and technology, labored for seven hundred long years to make this earth friendly to man."

An enormous asymmetrical object, studded with tiny shining windows and bearing the holy name in letters which, full-scale, must have been two hundred meters tall, slid across the room. Tiny midge-things buzzed about it in furious industry. Limaal Mandella bounced up and down in his chair in excitement at the shapes in the sky.

"Be still," his father hissed. He looked at his mother for someone with whom to share all this excitement, but Eva Mandella had the look of non-understanding drawn on her face. His sister was wide-eyed and expressionless as an icon of a saint.

"What you are seeing are a few of the orbital devices by which ROTECH maintains our world's precarious environmental balance. Some are weather control machines, using infrared lasers to heat areas of the planet's surface to generate pressure differentials and thus winds. Others are magnetic super-cores, magnetos, generating the intense field that protects our world from the bombardment of charged solar particles and cosmic rays. Others still are vanas, the orbital mirrors that lighten the dark nights in the absence of moons, some are orphs, which work directly upon the world, even now seeding the barren places of the earth with life, some are shunters, which move cometary ice from the cloud we saw earlier, out at the edge of the solar system, and bring it to our world so that hydrostatic equilibrium may be maintained, and some are partacs, dreadful weapons of puissant destruction with which ROTECH can defend this fragile world against attack from . . . Beyond. Once there were many more but most have moved on with ROTECH to greater challenges; the taming of the hell-world we call Aphrodite but is better given its old name, Lucifer; the greening of the Motherworld's airless moon. Now look at this . . ."

It seemed to the children that they swooped like a great space-bird around the shoulder of the world and saw far beyond the cascading moonring something tremendous approaching the world, something like a butterfly kilometers and kilometers and kilometers across, something so huge and complex in its design that it defied imagining. It turned ponderously so that the sunlight caught it, and the twins and everyone around them gasped as three million square kilometers of sail were suddenly illuminated.

"Sails wide enough to wrap the world in," whispered Adam Black, and then let his voice rise to a dramatic pitch as he declaimed: "A SailShip of the Praesidium, arriving at the ROTECH orbital docking facilities. A year and a day ago she set sail from Metropolis with one and three quarter million colonists sleeping in stasis in the cargo-pods and now their journey is over. They have arrived at our world. They will find it a strange, topsy-turvy, confusing place, much as our fathers' fathers' fathers and mothers' mothers' mothers found it. Some will die, some will return home, some will fail and sink to the bottom of society, but most, when they arrive at the entrepot cities of Touchdown, Bleriot, and Belladonna, will take a long look at the world and think they have landed in paradise."

The disembodied viewpoint plunged toward the earth, down down, plunging ever faster until it seemed as if Limaal and Taasmin must smash to pulp on the hard earth. Knuckles went white and the Babooshka screamed. The lights came on again. Dust motes floated in the beams of the lamps. Adam

Black stepped into the lights and said, "That concludes our tour of the wonders of earth and sky and we now return you safely to familiar terra firma once more." Doors opened at the end of the carriage admitting a stream of dusty sunlight. The people were very quiet as they filed out into the afternoon sun.

"Well, what did you think of that?" said Rael Mandella to his children. They did not answer. They were immersed in their own thoughts.

Limaal Mandella's head was filled with falling planets pregnant with humanity, with spinning wheels of light thousands of kilometers across, with seemingly anarchic jumbles of shapes which nevertheless kept the world running like an oiled clock, and the rational part of him reached out and embraced all he had seen. He understood that both human and material universes operated according to fundamental principles and that these principles were knowable, then all the universes of matter and mind must be knowable too. He embraced the Grand Design and saw it copied in miniature everywhere his eyes rested. Everything was comprehensible, everything was explainable; there were no mysteries left, all things pointed inward.

Taasmin Mandella had likewise beheld the wonders of earth and sky but choose rather the path of mysticism. She had seen that all orders of organization obeyed higher orders, and those higher orders in turn obeyed orders of vaster and more splendid intelligence in an upward spiral of consciousness at the apex of which sat God the Panarch Unknowable: Ineffable, and Silent as Light, whose plans could only be guessed at from His revelations that dropped like some sweet distillate down the coils of the helix of consciousness. All things pointed outward and upward.

Rael Mandella could not know what he had done to his children, either at the instant of their births when he had cursed them with his family curse, or the germination of that curse-seed in Adam Black's Holographium. The twins seemed impressed. Maybe they had learned something valuable. If the roots of learning had taken in them, then the two bushels of strawberries and the chicken he had spent on his children's education had been money well invested.

14

On the night of Friday 21st Augtember, at twenty minutes of twenty, the Babooshka leaped up in the middle of one of their interminable word games just as Grandfather Haran was about to put "zoomorph" down on a triple word and exclaimed, "Is time! Is time! My baby, oh, my baby!" And she rushed into the room where the placentory had pulsed and pumped and swollen day by day, hour by hour, for two hundred and eighty days, 7520 hours, into a great bulb of blue-red flesh.

"What is it, flower of my heart?" cried Grandfather Haran. "What is the matter?" Receiving no reply, he hurried into the room and found his wife standing with her hands to her mouth, staring at the placentory. The artificial womb was shuddering and contracting and a foul, fetid stench filled the room.

"Is time!" gabbled the Babooshka. "My baby is come! Our baby! Oh, Haran! Husband."

Grandfather Haran sniffed the foul air. A trickle of black fluid squeezed out of the placentory and stained the nutrient liquid. A sense of great evil clutched at his heart.

"Out," he commanded the Babooshka.

"But Haran . . . our child! I, a mother, must be with my child." She reached for the fleshy obscenity on the window ledge.

"Out! I, your husband, command it!" Grandfather Haran seized his wife by the shoulders, turned her around, and thrust her out of the door, which he bolted behind him. Hideous belchings were now erupting from the spasming placentory. Grandfather Haran approached with trepidation. He tapped the jar. The placentory emitted a keening whine as if gas were streaming out under high pressure. Bubbles boiled to the surface of the Belden jar and burst, emitting a suffocating stench. Grandfather Haran covered his mouth and nose with a handkerchief and prodded the womb with a pencil. The placentory convulsed and, with a tearing, belching sound, spewed vile gray slime into the air. It spat a torrent of foul black fluid interspersed with stifling farts, then ripped down the middle and died. Holding his breath lest he vomit, Grandfather Haran poked about the decomposing remains with his pencil. There was no sign of there ever having been a child within. He did find some rotting black segments of what looked like mango skin. Satisfied that there was no child, alive or dead, he left the room and locked it behind him.

"A terrible, blasphemous thing has happened here to-night," he told his wife. "As long as I live, no one will ever enter that room again." He strode to the front door and threw the key as far into the night as he could.

"My child, Haran, my child, is she alive, is she dead?" The Babooshka swallowed. "Is she . . . human?"

"There never was a child," said Grandfather Haran, looking straight ahead of him. "Heart of Lothian has deceived us. The womb was empty. Quite empty." There and then he broke the vow his wife had made for him and went down to Tatterdemalion's B.A.R. to drink himself stupid.

At the precise moment the Babooshka leaped up and abandoned her game, Genevieve Tenebrae felt a tearing pain wrench at her. She let out a tiny, sobbing moan and knew that the time had come.

"Dearest, is there anything wrong?" said Gaston Tenebrae from his chair by the fire, where he sat of an evening smoking his hookah pipe and dreaming of sweet adultery.

Another contraction wrenched Genevieve Tenebrae.

"The child," she whispered, "it's coming."

"Child," said Gaston Tenebrae, "what child?"

Genevieve Tenebrae smiled through the pain. She had purposefully kept the pregnancy secret for nine months in anticipation of this delicious moment.

"Your child," she whispered. "Your child, you vain idiot."

"What?" roared Gaston Tenebrae, a thousand kilometers away, tall and futile as a wet reed.

"You slipped up, husband. Your child . . . you've denied me . . . and denied me, and kept . . . me . . . waiting, so I kept you waiting and now . . . the waiting's done." She gasped as a new pain gripped her. Gaston Tenebrae fluttered and flustered like a tiny, pathetic bird in a greenhouse. "Get me to Quinsana . . . Marya Quinsana."

She collected her remaining dignity and walked to the door. There the fiercest set of contractions yet racked her.

"Help me, you good-for-nothing pig," she moaned, and Gaston Tenebrae came and helped her through the cold dark night to Quinsana's Dental and Veterinary Surgery.

Seeing it loom out of post-anesthetic torpor, Marya Quinsana's face looked rather like a llama's, thought Genevieve Tenebrae. This plangent thought circled in the superconducting circuit of her mind until the gift-wrapped bundle of baby was placed in her arms and she remembered everything.

"Not that much harder than delivering a goat," said Marya Quinsana, smiling all over her llama face. "But I thought it best to knock you right out anyway."

"Gaston, where is Gaston?" asked Genevieve Tenebrae. Her husband's goateed face bent close to hers.

It said to her in a confidential whisper, "I'll speak to you when we're alone."

Genevieve Tenebrae smiled distantly, her husband of no more importance than an irritating fly. What mattered was the child in her arms, her child; had she not borne it herself, carried it within her for nine months, made it a part of her for almost half a year?

"Arnie Nicolodea," she whispered. "Little Arnie."

When the news of the surprise birth of the third natural citizen of Desolation Road broke in the Bethlehem Ares Railroad/Hotel, Persis Tatterdemalion declared drinks all around and there was toasting and merrymaking by all save Grandfather Haran, who came to realize as the night passed into morning exactly what had been done to him. He also came to realize that he could never prove anything.

"Isn't it strange," commented Rajandra Das, made loquacious by maize beer and wine from the hotel fermentory, "that the couple who wanted the baby didn't get one and the couple who didn't did?" Everyone thought that a pithy summarization.

15

Rajandra Das had once lived in a hole under Meridian Main Station. He still lived in a hole: in the Great Desert. Rajandra Das had once been prince of gutter boys, tramps, beggars, freebooters, goondahs, and bums. He still was prince of gutter boys, tramps, beggars, freebooters, goondahs, and bums. There was no one to compete with him for the honor. Too lazy to farm, he lived by his wits and charity of his neighbors, charming their broken cultivators and faulty sun-tracker units to renewed vigor, aiding Ed Gallacelli in the construction of mechanical devices of little practical value save the utilization of too much time. Once he had fixed a Bethlehem Ares Railroads Locomotive: a class 19, he remembered; it had limped into Desolaton Road with a badly tuned tokamak. It had felt like the old days again. In a fit of nostalgia he had almost asked the engineers for a ride: to Wisdom, shining dream of his heart.

Then he thought of the guard who had thrown him off the train and the hardships, hard kicks, and work, hard work he would encounter on such a journey. Desolation Road was quiet, Desolation Road was isolated, but Desolation Road was comfortable and the fruit could be picked fresh from the tree. He would stay awhile yet.

Upon the winter solstice, when the sun stood low upon the horizon and the red dust glistened with frost, Adam Black returned to Desolation Road. His coming was as welcome as spring to the winter-weary farming folk.

"Roll up, roll up," he bawled. "Adam Black's Traveling Chautauqua and Educational 'Stravaganza *once again*" (and here he banged his gold-topped cane on a small block for emphasis) "presents to you the wonders of the four quarters of the world in an *all new*" (bang bang) "show! Featuring for your delectation and delight *ladies*" (bang) "*gentlemen*" (bang) "*boys*" (bang) "and *girls*, a never-before-seen novelty, an Angel from the Realms of Glory! Captured from the Heavenly Circus, a real, bona fide, hundred-percent card-carrying gilt-edged *angel!*" (bang bang) "Yes, roll up, roll up, good citizens, only fifty centavos for five minutes with this wonder of the Age; fifty centavos, good people, can you really afford *not* to witness this *unique phenomenon*" (bang bang)? "If you would be so kind as to form an orderly line, thank you . . . no pushing please, there's time enough for everyone."

Rajandra Das had come late to the show. He had been comfortably asleep by his fire when the Chautauqua train drew up and as a consequence had to stand in the cold for over an hour before his turn came.

"Just the one?" asked Adam Black.

"Don't see anyone else."

"Fifty centavos then."

"Ain't got fifty centavos. You take two honeycombs?"

"Two honeycombs are fine. Five minutes."

It was warm in the coach. Black drapes covered the windows and whispered as the hot air from the ventilators stirred them. In the center of the car stood a large and heavy steel cage, most solid, without doors or locks. Sitting on a trapeze suspended from the roof of the cage was a melancholy creature Rajandra Das was meant to believe was an angel, though it was no angel he had ever been taught about as a child on the pious knee of his dear and departed mother.

Its face and torso were those of an extraordinarily beautiful young woman. Its arms and legs were made out of riveted metal. At shoulder and hip, flesh blended into metal. Rajandra Das could see that this was no mere fusion of human with prosthetic. This was something distinctly other.

A glowing blue aura outlined the angel and provided the only illumination in the black, warm carriage.

Rajandra Das did not know how long he stood and stared before the angel extended its mechanical legs into long stilts and stepped down from its trapeze. It telescoped to human height and pressed its face close to the bars, eye-to-eye with the staring Rajandra Das.

"If you've got only five minutes, I suggest you ask me something," the angel said in a thrilling contralto voice.

The staring spell was broken.

"Hoee!" said Rajandra Das. "Just what sort of thing are you?"

"That's usually the first question," said the tin-pot angel with the weariness of long-established routine. "I'm an Anael, a seraph of the Fifth Order of the Heavenly Host, hand-servant of the Blessed Lady of Tharsis. Now, would you like me to petition Our Lady on behalf of yourself or others, or take a message to a departed beloved beyond the veil of death? That's usually the second question."

"Well, it ain't mine," said Rajandra Das. "Any fool can see you're not taking any message anywhere, not while you're in that cage performing for Mr. Adam Black. No, what I want to know is what the hell kind of angel you are, sir, 'cause I was always taught angels were like ladies with long hair and pretty wings and glowing shifts and all that."

The angel pouted in petty offense.

"No damn dignity these days. Anyway, that's the third question most mortals ask. I expected better of you after you missed out question two."

"Well, how's about answering question three, then?"

The angel sighed.

"Behold mortal."

Out of its back unfolded two sets of collapsible helicopter vanes. The cage was too small to permit the rotors to open fully and the drooping blades made the angel seem even more pathetic and futile.

"Wings. And as for the gender question." The Anael's halo flickered. Peculiar swellings rose and moved under its fleshly parts. Its features melted and ran like rainwater off a roof. The subcutaneous moundings converged, solidified, and formed a new terrain of features. Rajandra Das let out a low whistle of appreciation.

"Nice teats. So you're either."

"Or neither," said the Anael, and repeated the facial-thaw trick, melting into an extraordinarily beautiful young person of indeterminate gender. Now worthy of the pronoun, it tucked its rotor blades into its back and smiled a disconsolate smile. Rajandra Das felt a needle of sympathy prick his heart. He knew how it felt to be in a place he had not chosen to be. He knew how it felt to be pissed on by life.

"Anything else, mortal" asked the Anael wearily.

"Hey hey hey man, not so touchy. I'm on your side, honest. Tell me, how come you can't bust out of this cage with one flick of your pinky finger? I was taught angels were pretty powerful things."

The Anael leaned confidentially against the bars of its cage.

"I'm only an Anael, Fifth Rank of the Heavenly Host, not one of the big shots like PHARIOSTER or TELEMEGON; they're the most recent models; First Orders, Archangelsks; they can do just about damn anything, but we Anaels, we were the first, we were the Blessed Lady's prototypes and she improved the design with each succeeding model: Avatas, Lorarchs, Cheraphs, Archangelsks."

"Hold on, hold on, you saying you were made?"

"We all get made, mortal, one way or another. My point is, we Anaels are designed to run on solar power, that's why Adam Black keeps this cage in darkness, otherwise I might be able to charge up enough sun power to sunder these bars. Though," the Anael added dolefully, "we Anaels are primarily designed for flight, not fight; most of my strength is channeled through my rotors."

"So what if I opened all the curtains?"

"Adam Black comes and closes them again. Thanks for the thought, mortal, but it would take about three weeks of constant sunshine for me to regain my full angelic might."

Adam Black put his head round the door and said, "Time's up. Come on out." He looked sternly at the Anael. "You been keeping them talking again? I've told you to keep it short."

"Hey hey hey, what's the rush?" protested Rajandra Das. "There's no one after me and we were just getting to an interesting stage in the conversation. One minute more, all right?"

"Oh, okay." Adam Black withdrew to count his takings: six dollars fifty centavos, a chicken, three bottles of peapod wine, and two honeycombs.

"All right, tell me more, man," said Rajandra Das. "Like how you came to be in this here cage in the first place."

"Simple carelessness. There I was in the Great Company

of the Blessed Lady, parading over some ten centavo High Plains town call Frenchman—we do that from time to time, make like a big circus parade, keeps mortals mindful of higher things, like who made the world, and anyway, the Blessed Lady's got this new policy of direct intervention with organic beings. Well, it was a pretty big show and what with the Great Powers and Dominions and the Spiritual Menagerie and the Big Blue Plymouth and the Rider on the Many-Headed Beast and all that, it took the best part of a day for it to pass over. I was in the final wave and what with all that waiting around I was getting pretty bored, and bored angels get careless. Next thing I knew, I'd flown smack into the high-voltage section of the Frenchman microwave link. Stunned me. Clear blew my fuses. Kayoed. Mortals cut me down and stuck me in this cage in a cellar and fed me cornpone and beer. Any idea what it's like to be an alcoholic angel? I kept telling them I was solar powered, but they couldn't take it in. Mortals were wondering what they could do with an Anael from the Heavenly Host, when along came Adam Black and bought me and my cage for fifteen golden dollars."

"Well, what about trying to escape?" suggested Rajandra Das, thinking evil thoughts.

"No lock. We are good with machinery, I'll say that for us, any lock on that cage I could pick, but that Adam Black knows his hagiography, for when I had regained my strength and grown new circuits, he had this door all welded up."

"That's bad," said Rajandra Das, remembering holes under Meridian Main Station. "No one should ever be in a cage because of a mistake."

The Anael shrugged eloquently. Adam Black put his head around the door again.

"Okay. Time's up, and I mean time's up. Out. I'm closing up for the night."

"Help me," the Anael whispered desperately, gripping the finger-thick steel bars. "You can get me out, I know it; I can read it in your heart."

"That's probably just question five," said Rajandra Das, and he turned to leave the darkened carriage. But out of his pocket he slipped his Defense Forces multiblade knife, stolen from Krishnamurthi's Speciality Hardware, and palmed it to the Anael.

"Hide that," he whispered without moving his lips. "And when you get out, promise me you'll do two things. First is don't come back. Ever. Second is remember me to the Blessed Lady when you see her, because she made me kind to machines and machines kind to me." The palm turned into a wave of farewell. Adam Black was waiting to lock the doors.

"Some sideshow you got there," Rajandra Das commented. "Tell you this, going to be a hard act to follow. What you got lined up for us next? St. Catherine in a cage, eh?" He winked at the showman. Already he thought he could hear the rasping of metal on metal.

16

The morning ROTECH came it entered the world as a dull drone in the dreams of the people and crept out of them as a heavy throbbing. It woke everyone from their sleep and it was then that they realized that they were not sharing the same communal nightmare, that the noise was a real objective phenomenon, so real and objective that it made every loose item in the house rattle and sent plates from their shelves to smash on the floor.

"What is it, what is it?" the people asked each other, throwing on their day clothes, throwing off nightmare superstitions of Apocalypse, Armageddon, nuclear destruction, interplanetary war, or the sky falling upon their heads. The throbbing grew until it even filled the spaces inside their skulls. It shook the rocks beneath their feet, it shook the bones beneath the skin, it shook heaven and earth, it shook the people up the stairs and out of their front doors to see what was happening.

Above Desolation Road hung a thousand silver saucers, so shiny-bright in the dawn sun that they blinded the eye: a thousand silver sky-craft shaking earth and heaven with the pounding of their engines. Each was a full fifty meters across, each bore the holy name of ROTECH in conjunction with a serial number and the subscript, in bold black: PLANETARY MAINTENANCE DIVISION. Searchlights snapped out and quartered the town, seeking the citizens who stood astounded on their porches and verandas. Illuminated from on high, the Babooshka fell to her knees and prayed that the Angel of the Five Vials of Destruction (plague of darkness, plague of hunger and thirst, plague of childlessness, plague of sarcasm, plague of all-devouring mutant goats) might pass from her presence. The children of Desolation Road waved to the crews in their forward control cabins. The pilots waved in return and flashed their searchlights. As people became used to the idea of ROTECH aircraft in the air above their town, they realized that there were not a thousand of them, nor a hundred, nor even fifty, but twenty-three. Twenty-three 'lighters filling heaven and earth with their pounding pounding engines was still an impressive sight first thing in the morning.

With a roar of stone-shattering power, twenty-two 'lighters lifted high into the air and banked away into the west, searchlights tracing long raking stains against the sky. The one remaining dirigible settled lower and came in for a landing on the far side of the railroad tracks, in the exact spot where Persis Tatterdemalion had crashed into Desolation Road. ROTECH's landing was fully controlled and performed with arrogant ease. The 'lighter's fans swiveled upward for landing and threw stifling clouds of dust into the air. When the coughing had stopped, the 'lighter was resting upon its landing pads and unfolding a flight of steps from its brightly lit interior. With the steps came the smell of breakfast cooking.

The citizens of Desolation Road were all gathered on the town side of the tracks, all save Persis Tatterdemalion, who had fled at the first touch of the searchlights on her skin, for the 'lighters were free to fly and she was not. The people watched the events around the airship with trepidation mixed with excitement. These could be the best visitors yet.

"Go on," said Mr. Jericho to Dr. Alimantando. "You're the boss." Dr. Alimantando brushed some dust from his perpetually dusty clothes and walked the hundred meters over the line to the 'lighter. There was not one encouraging cry to urge him on.

An extremely smart man in a beautiful high-collared white suit descended the 'lighter steps and stared at Dr. Alimantando. Dr. Alimantando, dusty and humble, bowed politely.

"I am Dr. Alimantando, Chairman Pro Tem of the Desolation Road Community, population twenty-two, elevation twelve hundred fifty, 'one step short of paradise.' Welcome to our town, I hope you will enjoy your stay here, we have a very good hotel for your comfort and convenience, clean, cheap, with full amenities."

The stranger, still staring (most rudely by a shy Deuteronomian's standards), nodded his head in the barest recognition of formality.

"Dominic Frontera, Settlement and Development Officer, China Mountain ROTECH Planetary Maintenance Division. What the hell are you doing here?"

Dr. Alimantando's quick temper rose.

"I might ask the same of you sir."

So Dominic Frontera told him. And Dr. Alimantando immediately convened a meeting of all citizens so that Dominic Frontera might tell them what he had told him. And this is what Dominic Frontera told them.

"On Tuesday sixteenth May, three days from today, at sixteen twenty-four, Desolation Road will be vaporized by the impact of a cometary nucleus weighing in the region of two hundred and fifty megatons, traveling at five kilometers per second, some thirty-four kilometers due south of here."

Pandemonium broke loose. Dr. Alimantando banged his Chairman Pro Tem's gavel until he cracked the block, then shouted himself hoarse and still the people roared and raged and waved Persis Tatterdemalion's best chairs in the air. Dominic Frontera could scarcely credit that twenty-two people could generate such bedlam.

None of this should have happened to him. He should have completed his survey of the impact site in one morning and by now be home in Regional HeadQuarters in Meridian. He should be playing backgammon in his favorite corner of Chen Tsu's tea rooms, sipping Belladonna brandy and watching the apricot blossom. Instead, he was facing a riotous mob eager to beat him to death with desert-pine bar stools—look at that old hag, she must be pushing forty if she's a day, but she'd like nothing better than to lick my blood off the floor—all because he had found a pissing little town where no pissing little town should be, in an oasis that was not even scheduled for environmental engineering until two years after the impact. Dominic Frontera sighed. He pulled a snub-nose Presney Reaction pistol from his pilot's holster and fired three quick shots into the roof of the Bethlehem Ares Railroad/Hotel.

The immediate shocked silence pleased him. The reaction charges hissed and fizzed in the rooftiles. Peace restored, he explained why Desolation Road must be destroyed.

It was all to do with water. There wasn't enough of it. The world was maintained by a series of ecological equations which must always balance. On one side of the equation was the engineered environment of the earth: air, water, weather, and those less tangible agents, like the orbital superconducting magnets that spun a protective web around the planet, banishing radiation and the storm of solar particles that would otherwise sterilize the surface of the earth, or the layer of metal ions suspended high above the tropopause that amplified ambient sunlight, and the orbital skymirrors, Vanas, that ironed out local temperature and pressure differentials: a stable equation, but fragile. On the other side of the equal sign stood the peoples of the earth, native and immigrant, their expanding populations, and the increasing demands they made upon the world and its resources. And this equation must always balance, should the population grow arithmetically, geometrically, logarithmically, the equation *must always balance* (here Dominic Frontera poked his pilot's gun muzzle at his audience for added emphasis), and if this equality meant importing water now and then from somewhere ("now and then" being every ten years or so for the next half millennium, "somewhere" being the gigatons of cometary ice waiting in the wings of the solar system for its gravitational cue), then imported it must be.

"In the past," explained Dominic Frontera to the rows of open mouths, "we impacted cometary heads willy-nilly on the surface of the world: what ice did not vaporize on reentry did so on impact, and the vast amounts of dust thrown up by the blast caused the water vapor to form into clouds and thus precipitate. In the early days comets were hitting at the rate of three per week, peak. Of course, there was no one around then for them to fall on." Dominic Frontera remembered he was not lecturing some secondary school geography class, but a bunch of stupid farmers, and grew angry. "As you might imagine, since settlement began it's been getting harder to find places to crash the ice; and we like to crash the ice if we can, it's by far the cheapest way of generating water vapor. Now, we had our target area picked, an area of the North West Quartersphere Region that had no environmental engineering planned for at least four years, maybe the odd traveler, the odd train, the odd 'lighter, but they could be warned out of the area before impact and afterward we could come in, fix up any track that got busted, and call down orphs from orbit to turn the desert into a garden. That's the plan. What do we find? What do we find?" Dominic Frontera's voice rose to a squeak., "You. What the hell are you doing here? There shouldn't even be an oasis here, much less a town!"

Dr. Alimantando rose to tell his tale of sailboards and mad orphs. Dominic Frontera waved him down.

"Save your explanations. You're not responsible. There's been a cock-up in the Orbital Environmental Engineering Division, some orph's programming gone up the spout. Cranky things. Okay, so it's not your fault, but there's nothing I can do. The comet is on its way, has been for the past seventy-two months. On Tuesday sixteenth of May, at sixteen twenty-four, it will impact thirty-four kilometers south of here and this little town and this little oasis will fold up like a . . . like a . . . cardboard house." There were howls of protest. Dominic Frontera raised hands for silence and calm. "I'm sorry. Truly I am, but there's nothing I can do. The comet can't be deflected, there's nowhere for it to go, not at this late stage. If only you'd let someone, anyone, know you existed earlier, we might have been able to compute different orbits. As it is, it's too late. I'm sorry."

"What about Heart of Lothian?" shouted Ed Gallacelli.

"She promised she'd tell someone about us," agreed Umberto.

"Yes, she said she'd tell China Mountain," added Louie.

"Heart of Lothian?" asked Dominic Frontera. His pilot shrugged eloquently.

"A traveling rep for the General Education Department," explained Dr. Alimantando.

"Ah. Different department," said Dominic Frontera. The citizens poured scorn on his feeble excusings.

"Bureaucratic bunglings!" shouted Morton Quinsana. "Planning blight!"

Dominic Frontera attempted to calm the situation.

"All right, all right, I agree there has been bureaucratic bungling at the highest level—that isn't the issue. What is the issue is that in three days the comet's going to hit and splatter this town like gravy, that's the long and short of it. What I can do is call back the 'lighter squadron and have them move you all out of here. Maybe then after we've cleared up the impact site, if you really like it here, then you can come back, but in three days you all have to be out of here, with all your goats, llamas, pigs, chickens, children, and fixings to boot. Now, any questions?"

Rael Mandella beat the rest of the house to their feet.

"This is our town, we made it, we built it, it is ours, and we will not see it destroyed. Everything I have is here, my wife, my children, my home, my livelihood, I will not leave it to be destroyed by your comet. You, you engineers who bounce planets around like billiard balls, you send your comet somewhere else."

There was a tempest of applause. Dominic Frontera weathered it out.

"Next."

Persis Tatterdemalion stood and shouted, "This is my business here, what you've been putting gunshot holes into, mister. Now, I've already lost one business, the flying business, and I don't intend to lose another one. I'm staying. Your comet can go someplace else."

Mikal Margolis nodded his head vigorously and shouted, "Hear hear."

Then Ruthie Blue Mountain stood up and hush fell around her like snow.

"Yes?" said Dominic Frontera wearily. "I'd appreciate a question please, not a monologue from the condemned dock."

"Mr. Frontera," said the simple Ruthie, who had understood from all the furor only that her friends were in danger, "you must not hurt my friends."

"Lady, the last thing I want to do is hurt your friends. If, however, they are intent on hurting themselves by not having the common sense to get out of the way of danger, that is a different question entirely." Ruthie did not understand the ROTECH representative's reply.

"I won't let you hurt my friends," she muttered dully. There was a shuffling silence in the room of the kind that precedes something out of the ordinary. "If you loved them as much as I do, then you wouldn't hurt them. So I'm going to make you love me."

Up on the podium Dr. Alimantando saw her face brighten the split-second before Ruthie Blue Mountain released four years of accumulated beauty on Dominic Frontera. The Chairman Pro Tem ducked under the Chairman Pro Tem's table and put his hands over his eyes. Dominic Frontera had no such warning. He stood a full thirty seconds in the nova-light before emitting a curious squawk and falling like a sack of beans to the floor.

Dr. Alimantando took control. He pointed to the 'lighter pilot, saved by his polarizing contact lenses. "Get him out of here down to one of the rooms," he ordered. "You two show him where." He indicated for Persis Tatterdemalion and Mikal Margolis to help the pilot carry the love-stunned ROTECH agent to a place of recuperation. He quelled the popular hubbub with a glance.

"Well, you've all heard what our friend here has to say, and I don't for one moment doubt that it's true. Therefore, I am ordering each and every one of you to prepare for evacuation." Consternation rose. "Quiet, quiet. Evacuation, as a last resort. For I, Alimantando, am going to try and save our town!" He stood and acknowledged the public acclamation for a few minutes, the swept out of the B.A.R./Hotel to save the world.

17

For a night and a day Dr. Alimantando filled the walls of his weather-room with chronodynamic symbols. The stream of logic had started three years before in the bottom left-hand corner of his kitchen, wound through parlor, dining room, and hall, up the stairs, taking small digressionary detours into number one and number two bedrooms, through the bathroom, across the toilet walls, up another flight of stairs, and into the weather-room, where it wound round the walls, round and round and up and up until only a blank area about the size of a dollar bill was left in the center of the ceiling.

Beneath this spot sat Dr. Alimantando with his head buried in his hands. His shoulders shook. It was not tears that shook them but rage, monumental rage at the mocking universe which, like a painted rumbo dancer in a Belladonna opium hell, casts off successive layers of concealment only for the lights to black out at the moment of ultimate revelation.

He had told his people he was going to save their town.

And he couldn't do it.

He couldn't find the missing inversion.

He couldn't find the algebraic formula that would balance out fifteen years of wall-filling in Desolation Road and Jingjangsoreng and the Universuum of Lyx and reduce it all to zero. He knew it must exist. The wheel must turn, the serpent swallow its own tail. He suspected it must be simple, but he could not find it.

He had failed himself. He had failed science. He had failed his people. That was the most crushing of all failures. He had come to care deeply for his people; that was how he saw them, his people, the children he had thought he'd never desire. When they had not needed saving, he had saved them. Now that they must be saved, he could not.

The realization brought Dr. Alimantando a great release of tension. Like the animal that fights and fights and fights and then in the jaws of inevitability surrenders to death, his anger drained out of him, down through his house, down through the sinkholes in the rocks out into the Great Desert.

It was six minutes of six in the morning of Monday sixteenth. The gas lamps were popping and the insects beating themselves against the glass. From the east window he saw Rael Mandella going about his solitary six-o'clock-in-the-morning labors. They were not necessary now. He would come down from the mountain and tell his people to go. He did not want their forgiveness, though they would give it. All he wanted was their understanding. He squeezed his eyes shut and felt a great peace blow out of the desert, a wave of serenity breaking over him, through him. The morning mist carried an aroma of things growing in wet, rich earth, black as chocolate, rich as King Solomon. A sound like tinkling wind chimes caused him to look away from the windows.

He should have been shocked, or stunned, or some variation on the human emotion of surprise, but the presence of the greenperson sitting on the edge of his table seemed quite the most natural thing.

"Good morning," said the greenperson. "I must have missed you at that next camp . . . five years is it?"

"Are you a figment of my imagination?" said Dr. Alimantando. "I think you are something of that ilk: an archetype, a construction of my mind while under stress: a hallucination, that's what you are—a symbol."

"Come now, would you like to think of yourself as the kind of man visited by hallucinations?"

"I would not like to think of myself as the kind of man visited by animated leftover vegetables."

"Touché. Which way will this convince you, then?" The greenperson stood up on the table. It produced a stick of red chalk out of somewhere unseen and wrote a short equation in symbolic logic in the dollar-bill-sized space in the center of the ceiling. "I think that's what you're looking for." The greenperson swallowed the stick of red chalk. "The nutrients are very useful, you know." Dr. Alimantando climbed onto the table and peered at the equation.

"Yes," he muttered, "yes . . . yes . . ." He traced the spiral of black charcoal equations outward across the ceiling, around the walls, round round and round, across the floor on hands and knees, all the while muttering, "Yes . . . yes . . . yes" down the stairs, round the toilet, through the bathroom, detoured into number two and number one bedrooms, down more stairs, across the hall, the dining room, and the parlor, into the kitchen. Up in the weather-room the greenperson sat on the table with a very smug smile on its face.

A great cry of triumph came up from the depths of Dr. Alimantando's house. He had followed the trail of reason to its source in the bottom left corner of his kitchen.

"Yeehah! It fits! It fits! Zero! Pure, beautiful, round, absolute zero!" By the time he reached the weather-room the greenperson was gone. A few dry leaves lay scattered on the table.

18

The Mark One Alimantando time winder looked like a small sewing machine tangled up in a spider web. It sat on Dr. Alimantando's breakfast table awaiting the approval of its designer.

"One hell of a job to build," said Ed Gallacelli.

"Half the time we really didn't know what we were doing," said Rajandras Das. "But there it is."

"It's basically two synchronized unified field generators working in tandem but with variable phase control," said Mr.

Jericho, "thus creating a temporal difference between the two unphased fields."

"I know how it works," said Dr. Alimantando. "I designed it, didn't I?" He studied the time machine with growing delight. "It does look the job, though. Can't wait to try it out."

"You mean you're going to use that thing on yourself?" said Rajandra Das.

"Could I really ask anyone else? Of course, and as soon as possible. After lunch, I think."

"Wait a moment," said Mr. Jericho. "Are you going to do what I think you're going to do, that is . . ."

"Go into the past and change history? Of course." Dr. Alimantando fiddled with some knobs and fine settings and the time winder rewarded him with a potent hum. "It's only history, and when I change it, everything gets changed with it, so no one'll ever know. Certainly nobody in Desolation Road."

"My God." It was Ed Gallacelli who said that.

"That's sort of the effect I'm looking for," said Dr. Alimantando. He had managed to surround the time winder in a glowing blue bubble. "Of course, there are some temporal paradoxes that have to be resolved, but I think I have that all taken care of. The main paradox is that if I succeed, then the purpose for my time traveling becomes nullified; you can see what I mean, the whole thing begins to loop around, but I think I should disappear from Desolation Road and stay disappeared; some other excuse for my disappearance will crop up, something to do with time traveling, as like as not. These things converge. Also, there'll be a lot of cross-temporal leakage; don't let it worry you, at the time of break there'll be a lot of time-echoes resonating around nodes of significance and you may find little bits of alternative histories, those old parallel universes, get superimposed on this one, so be prepared for the odd little miracle to happen. It tends to create a lot of fallout, tinkering with history."

While he had been speaking, his deft fingers had discovered the setting on the time transfer controls he desired. He stood back from the time winder; it gave a sigh, a shudder, and vanished in a series of blurred afterimages.

"Where did it go?" asked Rajandra Das and Ed Gallacelli.

"Three hours into the future," said Dr. Alimantando. "I'll pick it up about lunchtime. Gentlemen, you have seen with your own eyes that time travel is a practical possibility, if you join me at thirteen twenty, you can help participate in the first manned time trip in history."

Over his lunch of leeks and cheese Dr. Alimantando planned how he might change history. He thought he might start with the orph who had willed him the oasis. From there, well, all time and space was his to wander. He might spend a lifetime in one evening saving his town. It would be a lifetime well spent. He went to a special cupboard in his kitchen and opened it. Inside was piled his amateur time traveler's outfit. He had spent five years and a lot of his credit lodged in the Bank of Deuteronomy amassing it. At first it had been an idle fancy, the kind of hobby that men take up as proof of the ultimate fulfillment of their impossible dreams, then as the items began to arrive from the Meridian Mail Order companies, the fancy had dragged the dream after it until now here he was, preparing to travel to times and places in a way no one had ever traveled before.

Dr. Alimantando smiled over each item as he laid them out.

A folding one-man survival tent, military issue, with double-seal gaskets and integral groundsheet.

One sleeping bag, mummy-style: military issue.

One transparent plastic insulation suit, complete with bubble helmet and oxygen rebreather mask.

Two sets of clean underwear, one long for cold weather. Socks.

One complete change of clothes.

One military-issue camp kitchen, collapsible, adapted to run off his portable power supply. Compressed rations for desperation only.

Five hundred dollars in cash.

Sun hat and two tubes of sun-block cream.

Soap bag, sponge, and towel.

Toothbrush and paste (spearmint).

First aid kit, including antihistamines, morphine, and general antibiotics.

For use with above, one pewter hip flask Belladonna brandy.

One pair sunglasses, one pair sand goggles.

A pure silk scarf: blue paisley.

One pocket shortwave transceiver.

Compass, sextant, and inertial direction, together with Geological Survey maps to enable him to find his position on the planet's surface on emerging from the flux fields.

One small tool kit, glue and vinyl patches for the pressure suit and tent.

One packet water-sterilizing tablets.

A camera, three lenses, and twelve rolls of assorted self-developing film.

Five leather-bound notebooks and one guaranteed everlasting ball-point pen.

One wrist ionization dosimeter.

Six bars of emergency chocolate.

One Defense Forces knife, with a blade for every day of the year, and a tin of dry matches.

Emergency flares.

One copy *The Collected Works of Watchman Ree*.

One portable trans-stable muon power unit with multi-charge syphon for reenergizing from any power source: home-made.

Running off the above, one homemade portable tachyon blaster, about the size and shape of a folding umbrella, with enough clout to vaporize a small skyscraper.

One large frame backpack, military issue, to hold everything.

Dr. Alimantando began to store his equipment. It all folded down remarkably small. Then he glanced at his watch. It was almost thirteen o'clock. He went to the kitchen table and counted the seconds off on the wall clock.

"Now." He pointed at the table. In a cascade of multiple imaging, the time winder arrived out of the past. He picked it up and added it to the time traveler's kit. Then he went and changed into his old much worn, much loved desert clothes and as he struggled into his long gray desert coat he invented eight hundred and six reasons why he should not go.

Eight hundred and six cons, and one pro. It was simply that he had to. He strapped on his bulky pack and fastened the control verniers around his wrist. Mr. Jericho, Rajandra Das, and Ed Gallacelli entered, prompt as only Mr. Jericho could be prompt.

"Ready?" asked Mr. Jericho.

"How ready can you be for something like this. Listen, if I succeed, you'll never know, understand?"

"I understand."

"Because of the nature of chronodynamics, I'll have changed all history and you'll never know you were in danger because that danger will never have been. From an objective point of view, my point of view, because I'll be time free, the universe, rather, this subjective world-line, will shift onto a new world-line. I'll try to leave a note of what I've done, if I can, somewhen in the past."

"You talk too much, Doc," said Rajandra Das. "Just get on with it. You don't want to be late."

Dr. Alimantando smiled. He said good-bye to each man in turn and gave them a bar of his emergency chocolate. He cautioned them to eat it soon, before some transtemporal anomaly uncreated this moment. Then he flicked some switches on his wrist controls. The time winder began to hum.

"One final thing. If I succeed, I won't be back. There's too much out there that I want to see. But I may call in from time to time, so look out for me and keep a chair empty for me."

Then to Mr. Jericho, he said, "I've known who you were all along. Made no odds to me, the past never has, though I'm obsessed with it. Funny. Just look after my people for me. Right. Time to be off." He pressed the red stud on his wrist control. There was a shriek of tortured continuum and a fading trail of Alimantando-shaped afterimages and he was gone.

On the night before Comet Tuesday everyone dreamed the same dream. They dreamed that an earthquake shook the town so hard that a second town was shaken out of the walls and the floors, like the double image you sometimes see when your eyes won't focus first thing in the morning. The ghost town, complete with its company of ghost inhabitants (who so closely resembled the true citizens that they could not be told apart) separated from Desolation Road like curds from whey and drifted away, though not in any direction anyone could have pointed to.

"Hey!" the people cried in their dreams. "Give us back our ghosts!" For ghosts are as much a part of a community as its plumbing or its library, for how can a community be without its memories? Then there was a shock which shook every sleeper momentarily from his rapid eye movements. They could not know that they had died in that moment and been reborn into new lives. But when they regained the sanctuary of their common dreaming, they found a subtle revolution had taken place. They were the ghosts, real, solid, flesh-and-blood ghosts and the town drifting away in the incomprehensible direction was the Desolation Road they had built and loved.

Out of the dream woke Dominic Frontera, shaken by the alarm call of his communicator. He rubbed sleep and Ruthie Blue Mountain out of his eyes.

"Frontera."

"Asro Omelianchik." His chief officer. One hard bitch of a woman. "All hell's breaking loose; the orbital boys have picked up an enormous surge of probabilistic energy focusing five years, fifteen years, and eighteen years into the past with chron-echoes resonating all the way up and down the time-line."

"Uh."

"Damn it, man, someone's playing around with time! The orbital boys have given it a ninety percent plus probability of our universe being thrown onto a different time-line: whatever it is, it's going to change history, the whole damn history of the world!"

"I didn't get that . . . what's this to do with me?"

"It's damn well coming from your area! Someone within five years of you is pissing around with an unlicensed chronokinetic shunter! We've traced the probability net back to you!"

"Child of grace!" exclaimed Dominic Frontera, suddenly awake and aware. "I know who it is!"

And then he was asleep again, dreaming of Ruthie Blue Mountain as he had dreamed of her every night since . . . when? Why? Why did he love her?

The universe was changed. Ruthie Blue Mountain had never opened the blossom of her beauty upon Dominic Frontera, who indeed had no reason to be in Desolation Road now that the past was changed, yet he slept in his room in the Bethlehem Ares Railroad/Hotel and dreamed of Ruthie Blue Mountain because universes may come and go but love remains; such is the teaching of the Panarch from whom all love proceeds, and also Dr. Alimantando had promised the odd little miraculous interdimensional leakage on the night he changed the world.

And in the morning it was Comet Tuesday and everyone woke and rubbed the strange dreams of the night from their eyes and looked at the town charter, proud on their walls, the charter Dr. Alimantando had signed with ROTECH all those years ago to build a town here, the charter that meant that the approaching comet would be vaporized in the upper atmosphere instead of crashing into the ground with emormous destructive force as had been ROTECH's previous practice. Everyone gave heartfelt thanks to Dr. Alimantando (whenever he might be) for having made everything fair and square.

At fourteen minutes of fourteen everyone without exception was up at the high place on the bluffs called Desolation Point with warm rugs and flasks of hot Belladonna brandy-laced tea and readied themselves for what Dominic Frontera had assured them was going to be the spectacle of the decade.

According to Ed Gallacelli's watch, Comet Tuesday was two minutes late but Mr. Jericho's half-hunter made it forty-eight seconds early. Irrespective of terrestrial timepieces, the comet came when it came and it came with a dull thundering that shook the rock beneath the spectator's feet while above their heads, high in the ionosphere, auroral discharges wavered insubstantially, meteors showered like rocket bursts, and sheets of purple ionic lightning back-lit the entire desert for split-seconds of phantom illumination.

The sky was suddenly streaked with blue beams that converged upon the still-invisible comet like spokes upon a hub. Gasps of collective amazement greeted this scene.

"Particle beams," shouted Dominic Frontera, struggling to make himself heard over the noises in the sky. "Watch this!" As if he had spoken an abracadabra, a sudden blossom of light filled the sky.

"Coo!" said everyone, blinking away the blobs before their eyes. A great golden glow filled the horizon and slowly faded. The ionic lightning crackled fitfully and passed, the occasional meteors burned away to nothing. The show was over. Everyone applauded. Forty kilometers up, Comet 8462M had been shattered by ROTECH's particle beams into chunks of ice the size and shape of frozen peas and then flashed to vapor by the streams of agonized particles. A gentle rain of ice dropped through the ionosphere, troposphere, tropopause, and stratosphere over days and weeks to build a layer of cloud. But that was not part of Comet Tuesday.

When the last shooting star had flared over the horizon, Rajandra Das pursed his lips thoughtfully and said, "Now, that weren't bad. Weren't bad at all. I could live with that if I had to."

And that is the story of Comet Tuesday.

And this is the story of Comet Tuesday.

In a place as far removed from Desolation Road and yet as intimate to it as the print on either side of a page, two hundred and fifty megatons of dirty water ice, like an unhygienic sorbet, tunneled out of the sky at five kilometers per second and threw itself into Great Desert. Now, the application of Newton's formula for kinetic energy gives us a figure for the energy released by this act of 3.126×10^{16}J, enough to run a valve wireless until the end of the universe, or the equivalent calorific value of a pile of rumpsteak the size of the planet Neptune; certainly enough for Comet 8462M to be instantly vaporized, for that vapor and resulting dust to be thrown tens of kilometers into the atmosphere, and for the shock wave, traveling at four times the speed of sound through the rocks beneath the desert, to heave a great tidal wave of sand into the air and bury Desolation Road with all its cargo of dreams and laughter under fifteen meters of sand. Certainly the accompanying mushroom cloud could be seen by the ghosts of Desolation Road in their exile in the cities of Meridian and O; certainly they felt the red dust rains that fell sporadically for a year and a day after Comet Tuesday. But this was long away and far ago and of as little consequence as a dream.

And that is the other story of Comet Tuesday.

Who can say which is true and which is false?

19

In his days of deepest darkest duplicity Mikal Margolis often took himself on long walks into the Great Desert so that the wind might blow the women out of his head. And the wind blew as it had for a hundred and fifty thousand years and would for another hundred and fifty thousand years but that would still not be long enough to blow away the guilt Mikal Margolis felt in his heart. He had three women: a lover, a mistress, and a mother, and just as the learned astronomers of the Universuum of Lyx maintain that the dynamics of a system of three stars can never be stable, so Mikal Margolis wandered, a rogue planet, through the fields of attraction of his three women. Sometimes he ached for the enduring love of Persis Tatterdemalion, sometimes he longed for the piquancy of his lascivious relationship with Marya Quinsana, sometimes when the guilt gnawed at the base of his stomach he sought his mother's forgiveness, and sometimes he wished he could escape their whirling gravitations entirely and wander free through space.

His desert walks were his escape. He did not have the courage to escape completely from the forces that were destroying him; a few hours alone among the red dunes were the farthest he could go from the stellar women of his life, yet in those hours he was alone in delightful solitude and he could play out his fantasies in the cinema of the imagination: desert raiders; grim, unspeaking gunmen; bold adventurers seeking lost cities; tall riders; lonely prospectors close to the mother lode. He trudged for hours up slopes and down, being all the things the women would not let him be and tried to feel the wind blow and the sun sweat the guilt out of him.

On this day no wind blew and no sun shone. After a hundred and fifty thousand years of light and air unceasing, the sun and wind had failed. A dense bank of cloud lay over the Great Desert, wide as the sky, black and curdled as devil's milk. It was the legacy of Comet 8462M, a layer of condensing water vapor that covered most of the North West Quartersphere and which had turned to rain and fallen on Belladonna and Meridian and Transpolaris and New Merionedd and everywhere except Desolation Road, where it had somehow forgotten to rain. Mikal Margolis, walker of dunes, knew little of this and cared less: he was an earth-scientist not a sky-scientist and anyway he was preoccupied because he was about to make a serendipitous discovery.

Sand. Contemptible sand. Red grit. Worthless, but Mikal Margolis, with the light of revelation in his eyes, bent down to pick up a handful and let it run through his fingers. He closed his fist on the remaining dribble, stood up, and shouted his delight to the ends of the Great Desert.

"Of course! Of course! Of course!" He stuffed his lunch satchel full of sand and danced all the way back to Desolation Road.

20

imaal and Taasmin Mandella, Johnny Stalin, and little Arnie Tenebrae, six days past her second birthday, were up at Desolation Point building paper gliders and launching them over the bluffs when The Hand came. They did not know it was The Hand then, not at first. Taasmin Mandella, whose eyesight was keenest, thought it was just a trick of the heat, like the hazy thermals that spiraled the paper gliders up into the heavy gray clouds. Then everyone noticed the thing and were amazed.

"It's a man," said Limaal Mandella, who could barely distinguish its shape.

"It's a man of light," said Taasmin Mandella, noticing the way the figure shone brighter than the cloud-hidden sun.

"It's an angel," said Johnny Stalin, seeing the pair of red wings folded on its back.

"It's something much much better!" squeaked Arnie Tenebrae. Then all the children looked and saw not what they wanted to see but what was there wanting to be seen, which was a tall thin man in a high-collared white suit upon which moving pictures of birds, animals, plants, and curious patterns were projected, and the wings upon his back were not wings at all but a great red guitar slung across his shoulders.

The children ran to meet the stranger.

"Hello, I'm Limaal and this is my sister, Taasmin," said Limaal Mandella. "And this is our friend, Johnny Stalin."

"And Arnie Tenebrae, me!" said Little Arnie Tenebrae, bouncing up and down in excitement.

"We're called The Hand," said the stranger. He had a strange voice, as if he were speaking from deep down in a dream. "Where is this place?"

"This is Desolation Road!" chorused the children. "Come on." And two grabbed hands and one ran outrider and one ran van and they galloped up the bluffs and through the green tree-hung alleys of Desolation Road to the Bethlehem Ares Railroad/Hotel, for that was the place all strangers came to first.

"Look what we've found," said the children.

"He's called The Hand," piped Arnie Tenebrae.

"He's come all the way across the Great Desert," said Limaal. A rumble passed among the clients, for only Dr. Alimantando (lost in time chasing a legendary green man, God be kind to him in his folly) had ever ever ever come across the Great Desert.

"He'll be wanting a drink then," said Rael Mandella, and nodded for Persis Tatterdemalion to draw off a glass of cold maize beer.

"Thank you kindly," said The Hand in his funny faraway voice. The offer of acceptance was made and received. "Might we take off our boots? The Great Desert's hard on feet." He unslung his guitar, sat down on a table, and the glow from his picture-suit cast odd shadows over his shark features. The children sat around him, waiting to be praised for their wonderful find. The man called The Hand pulled off his boots and everyone gave a cry of consternation.

His feet were slim and fine as ladies' hands, his toes long and flexible as fingers and his knees, his knees bent backward as well as forward, like a bird's.

Then Persis Tatterdemalion spoke and calmed the storm. "Hey, mister, play us a tune on your guitar, will you?"

The Hand's eyes sought out his questioner, far away in the back-bar shadows. He stood and executed a complex bow, impossible for any less flexible than he. Time-lapse images of flowers blooming passed over his picture-suit.

"Because the lady asks, we think we will." He picked up his guitar and struck a harmonic. Then he touched his long slender fingers to the strings and released a swarm of notes into the air.

There was never such music played as played that afternoon in the Bethlehem Ares Railroad/Hotel. The music found notes in the tables and the chairs and the mirrors and the walls; it found melodies in the bedroom and the kitchen, the cellar and the shit-house, and dragged tunes out of the places where they had lain hidden undiscovered for years, found them, took them, and made them part of the greater self. There were tunes that made feet tap and tunes that brought out bouts of dancing. There were tunes that kicked over the tables and tunes that made the glassware rattle. There were tunes to make you smile and tunes to make you cry and tunes that sent delicious shivers down your back. There was the grand ancient music of the desert and airy, breathy music of the sky. There was the music of dancing firelight and the infinite whistle of distant stars, there was merriment and magic and mourning and madness; music leaping, music crying, music laughing, music loving, music living, music dying.

When it was finished no one could believe it was over. No one could believe that just one man, with a guitar lying in his lap, could have made such mighty music. A ringing stillness filled the air. The Hand flexed his curious fingers, his curious toes. Desert sunsets glowed red and purple on his picture suit. Then Umberto Gallacelli called out, "Hey, Mister, just where do you come from?"

No one had heard Mr. Jericho enter. No one had seen him take a seat at the bar. No one even knew he was there until he said, "I'll tell you where he's from." Mr. Jericho pointed at the ceiling. "Am I right?"

The Hand stood up, tense and sharp-edged.

"Outside, right?" Mr. Jericho pressed home his reasoning. "The feet, that's the way they're born for use in open gravity, isn't it? Extra hands? And the picture-suit, that's a universal tool among ROTECH orbital personnel for reviewing visual information at a glance: I reckon it's just running a random test pattern in the absence of data, am I right?"

The Hand did not say yes or no. Mr. Jericho continued.

"So, what are you doing here? Exclusion orders prohibit space-adapted humans from coming to the surface except under permiso. You got a permiso?" The man called The Hand tensed, ready to flee, his red guitar held defensively before him. "Maybe you should have a talk with our district supervisor, the mayor Dominic Frontera. He can have the ROTECH boys in China Mountain check you out."

Not even the prodigious experience of Mr. Jericho's Exalted Ancestors could have prepared him for what The Hand did next. A screaming power-chord from the red guitar twisted the world away and tore at the mind with chromium teeth. Under cover of the guitar-scream, The Hand was gone, the children with him.

21

Limaal, Taasmin, Johnny Stalin, and Arnie Tenebrae hid The Hand in a small cave behind Mr. Blue Mountain's house. It was the very best of hiding places. No one would find The Hand here because no one grown up even knew there was a secret cave here. There were a lot of places around Desolation Road which no one grown up knew were there, dozens of really good places where a toy or an animal or a man could be hidden away for a long long time. Once Limaal and Taasmin had tried to hide Johnny Stalin away in a secret cave, but he had thrown a screaming tantrum and his mother had come flapping to the rescue. That was one hiding place they could not use again.

They had brought The Hand stolen things they thought he would need to make him comfortable: a rug, a cushion, a plate and a glass, a jug of water, some candles, some oranges and bananas. Arnie Tenebrae gave him her coloring book and new wax crayons which she had been given for her birthday and which had come all the way from the catalog sales shop in the big city. Miniature Magi, they presented their gifts to The Hand. He accepted their tribute graciously and rewarded them with a tune and a story.

This is the story The Hand told.

In the flying cities that circled the earth like shards of shattered glass there lived a race of men who still laid claim to the bond of common humanity with their world-bound brothers but who, in their centuries of self-imposed high exile, had grown so strange and alien that they were in truth a separate species. This magical race had been charged with two great tasks. These tasks were the reason for their peoples' existence. The first was the care and maintenance, and, until such time as it might govern itself, the administration of the world their ancestors had built. The second was its defense against those alien powers which might wish, out of jealousy, greed, or outraged pride, to destroy man's greatest work. The fulfilling of these sacred mandates, imposed by the Blessed Lady herself, demanded such concentration of effort by the sky-folk that none could be spared for lesser tasks. Therefore one simple law was made.

It was that at the age of majority and reason, when a person assumes the mantle of responsibility, each individual must choose between three futures. The first was to follow the ways of the ever-living ancestors, take the Cathrinist vows and serve ROTECH and its celestial patroness. The second was to submit to the adaptive surgery of the physicians and choose exile and a new life, wiped clean of the memories of all that was before, upon the world below. The third was either to break free from the flesh and merge with the machines to live a disembodied ghost in the computer-net, or set the controls of the transmat machine to a well-guarded set of coordinates known as Epsilon Point, where the quasi-sentient Psymbii, vegetative creatures of light and vacuum, would come and take that individual and wrap themselves around, into, through him until they became a symbiote of flesh and vegetable, living free in the vast spaces of the moonring.

Yet there were those who found all of these futures horrible to contemplate and chose their own. Some wished to remain the folk they were and went unadapted to the world below, where they lived only a short while and died in great misery. Some took ships and sailed away into the night toward the nearer stars and were never heard of again. And some sought refuge behind the walls of the world in the air-shafts and light-wells, brothers and sisters of the rats.

Such a one was The Hand. Upon his tenth birthday, the traditional day of decision, he stole his brother's picture-cloth suit and slipped behind the walls to run the tunnels and catwalks, for it was not the Blessed Lady he wished to serve, but Music. And he became Lord of the Dark Places, a thing quickly said in few words, not so quickly done: King in a world where music was law and the electric guitar master of light and darkness.

As evening shadows grew to infinite lengths down the light-wells of Carioca Station, bright-winged creatures like heroin angels would flash across the echoing spaces and cluster like vampires, their wings shrouded about them, upon spars and rigging wires to witness the duels of music. All darktime long until, like vampires, the strengthening sunlight drove them into the shadows, they would listen to the guitars clash. The shafts and tunnels would ring to the crazy music, the guitars would wail and scream like sweating lovers, and responsible citizens who lived by law and duty would wake from their free-fall dreams to catch tailing echoes of wild, free music wafting from their air-conditioning slots, music like they had never dreamed before. And when all the fights were fought and the last droplets of blood squeezed from shattered fingertips, when the last seared guitar corpse had been sent spinning out of the locks into space, the King was crowned and everyone proclaimed that The Hand and his red guitar were the greatest on Carioca Station.

For a season The Hand ruled the tunnels and runways of Carioca Station and there was none to challenge him. Then word came that the King of MacCartney Station wished to call out the King of Carioca Station. The gauntlet was down. The purse was the Kingdom of the loser, and all his subjects.

They met in an open-gravity observation blister beneath slow-wheeling stars. All that day the King of Carioca Station's picture-suit (which he wore in preference to the rags, plastics, metals, and synthetic furs of the behind-wallers) had projected black and white pictures of incredible antiquity: a visual entertainment whose name, translated from the ancient languages, meant "White House." Then the King of Carioca Station's steward handed him his freshly tuned guitar. He touched his fingers to the strings and felt the evil genius thrill up his arm and liquify his brain. The King of MacCartney Station's stewards passed him his machine: a nine-hundred-year-old Stratocaster. Sunlight flared from its sunburst finish and awed the spectators, clinging by feet and tails to the traverse wires, into holy silence.

The adjudicator gave a signal. The duel began.

All through the compulsory fugues the King of MacCartney Station matched the King of Carioca Station. Their melodies curled and twined around each other's themes like birds in flight with such precise skill that no one could tell where one ended and another began. Their free-form improvisations sang into the cathedral vastness of Number Twelve airshaft and flakes of crystallized power-chords sifted down like snow to powder the heads of the girls with stardust. The guitars stalked each other through the harmonic landscapes of the modes: the Ionian, the Dorian, the Phrygian, Lydian and Mixolydian, the Aeolian and the Locrian. Time slowed in a jungle of scales and arpeggios: there was no time, the stars froze in their arcing paths, tracing slow silver snail tracks across the glassite cap-dome. The guitars flashed like switchblades, like methadone dreams. The guitars cried like violated angels. Back and forth the battle swayed, but still neither could gain advantage over the other.

The King of Carioca Station knew he had met his match in the King of MacCartney Station. Now there was only one way left for him to win, and the price of that victory would be terrible indeed. But the guitar, having smelled blood and steel on the wind, would not now permit its slave the weak luxury of surrender.

The King of Carioca Station, who was The Hand, reached inside him to the dark place where the wild things were and with a prayer to the Blessed Lady he opened the dark place to the light and let the blackness pour out of him. Released, the red guitar roared like a demon in heat and sucked the dark fluid up into its internal amplifiers and synthesizers. Its strings ran with purple lightning and rang with alien harmonics like no one had ever dreamed could be. The dark music struck out like the fist of God. The audience fled screaming from the black, living unclean thing The Hand had unleashed. A tongue of dark lightning stabbed out from the red guitar and burst the stranger's Stratocaster into smoking chunks. For an instant the inside of the stranger's skull lit up with heavenlight and then his eyesockets burned out in a flash and smoke trickled from them and he was dead dead dead and the King of Carioca Station was King indeed, King of two worlds, but what was the price, of what was the price, the price he paid for his crown?

Then grim-faced winged women in tight yellow stretch suits swarmed out of every hatchway: Station Security, armed with shock-staves and love-guns. They rounded the King's subjects into neat groups of six and took them away to an uncertain but assured future. They sprayed the charred, cartwheeling corpse of the King of MacCartney Station with fire-retardant foam. They took away the King of Two Worlds in a bundle of narcotic floss, and his red guitar with him. They took the King to the healers of St. Catherine's, who would execute the judgment of the Group of Nineteen by the administration of tiny, oh-so-carefully measured doses of myelin suppressants, through which they would restore the soul of the murdered man to life once more, within his murderer's body, and that murderer would pay with his laughing screaming soul and be no more.

This would have been the end of The Hand had he not escaped from the holy doctors of St. Catherine's. How he escaped from them, he will not say, suffice that he escaped and saved his red guitar from the furnaces and together they set the controls of the station transmat cubicle for the forbidden earth beneath. With the speed of thought he, his guitar, and the embryonic soul of the King of MacCartney Station were transported into the industrial ghetto of Touchdown, where they were shown mercy mild by the Little Sisters of Tharsis and taken into their charity home for crippled mendicants. An old legless beggar had taught him to walk free from his wheelchair, another thing soon said but slowly realized, and guessing The Hand's origin, taught him all the old man knew of this world's ways, for he must learn such things or perish, and organized his escape from the Little Sisters of Tharsis. The Hand begged a ride on a truck convoy across the Ecclesiastes Mountains into the ancient heartland of the Great Oxus, where he wandered for a year and a day among the rice farms offering to plant seedlings in the flooded paddies with his dextrous feet. At night he would entertain the farm folk with tunes from his red guitar and earn a bowl of soup or a glass of beer or a few centavos in his pocket.

But he knew no peace, for the soul of the man he had murdered would give him no peace. At night it would wake him from his sleep in a scream and a sweat from the dreams of his own dying. Pricking him with guilt every time he touched the strings of the red guitar, the ghost drove him onward through constant reminders of what the holy doctors of St.

Catherine's had yet to do to him. So The Hand wandered the length and breadth of the wide world, for the holy doctors of St. Catherine's were searching for him across the face of the globe and if he ever stopped moving they would find him, take him back to the sky, and destroy him. This was the curse of The Hand, forever to wander the world with his red guitar on his back, pursued by the ghost of a murdered man waiting behind his eyes to take his soul.

"That was a good story," said Arnie Tenebrae.

"Every man's story is a good story," said Rael Mandella. The children shrieked in alarm. The Hand reached for his red guitar to fire another paralyzing chord. "Easy," said Rael Mandella. "I wish you no ill." To the children he said, "You should be more careful with the water next time you want to hide someone. I followed the trail of drips right to this place. Why did you do it?"

"Because he was our friend," said Limaal Mandella.

"Because he needed someone to be kind to him," said Taasmin Mandella.

"Because he was scared," said Arnie Tenebrae.

"You're not going to tell anyone he's here, are you?" said Johnny Stalin. The children chorused their protest.

"Quiet," said Rael Mandella, suddenly filling the cave with his presence. "I've heard your story, Mr. Hand, and I tell you this, what a man's done in his past is no matter to me, nor should it be to anyone else. When Dr. Alimantando (you remember him, kids?) invented this place, he said that no one would ever be turned away because of what they had done before. This was to be a place of fresh starts. Well, Dr. Alimantando's gone now, into the past or the future I don't know, but I think he was right. This is a place for fresh starts. Now, I don't hold with all this newfangled mayor stuff; things went much better when Dr. Alimantando looked after the place. And I don't hold with people running up to this mayor and asking him for all the right answers; I say the right answers are inside you all along or they aren't there at all, which is just another way of saying that I'm not telling anyone you're here. I'll tell them if they ask, and so will you, kids, that you saw him walking off across the tracks, because if what you say is true, you'll have to be moving on soon enough anyway."

The Hand nodded, a small bow of gratitude.

"Thank you, sir. We'll be moving on tomorrow. Is there anything we can do for you to demonstrate our gratitude?"

"Yes," said Rael Mandella. "You say you're from the Outside, maybe then you'll know why it hasn't rained for one hundred and fifty thousand years. Come on, kids, practice your alibis and come for dinner at my house."

22

The ground was sparkling with frost under a steel-gray sky when Rael Mandella took the pot of porridge and two bananas to the refugee in his cave. Rael Mandella enjoyed the peace of the hours before the rest of the world woke with a yawn and a fart. Usually only the birds ever woke before he; therefore he was much surprised to find The Hand awake and alert and intent upon some inscrutable private business. His picture-suit had gone black as night, and upon it lines, like the spokes of a wheel, crowded with flashng digits and scurrying graphs and colored sentences, spun across the remarkable fabric. The small cave was filled with shimmering light.

"What's happening?" said Rael Mandella.

"Shh. Graphic readout of the Solstice Landing climatic and ecological regimes for the seven hundred years since terraforming commenced. We've tapped into the Anagnostas aboard the Pope Pious Station to see if we can locate the breakdown of discipline in the local microclimate, and not only is it coming at zip speed but I have to read it backward in the reflection from this water jug so we'd appreciate some shush while we concentrate."

"That's impossible," said Rael Mandella. Colors flew, words whirled. The dizzying display suddenly clicked off.

"Got it. Problem is, they've also got us. They'll have traced us through the computer link, so we'll take our breakfast, thank you, and go."

"Sure, but why hasn't it rained?"

The Hand helped himself to porridge and said through mushy spoonfuls, "All kinds of things. Temporal anomalies, barometric gradients, precipital agents, jet-stream deflection, microclimatic zones of probability, catastrophe fields: but chiefly, you've forgotten the name of rain."

And at that the children who had secretly followed Rael Mandella to the cave all cried, "Fogotten the name of the rain?"

"What's rain?" asked Arnie Tenebrae. When The Hand explained, she said sternly, "Silly, how can water come out of the sky? The sun's in the sky, water can't come from there, water comes out of the ground."

"See?" said The Hand. "They've never learned the name of the rain, the true name, the heart-name, which everything has and to which everything comes when called. But if you've forgotten the heart-name, the rain can't even hear you."

Rael Mandella shivered for no reason he could give.

"Tell us the name of the rain, mister," said Arnie Tenebrae.

"Yes, go on, show us how water can come out of the sky," said Limaal Mandella.

"Yes, make it rain for us so we can call it by its name," said Taasmin.

"Yeah, show us," added Johnny Stalin.

The Hand put down his bowl and spoon.

"Very well. You've done us a turn, so we'll do you a turn. Mister, any way of getting out into the desert?"

"The Gallacellis have their dune buggy."

"Could you borrow it? We need to get quite far out: we'll be playing with forces on a pretty cosmic scale. Sonic cloud-seeding's never been tried before as far as we know, but the theory's sound. We'll make it rain in Desolation Road."

The Gallacelli brothers' dune buggy was an odd mongrel of a vehicle. Knocked together by Ed in spare moments, it looked like a six-seater all terrain motor-trike with a large shopawning over it. Rael Mandella had never driven it before. The children giggled and cheered as he bounced along the rough track down the bluffs and headed out into the dune fields. As he threaded the cumbersome vehicle along the channels between the red sand mountains, his handling grew more confident. The Hand entertained the children with the tale of his desert crossing and pointed out highlights and landmarks. They drove and they drove and they drove beneath the great gray cloud, away from the habitation of men into a landscape where time was as fluid and morphic as blown sand, where the bells of buried cities chimed out from beneath the shifting surface of the desert.

Everyone's watches had stopped at twelve minutes of twelve.

The Hand gestured for Rael Mandella to stop, stood up, and sniffed the air. Television clouds raced across his picture-suit.

"Here. This is the place. Can't you feel it?"

He jumped from the dune buggy and scrambled to the top of a great red dune. Rael Mandella and the children followed, slipping and sliding in the shifting sand.

"There," said The Hand, "do you see it?" Half-buried in the dune hollow stood a spidery sculpture of rusting metal, eaten by age and sand. "Come on." Together they bounded down the slip-slope of the dune in cascades of dislodged sand. The children ran up to the metal sculpture to touch their hands to its alien surfaces.

"It feels alive," said Taasmin Mandella.

"It feels old and cold and dead," said Limaal.

"It feels like it doesn't belong here," said Arnie Tenebrae.

"I don't feel anything," said Johnny Stalin.

Rael Mandella found some writing in a strange language. No doubt Mr. Jericho could have translated it. Rael Mandella did not have the gift of tongues. He sensed a strange flat silence in the place between the dunes, as if some enormous power were draining the life out of the air and the words that hung in it.

"This is the heart of the desert," said The Hand. "This is where its power is strongest, this is where its power flows from and returns to. All things are drawn here; we were as we passed through, undoubtedly so was your Dr. Alimantando as he

crossed the Great Desert, and so, hundreds of years ago, was
this. It's an ancient space vehicle. It landed here about eight
hundred years ago as man's first attempt to assess this world's
suitability for life. Its name, which is written there, Mr.
Mandella, means Northern Seafarer, or to translate it literally,
'one who inhabits bays and fjords.' It's been here a long long
time, here at the heart of the desert. The sand is strong here at
the heart."

Overhead the clouds had grown thick and pregnant. Time
snagged around the needle point of twelve minutes of twelve.
No words were spoken; there was no need for them and those
which had been needful the desert had taken away. The Hand
unslung his red guitar and struck a harmonic. He listened
intently.

Then the rain-music began.

*Sandwhisperwindwhisperblowthereddduneface,
carryanddrop carryanddrop, the granular march of the desert
verbed in a risingswirlingeddying, devildrivingstoneshaping all
things come from sand and to sand they return,* sang the red
guitar, *listen to the voice-of-the-sand, listen to the wind, the
voice of the lion, the wind from around the shoulder of the
world, cloudcarrying jetstreaminglifftingfalling, airy barometric
layers of occluded fronts spiraldepressions: element of zones and
boundaries while yet boundaryless, shifting frontiers of the
mutable kingdoms of air howling their path roundandround
and round the roundroundglobe:* the guitar sang the song of the
air and the sand, *now sing the song of light and heat: of shafts
and planes and the geometrical precision of their intersections,
domain of perpetualperpendiculars, shafts of light, shields of
heat, solid suffocation of desert carpets and breadovens, the
silver eyebrow of the sun raised quizzically over the veiling
clouds' dark perimeter: this is the song of the light, this is the
song of the heat, yet there are still songs to be sung,* sang the
guitar, *before rain can fallfallfall and the song of the clouds is
one of these, song of pillowfleecycottoncandyhighwispy exhala-
tions of steamtrains and saucepans and bathrooms on winter
mornings whipped by the wind and sent sailingscudding
slipping in white armadas across a blueblueblue sea; and hear
also the voice of the water drawn into the air, riverrundipple-
dappleonwardflowingemptiedtrickles multiplying into streams-
brookstributariesrivers into thesea thesea! where shafts of light*

and heat move upon it like God's fingers and the wind draws it upup up into the realm of barometric boundaries where the sea is shaped into chords of StratusMajor and CirrusMinor and Augmentedcumulus: there were songs to each of these things, and a music that was the name people gave them in their hearts, hidden like the harmonies in the strings of a guitar. These songs were the true names of things, spoken by the soul, so easily buried under the little busynesses of everyman everyday.

The music raged into the sky like an elemental thing. It threw itself with a roar and a howl at the walls of the clouds: wild and unbounded, growing and growing until it burst the bounds of human understanding into the place beyond understanding, where the true names are. The guitar cried for release. The clouds fretted at their tight constriction. Time strained at twelve minutes of twelve but the song would not let them go, any of them. Reflected images of insanity flickered across The Hand's suit of white picture-cloth. The children hid themselves under the flaps of Rael Mandella's desert coat.

The world could not take very much more truth.

Then a raindrop fell. It ran down the flank of the derelict space-explorer and made a dark splash on the sand. Another joined it. Then another. Then another and another and another and another and suddenly it was raining.

The rain song ended. The acappella voice of the rain filled all the earth. The children held out disbelieving hands to catch the heavy drops. Then the clouds burst open and one hundred and fifty thousand years of rain hurled itself to the ground. Rael Mandella, blind and gasping, the wind driven from his lungs, sought the terrified children and hid them under his coat. The sky emptied itself on the huddled, miserable pile of people.

Concentric walls of water swept out from the secret heart of the desert. At the high place called Desolation Point the Babooshka and Grandfather Haran had prepared a private siesta-time picnic. The rain transformed it into a rout. Pathetic in drenched taffeta, the Babooshka dazedly stuffed plates and rugs into a wicker hamper rapidly filling with water. Torrents of red water poured into every home and swept away carpets, chairs, tables, and loose sundries. The people were astonished. Then they heard the drumming on the rooftiles and they all shouted, "Rain, rain, rain!" and rushed out into the lanes and alleys to turn their faces to the sky and let the rain wash the dry years out of them.

The rain rained as it had never rained before. Red rivers coursed down the narrow alleyways, a small but spectacular waterfall leaped over the bluffs, the irrigation channels in the gardens swelled into torrents of thick brown chocolaty loam studded with uprooted seedings and vegetables. Everything leaped and hissed under the deluge. The rain punished Desolation Road.

The people did not care. It was rain: rain! Water from the sky, the end of the drought that had gripped their desert land for one hundred and fifty thousand years. The people looked at the town. They looked at the rain. It was so heavy they could barely see the relay beacon light on top of Dr. Alimantando's house. They looked at one another, clothing clinging to their bodies, hair plastered to their heads, faces streaked with red mud. Someone laughed, a little ridiculous laugh that grew and grew and grew until it was a great guffawing belly laugh. Someone else caught the laugh, then someone else and someone else, and in a moment everyone was laughing, wonderful good good laughter. They threw off their clothes and ran naked into the cloudburst to let the rain fill up their eyes and mouths and run down their cheeks and chins, their breasts and bellies, their arms and legs. The people laughed and cheered and danced in the splashing red mud and when they looked at one another, red-painted and naked as the hill-dwelling revenants of Hansenland, they laughed all the longer.

Drop had led to drop to drop in the rain's beginning: likewise it ended, drop by drop. There came a moment in the people's revels when they could see clearly and hear each other's voices over the roar. The deluge slackened, then eased, and it was no more than a light shower. Drop by drop the rain cleared. The last raindrop fell. After the rain it was as quiet as the hush before Creation. Water dripped from the black lozenges of the solar collectors. The clouds ROTECH had made were rained dry. The sun broke through and cast puddles of light across the desert. A double rainbow stood with its feet on the distant hills and its head in heaven. Wisps of vapor ghosted up from the ground.

The rains were over. The people were just people again taking up the lives of men and women. Shamed by their nakedness, they pulled on their saturated, filthy clothes. Then the wonderful thing happened.

"Oh, look!" cried Ruthie Blue Mountain. She pointed to the far horizon. Out there a mystic transformation was taking place: before the amazed eyes of the people of Desolation Road the desert was turning green. The line of alchemy advanced like a breaking wave across the dune fields. Within minutes it was green as far as even Mr. Jericho's eye could see. The clouds dissolved away and the sun shone in the bold blue sky. The people held their breath. Something enormous was about to happen.

As if by divine command the Great Desert exploded into color. At the touch of the sun behind the rain the dunes unfolded into a pointillist landscape of reds, blues, yellows, delicate whites. The wind stirred the ocean of petals and wafted the perfume of a hundred million blossoms over the town. The people of Desolation Road poured down from their bare stony bluffs into the endless meadows of flowers. Behind them their abandoned town steamed in the afternoon sunshine of two minutes of two.

At the heart of the desert Rael Mandella noticed it had stopped raining. The children peeped out from under his coat like chicks. Beneath their sandals green shoots uncoiled like watchsprings and waved pale stalks in the breeze.

The flowers had pushed their way around the red guitar. Rael Mandella went to the instrument and picked it up. In the sterile place where it had lain, thin white stems struggled for the light.

The red guitar was dead. Its slick plastic skin was blistered and seared, its frets mangled, its strings blackened, its rosewood neck split down the middle. Smoke trickled from its fused internal synthesizers and amplifiers. As Rael Mandella turned the dead thing over in his hands, the strings snapped: precise, terminal noises. There was something clean about the red guitar after its death. It was as if the rain had washed away its sins.

Of the man who had called himself The Hand, once King of Two Worlds, there was not so much as a single scrap of picture-cloth torn from a television suit.

"Too much music," whispered Rael Mandella to the red guitar. "You made much too much music this time."

"What's happened to The Hand?" asked Limaal.

"Where's he gone?" asked Taasmin.

"Have the bad doctors got him?" asked Arnie Tenebrae.

"Yes, the bad doctors have him," said Rael Mandella.

"Will they push the dead man into him?" asked Johnny Stalin.

"I don't think so," said Rael Mandella, looking to the sky. "And I'll tell you why. Because I think what they have is neither The Hand nor the dead man. I think it is both, that at the very peak of the music they fused together like sand into glass, and now it's like starting out all over again for them."

"Like being born again?" asked Arnie Tenebrae.

"Just like being born again. It was a pity they found him and took him back so soon; we never thanked him for the rain. That was bad of us. I hope he doesn't hold it against us. Well, kids, let's go."

Limaal Mandella tried to drag the red guitar after him to take home as a souvenir, but it was too heavy and his father told him to leave it there at the heart next to the old space-explorer and he went back to the world with empty hands.

23

Persis Tatterdemalion was married to Ed Gallacelli, Louie Gallacelli, and Umberto Gallacelli at ten o'clock on a Sunday morning in the early spring of the year 127. By the power invested in him as town manager, Dominic Frontera declared them polyandrously wed and saw them off on the train to Meridian to honeymoon under the volcanoes. The wedding had been a moving experience for him. The

minute the train left he went and asked Meredith Blue
Mountain for the hand of drab Ruthie. Meredith Blue
Mountain was reluctant. Dominic Frontera confessed his
mystic love born in another dimension, his obsessive vision of
beauty that tormented him night and day, and burst into tears.

"Ah, the poor man, what can I do to make you happy
again?" asked innocent Ruthie, entering the room at the sound
of blubbing.

When Dominic Frontera told her she said, "If that's all, of
course I will."

The second happily wedded couple in as many days
honeymooned among the thousand exquisite and unique
villages of China Mountain.

A sign was hung on the door of the B.A.R./Hotel. It read:
CLOSED FOR ONE WEEK: REOPENING SUNDAY 23RD, 20
O'CLOCK, PROPS: P. TATTERDEMALION, E., L., & U. GALLA-
CELLI. The sign had been painted by Mikal Margolis. As he
painted out his name and replaced it with those of his
successful rivals in love, he felt no jealousy, no hatred, only a
numb sense of fate closing in around him. He locked the door
and dropped the key down a well. Then he went and knocked
on Marya Quinsana's door.

Marya Quinsana rapidly grasped the situation.

"Morton, I'm taking on Mikal as an extra hand in the
surgery. Right?"

Morton Quinsana said nothing but stormed out in a
petulance of slamming doors.

"What was that all about?" asked Mikal Margolis.

"Morton's very attached to me," said Marya Quinsana.
"Well, he'll just have to get used to the fact that things have
changed a bit now that you're here."

A week later Persis Tatterdemalion returned to Desolation
Road with her old, proud name, her three husbands, and a
full-size professional-quality snooker table made by MacMurdo and Chung of Landhries Road. All hands were set to
hauling it from the station to the Bethlehem Ares Railroad/
Hotel. Complimentary refreshments were promised and the
children, who had danced around pulling ropes and carrying
cues, gave a hooray in anticipation of bottomless jugs of clear
lemonade. When Persis Tatterdemalion/Gallacelli saw the
locks and the sign, she went straight to find Mikal Margolis.

"You don't have to go."

Mikal Margolis was sterilizing a pair of pig castrators. He found it impossible to hold any anger against her, though rationality demanded that he should. It was fate, and being angry at fate was as futile as being angry at the weather.

"I thought it was best that I leave." Mikal Margolis's voice was heavy with congested love. "It wouldn't have worked, we couldn't have gone back to the old days, not knowing that you belonged to someone else, were bearing someone else's child. It won't work again. Take my share of the hotel as a wedding present and I hope it brings you joy. Honestly. One thing though . . . tell me, why did you have to do it?"

"What?"

"Get pregnant by . . . by the Gallacelli brothers, of all people! What were you doing that day the rains came? That's what I can't understand, why them, have you seen the place they live in? It's like a pigsty . . . I'm sorry."

"It's all right. Look, I was crazy then, we were all crazy then. . . ."

She remembered lying flat on her back in a bed of red poppies the day the rains came, staring at the sky, twirling a little red poppy in her fingers, humming a silly little tune while a million million light years away something went ump-wump, ump-wump, ump-wump inside her. She had gladly ripped off her clothes when the rain fell and rubbed the beautiful red mud into her hair; it had felt good, it had felt free like flying, it had felt like she could fall forever like a fat, pregnant raindrop and burst her womanly fluids over the dry land. She had put her arms out like wings weeeeee round and round and round, down into the fields of flowers, her propellors sending daisies marigolds poppies flying in twin arcs from her round nippled engines. Child of grace, she had been crazy then, but hadn't everyone, and if this crazy town with all its same same faces wasn't an excuse to go crazy time and again, what was? Maybe she had gone a little too far: the Gallacelli brothers had never needed much encouragement, but when EdUmbertoLouie had gotten on top of her, she'd flown!

"I didn't know what I was doing; hell, I thought I was flying." The excuse did even convince her. After they parted, Mikal Margolis felt the guilt rise like fog. He must walk away, and walk away soon, from these women who were drawing him close to the Roche limit of the heart.

In the new snooker annex of the B.A.R./Hotel Mr. Jericho was potting balls with the consummate ease of a man who had his Exalted Ancestors calculating the angles for him. Limaal Mandella, aged seven and three-quarters watched him. When the table was free, he picked up a cue and while attention was focused on beer and bean stew, made a break of one hundred and seven. From behind the bar Ed Gallacelli heard the sound of balls falling into pockets and took interest. He watched Limaal Mandella complete his hundred and seven, then go on to make one hundred and fifteen.

"Child of grace!" he exclaimed quietly. He went over to the boy, busy setting up the triangle of reds for another practice. "How do you do that?"

Limaal Mandella shrugged.

"Well, I just hit them where it seems right."

"You mean you've never touched a cue before now?"

"How could I?"

"Child of grace!"

"Well, I watched Mr. Jericho and did what he did. It's a very good game, you're totally in control of what's happening. It's all angles and speed. I think I might go for the big break this frame."

"How big?"

"Well, I think I've got the hang of it. The maximum."

"Child of grace!"

And Limaal Mandella made a maximum break of one hundred and forty-seven and Ed Gallacelli was utterly amazed. Ideas of bets, challenges, and purses began to trickle through his mind.

The months of Persis Tatterdemalion's pregnancy passed. She grew great and bulbous and unaerodynamic, which depressed her more than anyone suspected. So great and bulbous grew she that her husbands took her to Marya Quinsana's veterinary surgery for a second opinion. Marya Quinsana listened for almost an hour through a device used for monitoring llama pregnancies and at the end of that time diagnosed a case of twins. The town cheered, Persis Tatterdemalion waddled ponderously around the B.A.R./Hotel in gravid misery, the rains rained, and the crops grew. Under Ed

Gallacelli's management Limaal Mandella turned teen-shark, fleecing gullible visiting soil-scientists, geophysicists, and plant pathologists out of their beer dollars. And Mikal Margolis drew foolishly close to Marya Quinsana's mother-mass and by the laws of emotional dynamics cast Morton Quinsana into the dark.

On a sharp and freezing autumn night, Rajandra Das went around knocking on every front door in Desolation Road.

"They're coming, it's time!" he said, and dashed away to spread his warning to the other households. "They're coming, it's time!"

"Who's coming?" asked Mr. Jericho, slyly arresting the fleet-footed Mercury with a cunning arm lock.

"The twins! Persis Tatterdemalion's twins!"

Within five minutes the whole town, with the exception of the Babooshka and Grandfather Haran, were being served complimentary drinks in the B.A.R./Hotel, while in the master bedroom Marya Quinsana and Eva Mandella got in each other's way as Persis Tatterdemalion squeezed and huffed and huffed and squeezed and huffed a pair of fine sons into the world. As might have been expected, they were as alike in every detail as their fathers.

"Sevriano and Batisto!" declared the Gallacelli brothers (senior). The two celebrated and while the Gallacelli bothers (senior) were in with the mother and the Gallacelli brothers (junior), Rajandra Das posed the question everyone wanted to ask but had lacked the courage to voice.

"All right then, which one of them is the father?"

The Great Question buzzed around Desolation Road like a swarm of annoying insects. Ed, Umberto, or Louie? Persis Tatterdemalion did not know. The Gallacelli brothers (senior) would not say. The Gallacelli brothers (junior) could not say. Rajandra Das's question reigned absolute for twenty-four hours, then a better question replaced it. That question was: Who killed Gaston Tenebrae and left him by the side of the railroad line with his head smashed like a breakfast egg?

24

There was to be a trial. It was eagerly anticipated by all. It would be the event of the year. Possibly the event of all time. It would mark Desolation Road as a real place, for no place was real until someone had died there and put a big black pin on the monochrome maps of the dead. It was of such importance that Dominic Frontera spoke with his superiors on his microwave relay and hired the services of the Court of Piepowder.

Two days later a black and gold train climbed up over the horizon and was waved into a siding by Rajandra Das, station master Pro Tem. It promptly disgorged a bustle of periwigged lawyers, judges, recorders, and ushers, who subpoenaed everyone over the age of ten to form a jury.

The courtroom of Piepowder was constructed inside one of the carriages. This made it rather long and narrow as courtrooms went. The judge presided at one end with his books, counsels, and flask of brandy; at the other stood the defendant. Public and jury faced each other across the center of the carriage and developed severe cases of tennis neck during cross-examination. The Honorable Justice Dunne took the chair and the court was in session.

"This legally constituted Mobile Court Service under the jurisdiction of the North West Quartersphere Justicciary (as provided by the Bethlehem Ares Corporation) for the settlement of such cases and claims as have not access to Official Circuit Courts and corresponding legal facilities is now in session." Justice Dunne suffered dreadfully from hemmorhoids. In times past they had often adversely influenced the outcome of trials.

"Representing the State and Company?"

"Messrs. Prye, Peake, and Meddyl." Three weasel-faced lawyers stood up and bowed.

"Representing the defendant?"

"I, Your Honor, Louis Gallacelli." He stood and bowed. Persis Tatterdemalion thought him very smart and assured in his legal costume. Louie Gallacelli was trembling, sweating, and suffering from an overtightness in the crotch of his pants. He had neither worn his mothball-redolent suit nor practiced his art before.

"And what is the charge?"

The recorder rose and bowed.

"That on the night of thirty-first Julaugust, Mr. Gaston Tenebrae, citizen of the Officially Registered Settlement of Desolation Road, was murdered in cold blood and with malice aforethought, by Mr. Joseph Stalin, citizen of Desolation Road."

Seldom in the history of jurisprudence had there been a suspect as clearly guilty as Mr. Stalin. He was such an obvious choice for the murder of his hated rival Gaston Tenebrae that most people thought a trial was a waste of time and money and would have gladly lynched him from a wind-pump.

"We will have a trial," Dominic Frontera had said. "It must all be legal and proper." He added, "First the trial, then the hanging." Despite his protests of innocence, all the evidence piled up against Mr. Stalin. He had the motive, the opportunity, and absolutely no alibi for the night. He was guilty as hell.

"How does the accused plead?" asked Justice Dunne. The first hemorrhoidal twitchings plucked at his rectum. This was going to be a difficult trial.

Louie Gallacelli rose, adopted the proper legal stance, and declared in a loud voice, "Not guilty."

Order was restored five gavel-banging minutes later.

"Any further disturbances and I will have the court cleared," scolded Justice Dunne. "Further, I am not totally satisfied with complete impartiality of the jury, but lacking any other we must proceed with the jury we have. Call the first witness."

Rajandra Das had been taken on as a temporary usher for the duration of the trial.

"Call Genevieve Tenebrae!" he shouted. Genevieve Tenebrae took the witness stand and gave her testimony. As witness after witness was called it became manifestly clear that Mr. Stalin was as guilty as hell. The prosecution demolished his alibi (that he had been playing dominoes with Mr. Jericho) and unearthed the long-standing feud between the Stalins and Tenebraes. They settled upon the lone wind-pump for both gardens with the glee of vultures settling upon a dead llama. "Prime motivation!" they chorused, forefingers raised in triumph. In speedy succession they threw the rumored dalliance on the train to Desolation Road, the envy over the children (at which point Genevieve Tenebrae left the court), and a thousand and one petty loathings and hatreds into the laps of the jury. Messrs. Prye, Peake, and Meddyl were triumphant. The defense was demoralized. Everything was set for the conviction of Mr. Stalin for the murder of his neighbor Gaston Tenebrae.

In desperation Louie Gallacelli, having realized that he was well out of his league in the company of Messrs. Prye, Peake, and Meddyl, moved for an adjournment. To his surprise, Justice Dunne agreed. Two motives moved His Honor. The first was that the Court of Piepowder worked on daily rates, the second that his piles had reached a point of such excruciation that he could not face another hour on the judge's bench. Court was adjourned, all rose, and Justice Dunne retired to a dinner of cutlets and claret followed by an intimate appointment with a jar of Mammy Lee's Calendula Pile Ointment.

In the Bethlehem Ares Railroad/Hotel Louie Gallacelli sat in a quiet corner and reviewed the day's proceedings over a bottle of complimentary Belladonna brandy.

"Holy Mother, I was lousy."

He saw Mr. Jericho enter and order a beer. He did not like Mr. Jericho. None of the Gallacelli brothers liked Mr. Jericho. He made them feel coarse and clumsy, more animals than men. But it was not dislike that made Louie Gallacelli call loudly for Mr. Jericho to get himself over here, but the fact that Mr. Jericho had refused to stand witness and corroborate his client's alibi.

"Why the hell, I say, why the hell didn't you substantiate Joey's alibi? Why the hell didn't you come forward as a witness and say, 'We were playing dominoes at such and such a time on such and such a night' and end the case?" Mr. Jericho shrugged.

"Well, were you playing dominoes together the night of the murder or weren't you?"

"Of course we were," said Mr. Jericho.

"Well, then damn well say so in court! Listen, I'm going to subpoena you as a defense key witness and then you'll damn well have to say you were playing dominoes the night of the murder!"

"I will not appear as a witness, even under subpoena."

"Why the hell not? Afraid of someone recognizing you? The judge perhaps? Afraid of cross-examination?"

"Precisely." Before Louie Gallacelli could ask any difficult lawyer's questions, Mr. Jericho said in a confidential whisper, "I can get you all the evidence you need without my having to take the witness stand."

"Oh? How?"

"Come with me, please."

Mr. Jericho led the attorney to Dr. Alimantando's old house, empty and dusty since the day two years before when Dr. Alimantando had magically vanished into time to hunt down a mythical greenperson. In Dr. Alimantando's workshop Mr. Jericho dusted off a small machine that looked like a sewing machine tangled up in a spider's web.

"No one knows this exists, but this is the Mark Two Alimantando time winder."

"Get on. You mean all that about the time traveling little green man's true?"

"Should have talked more to your brother. He helped us build it. Dr. Alimantando left instructions for us to build this Mark Two unit in case something went wrong in time; he could put himself into stasis for a couple of million years and arrive here to pick up the replacement unit."

"Fascinating," said Louie Gallacelli, not in the least fascinated. "How does this relate to my expert witness?"

"We use it to wind time backward so that we can take a look at the night of the murder to see who really committed the crime."

"You mean you don't know?"

"Of course not. Whatever made you think I did?"

"I don't believe this."

"Watch and wait."

Rajandra Das and Ed Gallacelli were fetched from their suppers and taken to the place by the railroad line where Rajandra Das had found the body. It was a cold night, as it had been the night of the murder. The stars shone like steel spearpoints. Lasers flickered fitfully across the vault of the sky. Louie Gallacelli flapped his arms for warmth and tried to read the heliograph of the heavens. His breath hung in great steaming clouds.

"You folks near ready?"

Mr. Jericho made some fine adjustments to the field generator settings.

"Ready. Let's do it."

Ed Gallacelli tripped the remote switch and imprisoned Desolation Road within a translucent blue bubble.

"Child of grace!" exclaimed brother Louie. Ed Gallacelli looked at him. That was his expression.

"That's not what's meant to happen," said Rajandra Das needlessly. "Do something before anyone notices."

"I'm trying, I'm trying," said Ed Gallacelli, frozen-fingered clumsy at the fine settings.

"I think we must have overlooked the Temporal Inversion Problem," speculated Mr. Jericho.

"Oh, what is that?" said Lawyer Louie.

"A variable-entropic gradient electromagnetogravitic field," said Ed Gallacelli.

"No, what is *that*." Something like a miniature thunderstorm was bombarding the upper curve of the bubble with rather pretty, if totally ineffectual, blue lightning.

The three engineers looked up from their time machine.

"Child of grace!" said Ed Gallacelli.

"I think it's a ghost," said Rajandra Das. The storm of entropic ectoplasm knotted into a translucent blue lifestudy of Gaston Tenebrae. His head was bent over at an improbable angle and he seemed to be boiling with suppressed rage. This could have been because he was quite naked. Garments clearly did not pass beyond the grave, not even the decorous white shifts with which public imagination covered its spooks' modesty.

"He looks pretty mad," said Rajandra Das.

"So would you if you'd been murdered," said Louie.

"No such things as ghosts," said Mr. Jericho firmly.

"Oh, no?" said three simultaneous voices.

"It's a time-dependent set of persona engrams stored holographically in the local spatial stress matrix."

"Like hell," said Rajandra Das. "It's a ghost."

"Will that bubble hold him?" asked Louie.

"Looks like it is," said Mr. Jericho.

"All right. Then we have our expert witness. Fiddle with that thing and see if you can bring him in. I'm looking forward to presenting the ghost of the murder victim to testify on his own behalf tomorrow." Six hands reached for the field generator controls. Mr. Jericho slapped less dextrous fingers away and stroked the verniers. The blue bubble contracted to half its volume, bisecting a wind pump and cutting off a third of the community solar farm.

"Do that again," said Louie Gallacelli, drawing up a line of questioning in his mind. He would make legal history. The first attorney ever to cross-examine a ghost. The bubble shrank once again. Now less than one hundred meters distant, the ghost glowered at its captors and pelted the imprisoning dome with pixie lightning.

"I hope he doesn't decide to use that stuff on us," said Rajandra Das. The ghost was now circling at high speed under the apex of the dome, seething with unutterable fury.

"Bring him in," said Louie Gallacelli, unconsciously adopting his courtroom stance. The case was already successfully concluded in his mind. The name of Gallacelli was whispering up and down the line wherever injustice was being fought and the rights of man championed.

The electromagnetogravitic variable entropy field was now no more than a meter across. The ghost, cramped and contorted into a painful knot of ectoplasm within, mouthed oaths which Mr. Jericho, being an accomplished lipreader, found quite shocking and utterly inappropriate for one supposedly passed into the nearer presence of the Panarch. Louie Gallacelli tried some preliminary questions, but such was the ghost's indignant ingratitude that he had Rajandra Das shut the field down to an agonizing fifteen centimeters and left it that size all night until the ghost learned some respect for the due processes of law. The Mark Two time winder and incumbent phantom were taken to the Bethlehen Ares Railroad/Hotel to await the morning. Umberto Gallacelli amused himself for several hours by spitting at the force field and showing the ghost some of his vast collection of photographs of women either having, about to have, or thinking about having sex with themselves, other women, a variety of farm animals, or massive-membered men.

25

J ustice Dunne was in poor humor for a sentencing. The local water had given him diarrhea, which, coupled with his hemorrhoids, had felt like shitting sheets of flame. His breakfast had been cold and inadequate, he had learned from his radio that his racehorse had fallen and broken its neck in the Morongai Flats Ten Thousand Meters, and now two of his jurors were missing. He had his usher, that ragged scamp Rajandra Das, search the town for them, and when that proved to be in vain he ruled that the trial could proceed with a jury of eight. He made a mental note to add a charge of fifty golden dollars to the town's already substantial bill for this additional ruling. And now the defense counsel, a ludicrous semi-educated bumpkin with an overinflated opinion of his legal prowess, was seriously proposing that a key witness be admitted at this late stage in the proceedings.

"What is the name of this key witness?"

Louie Gallacelli cleared his throat.

"The ghost of Gaston Tenebrae."

Messrs. Prye, Peake, and Meddyl were on their feet instantly. Genevieve Tenebrae fainted and was carried out.

Justice Dunne sighed. His anus was beginning to itch again. The counsels argued. The accused ate a breakfast of fried bread and coffee. After an hour, jury, spectators, and witnesses went to tend their fields. Arguments clashed and parried. Justice Dunne fought an insistent urge to insert a forefinger into his backside and scratch the frustration until it bled. Two hours passed. Seeing no end to the wrangling unless he intervened, Justice Dunne banged his gavel and declared, "The ghost may testify."

Rajandra Das skipped around the fields and houses of Desolation Road rounding up jurors, witnesses, and spectators. There was still no sign of the two missing jurors: Mikal Margolis and Marya Quinsana.

"Call the ghost of Gaston Tenebrae."

The ghost-catchers exchanged clenched-fist signs of triumph. Ed Gallacelli wheeled in the Mark Two time-winder and checked the transducers he had fixed around the edge of the bubble.

"Can you hear me?" squeaked the ghost. Newly revived, Genevieve Tenebrae promptly fainted again. The phantom's voice came scratchy but audible through Ed Gallacelli's radio amplifier.

"Now, Mr. Tenebrae, or rather, Late Mr. Tenebrae, did this man, the accused, murder you on the night of thirty-first Julaugust, at approximately twenty minutes of nothing?"

The ghost somersaulted gleefully in its blue crystal ball.

"Joey and I have had our differences in the past, I'd be the first to admit it, but now that I've passed into the nearer presence of the Panarch, all that's forgiven and forgotten. No, it wasn't him that killed me. He didn't do it."

"Then who did?"

Genevieve Tenebrae regained consciousness to hear her husband name his murderer.

"It was Mikal Margolis. He did it."

In the ensuing uproar Genevieve Tenebrae fainted for the third time and the Babooshka crowed triumphantly, "I told you so, he was no good, that son of mine," and Justice Dunne banged his gavel so hard the head came off.

"If there is any more of this behavior, I'll have you all fined for contempt," he thundered.

Order restored, the ghost of Gaston Tenebare unraveled its

sordid testimony of adultery, glowing passion, violent death, and illicit tripartite relationships between Gaston Tenebrae, Mikal Margolis, and Marya Quinsana.

"I suppose I should never have done it," the phantom squeaked, "but I still thought of myself as an attractive man: I wanted to know I had not lost my touch with the ladies, so I flirted with Marya Quinsana because she's a fine, fine woman."

"Gaston!" shrieked his widow, up from her third faint, ready for her fourth. "How could you do this to me!"

"Order," said Justice Dunne.

"What about the baby, eh, darling?" said the ghost. "Since I passed into the world beyond I've learned a lot of interesting things. Like where little Arnie came from."

Genevieve Tenebrae burst into tears and was led from the courtroom by Eva Mandella. The ghost resumed its tale of clandestine trysts and whispered intimacies beneath silk sheets to the utter amazement of the citizens of Desolation Road. Amazement, and admiration that an illicit adulterous relationship of such intensity (and with such a publicly promiscuous figure as Marya Quinsana) could have been so successfully concealed among a population of only twenty-two people.

"She led me along good. But now I know better." Since metempsychosing to the Heavenly Exalted Plane, Gaston Tenebrae had learned of Marya Quinsana's simultaneous relationship with Mikal Margolis. "She was playing us off, one against the other; me, Mikal, and her brother Morton; playing us off just for the fun of it. She enjoyed manipulating people. Mikal Margolis, well, he was always a headstrong boy and never really made it in love: having me to contend with was too much for him." Suspicious, Mikal Margolis had followed Marya Quinsana and Gaston Tenebrae and spied upon their lovemaking. It was then that the trembling started. In the surgery he would shudder with repressed rage and drop instruments and spill things. The tension built until he could feel the blood seething around his bones like the ocean breaking upon rocks until something old and foul like a black ulcer burst inside him. He found Gaston Genebrae walking home from a tryst along the side of the railroad line.

"Then he picked up a short piece of rail, about half a meter long, that was lying beside the track and smashed me on the side of the neck with it. Severed my spine at once. Killed me instantly."

The ghost concluded its evidence here and was wheeled away. Justice Dunne delivered his summing up and after begging them to please be objective about what they had seen and heard, gave leave for the jury to retire and consider its verdict. The jury retired to the Bethlehem Ares Railroad/Hotel, now reduced to seven jurors. Unseen by any, Morton Quinsana had slipped away during the final testimony.

At fourteen minutes of fourteen the jury returned.

"How do you find the accused, guilty or not guilty?"

"Not guilty," said Rael Mandella.

"And that is the verdict of you all?"

"It is."

The judge acquitted Mr. Stalin. There was cheering and clapping. Louie Gallacelli was carried shoulder-high from the Court of Piepowder and paraded all around the town so that every goat, chicken, and llama might see what a fine lawyer Desolation Road had produced. Genevieve Tenebrae took her daughter and went to ask Ed Gallacelli for her husband's ghost.

"The time-dependent set of persona engrams stored holographically in the local spatial-stress matrix?" said engineer Ed. "Sure." Genevieve Tenebrae took the time-winder and the tiny bubble containing her late husband home, put them on the shelf, and nagged the ghost for its unfaithfulness for twelve years.

Justice Dunne returned to his disrobing carriage and had his personal servant, an eight-year-old sloe-eyed Xanthian girl, apply soothing lotion to his piles.

Mr. Stalin was joyously reunited with wife and blubbering adolescent son, whose nose had generated a stream of shining goo all through the trial. Celebrating with roast turkey and peapod wine that night, the Stalins' buoyant mood was shattered when four armed men dressed in black and gold leather smashed the door in with rifle butts.

"Joseph Mencke Stalin?" the leader asked.

Wife and son pointed simultaneously to husband and father. The man who had spoken held out a piece of paper.

"This is your bill for services rendered by the Bethlehem Ares Corporation Legal Services Division, incorporating hire of courtroom, court charges, hire of court personnel for two days, wages for same, use of power and light, use of papers, file reference charges, prosecution fees, recorder's fees, judge's fees, comestibles, including sundries, including meals, pile ointment, and claret, justice's servant's fees, arrival and departure fees for the locomotive, insurance of same, hire of same, interrogation fees, acquittal fees, jury tax, and replacement of one judicial gavel: total, 3548 New Dollars twenty-eight centavos."

The Stalins gaped like ducks in a thunderstrom.

"But I've paid. I've paid Louie Gallacelli his twenty-five dollars," stammered Mr. Stalin.

"Normally all court fees are paid by the guilty party," said the sergeant-at-arms. "However, the guilty party having absconded, the charges, under sub-section 37, paragraph 16 of the Legal Charges Deferment Act (Regional and Sub-Contractee Courts) all pass to the defendant, as the legal next-to-guilty party. However, the Company being generous to those of limited means, will accept payment in either cash or kind and will issue you, upon your request, with a court order for the restitution of payment from Mr. Mikal Margolis, the actual guilty party."

"But we've no money," pleaded Mrs. Stalin.

"Cash or kind," said the sergeant-at-arms, already quartering the room with his bailiff's eyes. His gaze rested on Johnny Stalin, a forkful of turkey frozen between plate and open mouth. "He'll do." The three armed sequestrators marched down into the dining room and lifted Johnny Stalin bodily from his chair, fork still in hand. The sergeant-at-arms scribbled something on his clipboard.

"Sign here and here," he said to Mr. Stalin. "Right. That . . ." he continued, ripping a pink form off at its perforations, "is one certificate for the indenture of your son against incurred court charges liable to the Court of Piepowder, for an indefinite amount of time no less than twenty years and no greater than sixty. And this"—he slapped a piece of blue paper into Mr. Stalin's hand—"is your receipt."

Shrieking and blubbering like a stuck pig, Johnny Stalin, aged 8¾, was marched out of his house, up the alley, and onto the train. With an ear-shattering roar of power the locomotive fired up its fusion engines and drew away from

Desolation Road. The Court of Piepowder was never seen again.

Morton Quinsana returned to the empty office. He took all his dental tools, his dental books, his dental coats, his dental chair, and made a pile of them in the middle of the office and set fire to them. When it had died to ashes, he took a piece of hemp rope from a cupboard, made a strong noose, and hanged himself in the name of love from the roofbeam. His feet pendulumed through the pile of ashes and fused metal and drew little gray trails across the floor.

26

For a year now it had been the same all day every day: how unfaithful he had been to her, how she had loved only him, only him, always and only, never a thought crossed her mind of another man, no, never, not once in all those years, not ever, and while she was sitting at home worshipping him in the temple of her heart, what had he been doing, oh, yes, you know only too well; yes, that, with that jade of a woman, that scarlet woman of bad parentage (may her womb rot within her and her breasts wither like dry eggplants) and he had earned no better than he deserved, yes, justice had been done, for the betrayal of a wife as adoring as she and what had he done, what had he done; shamed her before the whole town, yes the whole town, where she could no longer hold up her head in dignity or pride again, where she must hide from the people who said of her as she passed by "there she goes, there, look at her, the woman whose husband cheated on her and who never knew"; well, now everyone knew thanks to

him, thanks to the goodness of his heart, his wonderful lofty
intentions getting that Stalin man off the hook, his own rival
and enemy, no less, he had given plenty of thought for rivals
and enemies, yes, but was there ever a single thought for poor
devoted wives, the kind who love with a love incomparable,
and what had he done with all that love, eh? what had he
done?: only squandered it on some cheap bawd who was not
nagnagnagnagnagnagnagnagnag from rising to set the fire at
dawn until she went to bed at sunset, and he saw how the
nagging had made her ugly in body and soul and he hated her
for it, hated the maliciousness that made her nag nag nag him
for eternity in the bosom of the Panarch, he hated her and so
he decided to punish her, so one day he whistled and called to
his daughter until she put down her book and pushed her face
against the blue bubble and he said to her, "Arnie daughter,
have you ever wondered where you came from?" and Arnie
replied, lips brushing the blue force field. "You mean sex and
all that?" to which he said, "Oh, no, I mean, you, personally,
because, Arnie, I'm not your daddy" and then he told her what
he had learned from his brush with the Panarchical Omnisci-
ence of how a woman had stolen a baby from a childless old
woman and how that woman wanted that baby more than
anything else in the visible or invisible world and enfolded and
nurtured and birthed that baby as if it were her own, and after
he had told her all this he said, "Go look in the mirror, Arnie,
and ask yourself, do you really look like a Tenebrae, or do you
look like a Mandella, for that is what you are; Rael's sister,
Limaal and Taasmin's aunt," and when she went to the mirror
in her room and he heard her sobbing, he was much pleased,
for he had sown the seeds of his wife's destruction in the girl
who was not and never had been his daughter's heart and such
was his malignant glee that he turned little cartwheels of
delight in his shimmering blue bubble.

27

His name was Trick-Shot O'Rourke. He had diamond fillings in his teeth and a gold inlaid cue. His suit was of the finest organza silk and his shoes of Christadelphia leather. He called himself many grand things: "The Champion of the World," "Sultan of Snooker," "Master of the Green Baize," "The Greatest Snooker Player the Universe Has Ever Known," but he was a fading star and everyone knew it, for a man who was all those things he claimed to be would not be playing a ten-dollar jackpots in the snooker room of the Bethlehem Ares Railroad/Hotel. Yet even at its dimmest, his star was brighter than any of the other cuemen in Desolation Road and he had amassed a considerable pile of bills by the time he asked for any more challengers.

"I know one," said Persis Tatterdemalion, "if he isn't in bed yet. Anyone seen Limaal?"

A patch of darkness detached itself from the darkest table in the darkest corner and coiled toward the snooker table. Trick-Shot O'Rourke regarded his opponent. He guessed his age to be between nine and ten, that indefinable and painful age between boyhood and manhood. Young, confident; look at the way he folds his cue chalk back into his vest pocket. Which will he be: gritty grinder or master tactician, prince of potters or king of psywar?

"How much down?" he asked.

"How much do you want?"

"The whole wad?"

"I think we could match that." There were nods of consent from the faces at the bar. They seemed to be grinning. A pile of ten-dollar bills built up on the counter.

"Toss for break?"

"Heads."

"Tails. I break." Where did a nine-year-old man-boy learn such self-assuredness? Trick-Shot O'Rourke watched his opponent bend to the cue.

—He is like a snake, thought the hustler, lithe and elegant. But I think I can beat him.

And he played with all his might and spun the thread of his skill so fine that it seemed it must snap, but the thin, hollow-eyed boy must have drawn power from the darkness, for each shot he played was as carefully composed and executed as the one before. He played with a deadly consistency that wore Trick-Shot O'Rourke away like a grindwheel. The old hustler played five frames against the boy. By the end of the fifth he was tired and stale but the boy was as fresh and accurate as when he had broken off in the first. He stood back in blatant admiration of the boy's skill and when the final black gave the boy his three-two victory, the professional was the first to congratulate him.

"Son, you've got talent. Real talent. I don't mind losing a hundred dollars to an opponent like you. It was a joy to behold. Let me do you one favor, though. Let me tell your fortune."

"You tell fortunes?"

"By the table and the balls. Never seen it done before?" Trick-Shot O'Rourke took a wide roll of black baize from his case and spread it across the table. The baize was divided into sections, each marked with arcane symbols and peculiar names in gold lettering: "Self Unseeing," "Changes and Changing," "Vastness," "Behind him," "Before him," "Beyond him." Trick-Shot O'Rourke formed up a triangle of multicolored balls and placed the cue ball on a golden spot marked "To Come."

"Rules are simple. Just drive the cue ball at that pack. It's all up to you what side, what spin, what angle, what speed, what swerve, what screw, and from the way you scatter them I can interpret your fortune." The skinny boy picked up the cue and wiped it with a rag. "One word of advice. You play the rational game; you've probably got it all worked out where you want to put the balls. If you do that, it won't work. You've got to switch off the mind and let the heart decide."

The boy nodded. He sighted along the cue. A sudden crackle of dark energy made everyone shudder and the cue ball burst the pack of colored balls apart. For a second or so the table was a quantum nightmare of ricocheting spheres. Then all was rest again. Trick-Shot O'Rourke hummed and hawed around the table.

"Interesting. Never seen one like that before. Look, see. The tangerine ball, Journey, is resting in Golden Trove, next to the Crimson Heart ball, which lies equally in Golden Trove and God's Mansion. You'll leave here, soon, if the Fleetingness ball is anything to go by; also someone to love who you will find in this place of fame and fortune, but will not be of it. But this is the best bit. See that turquoise ball, Ambition; it's resting right on the cushion in Strife next to the gray Darkness ball. I would interpret this to mean that you're going to come into conflict with a mighty force of darkness—possibly even the Destroyer himself."

It was all-of-a-sudden cold in the Bethlehem Ares Railroad/Hotel. Limaal Mandella smiled and asked, "Do I win?"

"Your ball's next to the cushion. You win. But look, see there, the white ball, the Love ball, hasn't moved from the break-off point. And the Answers ball, the lime green one, lies in Great Circle while the purple Questions lies in Changes and Changing. You leave here to seek answers to your questions, they will be found only when you return home where your heart is."

"My heart? In this place?" Limaal Mandella's laugh was ugly, too old for a boy of nine.

"That's what the balls say."

"And do the balls say when Limaal Mandella must die, old man?"

"Look at the black Death ball. See how it lies next to Hope on the line between Word and Darkness. You will fight your greatest battle where you heart is and in winning it you lose everything."

Limaal Mandella laughed again. He clutched his heart.

"My heart, old man, is in my chest. That is the only place my heart is. In me."

"That is a true saying."

Limaal Mandella rolled the black Death ball with the tip of his forefinger.

"Well, we must all die and none of us can choose the time or the place or the way of it. Thank you for the fortune-telling, Mr. O'Rourke, but I want to make my own future out of the balls. Snooker's a game for rationalists, not mystics. Say, isn't that deep thinking for a nine-year-old? But you played well, mister, you played the best. Time this nine-year-old was in bed, though."

He left and Trick-Shot O'Rourke gathered up his magic balls and fortune-telling cloth.

After that night Limaal Mandella became convinced of his greatness. Though his rationalism would not allow him the generous oracle of the balls, his heart had seen his name written large in the stars and he began to play not for love or money but for power. His greatness was buttressed every time he smashed some visiting geologist, geophysicist, botanist, plant pathologist, soil engineer or meteorologist. The stake money was meaningless, he used it to buy drinks for the house. The name of Limaal Mandella passed up and down the line, together with the legend of the boy from Desolation Road who was unbeatable as long as he remained in his hometown. There was no shortage of young headhunters eager to disprove the legend: their defeat only reinforced it the more. Like the tumbling planets of his childhood nightmares, the rolling balls crushed all Limaal Mandella's opponents.

Sometime in the early morning of his tenth birthday, his coming of age, when the covers had been pulled over another victory on the baize and the chairs upturned on the tables, Limaal Mandella went to Persis Tatterdemalion.

"I want more," he said as she washed glasses. "There has to be more, there has to be somewhere outside of here where the lights are bright and the music's loud and the world doesn't close down at three minutes of three. And I want it. God, I want it more than anything. I want to see that world, I want to show it how good I am. There are folks out there, up there, who knock worlds around like snooker balls, I want to take them on, I want to match my skill against theirs, I want out of here."

Persis Tatterdemalion put down her glass and looked for a long time into the morning. She was remembering how it felt to be trapped in a small, confusing place.

"I know. I know. But listen to this, and listen for once.

Today you are a man and master of your own destiny. You decide what it will be, where it will lead. Limaal, the world can be any shape you want it to be."

"You mean go?"

"Go. Go now, before you change your mind, before you lose your nerve. God, I wish I had the courage and the freedom to go with you."

There were tears in the barwoman's eyes.

That morning Limaal Mandella packed a small backsack with clothes, put eight hundred dollars purse money he had saved into his shoe, and slipped two cues into a cue case. He wrote a note for his parents and crept into their room to leave it by their bedside. He did not ask their forgiveness, only their understanding. He saw the presents his mother and father were to give him on his birthday and faltered. He breathed deeply, quietly, and left forever. He waited in the frosty cold beneath the star-sparkling sky for the night-mail to Belladonna. By dawn he was half a continent away.

28

She never washed. She never cut her hair. Her finger-nails, her toenails, curled over at the ends, and the hair of her head hung to the small of her back in a greasy, dusty rope, thickly plaited. A legion of parasites found shelter there, and in the hair of her loins and the fetid sweat-glued mats in her armpits. She itched and festered but never scratched. To scratch would have been to surrender to the body.

She had commenced the war against her body on her tenth

birthday. That was the day Limaal had gone. The maple cue her father had planed himself stood wrapped by the kitchen table. When the evening came and it was apparent that Limaal would not return, it was put away in a cupboard and the cupboard locked and forgotten. Then Taasmin went up alone to the red rim rocks to look again at the shape of the world. She stood before the Great Desert and let the wind whip at her, trying to learn from it what it was to be a woman. The wind that never stopped blowing tugged at her as if she were a kite to be whisked away into the heavens.

She realized she would love that. She would love the spiritual wind to carry her away like a paper bag, a piece of human refuse swept higher and higher away from the burning dry dry land into a sky filled with angelic beings and pieces of orbital engineering equipment. She felt herself sailing, lifting before the Godwind and in panic she called with the voice inside for her brother but the closeness was gone, stretched beyond the breaking point, dissipated, gone. The twins were unbalanced. No longer did the one's mysticism govern the other's rationalism: like machines without control they flew apart into space. Unchecked, the mysticism rushed into the emptiness in Taasmin's mind where her brother had been, and transformed her into a creature of purest light; white, shining light eternal, fountaining into the sky.

"Light," she whispered, "we are all light, of light, to light we return." She opened her eyes and beheld the base red desert and the ugly little town crouched beside it. She regarded her body, newly womaned, and hated its round sleekness and muscular smoothness. Its endless hungers, its insatiable appetites, its blind disregard for anything but itself disgusted her.

Then it seemed to Taasmin Mandella that she heard a voice carried on the wind from very very far away, beyond the world, beyond time, and it cried, "The mortification of the flesh! The mortification of the flesh!"

Taasmin Mandella echoed that cry and declared war on her body and the material things of the world. There and then she cast off her clothes, finely woven by Eva Mandella upon the loom of her devotion. She walked barefoot, even when the rain turned the lanes to liquid filth or the frost pecked at the earth. She drank rainwater from a barrel, ate vegetables earthy from the garden, and slept unroofed beneath the cottonwood trees in the company of llamas. At noontime, when other citizens enjoyed the enshrined siesta, she would squat upon the burning rocks of Desolation Point, immersed in prayer, oblivious to the sun tanning her skin to leather and bleaching her hair the color of bones. She meditated upon the life of Catherine of Tharsis, whose quest for spirituality in a pagan worldly age had led her to cast off fleshly humanity and merge her soul with those of the machines that built the world.

The mortification of the flesh.

Taasmin Mandella passed beyond humanity. Her parents could not touch her, Dominic Frontera's attempts to order modesty of dress were ignored. Only the inner symphony mattered, the cascade of saintly voices pointing the way through the veil of flesh to heaven's gate. It was the way the Blessed Lady had walked before her, and if that walk meant earning the disgusted stares of the newcomers to Desolation Road, the farmers and shop owners and mechanics and railroad staff, then that was the price of it. They saw her ugly, these new faces from Iron Mountain and Llangonnedd, New Merionedd and Grand Valley, they whispered so behind her back. She saw herself beautiful beyond words, beautiful in spirit.

One day in the month of July, when the summer sun was at its peak and the noontime heat cracked pebbles and shattered rooftiles, Dominic Frontera came hot and sweaty to Taasmin Mandella, perched high like a leather bird on the red rim rocks.

"This can't go on," he told her. "The town is growing, there are new people coming in all the time: the Merchandanis, the Pentecost sisters, the Chungs, the Axamenides, the Smiths: what kind of place are they going to think this is where girls . . . women wander around naked all day, stinking like a hog wallow? It won't do, Taasmin."

Taasmin Mandella stared straight ahead of her at the horizon, eyes narrowed against the glare.

"Look, we have to do something. Right? Good. Now, how you say you come back with me to your parents, or if you don't want that, Ruthie'll look after you, have a bath, get cleaned up, put on some pretty clothes, eh? How would that be?"

A gust of wind carried a waft of fetor over Dominic Frontera. He gagged.

"Taasmin, Desolation Road is not what it was and we can't go back to what it was. It's growing, reaching for the fourteenth Decade. We can't accept certain kinds of behavior. Now, are you coming?"

Without breaking her stare, Taasmin Mandella said, "No." She had not spoken for fifty-five days prior to that word and the speaking of it disgusted her. Dominic Frontera stood, shrugged, and climbed down from the rim rocks to what remained of his siesta. The same night Taasmin Mandella took herself away from the people of the 13th Decade and wandered far along the bluffs until she found a cave where water trickled up from the subterranean ocean. Here she dwelt for ninety days, by day sleeping and praying, by night walking twelve kilometers to Desolation Road to raid the 13th Decaders' gardens. When dogs and shotguns began to appear, she felt the divine call to take herself farther away, and one bright morning she walked and walked and walked into the Great Desert, walked and walked until she had passed out of the desert of red sand into the desert of red stone. There she found a stone pillar upon which to stylitize herself, a needle of rock to impale herself. That night she slept at the base of the stone column that pointed her way to the Five Heavens and for moisture licked the dew that had settled on her naked body. From dawn to dusk of that day she climbed the stone pillar; lithe and agile as a desert lizard. The splintered nails, the torn toes, the blistered fingers, the shredded flesh: all meant as little to her as the hunger in her belly; all beautiful little mortifications, petty victories over the flesh.

For three days she sat cross-legged atop the red rock pillar, neither sleeping nor eating, drinking nor making the least movement, driving the body's scream down down down, out out out. Upon the morning of the fourth day Taasmin Mandella moved. In the long night she dreamed she had turned to stone but in the morning she moved. Not a great movement, only a swiveling of dry eyeballs to behold a cloud passing out of the south, a solitary dark cloud shot through with lightnings. From this cloud came a sound like that of a swarm of furious bees. As it drew nearer, Taasmin Mandella saw that it was composed of many tiny particles in desperate motion, indeed like a swarm of insects. Nearer drew the cloud, nearer still, and she saw to her astonishment (Taasmin Mandella yet being remotely capable of some human emotion) that the cloud consisted of thousands upon thousands of angelic beings beating their holy way through the upper air. They were similar to the angel freed by Rajandra Das from Adam Black's Chautauqua and were supported in their flight by a bewildering diversity of wings, vanes, rockets, airfoils, propellors, balloons, rotors, and jet engines. The angel host swept past her out of the South, so many of them that they might be looping high into the tropopause to parade past again. Then out of the buzzing cloud loomed a massive device, a boxy flying object glittering blue and silver, a full kilometer long. In its peculiar construction it reminded Taasmin of the pictures of rikshas and autocars she had seen in her mother's picture books. Upon its blunt prow was a chromium grin of a grille bearing the title "Plymouth" in letters as tall as Taasmin Mandella. Beneath the grille was a rectangular shield, bright blue, with the legend lettered in yellow:

STATE OF BARSOOM
ST. CATH

The Blue Plymouth halted above the rock pillar and as Taasmin tried to guess its possible function (ROTECH engineering facility, celestial chariot, flying market, trick of sun and stone) a choir of angels banked in beneath it and sang, to the accompaniment of zither, serpent, okarina, crumhorn, and stratocaster:

> *Doo wop a bee bop*
> *Shooby-dooby doo*
> *Doo wop showaddy-showaddy*
> *A-bop bam boo.*
> *Be-bop a lulah*
> *Shebob shooby-doo*
> *Re bob a lulah*
> *Bebop bam boo.*

A solitary angel detached itself from the celestial choir and dropped on its helicopter vanes until face-to-face with Taasmin Mandella.

> O Blesssede Mortalle, nowe thys Newes Receive:
> Prepare Thyselfe to Entertaine a Sainte,
> Oure Sainte, Oure Blessede Ladie, She of Tharsis
> Beholde the Advente of the Blessede Cathie!

It declaimed this in flawless iambic pentameter. Contrarotating blades snatched the angel up to heaven. The Big Blue Plymouth played an ancient, ancient tune called "Dicksee" on its quintuple airhorns and extended an access ramp. A small crop-haired woman dressed in a glowing white picture-suit descended the ramp and walked toward Taasmin Mandella, arms outstretched in the universal symbol of welcome.

29

Seeing for the first time the city of Kershaw, capital of the Bethlehem Ares Corporation, Johnny Stalin could not properly comprehend what he beheld. From the viewpoint of the guardroom of a train rattling through a range of hills the color of slate and rust, it seemed to him that he saw a cube, black as his closed eyelids, bearing on its topmost edges the words BETHLEHEM ARES CORPORATION BETHLEHEM ARES CORPORATION BETHLEHEM ARES CORPORATION BETHLEHEM ARES CORPORATION lettered in gold. Still, he could not assign any proportions to the cube, for it stood in a pond of dirty water which robbed it of any sense of perspective. Then he saw the clouds. They were dirty white cumulus clouds, like soiled cotton, gathering together three quarters of the way up the face of the cube. Johnny Stalin spun away from the window and hid away from what he had beheld.

The cube must have been almost three kilometers on a side.

Now the world took on its proper proportions: the hills scabbed with blast furnaces and foundries, the pool that was no pool at all but a great lake in the center of which stood Kershaw. A dreadful fascination drew him back to the scene outside. The tiny threads that tied the cube to lake shores he now saw to be wide earth causeways, wide enough to carry twin railroad tracks, and what he had thought to be birds swooping around the faces of the cube were helicopters and dirigibles.

The Court of Piepowder rattled onto a causeway. Proud black and gold expresses bulleted past, rocking the train with their pressure waves. In their wake Johnny Stalin received his first close look at the lake. It seemed to be full of oily sludge, bubbling and steaming gently. Patches of chrome yellow and rust red stained the surface, in the far distance an oil geyser spouted black filth and an area of lake the size of a small town exploded into yellow sulphurous boiling flinging cascades of acid mud hundreds of meters in all directions. Not half a kilometer distant from the causeway some enormous waxy pink object lifted out of a froth of polymerized bubbles, a complex thing of spires and lattices like a capsized cathedral, forever crumbling back into dissolution under its own weight.

Johnny Stalin whimpered in fear. He could not comprehend this hellish place. Then he saw what seemed to be a human figure, strangely clothed, walking on the far lake shore. The sight of humanity in the chemical wilderness cheered him. He did not know, much less care, that the figure was that of a Shareholder of the City of Kershaw strolling by the pleasant shores of Syss, the poisoned lake, in elephantine respirator and isolation suit. The lake's prismatic colors and rainbow sheen, its gushing geysers, eruptions, and spontaneous polymer accretions were much prized by the Shareholders of Kershaw: the melancholy air of Sepia Bay, properly filtered through respirator and rebreathed, was most conducive to reflections on love and love lost; Green Bay, rich in copper nitrates, promoted the tranquility of thought and serenity necessary for managerial decision-making; sickly decaying Yellow Bay, redolent of mortality, favorite spot for suicides; Blue Bay pensive, thoughtful; Red Bay, much beloved by Junior Executive Levels, aggressive, dynamic. The executives astroll upon the rusty shores saw the return of the Court of Piepowder, saw the strange polymer chemoid raise itself out of the chemical brew and chattered excitedly through their microphones. Such phenomena were considered fortunate, bestowing upon the beholder luck in love, success in business, and good omens. To the traveler arriving in Kershaw they were foretellers of great fortune. Johnny Stalin, locked in the guardsvan for eight days, knew nothing of omens and harbingers. He knew of the Bethlehem Ares Corporation nothing whatsoever. He would soon.

"Shareholder 703286543," they told him. "Don't forget it. 703286543." He would have been hard put to forget it. It was printed on the plastic badge they gave him, on the one-piece paper suit they gave him, on the door of the room they gave him, and it was stamped on every item in the tiny windowless room: the table, the chair, the bed, the lamp, the towels, the soap, the copy of *Toward a New Feudalism* under the number-stamped pillow: Shareholder 703286543. At corridor roll call every morning the fat woman in the gray paper junior executive suit called out, "Shareholder 703286543" and every morning Johnny Stalin would raise his hand and call out, "Present." He came just after Shareholder 703286542 and just before Shareholder 703286544 and learned where to stand in the row by number, not face. After the roll call the fat woman would read a short piece from *Toward a New Feudalism*, deliver a brief homily on the virtues of industrial feudalism, and shout out the day's production quotas which the Share-holders shouted back while performing forty press-ups, forty knee-bends and jogging on the spot to rather martial music blaring from the loudspeakers. Then they would doff paper caps and hold them over hearts to sing the Company song. As Shift C marched down the corridor to the gravity bus, the fat woman would shout out the state of the Company's shares in the world markets. It was Company policy for all Shareholders to feel personal satisfaction from their minuscule contribution to the Bethlehem Ares Corporation. The fat woman would check Shift C into the gravity bus, Shareholder blah blah blah, Shareholder blah blah blah, Shareholder blah blah blah. The doors would close and the gravity bus would shoot upanddownandforwardandbackwardandleftandright and Shareholder 703286543 would have his shift in ructions of laughter with his impersonation of the fat gray woman going blah blah blah. With a lurch that pushed everyone against everyone else the gravity bus would arrive at its destination, doors would slam open, and the laughter and smiles switch off like late-night radio programs as Shift C marched into the factory.

There were numbers on the machines too: machine number 703286543 stood on the conveyor between machine 703286542 and machine 703286544. The Shareholders would take up their positions, and when the hooter blew, the hatch at the end of the conveyor would open and components start to come down the serpentine production line. From 0900 to 1100 hours (when there was a break for tea) and from 1115 to 1300 (when it was lunchtime) Shareholder 703286543 took a piece of plastic shaped a bit like a human ear and a piece of plastic shaped like an ornate letter P and heat-welded them together on his bonding machine. From 1330 hours to 1630 hours he would weld some more ears and letter Ps and then Shift C would clock out and march out of the factory to meet Shift A marching in. They would enter the gravity bus once again, there would be more upping and downing and to-ing and fro-ing and then the Shareholders of Shift C would be back in their familiar corridors. There would be a noisy, joking hour-and-a-bit in the corridor bath house, then dinner in the refectory (so similar to the factory refectory that Shareholder 703286543 sometimes wondered if they were the same refectory), and after that the comrades of Shift C would go to a bar and run up phenomenal charge accounts buying ridiculous daquiri ices and ludicrous drinks make primarily from puréed mulberries. On Mondays, Wednesdays, and Fridays they went to the bar. On Tuesdays and Thursdays they went to see a movie or a live show, and on Saturdays they went dancing because the Palais De Danse was the only place they could meet girls. Shareholder 703286543 was a little bit too short and a little bit too young to enjoy the dancing. His teeth came uncomfortably close to nipple height on his dancing partners, but he liked the music, especially the new music by that man Glen Miller. Buddy Mercx was good too. On Sunday there was the Miracle Mall and in the evening everyone went to the Company relaxarium, where the young Shareholder learned all about Men's Fun well before his due.

Kid's too young for this, his comrades said, but they brought him along week in and week out because to have left him out would have broken shift solidarity. Shift solidarity was the guiding light of the production unit's life. You stuck by your mates or you didn't stick at all. That was before Johnny Stalin learned the meaning of the tiger-stripped suggestion box.

Johnny Stalin learned much in his early months in the corporation. He learned to bow to the manager and pull faces behind his back. He learned to please all men while pleasing himself. He learned the involutions of the pseudo-science called economics and its spurious laws, and he courted its idiot bastard daughter called industrial feudalism. He drank and joked with the boys at night and by day he welded pieces of plastic shaped like ears to pieces of plastic shaped like Ps and passed them on to Shareholder 703286544, who welded them to a piece of plastic shaped like a fat man. The weeks, the months passed drab and featureless as paper tissues pulled from a box until one day, in mid-weld, Johnny Stalin realized that he had no idea where the plastic pieces shaped like Ps, ears, and fat men went, or what they formed. For twelve months he had been welding two pieces of plastic together and now he had to know why. Dreaming in his numbered bed at night, plastic mouldings tumbled around him and fused into huge plastic mountains, into plastic cordilleras, into plastic continents, into crushing plastic moons at the heart of which lay a piece of plastic shaped like an ear welded to a piece of plastic shaped like a letter P.

One day, feigning mild diarrhea, he excused himself from the clocking-off shift and hid in the toilet until the gravity bus had rumbled and clanked away up its slot. Quietly slipping through the swinging doors, he sauntered past the stony silent Shareholders and reached the beginning of the line where the components came through the wall and embarked upon their journey of fusion. He followed the meandering production line, peering over Shareholders' shoulders as they welded, screwed on knobs, pressed together housings and casings, soldered electronics, and fitted trims. Intent on Company business, most ignored him; to those few who shot him a quizzical glance, 703286543 put on his best managerial expression (perfected through months of practice) and said in a foremanly fashion, "Very good, very good, carry on." He was beginning to gather what the device was—a combination radio, tea maker, and bedside lamp, a useful enough item to be certain, though he could not see where his plastic ear and letter P made a contribution. At the end of the production line the radioteamakerlamps passed through a slot in the wall and vanished. Beside the conveyor was a door marked Management Only. Johnny Stalin pushed the door open and found himself in a short corridor at the end of which was another door marked Management Only. Beside him the completed radioteamakerlamps moved along the conveyor toward another slot in the wall. Johnny Stalin pushed open the second door marked Management Only and found himself in a room so similar to the one he had left that he thought for a moment that he had taken the wrong door. Then he looked harder and saw that all was utterly different. The radioteamakerlamps appeared out of the wall and passed down a production line where Company Shareholders in paper worksuits and plastic identity badges reduced them to their component parts. A deproduction line, a disassembly line. Numb with surprise, Johnny Stalin found the point on the line where his counterpart placed the pastic ear and letter P under a radio beam and broke the bonds that held them together. The number of that Shareholder was 345682307. At the end of the line, down by position 215682307, a stream of plastic and chrome components passed through a slot in the wall beside which was a door marked Management Only.

That night, while drinking fizzes in the bar, Shareholder 703286543 wrote on a small slip of paper:

"In the interests of merchantable-product per labor-unit quotas, I suggest you investigate and subsequently close down all production lines for product 34216. Respectfully, Shareholder 703286543, J. Stalin, Esq."

Next morning he dropped his tiny bombshell into the yellow and black striped box marked Suggestions.

Within two weeks the members of Shift C were relocated to

new production lines. Johnny Stalin smiled to himself to think of the gray men in gray suits discovering to their horror the economic abomination of a factory that constantly built and dismantled the same article over and over and over again. When the relocation was done, Shareholder 703286543 found himself in a new room in a new corridor working on a new line at a new credit rating. He bought a little radio for his room so that he could listen to the *New Big Band Hour* on Sunday afternoons. He liked the new music very much; Hamilton Bohannon, Buddy Mercx, Jimmy Chung, and the greatest of the great, Glen Miller. He could afford to buy the little trinkets and bauds from the costermongers on Miracle Mall that made all the difference to Company work overalls. He could afford to get drunk three nights a week. He could afford a girlfriend; a thin, crop-haired child with glasses whom he took for romantic (and expensive) promenades by Sepia Bay and upon whom he lavished his money but starved of his trust. Some gray suit in managerial was taking an interest in him, he reckoned, and he decided to keep the fires of that interest well-stoked and the gray-suited guardian angels hovering near.

At lunch one day he overheard Shareholder 108462793 whisper something to Shareholder 93674306 while passing the sauce bottle around a Union meeting in the back of Delahanty's Bar. In the cubicle in the men's toilet Johnny Stalin penciled a little note to the angels in gray and relinquished it to the Suggestion box.

Shareholders 108462793 and 93674306 were absent from work the next day, and the next, and the next, and then the line supervisor informed the shift that they had volunteered for redeployment to another line because of manning shortages. Johnny Stalin would almost have believed it had he not heard the sounds of Company police raiding Delahanty's rattling from his air-conditioning slot. He had had to turn his radio up quite loud to drown out the shouts and cries. Shareholder 396243088 next door had banged on the wall most unpleasantly for an hour or more for him to keep it down.

Two days later Shareholder 396243088 made a joke over lunch about the sexual conduct of Company directors during board meetings. Johnny Stalin had roared with laughter like everyone else. Unlike everyone else, he sent a little note to the gray suit.

"I accuse Shareholder 396243088 of not subscribing to Proper Thought with regard to the Company, its Venerable Board of Directors, and the principles of industrial feudalism. He is disloyal and disrespectful and I suspect him of holding pro-union sympathies."

When Shareholder 396243088's job as Section Overseer suddenly became vacant ("Relocation and Promotion," said the line supervisor), Johnny Stalin was the youngest man ever to be promoted to the position in the light agricultural engineering division. He held the credit rating of a man five times his age and experience. The Model Worker of the Year (light engineering section) awards came upon their annual rounds. Johnny Stalin anonymously exposed a system of petty corruption and pilfering with connections as high as junior management and, by good timing, became Model Worker of the Year (light engineering section) just two days before the corporate ax fell on twelve jobs in the agricultural division. In a sound display of Shareholder solidarity, Johnny Stalin declined to attend the Company tribunal sessions in which the twelve defendants were charged by the court of workforce and management alike and summarily dismissed. "It could have been any of us," said the Model Worker of the Year to his colleagues on Shift A as they sipped tangerine daquiris in the newly refurbished Delahanty's Bar. "It could happen to anyone."

It did. It happened to Shareholder 26844437 (I suspect Shareholder _____ of engaging in industrial espioniage and gross betrayal for rival companies which I, being a loyal and true Shareholder, shall not mention by name, respectfully, J. Stalin) Shareholders 216447890 and 552706123 (I suspect Shareholders _____ of having illicit sexual congress on Company time respectfully, J. Stalin), and Shareholder 6649-73505 (I accuse Shareholder _____ Line Supervisor on Production Line 76543, Light Agricultural Engineering Division, of laxity, sloth, and absence of zeal in promoting the Ninefold Virtues of Industrial Feudalism, respectfully, J. Stalin).

It was merely a matter of time before the gray suits invited this paragon of industrial virtue to join the junior management. It was then that he discovered that there had not been one gray suit, but eleven of them, now covering three sides of an oak table, all of them rolled off whatever production line it was that manufactured junior managers. At the head of the table sat the oldest junior, the gray suit to whom the other gray suits deferred. At the bottom of the table, a respectful distance from the luminaries of the managerial castes, stood Johnny Stalin. Oldest gray suit made a short speech filled with expressions like "model worker," "shining example," "productive unit," "company loyalty," "higher values," and "Shareholder who understands the principles of industrial feudalism." Johnny Stalin carefully memorized these clichés to use in his own speeches of praise and exhortation. After the interview, sticky cocktails were served, congratulations delivered, and Johnny Stalin bowed himself out of the presence of the managerial caste. On his return to his numbered room he found an envelope containing his relocation documents to the production management training unit pushed under his door. On the back of the door he found a standard-sized paper suit, gray, hanging from a plastic hanger, gray.

30

Wisdom, capital of the world, stands upon forty hills by the edge of the Syrtic Sea and its crystal towers are draped in curtains of green vines and summer blossoms. Llangonnedd is built upon an island in a lake and over the centuries has burst these bounds to grow whole districts that float upon a lattice of pontoons or perch precariously upon thousands of pilings. Lyx stands upon both lips of a great chasm and across its twenty bridges, each the masterpiece and care of one of the departments of the

Universuum, go the hooded and gowned Masters of the Faculties, and from its short cylindrical towers fly ten thousand prayer-kites, supplications for the continued wisdom of the Masters of Lyx. The ROTECH redoubt, China Mountain, is a federation of a hundred small villages set in an exquisite parkland. There is a village suspended from the branches of trees like the woven nests of certain birds, another is made from exquisitely glazed and fired procelain, another stands upon a floating island in a lake, another is of gaily painted caravans and pavilions that wends and wanders through the woods, another is built upon a web of diamond filaments caught between the pinnacles of China Mountain peak.

These are some of the great cities of the world. To this list, Belladonna must be added. Without doubt, it is the peer of any mentioned here but its wonders are less apparent. To the traveler coming upon Belladonna across the dry and dusty Stampos all that can be seen of her are a few dish antennae, a tall air-traffic control tower, a few dirty adobe lean-tos, and several square kilometers of tire-marked runway. Yet Belladonna is there, present yet unseen like the Divine essence in the Paschal host: it is no lie, the wickedest city in the world awaits the traveler, just a few meters beneath his feet, like the ant-lion, hungry to draw men down its maw.

Belladonna is proud of its appetites, proud of its wickedness. It is an old hard bitch of a city; a port city, a sailor's whore of a city. It is always three o'clock in the morning in Belladonna under the concrete sky. There are more street corners in her than anywhere in the world. And in a city with more bars, sushi houses, tavernas, sex boutiques, wineries, whorehouses, seraglios, bath houses, private cinema clubs, all-night cabarets, cafés, amusement arcades, restaurants, pachinko parlors, billiard halls, opium dens, gambling hells, dance palaces, card schools, beauticians, craps joints, body shops, massage parlors, private detective's offices, narcotics refineries, speakeasies, saunas, bunco booths, gin palaces, bondage basements, singles bars, flesh markets, flea markets, slave auctions, gymnasiums, art galleries, bistros, reviews, floor shows, gun shops, book stalls, torture chambers, relaxariums, jazz clubs, beer cellars, costermongers' barrows, rehearsal rooms, geisha houses, flower shops, abortion clinics, tea rooms, wrestling rings, cock pits, bear pits, bull and badger pits, Russian roulette salons, barber shops, wine bars, fashion boutiques, sports halls, cinemas, theaters, public auditoria, private libraries, museums of the bizarre and spectacular, exhibitions, displays and performance areas, casinos, freak shows, one-armed-bandit malls, strip shows, sideshows, tattoo parlors, religious cults, shrines, temples, and morticians than any other place on earth, it can be hard to find a man if he does not want to be found. But if he is as famous as Limaal Mandella, then it is easier to find him in Belladonna than in any other of the world's great cities, for Belladonna loves to flatter famous men. There was not a street sweeper or shit shoveler who did not know that Limaal Mandella, the Greatest Snooker Player the Universe had Ever Known could be found in the back room of Glen Miller's Jazz Bar on Sorrowful Street. Likewise, there were few people who could not stream off Limaal Mandella's lists of conquests, Belladonna being a city where lists ascribe greatness. There is not a single great Belladonian who has not several great lists behind him.

What then, were the names of those Limaal Mandella defeated to become champion? It is soon told.

Tony Julius, Oliphaunt Dow, Jimmy "Jewel" Petrolenko, "Aces" Quartuccio, Ahmed Sinai Ben Adam, "Sack" Johnson, Itamuro (Sammy) Yoshi, Louie Manzanera, Raphael Raphael, Jr., "Fingers" Lo, Noburo G. Washington, Henry Naminga, Bishop R. A. Wickramasinghe, Mr. C. Asiim, "Jaws" Jackson Jr., "Iceman" Larry Lemescue, Jesus Ben Sirach, Valentine Quee, Mr. Peter Melterjones, "Frenchy" Rey, Dharma Alimangansoreng, Nehemiah Chung (The Ripper), Mr. David Bowie, Mikal "Micky" Manzanera (no relation), Saloman Salrissian, Vladimir "The Impaler" Dracul, Mr. Norman Mailer, Mr. Halran Elissian, Mercedes Brown, "Red" Futuba, Judge, (Judge Dread) Simonsenn, "Prof" Chaz Xavier, Black John Delorean, Hugh O'Hare, Mr. Peter Melterjones (again).

In victory Limaal Mandella was a modest man. He scorned the expensive affectations of his opponents; the mink-lined cue cases, the diamond-filled teeth, the mother-of-pearl inlaid cues, the shop-built bodyguards, the solid gold flechette pistols: all the trivia of losers. Of the fortune he amassed, sixteen percent went to his manager, Glen Miller, who launched his own "American Patrol" label for new underground bands and built a studio for them to record in, he kept enough to hold body and soul together and gave the rest anonymously to charities for the relief of retired prostitutes, hot stew for Belladonna's 175,000 registered mendicants, and the rehabilitation for alcohol, narcotic, and pornography addicts.

However modest, even charitable, his personal lifestyle, Limaal Mandella could not be said to possess a surfeit of self-effacement. He believed he was the best with a conviction unshakable as heaven. He grew zealous, he grew thin, he grew a beard which only highlighted the steely tint in his eyes. Concerned at his protégé's fanaticism, Glen Miller watched him one morning after the band had packed up and gone home, potting ball after ball after ball, practicing practicing practicing, perfecting, honing, never satisfied.

"You drive yourself too hard, Limaal," said Glen Miller, resting his trombone on the table. Balls clunked into pockets, impelled by relentless mathematics of cue. "No one could do more than you. Look, you've been here, a year, yes? Just over twenty-six months, to be precise; you're not long turned eleven, you've beaten men years more experienced than you; you're the champion, the toast of Belladonna, isn't that enough? What more can you want?"

Limaal Mandella waited to clear the table before answering.

"Everything. It all." The white rolled to rest in the center of the table. "Best in Belladonna's not enough while there's someone out there who might be better than me. Until I know that there either is or isn't, I can't rest." He picked the balls out of the pockets and squared them up for another match against himself.

The challenge was born. To the man who could defeat him Limaal Mandella would give his crown, half his personal riches, and his word that he would never touch a cue again. Of the man he defeated he asked only that he bow and acknowledge the victor. The challenge went out on the airwaves of Glen Miller's Sunday evening *Big Band Hour* and the nine continents rose to meet it.

And the challengers, they are another list.

There were young men, old men, middle-aged men, tall men, short men, fat men, thin men, sick men, healthy men, bald men, hairy men, clean-shaven men, bearded men, men with moustaches, men without hats, black men, red men, brown men, yellow men, off-white men, happy men, sad men, clever men, simple men, nervous men, confident men, humble men, arrogant men, serious men, laughing men, silent men, men who liked to talk, straight men, gay men, men who were both, men who were neither, blue-eyed men, brown-eyed men, green-eyed men, radar-eyed men, bad men, good men, men from O and Meridian and Wisdom, men from Xanthe and Chryse and the Great Oxus, men from Grand Valley and Great Desert and the Archipelago, Transpolaran men and men from Borealis, the men of Solstice Landing, men from Llangonnedd and Lyx, from Kershaw and Iron Mountain, men from Bleriot and Touchdown, men from great cities and tiny hamlets, men from the mountains and men from the valleys, men from the forests and men from the plains, men from the deserts and men from the seas; they came and they came and they came until the towns were emptied and the machines stood idle in the factories and the crops filled and ripened in the fields under the summer sun.

The old men came, the old ones with death in their eyes who reminded Limaal of his Grandfather Haran, and the women, the wives and lovers and strong ones who bore the weight of the world on their backs, the great, strong women of the nine continents and the children came, out of the schools and nurseries and play groups, with cut-down cues and beer boxes to stand upon as they took their shots.

Limaal Mandella beat them all.

There was not a man, woman, child on the planet who could beat Limaal Mandella. He was the Greatest the Universe Had Ever Known. And when the last challenger had fallen, he stood up on the table, held his cue above his head in his two hands, and proclaimed, "I am Limaal Mandella, the Greatest Snooker Player the Universe Has Ever Known: who is there, man or god, who will challenge me, who is there mortal or immortal, sinner or saint, that I cannot defeat?"

In the darkest corner of the room, by the gentlemen's toilet, a voice spoke in syllables clear as desert raindrops.

"I am the one, I am he. Play me, Limaal Mandella, and learn some humility, little crowing cockerel."

The speaker stood up so that Limaal Mandella might see

his challenger. He was an elegant olive-skinned gentlemen, dressed in red satin and leaning on a cane as if a trifle lame.

"Who are you who would challenge me?" boasted Limaal Mandella.

"I am not required to give my name, only to challenge you," said the elegant man; indeed, he did not need to give his name, for a momentary flicker of hellfire in his black satin eyes identified him to all: Appolyon, Put Satanachia, Ahriman, the Goat of Mendes, Mephisto(pheles), Archfiend, Antichrist, Hermes Trismegetus, Old Clootie, the Adversary, Lucifer, Father of Lies, Satan Mekratrig, Diabolus, the Tempter, Old Nick, the Serpent, Lord of the Flies, the Old Gentleman, Satan, the Enemy, the Devil, the evil which needs no name to cover it.

Perhaps Limaal Mandella was too drunk on victory to recognize his enemy, perhaps his rationalism forbade him to permit the gentleman's infernal incarnation, perhaps he could just not resist any challenge, for he cried, "How many frames? By how much do you wish to be humiliated?"

"The best of seventy-seven?" suggested the Enemy.

"Done. Toss for break."

"One moment. The stakes."

"Same as for any other challenger."

"Not quite enough, if you'll pardon me. If you win, Satan Mekratrig will bow the knee to you, Limaal Mandella, but if you lose, he will take your crown, your riches, and your soul."

"All right, all right. Enough theatrics. Heads or tails?"

"Tails," said the Enemy, smiling to his Infernal self. Limaal Mandella won the toss and broke off.

Very soon Limaal Mandella found himself pitted against an opponent the like of whom he had never met before. For by his once-divine nature, all human wit and science were the Enemy's to use and abuse, though for reasons of demonic honor inexplicable to humans but binding upon devils and Panarchs, he could not use these supernatural wisdoms to improperly influence the game. His natural powers were still sufficient to battle Limaal Mandella to a standstill. The tide of combat surged back and forth across the green baize; here the Enemy led by two frames, there Limaal Mandella pulled back the deficit and went one ahead. There were never more than a handful of frames separating the combatants.

Every four hours they would take a sixty-minute break. Limaal Mandella would eat or bathe or drink some beer or catch a few winks of sleep. The Enemy would sit alone in his chair and sip from a glass of absinthe topped up by a nervous bartender. As word passed around the corridors and alleyways that Limaal Mandella was playing the devil for his very soul, crowds of the curious pressed into Glen Miller's Jazz Bar, concentrated and compressed almost to the point of suffocation and implosion, mounted policemen rode back and forth along the boulevard outside, keeping the crowd away from the doors. Teenage runners hotfooted it to the press agencies with the latest frame scores and excited Belladonians watched posters go up reading "Mandella leads by one frame" or sat in bars and cafés listening to Maelstrom Morgan's radio commentary on the epic contest. In barber shops, sushi bars, bath houses, and rikshas the city of Belladonna cheered on the Greatest Snooker Player the Universe Had Ever Known.

But the Greatest Snooker Player the Universe Had Ever Known knew that he was losing. The quality of his play strained the credible, but he knew he was losing. There was a dreadful precision to the Enemy's shots, a foresightedness to his play that echoed the omniscient, and Limaal Mandella knew that play as he might, his human talent could never match the demonic perfection of Satan. He lost the initiative, slipped behind, and began to trail the Devil, always making up the frame's deficit to stay in touch with the match but never forging ahead to take control of the table. The cries and shouts of the well-wishers now held a note of desperation.

After thirty-two hours at the table Limaal Mandella was a man destroyed. Haggard, unshaven, fatigue oozed from every pore as he bent to the table again. Only his rationalism, his unshakable faith that skill must triumph over dark sorcery in the end, kept his cue arm moving.

The final frame ground into play. The third change of referees announced the frame score: Limaal Mandella 38 frames, the Challenger 38 frames. The game was down to the colors. Limaal needed blue, pink, and black to win. The Enemy needed black and pink. Sipping his absinthe, he was as fresh and bright as a dandelion in a summer hedge. The green baize universe with its tiny colored solar systems swirled before Limaal Mandella's eyes, and suddenly it was a black ball game.

Limaal took a deep breath and let the dregs of his rationalism flow through him. The black ball glided along the table, wriggled in the jaws, wriggled free.

The audience moaned.

The devil sighted down his cue. And then Limaal Mandella had it. He stood on his side table, pointed his cue at the Enemy, and shouted, "You can't win! You can't win, you're not real! There is no devil, there is no St. Catherine, there is only us, we ourselves. Man is his own god, man is his own devil, and if I am being defeated by the devil, it is by the devil within me. You are an impostor, an old man who dresses up and says 'I am the Devil' and you all believe him! We believe him! I believe him! But I don't now, I don't believe in you! There's no room for a devil in the rational world!"

The referee tried to restore the contemplative calm of the snooker hall. Glen Miller's Jazz Bar settled after the untoward outburst. The Goat of Mendes sighted down his cue once more and struck. Cue ball struck black ball, black ball ran toward the pocket. As the balls ran down the table, the hellfire flickered in the gentleman's eyes and snuffed out. The infernal power, the unworldly perfection, had gone out of him, wiped away by Limaal Mandella's act of unbelief. The city of Belladonna held its breath. The black ball was losing momentum, losing impetus. A breath short of the pocket the black ball came to rest. There was utter silence. Even gabbling garrulous Maelstrom Morgan fell silent, words frozen in his microphone. Ten kilometers tall, Limaal Mandella stepped to the table. The city of Belladonna let out a shriek of anticipation.

Suddenly the Devil was just a tired, scared old gentleman.

Limaal Mandella swept his cue down into the striking position, oblivious of the fatigue tearing at every muscle. The room fell quiet again, as if his gesture had stopped time. His arm pistoned back, the same precise machine motion that he had performed ten thousand identical times in the past day and a half. He smiled just for himself and let the cue barely touch the ball. The white wall rolled down the table and stroked the black ball soft as a lover's caress. The black shivered and tumbled into the pocket, like the plummeting porcelain planetoids of his nightmares.

31

After she walked away from Mikal Margolis at a soba bar in Ishiwara Junction, Marya Quinsana pointed her heart in the general direction of Wisdom and let her freedom waft her away.

Freedom. She had been so long the prisoner of other people's needs that she had forgotten the flavor of freedom. But freedom had a taste. It tasted like a centimeter of Belladonna brandy in the bottom of a glass when you think the glass is empty. It tasted like hot soba noodles with gravy on a cold morning after a colder night. It tasted so good that she got up from her breakfast and walked away from Mikal Margolis, away from the soba bar, across the street where the old men aimed jets of brown hemp juice at a battered brass spitoon to the freight train slumbering in the siding. She felt Mikal Margolis's eyes on her every step as she went up to the cab where two engineers, neither more than ten years old, loafed, waiting for the signal.

"Any chance of a ride?" she asked. As the two paan-chewing youths looked her up and down, she shot a glance across the street to MacMurdo's soba bar and was rewarded by Mikal Margolis's betrayed eyes behind the glass window.

"Might say the same to you," said the dark brown engineer-boy whose cap bore then name Aron.

"Sure. Why not? Marya Quinsana rolled the flavor of freedom around her mouth like rolled up paan leaves. Whoring was small change in the currency of ambition.

"In that case, sure, why not?" Engineer Aron opened the cab door. Marya Quinsana climbed up and sat between the suddenly tense boy engineers. The signal changed, the tokamaks roared, and the train pulled away from Ishiwara Junction.

Changing trains in the dawn hours, waiting for half days on end at the side of Grand Trunk Roads holding aloft the totem of the windswept thumb, hitching rides on overnight transport dirigibles, Marya Quinsana pursued the ghost of freedom across half the world until she caught up with it in a freight siding behind l'Esperado Main Station.

The train was shabby, paint-peeled, and dowdy, eroded by years of exposure to the marvelous and wonderful, but Marya Quinsana could make out the legend by the yellow sodium glow: Adam Black's Traveling Chautauqua and Educational 'Stravaganza. A small crowd of station bums stood idly around at the foot of the steps, lacking even the small change to share in the wonders of Adam Black's show. Marya Quinsana could not have said what it was that made her go there that night; perhaps mellow nostalgia, perhaps some atavistic urge, perhaps the desire to pick at scabs. She pushed the bums aside and entered. Adam Black was a little grayer and a little sadder but otherwise unchanged. It pleased Marya Quinsana that she should know him and that he should not know her.

"How much is it?"

"Fifty centavos."

"In cash or kind. As ever."

Adam Black regarded her with the expression of one trying to place a memory. "If you will come with me, I will show you the wonders of my Hall of Mirrors." He took Marya Quinsana by the hand and led her into a darkened carriage. "The mirrors of Adam Black's Hall of Mirrors are no ordinary mirrors, they have been cast by the Master Mirror Moulders of Merionedd, who have refined their art to such a pinnacle of perfection that their mirrors reflect not the physical image, but the temporal one. They reflect chronons, not photons, time images of the myriad possible futures that may befall you, which diverge through time when the searcher gazes upon them. To you they will display the futures possible for you at life's diverse junctures, and the wise man will mark, meditate, and amend his life accordingly." As he delivered his stale spiel, Adam Black had guided Marya Quinsana through a pitch-dark maze of claustrophobic twistings and turnings. With the conclusion of his speech he stopped.

Marya Quinsana heard him draw breath and then he declared, "Let light fall upon the future!"

The chamber was filled with gritty purple light cast from a peculiarly shaped lantern above their heads. By this strange lanternlight Marya Quinsana saw herself reflected a thousand thousand thousand times in an endless mirror-maze. The images were fleeting, fleeting, twisted away the instant the eye comprehended them by the complex mechanisms that kept the mirrors turning. Marya Quinsana learned that there was a trick of holding the images in her peripheral vision and by this visual deception she beheld numinous glimpses of her future selves: the woman in combat duns with the MRCW slung across her shoulder, the woman with the five children under her skirts and her belly swollen with the sixth, the woman noble and powerful in judge's gowns, the woman naked upon the glycerine-filled bed, the woman weary, the woman joyful, the woman tearful, the woman dead . . . no sooner seen than turned away like strangers. on a train, into their own futures. There were the faces of frustrated ambition, the faces of despair, the faces of hope, and the faces that have put away all hope because they know their present lot is the most they can ever possess: there were the faces of death, a thousand faces bloody or ashen pale, seared black like coals or burst into festering boils by disease, sunken by age and wasting or calm with the false tranquility death grants those who fight it most.

"Death is every man's future," said Marya Quinsana. "Show me the future of the living."

"Look here then," said Adam Black. Marya Quinsana looked where he pointed and saw a laughing sardonic figure glance over her shoulder at her and walk away into the maze, stepping from mirror to mirror with the easy gait of the jaguar, power slung low in her belly. She walked with the steps of the powerful; the makers and molders of worlds walked like that. It was the image of how she had always imagined herself.

"That's the one I want."

"Then walk forward and take it."

Marya Quinsana stepped forward in pursuit of the future self and with every step she took, confidence swelled up in her like a bud. She broke into a run, the run of the huntress, and as the mirrors swung out of her way to show only empty reflections of each other, she saw her prey was slowing. The power and authority were ebbing out of the image's steps into her own. Marya Quinsana drew to within an arm's reach of the fleeing image.

"Got you!" she declared, and seized the image's shoulder in an arresting grip. With a gasp of terror the image wheeled and she saw herself as she had been, certain yet uncertain, knowledgeable but ignorant, a slave to freedom, and she knew that at some time in the pursuit she had become the image and the image her. The image collapsed with a pop of inrushing air into glittering dust and Marya Quinsana found herself by the entrance to the Hall of Mirrors once more.

"I trust you found the experience rewarding," said Adam Black politely.

"I think so. Here, I forgot, fifty centavos."

"For you, madam, there is no charge. For a satisfied customer, there is never a charge. Only the dissatisfied pay. But then, they always pay, don't you think? But now I think I remember you, madam, your face seemed familiar to me; have you any connection with a place called Desolation Road?"

"Long ago and far away, I fear, and I am not the woman now I was then."

"Such can be said of us all, madam. Well, a good evening to you, thank you for your patronage, and if I might ask one favor, it would be for you to pass on to your friends and relatives the fascinations of Adam Black's Traveling Chautauqua and Educational 'Stravaganza."

Marya Quinsana crossed the tracks toward a sodium-lit siding where a chemical train with "Wisdom" on its tanker-boards was powering up its fusion engine. It began to rain, a thin, cold, needling rain. Marya Quinsana tumbled the images of what she had seen over in her head. She knew what she was now. She had a purpose. Freedom was still hers, but it was a purposeful freedom. She would seek responsibility, for freedom without responsibility was worthless, and to that duality she would add power, for responsibility without power was impotence. She would go to Wisdom and enthrone the trinity of liberties within herself.

Close to the chemical train now she could see the engineer waving at her. She smiled and waved back.

Two peculiarities of the evening could not be fitted into her scheme. The first was that Adam Black's reflection had not shown in any of the time mirrors. The second was that the image she had embraced had been walking in the general direction of Desolation Road.

3 2

Ever since her father's ghost had told her she was a changeling, Arnie Tenebrae had refused to live under the same roof as either of her parents, living or dead. If she was a Mandella, she would live a Mandella in the Mandella household. She found Grandfather Haran asleep on his porch among his seedlings (for of late he had developed a passion for gardening, born in part out of his frustrated fatherhood). His mouth was wide and snoring. Arnie Tenebrae popped a hot chili pepper in the open mouth, and when the fire and fury had been extinguished, curtsied and said, "Mr. Mandella, I am your daughter, Arnie."

So she left the Tenebrae household and entered under the roof of the Mandella family and called herself by a new name, though everyone else called her little Arnie Tenebrae, as they always had. She hated them calling her little Arnie Tenebrae. She was nine years old and mistress of her own destiny, as her adoption of families had proven, and as such she was to be taken seriously. Had she not provoked the greatest scandal to break in Desolation Road since her father's murder, with the result that her own mother now lived a virtual outcast with only the Stalins talking to her, and those few words only to taunt and blame? She was a person of some significance and she hated people who laughed at her vanities.

"I will show them," she told her mirror. "Mandella or Tenebrae, I will make the heavens ring with my name. I am a person of consequence, I am."

Desolation Road was a town without consequence or heaven-ringing names. It was, simply was, and its contentment to merely be infuriated Arnie Tenebrae, who could not be without becoming. Desolation Road bored her. Her adoptive parents bored her. She hated their little lovingnesses; their multitudinous kindnesses made her cringe.

"I will break free," she confided to her image. "Like Limaal, making a great name for himself in Belladonna, or even Taasmin; she was strong enough to break away from the mold of society and live among the rocks like a hyrax, why can't I?"

She shunned the presence of people, even her doting father and mother, for she knew that people thought she was a little gold-digger playing on the fond fancies of an old man and woman. She found a way into Dr. Alimantando's house and spent long hours of blissful solitude reading his volumes of speculations on time and temporality in the privacy of the abandoned weather-room. Gone, gone gone gone, everyone was going in Desolation Road, everyone who was interesting and adventurous: what of Arnie Tenebrae?

One day she spied rollers of dust advancing across the desert plains and knew, even before they transformed into a dozen MRCW-armed men and women in combat duns mounted on all-terrain motor trikes, that this was salvation riding across the desert for her.

At first she was wary of scaring that salvation away like a little nervous bird, so she kept to the back of the crowd when the armed soldiers read the proclamation that they were the North West Quartersphere Truth Corps of the Whole Earth Army and that this town was under temporary occupation by the same. She held her silence as the soldiers explained the declared aims of the Whole Earth Army: the closure of the world to further immigration, the passing of control of the environmental maintenance equipment from ROTECH to the planetary authorities, the delegation to each continent of a regional autonomous parliament, the promotion of a truly indigenous planetary culture untainted by the dross and degeneracy of the Motherworld, and the smashing of the transplanetary corporations whose grasping corruption was draining the earth white. She did not join the protestors when Dominic Frontera and three employees of Bethlehem Ares Railroads were taken and placed under house arrest for the duration of the occupation, neither was she present when Ruthie Frontera, distraught and smeared with tears, rolled around on the earth in front of the house where the prisoners were guarded.

Rather, she hid under the shade of an umbrella tree and watched the guerrillas swarm over Dr. Alimantando's house doing things to the microwave tower. She saw the logo on the crates of radio equipment and suddenly the occupation was clear.

"All Swing Radio," she murmured to herself, tracing the words on the crates with her fingertips. "All Swing Radio."

All Swing Radio was vampire music. In some towns to be caught listening to All Swing Radio would earn you a fine, fifty days community service, confiscation of the radio, or even a public flogging. It was the music of subversives, terrorists, anarchists who roamed the empty places of the world on their terrain trikes looking for microwave towers into which they could plug their illegal transmitters and broadcast their subversive, terrible, anarchic music to the kids in the dead-end alleys, the empty gym-halls, the backseats of rikshas, closed-down bars, shut-up co-ops, and little Arnie Tenebrae/Mandella listening to the Big Big Sound of the New Music under the quilts at two minutes of two in the morning. It was the best music in the world, it set your feet on fire, friend, it made you want to dance, friend, it made the girls hitch up their skirts or roll up their overalls and dance and the boys somersault and back-flip and spin around the floor, or the concrete, or the packed brown earth: the bold, bad basement music of Dharamjit Singh and Hamilton Bohannon, Buddy Mercx and the King of Swing himself, the Man Who Fell Through the Time Warp: Glen Miller, and his Orchestra. It was basement music from smoky cellars deep under Bella-donna and hole-in-the-wall recording studios with names like American Patrol and Yellow Dog and Zoot Money: it was music that shocked your mother, it was All Swing Radio, and it was illegal.

It was illegal because it was propaganda though it carried

no political message. It was subversion through joy. It was the best PR job in the history of the profession, and its success could be measured by the fact that half a million kids a day whistled its famous call sign, and as many parents found the tune on their lips without ever knowing what it was. From the rice paddies of the Great Oxus to the towers of Wisdom, from the favelas of Rejoice to the cattle stations of Woolamagong, as the hour of twenty o'clock approached, the kids would tune their dials to the Fun 881, and tonight that famous call sign would thunder across the globe from Desolation Road.

"Fun 881," said Arnie Tenebrae. "Here, in Desolation Road." It was as if God had sent down his holy angels to sing and dance just for her.

"Hey!" A burly young woman was waving a Multi-Role Combat Weapon at her. "Don't poke around with the gear, kid." Arnie Tenebrae fled back to her hiding place beneath the umbrella tree and watched the soldiers at work until dinner time. That night she listened to *All Swing Radio* at two minutes of two under the quilts so that her adoptive parents would not hear. Tears of frustration ran down her cheeks as the mad, bad music played and played and played.

There was a certain Engineer Chandrasekahr, a farm boy not much older than herself from Great Oxus who smiled at her next morning as she pulled carrots from the garden. Arnie Tenebrae smiled back and bent lower so he could see all the way down the front of her overalls. That afternoon Engineer Chandrasekahr came over to engage her in conversation and tried to touch her, but Arnie Tenebrae was a little frightened by the forces she had released in the boy soldier and rebuffed his puppylike approaches. But that evening she went to the wooden hut the Truth Corps used as a broadcasting studio and asked for Sublieutenant Chandrasekahr. When he came to the door, Arnie Tenebrae flashed her shining white teeth at him and opened her blouse to display her proud nine-year-old breasts gleaming like temple domes in the light of the morning.

Afterward they lay in slots of skylight beaming through the shutters. Arnie Tenebrae turned on the radio and said, "Take me with you."

Engineer Chandrasekahr's foot tapped unconsciously in time with the Big Swing Beat.

"That is not so easy."

"It is too. You have to move to a new relay in a couple of days. Just take me with you."

"We are a secret, high-mobility unit, we cannot take just anyone who wants to come along. You are asking for much trust."

"I've just given you the most trust any woman can give. Can't you give me some in return?"

"What about your ideological commitment?"

"You mean all that 'close the sky' stuff? Sure, I know the facts. Listen to this." Arnie Tenebrae sat up and dominated Engineer Chandrasekahr with her light-slatted body as she counted off ideologies on her sticky fingers. "It's like this, isn't it? One Praesidium SailShip can hold a million and a half colonists, and when they come to our earth there has to be houses and farms and food and water and jobs for them. And if ten of these vehicles arrive every year, that's fifteen million people, which is five cities the size of Meridian, every year. And if this goes on for a hundred years, that's three hundred cities, a thousand SailShips, a billion and a half people, and where is the food, the water, the jobs, the houses, the factories, the farms going to come from for all these people? And that is what the Whole Earth Army is about, keeping the earth for its own people, keeping away all the greedy people who would take our beautiful world away from us and fill it up with their horrid bodies. Isn't that right?"

"That's putting it simply."

"So, I know the principles. Am I in, then?"

"No . . ."

Arnie Tenebrae shrieked her frustration and bit Engineer Chandrasekahr's chest. Grandfather Haran banged on the wall and shouted for her to keep the radio down a bit.

"I want in!"

"It's not up to me."

"Look, I can do things for you you wouldn't believe."

"You already have, my little cherry-pip."

"I don't mean that way. I mean like weapons, like things that would make you unbeatable. Listen, there was an old man used to live here years ago. He invented this place and the story goes that he met a green man and went off to travel through time with him, though I don't know about that bit. But his house is right over there where you've got the transmitters and it's full of ideas for things like you wouldn't believe."

"Like what wouldn't I believe?"

"Like sonic blasters, like electromagnetogravitic field inducers you can use either offensively or defensively, you can even use them to shut down gravity over short ranges; like light-scatter fields that make you the next best thing to invisible. . . ."

"Good God."

"I know it's there, I've seen it. Now, this is the deal. If you want it, you've got to take me with it. So, am I in or am I out?"

"We leave tomorrow at dawn. If you want to come, be there."

"Bet your ass I do. Now, get your clothes on and tell your chief Arnie Mandella's coming."

Arnie Tenebrae believed in paying only as much as a thing was worth to her. That was why she found the unfamiliar discomfort between her thighs good value received for being able to sit behind Engineer Chandrasekahr on his terrain trike as the Truth Corps revved and roared into the pre-dawn glow. She clung close to Engineer Chandrasekahr and felt the desert wind burn her cheeks and try to tug the tube of rolled documents from her shoulder.

—No, no, she told the wind, that is mine, with these papers I can make the heavens ring with my name. She looked down at the Whole Earth Army badge pinned to her khaki overalls and felt a glow of excitement swell up inside her.

The horizon dipped beneath the sun and the world was flooded with shape and light. Arnie Tenebrae turned to look back on Desolation Road, a jumble of amber, red, and shining silver. Nothing could have looked more like an insignificant, stultifying little hole and as she realized she was leaving it behind, Arnie Tenebrae knew a savage and keening joy. She had trapped the bird of salvation, sung to it, tamed it, and wrung its neck. This was her consummation, bouncing along on the back of a rebel terrain trike into exile with the romantic revolutionaries. This was the pinnacle of Arnie Tenebrae's insignificant, stultified little life.

33

Despite the halo around her left wrist and all things mechanical hers to command, Taasmin Mandella was finding sainthood rather boring. She resented spending hour after hour in the little shrine her father had added onto his already haphazard domicile: outside, the sun was shining and the green things were growing and here she was in her small dark room taking lists of supplications from old women with dead husbands (properly dead husbands; from time to time she wondered where her erstwhile aunt had gone on the morning she vanished from Desolation Road with the ragtag rebels) or placing her healing left hand upon broken radios, autoplanters, riksha engines, and water pumps to make them whole again.

As one devout old woman left and another entered, a shaft of yellow sunlight would beam through the door and Taasmin Mandella wished she could return to her lizard days, basking naked and spiritual on the hot red rocks; free of any responsibility save to God the Panarchic. But the Blessed Lady had laid a holy onus upon her.

"My world is changing," the little crop-haired urchin of a woman dressed in picture-cloth had said. "For seven hundred years I was a saint of machines and machines only, for machines were all there were, and through them I shaped this world and made it a good and pleasant place for man. And now that man has come, my relationships must be redefined. They have made me their god: I did not ask them to make me their god, much less desire to be that god, but it is what I am and I must bear the responsibility. Thus I have chosen selected mortals; if you'll forgive the expression, but it comes rather readily to me, to be my agents upon the earth. You see, I have no voice with which to speak to humans but human voices. Therefore to you I am freely giving my prophetic voice and my power over machinery: this halo"—and it had sprung into luminescence around her left wrist—"is the sign of your prophethood. It is a pseudo-organic informational resonance field, by its power all machinery is yours to command. Use it wisely and well, for you will be called to account for your stewardship of it someday."

It seemed like a dream now. But for that same halo around her left wrist none of it might ever have happened. Small-town girls do not meet saints. Small-town girls who wander crazy and soul-driven into the Great Desert are not transported home in a beam of light from a flying Blue Plymouth. They die in the desert and are turned to bone and leather. Small-town girls do not possess the power to control all machines through halos around their left wrists. Small-town girls are not prophets.

That much was true. The Blessed Catherine ("call me Cathy, for God's sake: never, ever let anyone give you a title you haven't chosen yourself") had demanded no especial virtue of her, merely to be wise and true. But there had to be more to Taasmin Mandella's prophetic mission than sitting in an incense-smoky room performing one-a-minute miracles for superstitious grandmothers from up and down the line.

The magazine reporters had not helped either. She hadn't seen the magazine yet, for some reason her parents had hidden the advance copies from her, but she was sure that when it went onto the world's newsstands the pilgrims would be lined up all the way to Meridian. She would never see daylight at all.

So she rebelled.

"If they want me, they can come and find me."

"But Taasmin darling, you have responsibilities," cooed her mother.

"Use it wisely and well, for someday you will be called to account for your stewardship of it; that was all she said. Nothing about responsibility."

"She? Is that what you call Our Lady of Tharsis?"

"That, and Cathy."

The Prophetess Taasmin began lunching in the Bethlehem

Ares Railroad/Hotel, snoozing with the radio on at siesta time, planting rows of beans in her father's garden, and painting the white walls even whiter. If a miracle was needed, or a healing, or a prayer, she would perform it there and then, in the hotel, on the veranda, in the field, by the wall. When the demands of the faithful grew too much, she would take herself off to a quiet corner of Grandfather Haran's garden and, finding a quiet spot among the trees, slip out of her clothes into the simple pleasure of simply being.

One summer morning an old man appeared on the edge of town. He had a mechanical left arm, leg, and eye. He borrowed a spade from the Stalins, whose feud, in the absence of a worthy enemy, had internalized into mere husband/wife strife, and dug a large hole in the ground beside the railroad tracks. He walked round and round and round in this hole all day and all night, drawing much comment from the bemused citizens of Desolation Road, and all the next morning until Taasmin Mandella came to have a laugh at the curiosity. Seeing her, the old man stopped, looked long and hard at her, and asked, "Well, are you the one then?"

"Who wants to know?"

"Inspiration Cadillac, formerly Ewan P. Dumbleton of Hirondelle; Poor Child of the Immaculate Contraption."

Taasmin Mandella was unsure whether his final comment had been about himself or her.

"Are you serious?"

"Deadly serious. I have read about you in the magazines, young woman, and I must know, are you the one?"

"Well, I might be."

"Give me a hand up, will you?"

Taasmin stretched out her haloed left hand. It closed on Inspiration Cadillac's metal hand and blue fire crackled along his mechanical limbs and forked from his artificial eye.

"You are the one, no mistaking," he declared.

Two days later a train drew up in Desolation Road. It was like no train anyone had ever seen before. It was a clanking, rattling, hissing old contraption threatening to burst its boilers at every stroke of its laboring drive-shafts. It hauled five dilapidated carriages trailing a squadron of prayer kites and prayer blimps and was decked out in a junkpile of religious flags, banners, emblems, and holy paraphernalia of all types.

The carriages were jammed with passengers. They poured from the doors and windows as if under pressure, and at Inspiration Cadillac's command tore carriage and train apart and built from the fragments a hasty shantytown of tents, lean-tos, and favelas. In the midst of the furious activity none of the spectators failed to notice that all the workers possessed at least one mechanical part to their bodies.

An official delegation soon arrived headed by Dominic Frontera and his three newly appointed constables, whom he had requisitioned from Meridian in case the Whole Earth Army should attempt another coup.

"Just what the hell are you doing?"

"We have come to be servants of the prophet of the Blessed Lady," said Inspiration Cadillac, and on cue the cyborg shanty-builders genuflected.

"We are the Poor Children of the Immaculate Contraption," continued Inspiration Cadillac. "Formerly known as Dumbletonians, we believe in the emulation of St. Catherine's example of the moritification of the flesh by replacing our sinful fleshly parts with pure, spiritual mechanical ones. We believe in the spirituality of the mechanical, the total transubstantiation of flesh into metal, and equal rights for machines. Alas, our zeal for this last principle led to our expulsion from the Ecumenical Enclave of Christadelphia: the burning of the factories was quite unintentional, we were sadly misunderstood and much abused. However, we have learned through various channels, spiritual and secular, of a young woman blessed by the Lady to be a prophet and so we have come in response to an angelic vision to serve her and through her attain our perfect mortification." As Inspiration Cadillac concluded, Taasmin Mandella arrived, disturbed from her meditations by the growing din. As she beheld the shantytown and its ragged tenants, a cry went up from the Poor Children of the Immaculate Contraption.

"It is her! She! She's the one!" The entire mass of Dumbletonians fell to their knees in attitudes of adoration.

"Blessed Child," said Inspiration Cadillac, smiling a horrid smile, "behold your flock. How may we serve you?"

Taasmin Mandella looked at the metal limbs, the metal heads, the metal hearts, the empty steel mouths, the plastic eyes. They revolted her. She cried out. "No! I don't want your service! I don't want to be your prophetess, your mistress, I don't want you! Go back to wherever you came from, just leave me alone!" She ran away from the furious worshippers, out along the rim rocks to her old refuge.

"I don't want them, you hear?" she screamed at the walls of her cave. "I don't want their hideous metal bodies, they disgust me, I don't want them to serve me, worship me, have anything to do with me!" She threw her arms above her head and released all her holy power. The air glowed blue, the rock groaned and shuddered, and Taasmin Mandella screamed bolt after bolt of frustrated force into the roof. At length she was drained and as she sat in a knot on the stone floor she thought about power, freedom, and responsibility. She pictured the Poor Children of the Immaculate Contraption in her mind's eye. She saw their metal hands, metal legs, metal arms, metal shoulders, their steel eyes, their tin chins, their iron ears, their half-and-half faces peeping out of their ugly, cheap little hovels. She was moved to pity. They were pathetic. Poor weak fools, pathetic children. She would show them a better way. She would lead them to self-respect.

After four days of thoughts and resolutions in her cave Taasmin Mandella was hungry and returned to Desolation Road for a bowl of lamb chili in the B.A.R./Hotel. Her halo glowed so brightly, no one could look at it. She found her town aswarm with construction workers in hard yellow hats, driving big yellow earthmovers and big yellow diggers. Big yellow transport dirigibles were setting down twenty-ton loads of pre-stressed steel girders and big yellow trains were unloading pre-mixed concrete and building sand into small yellow dumpsters.

"What the hell is going on?" said Taasmin Mandella, unconsciously echoing the mayor's words of greeting. She found Inspiration Cadillac surveying the pouring of foundations. He was dressed in yellow coveralls and a yellow hard hat. He gave Taasmin a similar hat for her to wear.

"Do you like it?"

"Like what?"

"Faith City," said Inspiration Cadillac. "The spiritual hub of the world, place of pilgrimage and finding to all who seek."

"Come again?"

"Your basilica, Lady. Our gift to you: Faith City."

"I don't want a basilica, I don't want a Faith City, I don't want to be the hub of the spiritual world, the finding of all who seek."

A load of construction girders swung overhead beneath a descending transport 'lighter.

"Where is the money coming from for all this? Tell me that."

Inspiration Cadillac's eyes were on the work. By his expression Taasmin knew he was already viewing the completed basilica.

"Money? Ah, well. Why do you think it's called Faith City?"

34

The Greatest Snooker Player the Universe Had Ever Known and the King of Swing were walking down Belladonna's Tombolova Street one day, when the Greatest Snooker Player the Universe Had Ever Known stopped dead outside a little street shrine wedged between a male strip club and a tempura bar.

"Look," said the Greatest Snooker Player the Universe Had Ever Known. Before the nine-pointed starburst of St. Catherine a young woman was at prayer, her lips moving silently as she whispered the litany, her eyes catching the light from the candles as she turned her gaze toward heaven. The Greatest Snooker Player the Universe Had Ever Known and the King of Swing watched her finish her prayer, light an incense wand, and pin a prayer to the door lintel.

"I'm in love," said the Greatest Snooker Player the Universe Had Ever Known. "I must have her."

Her name was Santa Ekatrina Santesteban. She had soft olive skin and hair and eyes as dark as the secret place next to the heart. She lived with her mother, her father, her four sisters and three brothers, her cat, and her singing bird in an apartment above Chambalaya's Speciality Spice and Condiment Store on Depot Lane. Through years of living above Mr. Chambalaya, her skin had taken on the perfume of spices and incenses. "I'm half-curried," she used to joke. She liked to joke. She loved to laugh. She was eleven years old. Limaal Mandella loved her madly.

Drawn by the trail of cardamon, ginger, and coriander, he followed her down lanes and alleys to her home above Mr. Chambalaya's shop and there, before her father, her mother, her four sisters and three brothers, her cat, and her singing bird, fell into a humble bow and asked for her hand in marriage. Ten days later they were wed. Glen Miller was best man and bride and groom walked from the registry to the waiting riksha under a canopy of raised snooker cues. The Glen Miller orchestra followed the wedding procession on a special float as far as Bram Tchaikovsky Station and played a selection of their greatest hits as bride and groom boarded the train. Rice and lentils rained down on them and well-wishers taped paper prayers of good omen to the back of the riksha and the side of the train. Smiling and waving to the cheering crowds, Limaal Mandella squeezed his wife's hand and a vagrant thought struck him.

This was the only irrational thing he had ever done.

But the irrationality was gathering above him. It had been drawing close for many months; halted a little in its advance by his defeat of the devil, but again closing. In that moment between the male strip club and tempura bar it had struck and bound itself to him through Santa Ekatrina. . . . Happy with his wife, then his first son Rael, Jr., then his younger son, Kaan, he was blissfully blind to the fact that God was setting him up for the Big One.

Since his defeat of the Anti-God, Limaal Mandella had ruled the land of Snooker absolute and unchallenged. As no one could defeat him, no one would play him. His own excellence had effectively disqualified him from the game.

City and Provincial, even Continental and World Champion-
ships went on without him and champions were crowned
"Belladonna Masters, except for Limaal Mandella" or "Solstice Landing Professional Champion, apart from Limaal
Mandella."

Limaal Mandella did not really care. Absence from the
matchroom gave him time with his lovely wife and children.
Absence from the matchroom gave the irrationality time to
seep into him.

When the word of a challenger to Limaal Mandella's
supremacy passed along the snooker circuits of Belladonna,
everyone knew that the challenger must be someone, or
something, quite exceptional. Perhaps the Panarch Himself
was taking up cue in the hand that steered the galaxies to
humble the proud human. . . .

Nothing of the sort. The challenger was an insignificant
mousy little man who wore upside-down spectacles and
composed himself with the nervous air of an apprentice clerk
in a large corporation. And that would have been the long and
short of him but for the significant fact that he had cut his wife
into teeny tiny pieces and ground them into hamburger and
that as punishment he was now nothing more than the fleshy
vehicle for the projected personality of the ROTECH computer Anagnosta Gabriel. He was a psychonambulist, an
obiman, a creature of childhood ghost stories.

"How many?" asked Limaal Mandella in the back room of
Glen Miller's Jazz Bar, for he was a player whose skill was
firmly attached to his sense of place.

"Thirty-seven frames," said Casper Milquetoast, the obiman. Side bets were not discussed. They were not important.
The stake was the title of the Greatest Snooker Player the
Universe Had Ever Known. Limaal Mandella won the toss
and broke off to begin the first of the thirty-seven frames. As he
had so correctly surmised years before when Trick-Shot
O'Rourke had shown him the destiny he had refused to accept,
snooker was the supreme game of rationalism. But the
Anagnosta Gabriel was rationalism incarnate. To its superconducting soul the balls on the table were no different from the
ballet of orbital technology ranging from grape-sized monitors
to habitats tens of kilometers across, all of which it routinely
choreographed. Behind Casper Milquetoast's every cue action

a tiny fragment of that computive power made precise calculations of spin, impulse, and momentum. "Luck" had no analog in the glossolalia of the Anagnostas. Always before, there had been the lucky fluke, the chance mistake by an opponent that put Limaal Mandella in a frame-winning position; the accumulated run of misfortune that demoralized the enemy into self-defeat, but computers do not demoralize and they do not make mistakes. Limaal Mandella had always maintained that skill would always defeat luck. Now he was being proved correct.

In the mid-session break (for even obimen must eat, drink, and urinate) Glen Miller drew Limaal Mandella aside and whispered to him, "You made some mistakes there. Bad luck."

Limaal Mandella flew into a temper and pushed his sweating face close to the jazz musician.

"Don't say that, never say that, never let me hear that again. You make your own luck, you understand? Luck is skill." He released the shaken bandleader, ashamed and frightened at how high the tide of irrationality had risen around him. Limaal Mandella never lost his temper, he told himself. That was what the legends said. Limaal Mandella hid his soul. But his outburst had shamed and demoralized him and when play resumed the Anagnosta Gabriel capitalized on his every mistake. He was outrationalized. As he sat in his chair automatically wiping his cue while Casper Milquetoast's computer-guided hands built break after break, he learned how it felt to play himself. It felt like a great boulder rolling up and crushing him. That was how he had made others feel: crucified on their own self-hate. He hated the self-hatred he had summoned up on the countless opponents he had defeated. It was a dreadful, grinding, gnawing thing which ate the soul away. Limaal Mandella learned remorse in his quiet corner, and the self-hatred ate away at his power.

His hands were numb and stupid, his eyes dry as two desert stones; he could not hit the balls. "Limaal Mandella is losing, Limaal Mandella is losing:" the word spiraled out from Glen Miller's Jazz Bar through the streets and alleys of Belladonna and behind it came a silence so profound that the click and the clack of the balls carried through the ventilators into every part of the city.

The computer ground him fine as sand. There was no pity,

no quarter. Play would continue until victory was assured. Limaal Mandella lost frame after frame. He began to concede frames which with determination he might have won.

"What's wrong, man?" asked Glen Miller, not understanding his protégé's agony. Limaal Mandella returned in silence to the table. He was being destroyed before the spectators' gaze. He could not bear to look up and see Santa Ekatrina watching. Even his enemies ached for him.

Then it was over. The last ball was down. ROTECH Anagnosta Gabriel operating through the synapses of the condemned murderer was the Greatest Snooker Player the Universe Had Ever Known. City and world hailed him. Limaal Mandella sat in his chair shot with his own gun. Santa Ekatrina knelt to take him in her arms. Limaal Mandella stared ahead of him, seeing nothing but the full tide of irrationality that had engulfed him.

"I'm going back," he said. "I can't stay here; not with the shame around me every minute of every day. Back. Home."

Five days later he snapped all his cues in half and burned them. On top of the fire he threw his contract with Glen Miller. Then he took his wife, his sons, his bags, his baggage, and as much money as he could bear the sight of and with that black money bought four tickets on the next train to Desolation Road.

At Bram Tchaikovsky Station porters scratched at his coattails. "Carry your bags, Mr. Mandella, sir, please, carry your bags? Sir, Mr. Mandella, carry your bags?" He loaded the luggage onto the train. As it passed out from under the immense mosaicked dome of Bram Tchaikovsky Station, goondahs, gutter boys, and urchins too poor for even a third class bench dropped from the signal gantries onto the roof. They leaned over and banged on the compartment windows, calling, "For the love of God, Mr. Mandella, let us in, kind sir, good sir, please let us in, Mr. Mandella, for the love of God, let us in!"

Limaal Mandella pulled the blinds, called the guard, and after the first stop at Cathedral Oaks there were no further disturbances.

35

The cylinder of rolled documents hung from Mikal Margolis's shoulder twenty-five centimeters above the track. Mikal Margolis hung from the underside of a Bethlehem Ares Railroads Mark 12 air-conditioned first class carriage. The Bethlehem Ares Railroads Mark 12 air-conditioned first class carriage hung from the underside of Nova Columbia and Nova Columbia hung from the backside of the world as it circled the sun at two million kilometers per hour, carrying Nova Columbia, railroad, carriage, Mikal Margolis, and document cylinder with it.

Ishiwara Junction was half a world away. His arms were tough now, they could carry him all the world's way around the sun hanging from the undersides of trains. He no longer felt the pain, of arms and Ishiwara Junction. He was beginning to suspect that he had a selective memory. Hanging beneath trains gave him much time for thought and self-examination. On the first such occasion after Ishiwara Junction he had devised the scheme that had drawn him down the shining rails across junctions, switchovers, points, ramps, and midnight marshaling yards toward the city of Kershaw. There was an irresistible attraction of dark for dark. The roll of papers across his shoulders would not permit him any other destiny.

He shifted to the least uncomfortable position and tried to picture the city of Kershaw. His imagination filled the great black cube with cavernous shopping malls where the exquisite artifacts of a thousand workshops commanded eye and purse; level upon level of recreation centers where every whim could be indulged from games of Go in secluded tea houses to concertos by the world's greatest Sinfonia to basements filled with glycerine and soft rubber. There would be museums and auditoria, Bohemian artists' quarters, a thousand restaurants representing the world's thousand gastronomies and covered parks so cleverly designed you could believe you were walking under open sky.

He could see the clanging foundries where the proud locomotives of the Bethlehem Ares Railroads Company were constructed, and the Central Depot from which they were dispatched all across the northern half of the world and the subterranean chemical plants that bubbled their effluent into the lake of Syss and the factory-farms where strains of artificial bacteria were skimmed from tanks of sewage to be processed into the thousand restaurants' thousand cuisines. He thought of the rainfall traps and the brilliantly economical systems of water reclamation and purification, he thought of the air shafts up which perpetual hurricanes spiraled, the dirty breath of two million Shareholders exhaled into the atmosphere. He imagined the outer skin penthouses of the managerial castes, their views of Syss and its grimy shore increasingly panoramic with altitude, and the apartments in the quiet family residential districts opening onto bright and breezy light-wells. He thought of the children, happy and well-scrubbed, in the Company schools learning the joyful lessons of industrial feudalism, which was not hard for them, he thought, for they were surrounded every second of every day by its pinnacle of achievement. Suspended beneath the first class section of the Nova Columbia Night Service, Mikal Margolis beheld the whole of the works of the Bethlehem Ares Corporation in his soul-eye 'and cried aloud, "Well, Kershaw, here I am!"

Then the first acid breaths of Syss caught at his throat and blinded his eyes with tears.

There is a level lower than the level of machine drudgery at which Johnny Stalin entered the capital of the Bethlehem Ares Corporation. It is the level reserved for those who ride into the Central Depot hanging from the bottom of the first class section of the Nova Columbia Night Service. It is the level of the unnumbered. It is the level of invisibility. Not the practiced invisibility that enabled Mikal Margolis to escape from the Central Depot undetected among the masses of Company Shareholders, but the invisibility of the individual before the body corporate.

Up a flight of marble steps, through brass doors ten times the height of a man, Mikal Margolis found himself in a cavernous hall of shining marble and polished hush. Before him was a very large and ugly statue of Wingèd Victory bearing the legend "Laborare est Orare." Several kilometers distant across the marble plains stood a marble desk above which hung a sign reading INTERVIEWS, APPOINTMENTS AND AUDIENCES ENQUIRIES. Mikal Margolis's train-scuffed shoes clattered vulgarly on the sacred marble. The fat man in the Company paper suit stared down at him from behind the marble rampart.

"Yes?"

"I'd like to make an appointment."

"Yes?"

"I'd like to see someone in industrial development."

"That would be the Regional Developments Offices."

"To do with steel."

"Regional developments offices, iron and steel division."

"In the Desolation Road area . . . the Great Desert, you know?"

"One moment." The fat receptionist tapped at his computer. "North West Quartersphere Projects and Developments Office, iron and steel division, regional developments offices, Room 156302, please join line A for your preliminary application for an appointment with the sub-sub-planning department undersecretary." He handed Mikal Margolis a slip of paper. "Your number: 33,256. Line A through those doors."

"But this is important!" Mikal Margolis waved the roll of documents under the receptionist's nose. "I can't wait for 33,255 other people to go ahead of me just for some . . . some application to see some undersecretary."

"Preliminary application for a preliminary application for an appointment with the sub-sub-planning department undersecretary. Well, if it's that urgent, sir, you should join line B, for an application for the Priority Clearance Program." He tore off a fresh numbered strip. "There. Number 2304. Door B please."

Mikal Margolis ripped both numbers into shreds and tossed them into the air.

"Get me an appointment, now, for tomorrow at the very latest."

"That is quite impossible. The earliest appointment is next Octenber, the fifteenth, to be precise, with the water and sewage treatment manager, at 13:30 hours. You can't throw the system about, sir, it's for the good of us all. Now, here is a new number. Give me yours so I know who wants an appointment, and go and join line B."

"Pardon?"

"Give me your number and go and join Line B."

"Number?"

"Shareholder's number. You have a shareholder's number?"

"No."

"Then you'll have a temporary visitor's visa. Could I have that, please?"

"I don't have a temporary . . ." The fat receptionist's outraged shriek turned heads all the way across the marble cathedral.

"No number! No visa! Holy Lady, you're one of those . . . one of those . . ." Bells began to ring. Black and gold Company policemen appeared from unnoticed doors and advanced. Mikal Margolis looked for a place to run.

"Arrest this, this gutter boy, this tramp, this freebooter, goondah, and bum!" screamed the receptionist. "Arrest this . . . Freelancer!" Thick foam sprayed from his mouth. The police drew short shock-staves and charged.

A sudden explosion of automatic fire threw everyone to the ground. The customary shrieker in such events shrieked. A figure in a gray paper suit stood by the door to line A, intimidating the lobby with a small black MRCW.

"Nobody move!" he shouted. Nobody moved. "Get over here!"

Mikal Margolis looked around for someone else the gunman could have meant. He pointed at himself, mouthing the word *me*?

"Yes, you! Get over here! Move!" One of the Company policemen must have reached for his communicator, for another burst of fire sent marble chips screaming and whining. Mikal Margolis stood up sheepishly. The gunman motioned for him to come around by the side, leaving clear his field of fire.

"What's happening?" asked Mikal Margolis.

"You're being rescued," said the gunman in the business suit. "Now, whatever happens, follow me and don't bother me with any questions." From an inside pocket he flipped a smoke grenade into the lobby. "Run."

Mikal Margolis did not know how far he ran, along how many marble, oak, or plastic corridors: he just ran, with the high-stepping gait of one expecting a bullet in the spine at any moment. When the sounds of search and pursuit were sufficiently remote, the rescuer stopped and opened a section of plastic wall paneling with a rather clever tool.

"In here."

"Here?"

The sounds of search and pursuit suddenly increased.

"In here." The two men dived into the wall cavity and sealed the wall behind them. The rescuer thumbed the laser setting on his MRCW to random emission and by its blue light led Mikal Margolis through a jungle of cables, ducts, pipes, and conduits.

"Mind that," he said as Mikal Margolis reached for a cable to steady himself after teetering at the lip of a two kilometer airshaft. "There's twenty thousand volts going through that." Mikal Margolis snatched back his hand as if from a snake, or a cable carrying twenty thousand volts.

"Just who are you?" he asked.

"Arpe Magnusson, Systems Service Engineer."

"With an MRCW?"

"Freelance," said the systems service engineer, as if that word explained everything. "See those glowing dust motes there, mind them. There's a communications laser in there. Take your head clean off, it would."

"Freelance?"

"An independent in the closed Company economy. Term of abuse. See, like you, I wanted to see someone in the Company, I had this great idea for revolutionizing the Kershaw air-conditioning system, but no one wanted to see me, not without a number or a visa. So I came here, behind the walls, because you don't need numbers back here, and joined the Freelancers. That was about four years back."

"There's more than one of you?"

"About two thousand. There's places in this cube don't appear on any Company schematics. Time to time, I do some independent work for the Shareholders; domestic stuff mainly, something breaks, things are always breaking, Company policy, built-in failure rate, and they're not keen on repairing things, better for the Company if you buy new, so they pass the word and I come and fix it. Also, I keep a look out at Enquiries there for potential Freelancers: every so often someone like you turns up and I get them away behind walls."

"With an MRCW?"

"First time I've ever had to use it. Bit slow getting to you, the computer almost missed tracking that call to the police. Watch the draft from that ventilator . . . it's not easy living here, but if you make it past the first twelve months, you're all right." Magnusson turned and extended a hand to Mikal Margolis. "Welcome to the Freelancers, friend."

Between pitfalls, acid, chemical waste, power blackouts, and electrocution, the months that followed were the happiest of Mikal Margolis's life. He was in constant danger, from both the perils between the walls and the sporadic raids of Company Kleenteems and had never felt more comfortable or relaxed. This was what he had dreamed of in his long sojourns on the desert rim. Life was brutish, dangerous, and wonderful. The Freelancers' computer, Jitney, which lived in their headquarters, a web of support cables stretched across Airshaft 19, provided him with the identity numbers of dead Shareholders and thus equipped, Mikal Margolis could eat with impunity in any Company refectory in the city, bathe in Company bath houses, dress in Company paper suits dispensed from street-corner slot machines, and even sleep in a Company bed until the Company withdrew the deceased's number from circulation. At such times he would return to the world of the crawlways and access shafts and doze in his hammock suspended over a kilometer-deep airwell, rocked with the breathings of a hundred thousand Shareholders.

When the alarm came he almost vaulted out of his hammock. But for his Freelancer-trained wits, he would have jumped straight down the airwell. He paused to gain composure. Composure was survival. Think before you act. Forethought, not spontaneity. He checked that the roll of documents was on his shoulder, then seized the swing rope and tarzaned to the lip of the shaft. Proximity alarms. Kleenteems. The backlog of complaints about vermin in the circuitry had built up until the Department of Water and Sewage Treatment was pressured into action. He felt for his gas mask. It was exactly where he had left it. He slipped it on and swung up into a major power conduit running parallel to the service duct. Thousands of amperes pulsed next to his cheek. He squinted through a chink in the cladding and watched the clouds of riot gas roll down the tunnel. Flashlight beams lanced through the clouds of toxic gas. The Kleenteem waded into view: two men and a woman, paper-suited executive types from the department of water and sewage treatment, fat balloon men in their transparent plastic isolation suits. From their backpacks they poured a fog of neurotoxic gas down the tunnel and warped the air with their wrist-mounted sonic disturbers. One of the Kleenteem picked up Mikal Margolis's alarm and showed it to the others. They nodded and their helmet beams bobbed and curtsied.

Arpe Magnusson's gasmasked head poked out of a hatchway, followed by an arm and a written note.

FOLLOW ME, AND WATCH CLOSELY.

The two men scurried through the labyrinth of access ways, gantries, and airshafts until they arrived at the junction with the level ten airduct which the Kleenteem had recently passed. Bodies of dead mice lay stiffening on the metal grills, proof of the efficacy of the Kleenteems' weaponry. Arpe Magnusson pointed to three snaking plastic hoses. Mikal Margolis nodded. He knew what they were, the Kleenteem's umbilicals. Arpe Magnusson traced the umbilicals back to the air outlet. Motioning for Mikal Margolis to watch carefully, he uncoupled the airhoses and connected them to the level ten sewage pipe. Brown filth poured down the hoses and raced into the gas-milky distance. At once the headlamp beams froze in position, then began to wave frantically to and fro. Finally they fell to the ground and remained motionless. A few seconds later the two men distinctly heard three soft, brown, wet explosions.

Mikal Margolis had been two years in the tunnels when the opportunity came. The computer reported a death in the North West Quartersphere Planning and Developments Department, iron and steel division. Some junior sub-sub-production assistant secretary had thrown himself into a geyser in Yellow Bay because of a bad decision over the Arcadia project. Even before he was fished part-cooked out of the geyser by the Chrysanthemum Brigade, employed specifically for such duties, Mikal Margolis had taken his number, his name, his job, his desk, his office, his apartment, his life, and his soul. The risk in approaching the North West Quartersphere Projects and Developments Manager/Director in such a direct fashion was great: the likelihood of recognition was nearly one hundred percent, but Mikal Margolis was not prepared to spend several years and a virtual economy of black money weaving his way up through personal assistants, junior-sub-managers, temporary liaison officers, production assistant managers, sector organizers, junior systems analysts, sales directors, financial directors (junior and senior), area directors, chief directors, project directors, sub-managers and project directors' personal managers. The information on his roll of papers was important.

So it was that upon a Tuesday morning at approximately 10:15, this being the best morning for a businessman's peace of mind according to Lemuel Shipwright's *Psychology of Managerial Practices* two volumes, Ree and Ree, Mikal Margolis straightened his paper tie and knocked on the North West Quartersphere Projects and Developments Manager/Director's door.

"Come in," said the North West Quartersphere Projects and Developments Manager/Director.

Mikal Margolis entered, bowed politely, and said in a clear but not too loud voice, "The mineralogical reports on the Desolation Road project."

Busy with his computer terminal, the North West Quartersphere Projects and Developments Manager/Director's back was turned to him.

"I don't recall anything about a Desolation Road Project," said the North West Quartersphere Projects and Developments Manager/Director. Mikal Margolis's mouth suddenly felt like a parrot's crotch. There was something oddly familiar about the voice.

"The Desolation Road project, sir: the ore sand extraction

project. The feasibility studies the planning council requested."

The bluff was so enormous it must succeed through audacity alone. Mikal Margolis was certain that the North West Quartersphere Projects and Developments Manager/Director did not know the face and name of every employee in his division. He was equally certain the North West Quartersphere Projects and Developments Manager/Director was so busy that he could not possibly remember all his decisions.

"Remind me more."

The bait was being taken.

"It was found that the red sands in the region around the isolated settlement of Desolation Road contain a phenomenally high level of iron oxides, the sand being, in effect, virtually pure rust. The project was to study means of exploiting this resource through bacteriological action upon the rust sands, rendering it more easily processable. It's all laid out in this report, sir."

"Very interesting, Mr. Margolis."

Mikal Margolis's heart stopped dead for a perilous moment. The North West Quartersphere Projects and Developments Manager/Director turned to face him. At first Mikal Margolis did not recognize the elegant young man, smooth, powerful, dangerous, not the least bit blubbery or whining as Mikal Margolis remembered him.

"Good God. Johnny Stalin."

"Shareholder 703286543."

Mikal Margolis stood waiting for the Company police to come. He waited and waited and waited. At length he said, "Well, aren't you going to call them?"

"They won't be necessary. Now, your files."

"What about them?"

"I want to see them. If they're worth the risk of coming out of the walls and engaging in this charade, oh, I know all about you, Mr. Margolis, everything, then they must be worth seeing."

"But . . ."

"But you are a convicted murderer and a Freelancer . . . Mr. Margolis, my father was a fool and if I had stayed in Desolation Road I would be a dirt-poor farmer and not a man of business and industry. What you may have done in the past to my family is all past. Now, show me the files. I take it you have conducted a full mineralogical, chemical, biological, and cost-effectiveness study to back all this?"

Mikal Margolis fumbled with his stolen briefcase and spread the papers across the North West Quartersphere Projects and Developments Manager/Director's desk. He weighted the corners down with little paperweights in the shape of naked boys lying on their backs with their legs in the air.

36

"I will give her the earth," said Umberto Gallacelli, siestaing on his bed, his head resting on a pile of soiled underpants. "Only the whole earth is good enough for her."

"I will give her the sea," said Louie Gallacelli, fastening his bootlace tie before the mirror. Business had been brisk since the pilgrims started coming. "She is so like the sea, boundless, untamed, restless yet yielding. For her, the sea." He glanced at Ed Gallacelli, oily and immersed in a copy of *Practical Mechanic*. "Hey, Eduardo, what are you going to give our lovely wife for her birthday?"

Never much given to unnecessary speech, Ed Gallacelli lowered his magazine and smiled a subtle smile. That night he left on the Meridian Express without telling his brothers when he would be back. There were seven days to Persis Tatterdemalion's twentieth birthday. Those seven days passed in a flurry. Louie prosecuted sixteen hours a day in Dominic Frontera's petty sessions: the pilgrims had brought petty crime and petty criminals and with a tough mayor and harassed attorney hearing up to fifty cases per day the town lock-up was always full. The three good-natured constables Dominic Frontera had seconded from the Meridian constabulary barely contained the flow of small crime.

Umberto had made the short move from farming to real estate. Renting his fields had proven so profitable that he went into business with Rael Mandella converting bare rock and sand into tillable farmland and letting it out at rents only slightly less than ruinous. Even Persis Tatterdemalion was so hardworked that she had taken on extra staff and was considering opting for a lease on the house across the alley to extend the premises.

"Business is booming," she declared to her regulars, and nodded in the direction of the pinched pious pilgrims sitting in their corners with their guava cordials, thinking pure thoughts of the Lady Taasmin. "Business is booming." Then Sevriano and Batisto would skip out together the same time every night and she would look at them and sigh and wonder how they had gotten so big in only nine years. They had their fathers' devilish good looks and rakish charm. There was not a girl in the whole of Desolation Road who did not want to sleep with Sevriano and Batisto, preferably simultaneously. Remembering this, she would call them to the bar and fuss over them and smooth down their curly black hair which would spring up again the second they walked out the door, and while no one was looking slip packets of male contraceptive pills into their shirt pockets.

Nine years. Not even time was what it used to be. Nostalgia certainly wasn't. With a start Persis Tatterdemalion realized her twentieth birthday was only five days off. Twenty. The halfway point. After twenty there was nothing to look forward too. Funny how time flies. Ah, flies. She hadn't thought about flying for . . . she couldn't remember how long. The sting was gone but the itch remained. She was not a pilot. She was a hotelier. A good hotelier. It was no less honorable a profession than pilot. So she told herself. When people talked about a pilgrimage to Desolation Road, they talked Bethlehem Ares Railroad/Hotel. She should be proud of that, she told herself, but she knew in her heart of hearts she would rather be flying.

With a start she realized she had a customer.

"Sorry. Way long way away."

"It's all right," said Rael Mandella. "Two more beers. Any sign of that runaway husband of yours? Umberto says it's been seven days."

"He'll turn up." Ed was the black clone in the brood. While his brothers were hungry for success and had made themselves attorneys and realtors, Ed was content to remain in his shed fixing small things and asking no money for the privilege. Dear Ed. Where was he?

The twentieth birthday dawned and Umberto and Louie threw a surprise breakfast party for their wife with cakes and wine and decorations. Still Ed did not appear.

"No-good bum," said Umberto.

"What kind of husband is not present at his wife's birthday?" said Louie. They presented their gifts to Persis Tatterdemalion.

"I give you the earth," said Umberto the soily-fingered farmer, and gave his wife a diamond ring, hand-crafted by the dwarf jewelsmiths of Yazzoo.

"And I give you the sea," said Louie, and he gave her a voucher for a holiday on the Windward Islands in the Argyre Sea. "Ten years you've worked here without a holiday. Now, you take off all the time you want. You've deserved it." And they both kissed her. And there was still no Ed.

Then Persis Tatterdemalion heard a noise. It was not a very big noise, it would have been easily lost in the happy din of party-making had she not been listening for it for ten years. The noise grew louder but still only she could hear it. As if gripped by the compulsion of an Archangelsk, she stood up. The sound called her from the hotel into the open. She knew what it was now. Twin Maybach/Wurtel engines in push-pull configuration. She shielded her eyes against the sun and peered. There it was, coming out of the sun, a speck of black dirt that became first a bird, then a hawk, then a howling thundering Yamaguchi & Jones twin-engine stunter that blasted over her head and she stood in the cloud of dust and pebbles thrown up by the prop-wash and watched the airplane make its turn. She saw Ed Gallacelli wave from the passenger seat, quiet Ed, dark Ed, happy-to-be Ed. From that moment onward Persis Tatterdemalion loved only and utterly him, for all her husbands, he alone had understood her sufficiently to give her the one thing she wanted most. Umberto had given her the earth, Louie the sea, but Ed had given her back the sky.

37

A reminiscent weakness she had been unable to break brought her back time and time again to Raano Thurinnen's Seafood Diner on Ocean Boulevard. It was not the quality of the chowder, indisputable though that was. It was not the cheery countenance of Raano Thurinnen, rosy from Stahler's beer, even though he called her "Miss Quinsana" now. It was, she thought, that the three years she had worked here could not be washed away into forgetfulness.

"Usual, Miss Quinsana?"

"Thanks, Raani."

The bowl of steaming fresh chowder was served by a dull-eyed paan-chewing teenage girl.

—Kid won't last three months, let along three years, Marya Quinsana thought. But the chowder was very good. Strange that in all the years of working here when she could have had the stuff for nothing she'd never once tasted it.

The energy she'd possessed then amazed her still. Sixteen to midnight serving chowder, bouillabaisse, and gumbo, then up at eight in the morning and off to the Party offices on Kayanga Prospect to fill envelopes and campaign down on Pier 66. Party supporter, party member, party worker, then the time had come to decide between party candidate and fish chowder. No choice, really, but she was still thankful for Raano and his dollars. She had learned a lot from the chowder-stuffed mouths of his clients, enough to rewrite the party Manifesto for the Syrtia Regional Assembly Elections and sweep the party onto victory balconies all across the continent. She'd been there on the balcony with the other loyal party workers, applauding the successful candidates, but the thought in her heart had been "poor puppets, poor puppets." She had manipulated them into power by telling them to listen to the people.

Listen, she'd said, listen to the people, listen to what they like, what they hate, what makes them angry, what makes them happy, what they care about and what they don't care about. The party that listens is the party that wins. But what she'd really wanted them to listen was Marya Quinsana telling them to listen.

"You should run for office yourself," Mohandas Gee had suggested, "you who know so much about what the people want." She had declined. Then. It had looked like dedication. It was ambition. Her time would come with the world elections in two years. In the intervening years she was the hammer and her manifesto the anvil upon which the New Party was forged. A zealous mood of reform swept the cadres. A new Electoral College was adopted and many an old reactionary ("the professional politicians" Marya Quinsana denounced them) found himself without a nomination when the regional ballots came around again. Yet Marya Quinsana trod carefully. Her essential hypocrisy must never be disclosed: that she, the decrier of professionalism, sought to bring a whole new dimension of professionalism to the political arena. There were still too many political luminaries who possessed the power to destroy her.

She dipped her bread into the chowder and watched the fishing fleet busy with nets and sails at the piers across Ocean Boulevard. Years and decades. This election, she would be content with a counsel post. Three years after that would be the time when she would sweep to glory as party leader. Gulls squabbled and wheeled over the open hatches of the fishing boats. Years and decades. Politics was like a sea. The Manifesto was the net, the populace the catch, and she the trawlerman.

Raano Thurinnen sat himself down heavily across the table from her.

"How goes the dinner, Miss Q.?"

"Your usual estimable quality, Raani."

"Grand. You're on the radio in five minutes if you want to listen."

"Can't stand election broadcasts. I sound like a llama on them. Only spoil the folks' appetites. You voting tomorrow?"

"Of course. For you, Miss Q."

"Hush now, Raani. Privacy of ballot is a man's constitutional right."

"I'm not ashamed for everyone to know. Why, anyone disagrees with me, he can get out of my restaurant."

"Now, Raani, democratic rights, remember? A man can hold any opinion he chooses."

"Not in my restaurant. Why, today two punks came wandering in wearing Whole Earth Army badges, started handing out flyers, they did. Well, I'm not having that in my restaurant, so I threw them out. Got quite nasty, they did, had to butt a couple of heads for them. That girl they had with them, she tried to scratch my eyes, imagine that? I don't know about that Whole Earth Army, Miss Q., I mean, opinions is one thing, but killings and bombings, well, something's got to be done, hasn't it? You will do something about that Whole Earth Army, won't you, Miss Quinsana? Why, I'm half scared they'll come and burn this place down: I've heard they've done that. You will do something about them, Miss Q.? You've got to stop them, they're all mad, and that music they play, it isn't good for the kids. Drives them wild. I won't have it in here . . . when you get elected, I know you'll stop it."

"I will," said Marya Quinsana. "You have my word on that." Then the radio announced that there was going to be a party political broadcast on behalf of the New Party by Miss Marya Quinsana and she wondered as the music played just how many of her other election promises she would keep as surely as her promise to break the Whole Earth Army.

38

Now that the trees were full-grown and provided a lovely shade, Grandfather Haran spent more and more time in the garden he had made. He loved to spend time in the contemplation of things past. He thought of his boyhood in Thompson's Falls, he thought of his first wife, Evgeny, he thought of his son's boyhood and his son's son's boyhood. He thought of his adoptive daughter, that wild, animal child, he thought of his granddaughter, turned into a deity against her own will, and his grandson, the Greatest Snooker Player the Universe Had Ever Known. He wondered if he would ever see him again. He thought the thoughts a man of forty-five thinks. When he thought these thoughts he liked to have his meals brought to him so that he could eat in the tranquility of his garden in undisturbed reminiscence and once or twice the Babooshka had had to come out at dusk to fetch him home.

"You should open it up to the public," said Rael Mandella, mindful of the stuffed pockets of the pilgrims flocking to see his daughter. "The Gray Lady's Garden of Serenity. Twenty centavos in." Of late the Poor Children of the Immaculate Contraption had taken to calling her the Gray Lady.

"I will do no such thing," said Grandfather Haran. "It is my garden, for the private personal use of my wife, myself, and those guests I choose to invite." To maintain that privacy he hired a handful of desperately impoverished Poor Children from the shantytown called Faith City that surrounded the great gray basilica and paid them to build a wall around his garden. Pleased with their industry, he erected a gate which he locked with a stout padlock and put one key into his pocket and the other on a long golden chain around his wife's neck.

When the bustle and rush of the new Desolation Road with its entrepreneurs and vendors of religious gewgaws and rent-racking hoteliers grew too much, they would lock themselves in the garden and listen to the singing of the birds and the leaping of the fish in the little stream. They would plant flowers and shrubs, for a garden is never completed while its gardener lives, and as they worked their soily-fingered way along paths and flower beds they seemed to discover parts to it they could not remember having planted: secret dells, tiny waterfalls, groves of cool trees, a maze, a sand garden, a grassy lawn with a sundial at its center.

"Dearest wife, does it sometimes seem to you that our garden reaches out beyond the walls I have built around it?" asked Grandfather Haran. After walking for almost an hour along an intriguing flagstone path, they had come to a stone bench beneath a willow tree and here they were resting. The Babooshka looked at the sky, which seemed to her strangely soft, not like the harsh blue-black of Desolation Road at all, and full of pillowy clouds.

"Husband Haran, I think that as we have grown this garden, so this garden has grown us, and the unexpected things we are finding in it are the seeds it has sown in our imaginations."

They sat quietly for a long time on the stone bench beneath the willow, watching the clouds, quiet with the quietness of old people who do not need to speak to communicate. As the world began to turn its face away from the sun they left the stone seat and returned by ways more wild and beautiful than they had ever trodden before to the gate in the wall. There pastry vendors and whey-faced tourists pushed rudely past them in the laneway as they locked the gate behind them.

"I am thinking that if what you say is true, then our garden may be of infinite extent and variety," said Grandfather Haran. The Babooshka clapped her hands in delight.

"Why, husband Haran, then we must explore! Tomorrow we shall begin, yes?"

Early the next morning, before the lanes and alleys filled with strangers, the Babooshka and Grandfather Haran embarked upon their exploration of the garden. The Babooshka fastened one end of a large ball of twine to the gate and played it out. In her satchel she carried eighteen such balls, her drawing books and pencils, so that she might map the unexplored hinterland of the imagination, and two packed lunches. Grandfather Haran led the way, equipped with opticon, sextant, watch, and compass. Within ten minutes of leaving the gate, husband and wife were in unfamiliar territory.

"There should be a stand of accelerated-growth beech trees here," said Grandfather Haran. "I planted them myself, I remember clearly." Before him was a small wooded valley. Banks of rhododendrons gladdened the slopes and a small stream splashed over stones. "There are no rhododendrons here. They are over by the left of the gate . . . the garden, I think, must be constantly reshaping itself. Fascinating."

"Hush," said the Babooshka, "do you hear a voice?" Grandfather Haran strained his less-acute ears.

"It is Rael?"

"Yes. Hush, listen. Did you hear what he said?"

"I thought I heard my son shout something about Limaal coming home."

"He did. So, husband, shall we go back?"

Grandfather Haran let the twine run through his fingers. Behind him he could just discern the iron gate. Before him he saw the new valley and it seemed to him that beyond it lay a huge, virgin landscape, a land of wooded hillsides and rushing rivers, bright meadows and leaping deer.

"Forward," he said, and together they went down into the valley, he sighting on the sun and marking compass bearings, she reeling out the twine behind her. They crossed the stream and hand in hand climbed up into the wooded hillsides and flower-filled meadows and never came back.

When Rael Mandella came to look for them he found only the twine the Babooshka had played out behind her. He followed its devious course around trees and flower beds, fountains, and shrubberies in a great spiral inward from the walls toward the heart of the garden. He burst through the final screen of privet into a small, neat lawn and came to the end of the twine. It was tied around the trunk of a great elm tree, one of a pair that stood so close together that their branches and roots were intertwined beyond the power of any man to separate.

39

Limaal Mandella had come with his wife, children, and fixings to boot to Desolation Road to escape from the plague of people, but such was his fame that he spent most of his first year a virtual prisoner in his own home.

"I am not the Greatest Snooker Player the Universe Has Ever Known!" he shouted in frustration to the crowds of admirers who gathered every morning outside the Mandella house. "Not anymore. Go away! Go and give yourselves to the ROTECH Anagnosta Gabriel, I don't want you!"

Finally Rael Mandella, Sr., made daily patrols with his shotgun to keep the chaff away, and Eva Mandella, who in the summer wove out of doors beneath the great umbrella tree in front of the house, performed magnificently as receptionist and vetter of visitors. Then, just as Limaal Mandella was settling into the first period of peace he had known since he walked into Glen Miller's Jazz Bar, cue under arm, the plague of surveyors descended upon Desolation Road.

And the plague of surveyors begat the plague of plastic grid squares, the plague of plastic grid squares begat the plague of planners, the plague of planners begat the plague of construction workers, and the plague of construction workers drove Limaal Mandella back into isolation. Just as he had gotten used to the pilgrims and entrepreneurs, and they to him, the town was suddenly filled up with successive waves of surveyors, planners, and construction workers until the hotels, hostelries, taverns, inns and bunkhouses bulged with them. He could no longer walk to Pentecost's General Merchandise Stores to buy the *Meridian Herald* without a dozen voices calling out, "Hey, look, Sanchi, it's Limaal Mandella," "It *is* him, I tell you, the

Greatest Snooker Player the Universe Has Ever Known," "Is that . . . yes it is . . . Limaal Mandella," and dozens of hands reaching out scraps of paper, bills, wage slips, betting forms, for him to autograph and dozens of invitations for him to play exhibition matches in some hotel, bar, workers' social.

"Just what the hell is going on!" he fumed to Santa Ekatrina. "First of all the whole damn desert's carved up like a dartboard into squares with plastic tape, now there's enough heavy construction gear flying in night and day to build an extra continent. And just as the folks here learn that I've retired and that I don't want to talk about snooker or beating the Devil or the competition to be the Greatest Snooker Player the Universe Has Ever Known; just when I can go down to the bar again, or the shop, I have to go into hiding again. Just what the hell are they doing out there, building an extra space elevator or something?"

Kaan Mandella, four years old, bright, cheeky, and stuffed full of lamb pilaf, piped up, "Iron, Pa. Whole desert's full of iron. Virtually pure rust, says teacher, and she should know, she used to be a geolly . . . a geoggy . . ."

"Geologist. Iron! Sweet Lady, what next? So that's the Bethlehem Ares Corporation out there. I don't know . . . what's to become of Desolation Road?"

Enough had become of Desolation Road in his Belladonna years for it to be virtually unrecognizable to Limaal Mandella. Saints, prophets, basilicas, men with metal arms, hotel, inns, flophouses all aglow with gaudy neon, prayer kites, gongs and windharps, belfreys full of clamor, vanished grandparents, walled gardens, mystery relations who vanished as rapidly as they had appeared, putty-featured aliens astonished on street corners, five trains a day, and a lighter port, too, shops, bars, shanties and slums, people sleeping in the alley at night, people standing in line all day by the door marked "Supplicants"; theft, rape, abduction: police! Constables with shock staves, courts, and Louie Gallacelli draped in attorney robes, real estate, property, and leases. Pastry vendors on every street corner; barrow boys, costermongers, hawkers of religious curios: streets! Poured concrete and corrugated tin, glass, steel, and plastic; beer that tasted like piss: imported food! Lines at water pumps, acres of solar generators, the all-pervasive smell of ordure from overloaded methane digesters. Bicycles, rikshas, trikes: trucks! People shouting during the siesta, people entering without knocking, people, strangers, staring staring staring, talking, opening mouths, making noises. Even his sister was a stranger to him, shut up inside the ugly concrete carbuncle that called itself the Basilica of the Gray Lady; admission only to pious supplicants, penitents, and those with the heart of a pilgrim. Limaal Mandella still possessed enough worldly pride to refuse to join the line by the door marked "Supplicants."

"This house, this town, this world, what is it coming to?" he shouted, and banged out of the house across the courtyard to his parents' house. In the twenty seconds it took him to cross the llama-dunged yard, two flash photographs were taken of him and a darkness-hidden female behind a potted bay tree begged him to sexually abuse her.

"Mother, this town has me driven to distraction!"

At work upon her tapestry frame, Eva Mandella smiled and said, "Limaal! How nice to see you!"

"Mother, I have no privacy! Just thirty seconds ago some woman implored me to tie her up, gag her, wrap her in plastic film, and piss all over her! It can't go on! I must have privacy!"

"You have a famous face, Limaal."

"That part of my life is over, Mother."

"While you are alive, no part of your life is over. That is what this is for. Tell me, Limaal, what do you think of it?" She showed him the tapestry upon which she had been at work.

"Very nice," said Limaal Mandella, still trembling with rage.

"Isn't it? It's the history of this town. Everything that has ever happened I am putting into this tapestry so that when I am long gone your children and their children will be able to look at it and know they have a proud history. It's very important to know where you are coming from, and where you are going to. That is your problem, Limaal, you have come from, but as yet you have nowhere to go. You must have a purpose."

Limaal Mandella said nothing but stood twisting his foot on the dusty flagstones. Then he kissed his mother a brief smack on the cheek, spun on his heel, and ran out of the house, past the frustrated woman and the pirate photographers in the branches of the mulberry trees, through his kitchen, past his startled wife and sons, out into a night roaring with heavy construction machinery. He pressed on with grim determination, ignoring the workers' cries of recognition and praise, and entered the overgrown garden surrounding Dr. Alimantando's cave house. The door had been forced, the vestibule was dusty and rank. Bats fled from their ceiling roosts as the light panels came to life.

Somewhere in this place must be the key to the dissatisfaction, the irritability, the bad temper, the restlessness. As a child he had believed that Dr. Alimantando had all human wit and wisdom inscribed upon his walls, now all he needed was some target at which to aim his rationalism. Limaal Mandella stood before the wallfuls of chronodynamic hieroglyphics and a smile grew. A light was lit in him. He might no longer be the Greatest Snooker Player the Universe Had Ever Known, but before him lay the key to becoming Master of Space and Time. Here was a lifetime of mystery, achievement, failure, and triumph.

"Pa?" The voice startled him. "Pa, you all right?" It was Rael, Jr., and already cursed with the family curse. Limaal Mandella rested a hand on his son's head.

"I'm all right. It's just that since we came here I've not known what I wanted to do with myself."

"I know. You were like a paper glider in the wind."

Had he been that inept at concealing his frustration?

"Well, that's all over now. Rael, your father is going to be a Gentleman of Science and Learning, like Dr. Alimantando in the stories I told you about this place. See here . . ." Father and son knelt to examine the faded scribblings. "This is where it all begins." He traced the line of reasoning along the wall and up and around, Rael, Jr., following him, and embarked upon the years of line-following that were to lead him to the center of the ceiling in Dr. Alimantando's weather-room.

40

"**B**ehold!" cried Inspiration Cadillac, surgical lamps glinting off his steel cranium. "The first total mortification!" Surgeons, nurses, prostheticians went down on their knees, arms uplifted in adoration. Taasmin Mandella backed away from the metal thing on the operating table. It horrified her.

Beneath a plastic dome the brain pulsed, studded with electromechanical transducers. A neuron fired, a transducer twitched, a metal arm raised itself, metal fingers opened to grip the air.

"Glory glory glory!" shrieked the surgeons nurses prostheticians.

"Get it away from me," muttered Taasmin Mandella. "It sickens me." Inspiration Cadillac was at her side in an instant, whispering suave persuasions.

"Consider the achievement, Lady, the first total mortification! Flesh made metal! This is indeed a hallowed moment!" The undisguised envy in his voice made Taasmin Mandella flinch. The thing opened a metal eye-shutter and rotated a steel eyeball at her. The smooth steel orb was pierced by three black slits. The mouth opened and a stream of gurgled gibberish vomited forth. It tried to sit up, embrace her.

"Kill it, kill the filthy thing, get it away from me!" the Lady Taasmin screamed.

The Total Mortification sat up. A spasm shook it. The cybernetic gibberish rose to a shriek of metal on metal. Oil trickled from the trembling mouth. Surgeons nurses prostheticians leaped from their knees to the operating table. The

Total Mortification spasmed, shuddered, and collapsed with crashing of grinding gears. In the confusion Taasmin Mandella slipped out of the operating theater and fled down empty antiseptic corridors and sun-baked cloisters in a rustle of circuit-printed fabric.

She was meditating in the sand garden at twilight when she heard the chanting. The machine mantras of the Poor Children comingled with the coarser cries of the populace touched the edge of her perceptions with a silver chime and drew her back into the world of men again. Troubles never end. She stretched, arching her back against the strictures of the form-fit meditation stool. In one minute Inspiration Cadillac would come knocking on the door, calling her back to responsibilities. She rose from the stool, went to her room, and pulled on a pair of gray bib & braces. Inspiration Cadillac found her nudity unspiritual and distrubing.

She was ready for the knock.

"What is it?"

"A problem, Lady. The Poor Children . . ."

"I heard them."

"I think it best if you see for yourself." Inspiration Cadillac led her along sun-baked cloisters returning their daytime heat to the sky.

"How was your . . . experiment?" Taasmin could not conceal the shudder in her voice and Inspiration Cadillac evidently heard it, for he replied, "With respect, you should not denigrate the labor of the scientists, they are trying to perfect the new humanity, the future man. Alas, in this instance the patient's system terminated but his courage and faith have surely earned him immediate passage into the presence of the Great Engineer."

Inspiration Cadillac pushed open a heavily ornate door that led onto the street. The sound of chanting and cheering swelled.

"What is going on?"

"Please to follow me, Lady." Chamberlain and prophetess rounded a corner and came face-to-back with a dense throng of people.

"Up here the view is better," suggested Inspiration Cadillac, hastening Taasmin Mandella up a flight of stone steps onto a balcony. Beyond the encirclement of puzzled citizens, Taasmin Mandella could see machine limbs catching the evening sun. The Poor Children of the Immaculate Contraption knelt beside the chain link fence that surrounded the Bethlehem Ares Steel construction site. The air was filled with the humming of their binary mantras, and their ungainly arms moved in cranelike gestures of fervent devotion. Every few seconds a Poor Child would leave his place in the congregation and, in blatant disregard of the warning notices that the wire was electrified, press his metal prostheses to the mesh. Electricity sparked, the worshipper groaned and flexed in religious ecstasy. Then he returned to his place and resumed the chant of 10111010101111000001101101010 while another took his place.

"What are they doing?" asked Taasmin Mandella.

"I would think it is obvious, Lady. They are worshipping."

"A construction site?"

"Apparently a prophecy has been circulating among the lower orders in Faith City. This prophecy claims that what the Bethlehem Ares Corporation is constructing here is no less than the birthplace, if that is the right expression, of the Steel Messiah, the Liberator, the Machine with the Heart of a Man who will deliver the machines from their millennial bondage to the flesh."

"And that is why they are worshipping . . . a pile of foundations and earthworks?"

Beyond the wire an off-clocking shift of construction workers paused to stare at the adoring Dumbletonians.

"Precisely. The site is holy, a place of veneration and worship."

Taasmin Mandella looked again upon the steady stream of Poor Children going joyfully forth to immolate themselves upon the electrified wire.

"It's sick," she whispered.

A voice from the crowd of townfolk cried out.

"Look! It's her! The Gray Lady!"

Heads turned, fingers pointed. The Poor Children froze in their Adoration of the Wire and swiveled metal eyeballs toward the balcony. A young woman with a metal chest and left leg stood up and screamed.

"A message! Give us a message!"

The chant spread instantaneously across the congregation.

"Message! Message! Give us a message! Message! Message! Give us a message!"

Five thousand eyes crucified Taasmin Mandella.

"They await your leadership, Lady," wheedled Inspiration Cadillac.

"I can't," whispered Taasmin Mandella. "It's disgusting. Sick, idolatry. . . . It's not true spirituality, true worship . . . it must stop."

"You are their leader, their spiritual head, their shepherd, guide, and conscience. You must lead them."

The chanting rose to a frenzy. The ground shook beneath two and a half thousand pounding fists.

"No! I refuse! It's an abomination! I'm not God that I desire their worship . . . I detest it. I didn't ask you to follow me, I am the servant of the Blessed Lady, not the Dumbletonians, I'm a child of the Panarch, not the Poor Children of the Immaculate Contraption." She tried to bite back the words but they flew from her lips like sweet birds. "Or you, Ewan P. Dumbleton!"

Suddenly she did not hear the chanting or feel the force of the Poor Children's demands. She looked into Inspiration Cadillac's fleshly eye and saw such hatred burning there that she gasped.

—Has he always hated me so? she thought, and realized even as she thought it that yes, he had, from the moment he had taken her hand in the pit by the railroad line, Inspiration Cadillac had hated and envied her because she was the true vessel of God, not self-shaped and self-justified as he was. He envied her spirituality, for all he could afford was a weary worldliness masquerading in the robes of holiness. He envied her and hated her and dedicated his every waking moment to manipulating, corrupting, and ultimately controlling her.

"How you must hate me," she whispered.

"Pardon, Lady? I did not quite hear that. What message will you give to your people? They await you." His voice was hard with hypocrisy.

Taasmin Mandella clenched her left fist. Her halo brightened to an intense blue that could not be hidden from the watching eyes.

"We are enemies, Inspiration Cadillac, Ewan Dumbleton, whatever you call yourself: you are my enemy, and the enemy of God."

"That is the message you wish to give your people?" The chanting pounded on her spirit.

"Yes! No! Tell them this; I was chosen by St. Catherine to be her emissary to the world of men, that after seven hundred years of being the Saint of Machines she now wishes to point men to God. To God, not to a factory. Tell that to your faithful."

She strode from the balcony and returned to her private quarters. It felt good to have an enemy as well as a friend. After years of nonachievement she felt purposeful and puissant. She was a crusader for God, a fighter of the good fight, an angel with a flaming sword. That felt good. Very good, better than any prophet of the Blessed Lady should allow a feeling to feel.

41

Every morning at eleven minutes of eleven Arnie Tenebrae would stand on the end of her bed so that she could see the three things beyond the bars on her window. In order of perspective they were an orange tree in a terra-cotta pot, thirty-six kilometers of dry Stampos, and one blue sky. None of these three things ever changed in the slightest, but every day at eleven minutes of eleven Arnie Tenebrae stood on her bed not because she found those three items in the least bit interesting but because Migli had expressly forbidden her to stand on her bed (fear of hanging, she surmised) and as he arrived promptly every day at twelve minutes of eleven she liked to gain some petty victory before the ignominy of the daily rehabilitation sessions.

"Miss Tenebrae, please, ah, don't stand on the bed. The, ah, warders don't like it."

Sky was blue. Stampos brown and orange tree dusty green. She could get down now.

"Morning, Migli." "Migli" was Prakesh Merchandani-Singhalong, rehabilitation psychologist at the Chepsenyt Regional Detention Center: small, brown, mousy, flustered, clumsy with tape recorder and notebooks, he could be nothing but a Migli.

"What is it today, Migli?"

He experimented with various arrangements of tapes, recorder, and notebooks on the table.

"I, ah, thought we might, ah, continue from where we left off yesterday."

"Where were we?" These talk sessions were a waste of government time and money. She suspected Migli felt the same, but the charade must be played out with all the busy jottings-down and lies little and not so little that the game demanded.

"Your early days with the North West Quartersphere Truth Corps, the, ah, various sexual, ah, liaisons with its members." Migli leered owlishly through his bottle-end spectacles. Arnie Tenebrae folded her hands and sat back on the bed. She opened her mouth and let the lies flow.

"Well, after I'd had about half a year on the Truth Corps— it was okay but kind of boring—the romance wore off and it was just long hot dusty trike rides and a couple of days in some ass-end village plugged into the telecommunications net: it wouldn't have been so bad if we'd actually got to *record* the music. But all that traveling, I got bike itch between my legs; what I really wanted was to get onto an Active Service Unit."

"And what did you do?" Migli leaned forward eagerly. He'd probably already heard this from the interrogation tapes. Arnie Tenebrae stretched an arm to scratch the back of her nails against the plaster.

"Invited Paschal O'Hare, Commander North West Quartersphere Brigade, to sample the sweet joys of my nine-year-old body behind the communications shack at Oblivion-ville HQ. He was resupplying at NWQHQ same time we were and the opportunity was just too good to miss. Have you any idea how good a lover he was?" Migli slavered in classic Pavlovian fashion. Arnie Tenebrae was disgusted that a graduate of the Universuum of Lyx should be so credulous of her tale of seduction and khaki sex. Nothing of what she had described had ever happened, but Migli did not really want to know that. She had indeed met Paschal O'Hare at Oblivion-ville and traded all Dr. Alimantando's secrets for a place on an active service unit and only dribbled her sordid tale of sexual humiliation, torture, deprivation, torment, and discipline to titillate Migli. For a rehabilitative psychologist he was very much in need of some of his own therapy. Spotty deviate. She described her three months combat training in graphic detail while in the cinema of the imagination she reviewed the reality. Months of sitting on hands, of cold winter bivouacs in the Ecclesiastes Mountains, of boredom and dysentery and diving for slit trenches every time an aircraft passed overhead.

"And what happened then?" asked Migli, vicariously high on death and glory.

"It'll keep for tomorrow," said prisoner Tenebrae. "Time's up." Migli glanced at his watch and scooped up his armfuls of tape recorders, notebooks, and pens.

"Same time tomorrow, Migli?"

"Yes, and, ah . . ."

"Don't stand on the bed."

But she was standing on the bed same time tomorrow, and Migli's small tantrum of temper pleased her so much she closed her eyes and extemporized a lengthy and glorious fantasia on her first year's active service for the Whole Earth Army, a spectacular of gun battles, bombings, ambushes, bank robberies, kidnappings, assassination, and diverse atrocities in places with euphonious names like Jatna Ridge, Hotwater Valley, Naramanga Plain, and Chromiumville. But when Migli was gone and she sat on her bed weaving cat's cradles from her bootlaces, she remembered the way Group Leader Hueh Linh's blood had leaked away through her fingers into the muddy foxhole at Superstition Mountain. She remem-bered how, with his death all over her hands, she had looked up from the red mud to see the Black Mountain Militia charging, charging charging, their mouths wide wide open. She remembered the fear that had smelled like the blood on her hands and the shit in her pants and had driven her fear-crazy with its howling until she dragged up the MRCW and screamed and fired and screamed and fired until the fear was gone and it was still. She hadn't wanted the promotion. The citation had read "Gallantry against overwhelming odds," but she knew that it was the fear that had made her shoot. It was not until several months later that she discovered that Paschal O'Hare's first raid with the new field-inducer weaponry had been a turkey shoot and the citation had been his way of thanking her. Sub-major of the Deuteronomy division. Cat's-cradling in her cell in the Chepsenyt Regional Detention Center, she couldn't even remember what she had done with the medal.

On the third day Migli came again with his tapes and his notebooks. Arnie Tenebrae was sitting on her bed.

"Not at the, ah, window today?" His attempts at sarcasm were puny.

"Haven't seen what I'm looking for yet." She had decided that today she would tell nothing but the truth. There was no satisfaction in lying when only she knew she was lying. "Today, Migli, I am going to tell you about the raid on the Cosmobad landing guidance system. Got enough tape? Enough paper? Batteries all right? Wouldn't want you to miss any of this." She sat back against the wall, closed her eyes, and began her tale.

"Orders came down from the regional command for a major offensive during the planetary assembly elections. After the battle of Smith's Shack several of the Deuteronomy division's command levels got knocked out—we didn't have F.I. weapon systems yet—and I was left in charge of the fifth and sixth brigades. Because we hadn't been issued the new equipment, we thought, *I* thought, we'd aim for a low-level target, namely, the landing guidance systems at Cosmobad. They drop off the Skywheel on remote, so if we knocked out the guidance radars, no shuttles would be coming in at Belladonna. We synchronized our action with the others in the sector and moved into position at Cosmobad."

The raid had been adeptly planned and flawlessly ex-

ecuted. At twelve minutes of twelve the sixty-five radar
beacons were destroyed by mines and the guidance computer
scrambled with a hunter-killer program bought from the
Exalted Families. All ground-to-orbit communications in the
Belladonna landing sector were hopelessly scrambled. It had
been beautiful, not with the beauty of yellow explosions and
collapsing towers, but the intellectual inherent beauty of
something done right. Platoon leaders reported all primary
targets destroyed. Arnie Tenebrae gave the order to withdraw
and disperse. Her own command group, Group 27, had
retreated toward the town of Clarksgrad and ran straight into A
and C Company of the New Merionedd Volunteers who had
been on maneuvers in the area. The firefight had been short
and bloody. She remembered she hadn't fired a single shot
during the brief engagement. She had been too stunned by her
own stupidity for not checking the military presence in the area
to even raise her MRCW. Group 27 sustained eighty-two
percent casualties before Sub-major Tenebrae surrendered.

"Next time I'll make sure of my intelligence," Sub-major
Tenebrae said.

"There's, ah, not likely to be a next time."

"Whatever. Anyway, Group Twenty-seven was obliterated
and now I'm resident in the Chepsenyt Regional Detention
Center, talking to you, Migli, and telling you your time's up
for today. What would you like to talk about tomorrow?"

Migli shrugged.

That night Sub-major Tenebrae lay in a shaft of bar-broken
starlight, twirling a piece of string between her fingers. She
thought starlight thoughts of fear and loathing. Since the
morning she left Desolation Road on the back of Engineer
Chandrasekahr's terrain trike, a day had not passed that she
had not woken fearful and gone to sleep fearful. Fear was the
air she breathed. Fear came in greater or lesser breaths, like the
bowel-loosening fear of foxhole Charlie with Hueh Linh
bleeding himself away through her fingers, or the tense
skyward glance of identification at the beat of an aircraft
engine. She twined the bootlace around her fingers, round and
round and round, and feared. Fear. Either she used fear or fear
used her.

Her fingers froze in their dance. The thought struck her

with irresistible profundity of divine law. Her aimlessness was illuminated by its holy glow. Until that moment fear had used her and had bequeathed her incompetence, failure, loathing, and death. From this bootlace-twining moment forward she would use fear. She would use it because she feared fear using her. She would be more terrible, more violent, more vicious, more successful than any Whole Earth Army commander before her: her very name would be a curse of fear and loathing. Children yet unborn would dread her and the dead die with her name on their lips because either she used fear or fear used her.

She lay awake a long time that night, thinking in the slatted shaft of starlight.

On the fourth day, at twelve minutes of eleven, Group Nineteen of the Deuteronomy Division of the Whole Earth Army stormed the Chepsenyt Regional Detention Center, eliminated the guards, released the prisoner, and effected the rescue of Sub-major Arnie Tenebrae. As she buckled on the new field-inducer weapons pack her rescuers had brought for her and made her escape, a small, bespectacled young man, like a dirty-minded owl, jumped out of a doorway waving an immense Presney long-barreled reaction pistol he clearly did not know how to use.

"Stay, ah, where you are, don't, ah, move, you're all, ah, under arrest."

"Oh, Migli, don't be a silly Migli," said Arnie Tenebrae, and blew the back out of his head with a short burst from her field inducers. Group Nineteen burned the Chepsenyt Regional Detention Center behind them and rode off across the dull brown Stampos with the dull brown smoke hanging over them.

42

It was as if they had all been snatched up into the night: men, houses, big yellow machines, everything, all gone. That night there had been the worst storm anyone could remember and the brothers had laid in their beds feeling delicious thrills of scariness every time the lightning threw huge blue shadows on the wall and the thunder boomed so loud and so long it was as if it were in the room with them, in the bed beside them. They could not remember falling asleep, but they must have, for the next thing they knew their mother was pulling back the curtains to admit the peculiar sunshine you get only after huge storms that is so clear and light and clean it is as if it has been laundered. They tumbled out of bed into clothes through breakfast and up into the laundered morning.

"Isn't it quiet?" said Kaan. To ears accustomed to months, years of the din of day-and-night labor the quiet was intimidating.

"I can't hear them working," said Rael, Jr. "Why aren't they working?" The brothers hurried to the low place they had dug under the wire so that they could play in the most exciting of boys' playgrounds, the construction site. They stood at the wire and looked at nothing.

"They're gone!" cried Kaan. There was not one earth grader, concrete pourer, or tower crane, not a single site hut, not a dormitory, canteen or social, not one welder, mason, or bricklayer, not even a foreman, site supervisor, crane driver, or truck loader to be seen. It felt as if the storm had sucked them all into the sky, never to return. Rael, Jr., and his young brother rolled under the wire and explored the new and empty world.

They trod gingerly through shadowy streets between the stupendous buttresses of steel converters. They shied at every desert bird that croaked and every distorted reflection of themselves in the jungle of metal piping. As it became apparent that the plant was utterly deserted, the boys' daring grew.

"Yeehee!" shouted Kaan Mandella through his cupped hands.

"YEEHEE YEEhee Yeehee yeehee . . ." called the echoes in the settling tanks and ore conveyors.

"Look at that!" shouted Rael Jr. Neatly parked in laagers beneath the towering complexities of pipes and flues stood two hundred dump trucks. Agile as monkeys the boys climbed and crawled all over the bright yellow trucks, swinging from door handles and foot-steps, sliding down sloping backs into buckets big enough to hold the entire Mandella hacienda. Their energy led them from the big trucks onto the gantries and catwalks to play perilous games of three-dimensional tag among the pipes and ducts of the ore filtration system. Hanging by one arm over a shuddering drop into the bucket of a rear loader, Kaan Mandella let fly a whoop of glee.

"Rael! Wow! Look! Trains!"

The jungle gym of industrial chemistry was immediately abandoned in favor of the twelve waiting trains. The explorers had never seen such trains before, each was over a kilometer long and hauled by two Bethlehem Ares Railroads Class 88s hitched in tandem. The sense of slumbering power trapped within the shut-down tokamaks awed the boys into silence. Rael, Jr., touched one of the titans with the flat of his hand.

"Cold," he said. "Powered down." He had been given a book about trains by his grandfather for his seventh birthday.

"'Edmund Gee,' 'Speedwell,' 'Indomptable,'" said Kaan Mandella, reading the names of the black and gold behemoths. "What would it be like if one suddenly started up?" Rael, Jr., imagined the fusion engines exploding into life and the idea scared him so much he made Kaan leave the sleeping giants alone and led him into another part of the complex entirely, one they had never seen before on their clandestine playground visits.

"It's like another Desolation Road," said Kaan.

"Desolation Road like it ought to be," said Rael, Jr. They found themselves at the edge of a small but complete town of about six thousand inhabitants, or, rather, which would have housed six thousand inhabitants, for it was as empty as a graveyard. It was a well-ordered town with neat terraces of white adobe houses with red roofs (for some things were too sacred for even the Bethlehem Ares Corporation to change) lining spacious streets that radiated out like the spokes of a wheel from a central hub of parkland. At the end of every street where it joined the circular service road stood a Company commissary, a Company school, a Company community center and a Company depot for small gadabout electric tricycles.

"Hey! These are great!" shouted Kaan, turning tight circles within circles on his three-wheeled buggy. "Race you!" Rael, Jr., rose to the challenge, kicked a trike into action, and the two boys raced each other up and down the empty streets of Steeltown past the empty houses, the empty shops, the empty schools and socials and tea rooms and doctors' offices and chapels, all empty empty empty like the eyes of a skull, and they whooped and cheered as their wheels threw up clouds of the red dust that had found its way even into this sacred place.

At the hub of the wheel of streets was a circular park with the name "Industrial Feudalism Gardens" above its wrought iron gate. When the boys tired of their racing they threw off their dusty sweaty clothes and splashed in the ornamental lake and sunned themselves on the neatly rolled lawns.

"Hey, this is great!" said Rael, Jr.

"When do you think all the people are coming?" asked Kaan.

"Don't care long as it isn't today. I could stay here forever." Rael, Jr., stretched like a cat and yielded himself to the innocent sun.

"Do you think you'll work here when you grow up?"

"Might do. Might not. Haven't thought much about what I might want to do. How about you?"

"I want to be rich and famous and have a huge house like we had in Belladonna and a pool and a 'lighter and have everyone know me, like Pa was."

"Huh! Seven years old and he knows exactly what he wants. How you going to get all this then?"

"I'm going to go into business with Rajandra Das."

"That bum! He can't do anything!"

"We're going to open a hot food stall and when we make a lot of money on that one, we'll open another, and another, and another, and I'll be rich and famous, just you see!"

Rael, Jr., lay back on the neatly rolled grass and wondered how his little brother could have all his days charted out before him while he wished only to be blown like a moth on the mystical desert wind.

"Listen," said brother Kaan, sitting up, alert. "Sounds like 'lighters."

Rael, Jr., stretched his hearing and caught the beat of aircraft engines on the edge of the wind.

"Coming this way. Maybe it's the people."

"Oh, no, maybe it is," said Kaan, struggling into sticky clothes. The first LTA drifted over the steel pinnacles of the city. "Let's go." The brothers ran down deserted streets filled with the drumming of aircraft engines and over their heads airship after airship after airship drifted past. Rael, Jr., ran with one eye to the sky.

"There must be hundreds of them." There was both wonder and awe in his voice.

"Come on," said brother Kaan, cursed with pragmatism.

"No, I want to see what's happening." Rael, Jr., climbed a series of sheer staircases that led to the top of a catalytic converter column. After only an instant's hesitation Kaan followed. He was indeed pragmatic; but curious. From the walkway around the head of the column the plan of the operation became apparent. The 'lighters were taking up stations in a huge disc centered on Desolation Road.

"Wow, there must be thousands of them," said Kaan, revising his brother's earlier estimates. Still the airships passed over their heads. The 'lighters flew over Desolation Road for a further half hour before their formation was complete. The sky was black with them, black shot through with golden liveried lightnings, a storm of industry about to descend upon Desolation Road. As far as the boys' desert-sharp eyes could see, the aircraft were waiting. The dark presence of the 'lighters scared them. They had known the Bethlehem Ares Corporation was powerful, but powerful enough to turn the sky black, that was awesome.

Then it was as if a magic word had been spoken.

All at once, everywhere, the cargo hatches of the dirigibles opened and clouds of orange smoke poured out.

"Gas!" the brothers shrieked in imagined alarm, but the orange smoke did not drift like gas would but hung in rippling curtains around Desolation Road. The orange smoke hung for a few seconds, then settled to the ground with uncharacteristic speed.

"That's clever," said Rael, Jr. "They're using their fans to make a downdraft."

"I want to go home," said the boy with the future planned.

"Shhh. This is interesting." Within a minute of the cargo doors' opening the cloud had precipitated out to lie in a thick orange-on-red scum over the Great Desert.

"I want to go home, I'm scared," repeated the boy who wanted to be rich and famous. Rael, Jr., peered at the dunes and the high, dry plateau, but all there was to be seen were the 'lighters peeling away from formation one by one.

"I've seen enough. We can go now."

At home Pa was in ebullient good humor.

"Come and look at this," he said, and took his sons into his maize field. "What do you make of that?" It reminded Rael, Jr., most of the copper sulphate crystal he had grown in school but this was dull black, rusty, and about half a meter in length. It was also growing out of the middle of the maize field, a thing no copper sulphate crystal ever did. Said Limaal Mandella with a note of pride in his voice, "I think I might dig it up as a souvenir."

"What is it?"

"Haven't you been listening to the radio? It's an iron ferrotrope crystal! Boy, we're living smack bang in the middle of the world's biggest bacteriologically active zone!" They could not understand why their father sounded so pleased. "If you get the binoculars and go down to the edge of the bluffs, there are these things growing out of the sand as far as you can see! Crystal ferrotropes! It's the way the Bethlehem Ares Corporation's getting all the iron out of the sand, by bacteria, tiny little living organisms that eat the useless rust in the sand and shit out those things you see there. Clever? Brilliant! A real first for Desolation Road. Never been one anywhere else. We're the first!"

"Was that what was coming out of the 'lighters?" asked Kaan. Rael, Jr., kicked him to shut him up before he said anything about being under the forbidden wire in Steeltown, but his pa's eyes were too full of the light of technology to see anything lesser.

"Microbial spores. That's what they were, microbial spores. But you know what's most amazing of all? This . . . disease, I suppose you might call it, only affects rust, one very particular iron oxide. Won't touch anything else; you could walk through the desert for kilometers and kilometers and kilometers and not come to any harm. Bethlehem Ares has that stuff reaching out twenty kilometers in all directions. Richest ore deposit on the whole planet I heard one of the construction men say afore he left."

"Why is this one here?" Rael, Jr., bent to examine the alien thing in the maize field.

"Must be iron deep under the soil. Some of the spores blew here and got into the rust. Tell you this, boys, Ed Gallacelli's got them growing out of his shed roof!"

"Wow! Can I go and look?" asked Kaan.

"Sure," said Pa. "I'll come, too, we'll take the binoculars and go down to the bluffs. Everyone's down there watching the show. You coming, Rael, Jr.?"

Rael, Jr., did not come. He went inside and read his book about trains, and when his father and brother and mother and grandmother and grandfather came home full of descriptions of towering crystals thrusting out of the sand growing growing growing ten, twenty, fifty meters tall before their sheer weight shattered them, he pretended to be playing with the cat but he was really hating them, his father brother mother grandfather grandmother because he did not know how to hate those pilots and planners who had willed such a world-shaking change upon his universe. He did not understand why he felt this hatred, why he felt violated, emptied, soul-sick. He tried to tell his brother, his mother, even his faraway father, but they did not understand what he was trying to tell them, none of them, not even wise Eva Mandella with her wise old weaving hands.

The only one in the whole of Desolation Road who would have understood Rael, Jr.'s soul-deep malaise was his Aunt Taasmin, for she alone knew what it was like to be cursed with an unguessable mystic destiny.

43

At six minutes of six the sirens blew.

They blew like the horns of angels. They blew like summer storms through the pump gantries and over the red rooftiles. They blew like the Trump of Doomsday, like the sky cracking, like the breath of the Panarch breathing life into lifelessness.

At six minutes of six the shout of the sirens broke the desert air and on every street every door in the new town flew open at once and out poured the people, people from all the continents of the world and beyond, from Metropolis, ever running backward in its chase to keep up with itself, people even from the impoverished people-weary Motherworld herself, all come to make the steel for the railroads and farm machines and power looms and rikshas and bridges and buildings of the young, vigorous world, pouring from their doors to make steel for the mighty Bethlehem Ares Steel: workers streaming to the manufactories, tributary joining to tributary in a river of heads, hands, and hearts surging down the shadowy streets of the Steeltown. Junior executives in smart paper suits fresh that morning from the slot dispenser zipped past on electric tricycles, children dawdled to their schools and Company kindergartens, shopkeepers and commissary merchants pulled up door blinds and set the chairs out on the verandas to advertise that they were open for business.

At the shout of the sirens two hundred yellow trucks shook into life like weary dogs and rumbled out from their garages. In the crystal dunefields draglines and bucket-wheelers woke from prayerful repose to feed. With a roar and a thunder twenty-four black and gold Class 88 haulers fired up their fusion tokamaks and cunk-cunked over the points onto the mainline.

At the sirens' shout smoke puffed from a hundred stacks: puffed, blew rings, then poured into the Indian summer sky, black, white, orange, brown. Conveyors rattled into motion, furnaces ignited, white-hot carbon electrodes descended into swirling vats of molten heat, rolling mills came up to speed, and at the very heart of the complex, behind walls of concrete, sound, steel, lead, and magnetism, the plasmic djinn rattled its pinch-bottle and poured magical power into the city.

At the sirens' shout guards in black and gold uniforms with black and gold emblems on their shoulders swung wide the wire gates and the two hundred trucks burst through them and bounced through Desolation Road down the red dirt track into the ore fields.

At the sirens' shout the Poor Children of the Immaculate Contraption poured from their cardboard and plastic hovels around the Basilica and streamed through the alleys of old Desolation Road in a welter of psalms and mantras to ring the Steeltown gates and scatter prayer confetti under the house-high wheels of the trucks. The guards smiled and waved, the plaid-shirted drivers flashed their lights and blared their horns. The rag-clad Poor Children danced and sang for them. Prayer kites improvised from plastic refuse sacks were run up into the dawn wind and fastened to the wire fence: great was the celebration on that, the first day of the Advent of the Steel Messiah! The trucks thundered past, fifty, one hundred, two hundred. The shouting of their engines drowned out the hymns of the worshippers, the churning wheels showered them with red dust. The dawn light brightened, flooding through the factorial geometries, casting beautiful industrial shadows through the wire onto the dancing Poor Children. Floodlights switched off as the day grew stronger.

At the sirens' shout Sevriano and Batisto Gallacelli awoke and it was their tenth birthday. Ten today. Hooray hooray. The day of majority, the day of adulthood, the day of putting behind the things of boyhood: the days of play-tough nearly-nine-year-olds jostling on street corners, days of corn beer and sunshine and music from the B.A.R/Hotel radio, girls to glad-eye, pockets to pick, cards to bet on, jokes to tell, boys to fight, policemen to sass, the occasional guilty sniff of burning hemp from Mr. Jericho's garden and the Saturday night dances at the construction workers' social, where they sometimes had the Big Bands from the Big Cities, like Buddy Mercx and Hamilton Bohannon and once the legendary King of Swing himself, Glen Miller and His Orchestra, and sometimes even that new stuff they played on *All Swing Radio*, samba, salsa, whatever they called it. Ah, the Saturday night socials! From the moment the doors closed on Sunday morning the count was on until they opened at twenty minutes of twenty next Saturday. The dressing and the preening, the painting and the swaggering, the drinking and the vomiting, the posing and the passing and sometimes at the end of a really good night, the thrashing and heaving in the riksha lot behind the dance hall. All past now. All gone, all put away, for today the sirens shouted and the Gallacelli brothers (mutually indistinguish-able as peas in a pod or days in a prison . . .) were ten.

So it was that as Steeltown woke to its first morning Sevriano and Batisto's mother called her sons to her.

"Today you are ten," she told them. "Now you are men and must take on the responsibilities of adults. For instance, have you thought of what you might like to do with your lives?"

They had not. They had rather liked what up till then they had been doing with their lives. But they promised their mother and fathers that within five days they would know what they wanted to do with their lives. So they asked their school career adviser, they asked their friends, they asked the girls they had met at the Saturday night socials, they asked their neighbors, they asked priests, politicians, policemen, and prostitutes and at the end of five days they knew what they wanted to do with their lives.

"We want to be pilots like you, Ma," they said.

"What?" said Umberto, who had wanted them to go into real estate with him.

"What?" said Louie, who had wanted them to go into law with him.

"We want to fly," said Sevriano and Batisto, thinking of wind, wires, sunlight on wings, and the sensual roar of Yamaguchi and Jones aero-engines in push/pull configuration, remembering their own mother blissful and glowing after long afternoons thundering down desert canyons and skimming the rim rocks of haunted mesas. To them the earth held nothing more fair than the sky.

"If you wish to fly, you shall fly," said Ed, who alone understood how the wind could blow through the blood. "Have you thought about how you're going to go about this?"

"We talked to Mr. Wong, the career officer at school," said Sevriano.

"He said to join the Company as commercial 'lighter pilots," said Batisto.

"And you are sure this is what you want to do?" asked Persis Tatterdemalion, secretly delighted that her sons, at least, would follow her dreams.

"We are." The twins produced application forms.

"Then you must follow your hearts' desire," she said, signing the consents at the bottom. For some reason she kept seeing Limaal Mandella's face in the paper, like an ancient watermark.

And last of all on that day of beginnings, the sirens' shout called a man onto a high balcony fronted with a black and gold Company banner. The man watched the torrents of workers, the busy-bee-bustling managers, the machines blossoming into life and motion. He watched the animating spark spread throughout Steeltown, lighting flames of empire and industry wherever it touched. The North West Quartersphere Projects and Developments Manager/Director watched the very first day dawn on Steeltown and was well pleased. Very well pleased indeed.

44

May 27, 06:13, seven ten-kiloton nuclear devices detonated simultaneously aboard the Praesidium SailShip *Jonathon Byrde* preparing to offload passengers, crew, and cargo at the ROTECH orbital docking facility for transfer to the Skywheel space elevator. Three hundred and fifty-five thousand people were instantly vaporized in the blast. A further hundred and fifty thousand exploded bodies were recovered by ROTECH blitches and sheddles from lonely funeral orbits. Fifty-eight thousand survived the explosion in remote sections of the vessel or in cargo pods blown clear from the ship mainframe. Of these, twelve thousand five hundred died from exposure to intense radiation. A further seventeen hundred perished when their spinning ship-section burned to slag in the atmosphere before all could be transmatted to safety. Sixteen hundred ROTECH personnel, including the *Jonathon Byrde*'s service crew of twenty-eight and nineteen Skywheel shuttle pilots leaving the drop-off end of the cable were killed. Ninety-seven thousand immigrants had already been transported to the surface when the *Jonathon Byrde* was destroyed. One shuttle with fifteen hundred passengers was knocked out of orbit into the path of the spinning cable and cleaved in half. A further two hundred and thirty-eight casualties resulted when the town of Dolencias Cui was bombarded by a hail of debris falling from orbit. A five hundred ton section of ship mainframe traveling at eight kilometers per second hit the Dolencias Cui school and in a nanosecond rendered the town childless. Seventy-two thousand were never accounted for, among whom must have been the fanatic seven who smuggled the warheads aboard the Sail-Ship.

The number of casualties from the *Jonathon Byrde* was 589,545. A group calling itself the Whole Earth Army Tactical Group claimed responsibility for the bombing. In a tent under an oak tree on the utmost northern edge of the holy Forest of Chryse, where the land lifts up and tears like a folded chapati into the Hallsbeck Palisades, Arnie Tenebrae sat by her radio listening to the special news bulletin. She nodded, she smiled, she twiddled the tuner so she could hear it told again in a different voice. Her name would live forever now.

Marya Quinsana paused to take a sip of water and assess the situation. They were a good crowd: straightforward, uncomplicated talk. Wave the flag, beat the drum, let them think they have won you to their cause when you are winning them to yours; humiliate the bumpkin heckler, hammer the nail between the eyes and keep hammering, pound pound pound. Local elections were quite fun. She smiled to the local candidate, that sallow, clever young man, and took up hammer in hand.

"Citizens of Jabalpur! Do I really have to tell you these things? Do I really have to tell you that murdering thugs roam your country, burning factories and businesses, setting crops to the torch, driving settlers from their homesteads; do I have to tell you good citizens of the innocent folk slaughtered like animals in bomb attacks, shot down on their own doorsteps? No!"

The audience brayed its approval.

"No! I do not need to tell you these things, good citizens! You know it only too well! And you may ask yourselves, where are the armed constables patrolling your streets? Where are the Local Defense Units, where are the regular troops? Yes, where are the Jabalpur Volunteers, the First Oxiana Division, the Twenty-Second Airmobile? I will tell you where they are!"

She treated them to a few seconds' calculated pause.

"Sitting on their hands in their barracks, that's where! And why? Why? Because your local opposition-dominated assembly doesn't think the situation warrants that kind of intervention! So: three million dollars worth of finest military technology gathers dust and the local defense forces have neither arms nor uniforms to drill in because Campbell Mukajee doesn't think the situation warrants that kind of intervention! Let him tell that to the Garbosacchi family! Let him tell that to the Bannerjees, the Chungs, the MacAlpines, the Ambanis, the Cuestas, and they will tell him whether or not the situation warrants that kind of intervention!"

She let them howl while she nodded to the candidate, then palms-downed them into simmering calm.

"But best of all . . . best of all, my friends, the constables; *your* constables, your guardians of law and order, routinely escort Whole Earth Army demonstrators through the streets of this city! 'Preservation of the right of political expression' says Campbell Mukajee. Really, Mr. Mukajee? And what of the rights of Constantine Garbosacchi, Katia Bannerjee, Roi MacAlpine, Abram Ambani; Ignacio, Mavda, Annunciato, and Dominic Cuesta, all butchered this past week by the murder squads of the Whole Earth Army?" The audience drew breath to thunder a condemnation, but Marya Quinsana played them like Blue Mountain tilapia on the line. "Escorting them? They should be arresting them!" She smelled frenzy-sweat and hysteria in the hall but still she did not release them. "There are Whole Earth Army representatives sitting in each of the three houses of this regional assembly who openly condone murder and violence and Mr. Campbell Mukajee has never once tabled a motion for their dismissal! He openly consorts with murderers and terrorists, he and his party: because of his bleeding-heart liberalism hundreds of your fellow countrymen have been butchered; he refuses to mobilize the security forces because he does not think the situation warrants that kind of intervention: his own words, ladies and gentlemen! And now . . . now . . . now he asks you to reelect him and his party for another three years!

"And I know, I know in my heart of hearts that the people of Jabalpur District are going to say no, no, a thousand, ten thousand, a hundred, a million times no on Thursday to another three years of Liberal misrule and say yes, yes, a million times yes to the New Party, the party with the will, the party with the determination, the party with the power and your mandate, citizens, to sweep the Whole Earth Army from the face of the globe; on Thursday you will say yes to the New Party, yes to Pranh Kaikoribetseng, your local candidate, yes to victory and strength!"

And now she released them. As one the audience rose; audience, party nominees, party members, party workers, a storm of applauding hands. Marya Quinsana smiled, bowed. But her performance had not pleased her. She preferred subtlety to tub-thumping and welkin-ringing. Clumsy, unsophisticated, unsubtle. A dirty night's work. Unseen and unheard in the tumult, a messenger slipped onto the platform and handed her a piece of paper: a telegram.

RETURN WISDOM IMMEDIATELY COMMA EMERGENCY MEETING RE JONATHON BYRDE OUTRAGE COLON KAROLAITIS STOP.
Jonathon Byrde? Jonathon Byrde?

She only learned that *Jonathon Byrde* was not an assassinated dignitary when the cabin attendant on the Jabalpur–Syrtia Night Mail brought her the morning papers with breakfast and banner headlines toppled over each other in plumbing the thesaural depths of outrage and horror.

She met First Minister the Honorable Vangelis Karolaitis on the veranda of his town house overlooking the Syrtic Sea. He was a fine old gentleman, honorable as his title, and wise, and Marya Quinsana hoped he would die in his bed before it became necessary for her to depose him. A butler served mint tea. The breeze carried the scent of jasmine and wisteria from the gardens that reached down to the sea.

"Well," said the First Minister.

"I've said it all along. Get me out of Science and Education into Security and I'll have the Whole Earth Army on its knees in six months."

"I'll be announcing the ministerial reshuffle this afternoon. I'll also introduce the emergency bill outlawing the Whole Earth Army per se; shouldn't have any trouble getting it passed, the Liberals aren't sounding quite so liberal this morning. So: the army's yours. Remember, they've never fought a proper war, so try and bring them all back in one piece, but that aside, do whatever you have to do to rid these lands of this . . . cancer of terrorism."

"One question: who destroyed the *Jonathon Byrde*? I want him first."

"Some faction calling itself the Whole Earth Army Tactical Group. The Parliamentary Group's issued blanket denial of any involvement with this group: personally I don't believe them. Leader's called . . . yes, Arnie Nicolodea Tenebrae."

45

The world had lost its sense of wonder. The marvels that seven, six, five years ago excited gasps and sighs of amazement today prompted contemptuous yawns of tedium. Only one hundred and fifty years old, the world was already middle-aged and cynical, consigning its cast of wonder workers, tellers of tales, showmen, miracle men, medicine men, and carnival touts to the rusted sidings of forgotten stations.

"Old train, the world has lost its sense of wonder!" cried Adam Black. He poured himself another liberal brandy and stood in the center of his once-opulent now-shabby showmaster's carriage, glass raised high in an ironic toast. "The world has grown weary of Chautauquas and Educational 'Stravaganzas, my friend. What shall Adam Black do now?"

"Might I suggest pooling your resources with those of the Immam of Bey and his Circus of Glass?"

Adam Black hurled his brandy glass at the wall.

"That charlatan! That mountebank! That money-spinning titillator of public fancy! Adam Black is a man of education and learning, his mission is that of teacher and preacher, not hustler and whore!"

"Still, I maintain that his is the sole remaining carnival of wonders in this hemisphere." The train's voice was calm and patient, almost unbearably so.

"Maintain what you will. Adam Black will not stride the same midway as the Immam of Bey."

Two days later locomotive and three coaches pulled away from the freight sidings of Ahuallpa Station and headed onto the main southbound line, eight tracks wide. The Great South Line was buzzing that day with the rolling stock and haulers of the world's great railroads: Bethlehem Ares, Great Southern, Great Eastern, Grand Valley, Argyre Express, Transpolaris Traction, Llangonnedd and Northeastern, Trans-Borealis, and among their jewel-bright flashing liveries was the chipped and pimpled paintwork of Adam Black's Traveling Chautauqua and Educational 'Stravaganza. In his managerial car Adam Black stormed and hurled things.

Smash.

"Turn this train around immediately."

"You know as well as I that that is physically impossible." The train's voice was a model of imperturbability as it took a set of points at two hundred.

Smash crash.

"Don't be clever. You know what I mean. I forbid you to take me to Beysbad, I forbid you to go to the Immam of Bey." Adam Black pounded on the sealed doors. The carriage rocked and bounced, the train was piling on more speed. Adam Black feared for the tokamaks. It had been a long time since he could afford a service.

"May I clarify one small point?" said the train. "You are a passenger. I am not taking you to Beysbad. I am taking myself. I am sure that the Immam of Bey will have a proud and honored position in his Glass Circus for a unique, computerized, thinking train!"

"Ingrate!" roared Adam Black. Smash crash smash went his bottles of Belladonna brandy against the camera-eye. "To betray the one who made you, gave you life and awareness!"

"Don't be so melodramatic," said the train, and Adam Black thought he heard a strange tone of menace in its perfect diction. "I am not your son anyway."

"We shall see!" shouted Adam Black. He reeled across the

swaying carriage and unlocked a strong metal cabinet. He removed an antennae-feathery headpiece.

"I would not advise the use of the cyberhat," said the train, and now the menace was unmistakable.

"Oh, would you not?" said Adam Black. Fighting for balance, he jammed the helmet on his head. "Now you will turn back."

"Don't," said the train.

"I will."

"Don't . . . I reversed the polarity so you can't . . ."

Adam Black pressed his fingers to his temples. All at once senses one two three four five and six shut down. Hallucinations bubbled up in his imagination: pushing against a glowing wind, star-hot fires burning in his belly, tireless legs, tireless arms, a wall of stout brick.

—So the train resists me. He gathered his mental strength and hurled his imagination at the bricks. It flew apart, no stronger than tissue, and Adam Black went falling falling into the abyss of preconsciousness.

"Reversed polarity, reversed polarity, reversed polarity." The words circled around him like condors as he fell. He felt his body changing, growing, expanding, taking on new textures and surfaces, new hard planes, new alignments of power.

—No! howled Adam Black as his consciousness merged with the metal and oil and steam of the train. No no no no no no no nonono noooooo; like a train building up steam, his denial lost its words and become a whistle, a steam whistle, whistling out across the paddy fields of the Great Oxus.

In the managerial car the body of Adam Black gave a convulsive death-jerk as if a million volts of electricity had coursed through it, which indeed it had, for the computer personality of the train was too strong for the delicate synapses of Adam Black's brain and they fused one by one, cracking, snapping, smoking, swinging. In a flash his eyeballs burned out and smoke trickled from the empty sockets and open mouth. The dissolved brain ran out of his empty eyes onto his lap to lie like clotted soup and with a desperate cry the train realized it was dead dead dead and Adam Black its erstwhile father was trapped inside the steel body of a Great Southern Class 27 locomotive.

46

Listen now.

Once there was a man who lived in a house with a buff-colored front door. He did not much like the color buff. He thought it characterless and insipid. But every door in every street in the town was buff-colored and to change the color would have brought him to the attention of those people who liked buff-colored doors. Every morning he would lock his buff-colored front door behind him and walk to work, where he would drive a steel-pouring crane until the evening whistle, when he would walk home again and open his buff-colored door and every evening he would feel depressed by the dreariness of the buff. Every day he opened and closed the buff-colored door and he grew more and more miserable, for the buff-colored door came to symbolize everything that was dreary and monotonous and characterless about his life.

One Sunday morning he went to the Company commissary and bought a brush and a big bucket of green door paint. He did not really know why he went and bought a brush and a big bucket of green door paint, but he had woken up that morning with an insistent vision of green in his head. Green green green. Green was a restful, meditative color, easy on eye and soul, serene; green was the color of green and growing things, green was God's favorite color: after all, He had made an awful lot of it. So he put on his old old clothes and set to work. Soon people were gathering to watch. Some wanted a go at it, so the man who liked green gave them a brush and let them paint a bit of his door. With all the help it was not very long before the door was finished and all the people who watched agreed that green was a very good color for a front door. Then the man thanked his helpers, hung a sign reading "Wet Paint," and went indoors to have his lunch. All afternoon Sunday, walkers came past his house to look at the green front door and pay their compliments because in street after street of buff-colored front doors there was only one that was green.

The next day being Monday, the man who liked green put on his vest and his pants and his hard hat and walked out of his green front door to join the stream of workers all pouring into the factory. He poured steel all morning, ate his lunch, drank some beer with his friends, went to the toilet, then poured steel again until seventeen o'clock, when the siren blew and he went home again.

And he could not find his house.

Every house in the street had a buff-colored door.

Wrong turn perhaps: he checked the street name. Adam Smith Gardens. He lived in Adam Smith Gardens. Where was his house with the green door? He counted along the rows of buff-colored doors until he reached number seventeen. Number 17 was his house, the house with the green front door. Except the door was buff once again.

When he had left that morning, it had been green. When he came home, it was buff. Then he saw, where someone had put a clumsy handprint, a little glow of living green shining through the buff.

"You bastards!" shouted the man who liked green. The buff front door opened and a buck-toothed little man in a Company paper suit stepped out to deliver a short homily on the necessity of eliminating undesirable traits of individualism between labor units in the interest of greater economic harmony in accordance with the Project Manifesto and Development Plan which made no provision in the labor unit social engineering system for dysfunctional and individualistic colors: such as *green*, in opposition to and set against uniform, official, functional and socially harmonic colors, such as *buff* with reference to labor unit housing modules: sub-section entrance and exit portals.

The man who liked green listened patiently to this. Then he took a deep breath and punched the little man in the Company paper suit as hard as ever he could right in his buck-toothed gob.

The name of the man who liked green was Rael Mandella, Jr. He was a simple man, uncomplicated, destinyless, and ignorant of the mystery spreading its cursed roots around his spine. On the occasion of his tenth birthday he said as much to his mother.

"I'm a simple person really, I like simple things like sunshine, rain, and trees. I don't much want to be one of the great people of history, I've seen what that's done to Pa and Aunt Taasmin. I don't much want to be a man of substance and consequence, like Kaan with his food franchises, I just want to be happy, and if that means never amounting to very much, that's fine." Next morning Rael Mandella, Jr., took the short walk from the Mandella mansion down to the gates of Steeltown and passing through them became crane-driving steel-pouring Shareholder 954327186 and happily remained so, a simple man never amounting to very much until the Sunday morning the mystic urge drove him to paint his door green.

Shareholder 954327186 was suspended from his job pending a full inquiry by an Industrial Tribunal. He bowed to the summonings officer, respectful, not in the least bitter or resentful, justice being justice, and went home to his buff-colored front door to find half a dozen demonstrators marching around in a circle outside.

"Reinstate Rael Mandella!" they chanted. "Reinstate reinstate reinstate!"

"What are you doing outside my house?" demanded Rael Mandella, Jr.

"Protesting against your unjust suspension," said a zealous-looking young man carrying a placard reading "Buff is boring, green is glorious."

"We're the voice of those that have no voice," added a pinched woman.

"Excuse me, but I don't want your protests, thank you. I've never even seen any of you before, please go away."

"Oh, no," said the zealous young man. "You're a symbol, you see, a symbol of liberty to the oppressed slaves of the Company. You are the spirit of freedom crushed beneath the booted heel of corporate industry."

"All I did was paint my door green. I'm no symbol of

anything. Now, go away before you get into trouble with Company security."

They paraded around outside his house until night fell. Rael Mandella, Jr., turned his radio up very loud and closed his blinds.

The industrial tribunal found him guilty of antisocial behavior and assault on the person of a Company executive in the execution of his duties. The chairman, in his short summing up, used the phrase "industrial feudalism" thirty-nine times and concluded that even though Junior Labor Relations Liaison Manager E. P. Veerasawmy was a fearful little shit whose punch in the gob was richly deserved and long overdue, Shareholder 954327186 was not the one to execute such judgment and was therefore fined two months wages spread over the next twelve months and barred from promotion in his section for the next two years. His job as a crane driver was reinstated. Rael Mandella shrugged. He had heard of worse sentences.

The protestors were outside waiting for him, banners and slogans at the ready.

"Draconian oppression of Shareholders!" shouted the pinched woman.

"Stop the show trials!" shouted the zealous man.

"We have a right to green doors!" cried a third protestor.

"Rael Mandella is innocent!" a fourth bawled, and a fifth added, "Quash the sentence! Quash the sentence!"

"Actually, I thought I got off rather lightly," said Rael Mandella, Jr.

They followed him home. They marched around outside his house. They would have followed him into the social center that evening had they not been involved in a boycott of Company recreational facilities, so they marched around outside waving their banners, chanting their slogans, and singing their protest songs. Agreeably mellow, Rael Mandella, Jr., left by a back way so that the protestors would not follow him. He heard shouting and peeked around the side of the Company commissary to see if they had somehow learned of his evasion. What he saw sobered him instantly.

He saw armed and armored security police bundling protestors, slogans, banners, placards, and shouts into a black and gold armored van of a kind he had never seen before. Two black and gold guards burst out of the social shaking their heads. They piled into the back of the van and it drove away. In the direction of Rael Mandella, Jr.'s house.

He had sworn that he would never return to sleep under his parents' roof while he still had a job and independence, but that night he revoked the vow, slipped under the wire, and slept in the Mandella household.

The six o'clock Company news bulletin next morning carried a somber tale. The previous night a number of Shareholders had taken themselves on a drinking spree ("doing the ring" in popular parlance) and, utterly inebriated, had wandered too close to the desert bluffs and had fallen to their deaths. The newsreader concluded her salutary tale with a warning about the evils of drinking and a reminder that the True Shareholder permitted nothing to impair his effectiveness for the Company. She did not read names or numbers. Rael, Jr., did not need to hear them. He was remembering the spiritual malaise of his childhood days, and as he remembered it returned to him, summoned by his remembrance; a nausea, a need, a destiny, a mystery, and he knew, as Santa Ekatrina ladled out breakfast eggs and ricecakes, that he could no longer be silent, he had a destiny, he must speak, he must vindicate. Sitting in his mother's kitchen, the clouds parted for him and he glimpsed a future for himself both awful and dreadful. And inescapable.

"So," said breakfast-busy Santa Ekatrina. "What now?"

"I don't know. I'm scared . . . I can't go back, they'll arrest me too."

"I'm not interested in anything you have or haven't done," said Santa Ekatrina. "Just do what is right, that's all. Follow the compass of your heart."

Armed with a borrowed megaphone, Rael Mandella, Jr., crossed a field of turnips, ducked down into a culvert only he and his brother knew about, and splashed through the floating feces into the heart of Steeltown. When no one was looking, he stood up on a concrete flower tub in Industrial Feudalism Gardens and prepared to speak.

The words would not come.

He was no orator. He was a simple man; he did not have the power to make words soar like eagles or strike like swords. He was a simple man. A simple man, sick in the heart, and angry. Yes . . . the anger, the anger would speak for him. He took the anger from his heart and placed it on his lips.

And the mothers children old folk off-shift strollers stopped and listened to his stumbling, angry sentences. He spoke about green doors and buff doors. He spoke about people and soft, peopley things that did not appear on Company reports or Statements of Account; of trust, and choice, and self-expression, and the things which everyone needed because they were not *things*, material, Company-provided things, without which the people withered and died. He spoke about being a simple man and not a thing. He spoke about the terrible thing the Company did to people who wanted to be people and not things, he spoke of the black and gold police and the van he had never seen before and people taken away in the middle of a Friday night and thrown off a cliff because they wanted more than the Company was prepared to give. He spoke of neighbors and workmates taken from their homes or workplaces on the whisper of Company informers, he spoke the inarticulate speech of the heart and opened great gaping wounds in his listeners' souls.

"What do you suggest we do?" asked a tall thin man whose slight build marked him a man of Metropolis. The by now sizable crowd took up the cry.

"I . . . don't . . . know," said Rael Mandella, Jr. The spirit fled. The people wavered, taken to the edge, then abandoned. "I don't know." The cries rang around him what do we do what do we do what do we do, and then it came to him. He knew what to do, it was as simple, uncomplicated, and clear as a summer morning. He snatched up the fallen megaphone.

"Organize!" he cried. "Organize! We are not property!"

47

It was a beautiful day for a march.

So said the steelworkers buttoned up in their best clothes, full to the gills with breakfast pineapple and fried egg, striding out into the crisp morning sunlight.

So said the railroadmen, straightening their peaked caps and examining the burnish of their brass buttons before stepping out to join the growing throng.

So said the truckdrivers, all suspenders and check shirts, inspecting their worn denims for the professionally correct amount of dirt.

So said the crane drivers, so said the rolling mill operators, so said the steel puddlers and the drag-line drivers, the furnacemen and the balingmen, the separator men, the washers, the grinders, the fusion-plant operators; and their wives, and their husbands, and their parents and their children: they all said as they stepped out of their buff-colored front doors that it was a beautiful day for a march.

As they streamed toward Industrial Feudalism Gardens their feet stirred up pamphlets only minutes before bundled out of the rear seat of a small, fast propeller 'plane to snow down upon the roofs and gardens of Steeltown. The printing of these pamphlets was coarse, the paper cheap, the language blunt and uneducated.

There will be a mass meeting on Sunday 15th Augtember at ten minutes of ten. A parade will form up outside Industrial Feudalism Gardens on the corner of Heartattack and 12th and march to

the Company offices to demand an explanation of the deaths of (and here the crude broadsheet named the poor, silly protestors) **and recognition of the Rights of every Shareholder. Rael Mandella, Jr., will speak.**

Rael Mandella waited on the corner of Heartattack and 12th dressed in his father's most elegant black snooker suit.

"You must look the part," Santa Ekatrina had told him that morning. "Your father was a fine figure of a man when he took on the world, you must be no less when you do the same."

He looked at his father's fob watch. His five colleagues: pamphleteer, brother of martyr, disaffected junior manager, political firebrand, empathist, looked at their respective time-pieces. Ten o'clock. Tick tock. Rael Mandella, Jr., rocked forward and back on the heels of his father's black snooker shoes.

What if no one showed?

What if no one were prepared to defy the Company, to defy the warning messages broadcast from the black and gold vans, the new ones more like armored cars?

What if no one were disloyal? What if every hand was a Company hand, every heart a Company heart?

What if no one cared?

"Beautiful day for a march," said Harper Tew, and then they heard it, the sound of a thousand buff-colored front doors slamming, the sound of a thousand pairs of feet stepping into the morning and falling into line and the sound swelled and swelled into a gentle roar like that of a forgotten sea. The first of the marchers rounded Industrial Feudalism Gardens and Rael Mandella's questions were answered.

"They did!" he shouted. "They cared!"

The procession formed up under the banners of its constituent trades and professions. Here truck drivers gathered under the symbol of a snarling orange truck, here puddlers and pourers carried the likeness of a glowing white ingot, here a black and gold locomotive snapped proudly in the air above the freight handlers and drivers. Those without banner or emblem gathered under regional flags, holy icons, and various slogans from the humorous through the scatological to the venomous. Rael Mandella, Jr., and his five deputies positioned themselves at the head of the procession. They raised a furled banner. The release was pulled and the wind streamed out the pure white ground emblazoned with a green circle. A rumble of puzzlement passed through the procession. This was not the banner of any known trade, profession, region, or religion represented in Steeltown.

Then whistles blew, airhorns trumpeted, and the march made the short and pleasant walk from the Industrial Feudalism Gardens through the belching burning factories to the befountained and statued Corporation Plaza. It took twenty minutes for Corporation Plaza to fill, and as the marchers passed through the ringing steel canyons that led to the offices of the Company, shouts of encouragement volleyed from the shiftworkers on their gantries and catwalks. Counting heads, Rael Mandella, Jr., estimated a full third of the workforce was present.

"Can't see any police around," he said to Mavda Arondello. "Shall we begin?" The gang of five nodded. Rael Mandella, Jr., summoned up the mystic anger and let it pour through his loudhailer into Corporation Plaza.

"I'd like to thank you all, all of you, for coming here today. Thank you, from myself, from my friends here: I can't begin to tell you how much this means to me, how it felt to be marching with all of you behind me. The Company has bullied us, the Company has threatened us, the Company has even killed some of us, but you, the people of Steeltown, you rise above the bullying and the threats." He could feel the mystic current flowing now. He snatched the green on white banner and let it fly in the wind. "Well, today you can be proud of yourselves, today we are giving a name to that strength and determination, and when your grandchildren ask at your knee where you were on August fifteenth, you can say, yes, I was there, I was in Corporation Plaza, I was there when Concordat was born! Yes, friends, I give you: the Concordat!"

Puzzlement yielded to expression. Rael, Jr., turned to his deputies and shouted over the clamor, "Well, did I do it right?"

"You did it right, Rael."

When there was quiet he held high a crumpled sheet of paper.

"I have here our Manifesto; our Six Just Demands. They

are fair, they are just. I will read them to you, and to the Company, so that it can hear the voice of its Shareholders.

"Just Demand One: Recognition of a Shareholders' Representative Organization, namely Concordat, as the official voice of workforce and management alike.

"Just Demand Two: Withdrawal of Company specie redeemable only in Company commissaries and the introduction of government legal tender, New Dollars.

"Just Demand Three: Full labor force representation and consultation on all matters pertaining to the labor force, including deployment, shift work, overtime, production quotas, automation, and efficiency programs.

"Just Demand Four: The gradual scaling down of the system of industrial feudalism in private life, including the spheres of education, recreation, health, and public services.

"Just Demand Five: Full freedom of expression, association, and religion recognized for all Company members. All property to be held in common by all Shareholders rather than by the Company on the supposed behalf of all Shareholders.

"Just Demand Six: Abolition of the system of promotion based on spying and informing on workmates."

After reading the Six Just Demands, Rael Mandella, Jr., folded the sheet of crumpled paper, then his arms, and waited for the Bethlehem Ares Corporation's reply.

Five minutes passed. Five more and the early siesta sun began to pour heat and sweat into Corporation Plaza. Yet five more minutes passed. The people were patient. The five deputies were patient. Rael Mandella, Jr., was patient. After twenty minutes a glass and steel door in the glass and steel face of the Company offices opened and a man dressed in the black and gold of Company security stepped into Corporation Plaza. His cross-polarized helmet prevented his face from being seen by the demonstrators, but it was an unnecessary precaution for there was no one present who could have recognized him as Mikal Margolis.

"I am required to inform you that this assembly is unlawful and that its organizers and participants are guilty of an offense against section 38, paragraph 19, sub-section F of the Bethlehem Ares Corporation Assemblies and Associations Ruling. You have five minutes to disperse and return home to enjoy your rest days. Five minutes."

Not a figure moved. The five minutes ticked away on Limaal Mandella's fob watch and the tension wound tight around Corporation Plaza. Rael Mandella, Jr., sweating in his father's best championship suit, was horrified to realize how few of such brief five-minute periods went to make up a lifetime.

"One minute," said the black and gold security man. The internal amplification circuits in his helmet lent his voice the ponderous weight of the whole Bethlehem Ares Corporation. Yet the protestors radiated defiance mingled with a colossal disbelief that the Company would use force against its own Shareholders.

"Don't do it," whispered Rael Mandella, Jr., to the black and gold elemental.

"I must," said Mikal Margolis. "I have my instructions." Then he shouted at the very heaven-ringing peak of his amplification. "Very well. You have neglected the Company's warnings. There will be no more. Commandant Ree, disperse this unlawful assembly."

Then the shots rang out.

There were screams. Heads turned this way, that way, the crowd surged like stirred porridge. Security guards stepped from concealment and advanced on the crowd, black and gold fringe firing volleys of shots into the air. The crowd panicked, orderly demonstration turned to rabble. Placards waved wildly, banners were snapped and trampled, the people wheeled and heaved. The black and gold line fell upon the hem of the demonstration in a baton charge of shock-staves. Swearing roaring panic filled Corporation Plaza. The security men cleared wedges before them, but as they struck toward the heart of the demonstration, the resistance solidified before them. Shock-staves were ripped from hands, riot shields ripped away. Somewhere at the edge of the battle someone was using a fallen guard's flechette gun to fire erratically at the advancing line. Guards and demonstrators broke on each other like waves. Canisters of riot gas trailed orange streamers through the air. Handkerchiefs over their faces, demonstrators threw them back at their assailants. They were holding them . . . the demonstrators were holding them . . . security withdrew, regrouped, deployed riot shields, and advanced behind a withering broadside of flechettes and soft plastic splat bullets. A detachment burst from the doors of the Company offices and stormed the steps, intent upon Rael Mandella, Jr., and his colleagues. With a roar of defiance a young truck driver (plaid shirt, red suspenders, dirty denims, wife and two children) hurled himself at the black and gold assailants armed with a heavy shock-stave. The security commander lowered his flechette gun and point-blank blew the berserker's head into a red smear. The shot and the blood galvanized the attackers. Riot guns swung down into short-range positions and ripped shot after shot into the terrified pandemonium. Hands, legs, shoulders, faces, flew into red shreds. Those who fell were trampled by the swirling masses. Rael Mandella, Jr., ducked under the blast of a security guard aiming for his head and floored him with a full-blooded kick to the balls. He snatched up the riot gun and charged, roaring, at the advancing guards. His maniac fury broke them. They scattered. Mikal Margolis, isolated before Rael Mandella, Jr., and his crazed deputies, tactically withdrew.

Rael Mandella, Jr., took up his loudhailer.

"Get out of here, all of you! They'll murder you! Murder you all! There's only one thing the Company understands. Strike! Strike! Strike!"

Bullets splintered the concrete facade of the Company offices and showered Rael, Jr., with shards. His words carried above the song of battle and the cries of the crowd took on pattern and form.

"Strike strike strike!" they chanted, pressing counterwedges through the police lines and holding them open with shock-staves and riot guns. "Strike strike strike!" The crowd broke through the encirclement and fled down the open streets crying, "Strike strike strike." The security guards sniped at their heels with flechette shot.

Hours later the guards were still searching Corporation Plaza for Rael Mandella, Jr., poking between the crushed placards and the snapped banners and the discarded helmets, checking the bleeding and the wounded and yes, even the dead, for dead there were, and they looked into the faces of the keeners who knelt disconsolate by the sides of sons, fathers, husbands, wives, mothers, daughters, lovers to see if they wore the face of the traitor Rael Mandella, Jr., the fool who had brought this down upon innocent people. They expected to find him wounded, hoped to find him dead, but he had escaped in the black burnoose of an old woman from New Glasgow, dead of contagious panic. Clutched to his chest were the Six Just Demands and the furled green and white banner of Concordat.

48

At six minutes of six the sirens blew. They blew every morning at six minutes of six, but that was not what was different about this morning. Up and down the radiating streets buff-colored doors burst open and poured labor units into the dawn. But that was not really any different from any other morning. What was different was that for every door that opened five stayed shut. Where on any other day a river of steelworkers had poured into the canyon streets of Steeltown, a trickle passed under the archway proclaiming the Three Economic Ideals of the Company: Profit, Empire, Industry. Where on any other day two hundred trucks would have bounced arrogantly through the narrow laneways of Desolation Road, today less than forty made the clangorous trip dodging children, houses, and llamas. Where a hundred draglines had once trawled, only ten worked, where fifty bucketwheelers had scooped the scabs from the skin of the Great Desert there were today only five and it was the same from the locomotive sheds to the hell-mouth converters to the 'lighters shut up in their underground hangers.

All because it was strike day.

Strike day! Strike day! Strike day!

Rael Mandella, Jr., called his strike committee to order

around his mother's kitchen table. There were congratulations, brief eulogies, and declarations of resolution. Then Rael, Jr., asked for reports.

"Strike pay's good for three months," said Mavda Arondello. "Plus pledges of support from bodies as diverse as the Spoonmaker's Guild of Llangonnedd and the Little Sisters of Tharsis."

"Nothing much to report on the picketing front," said B. J. Amritraj. "Company security is still itchy on the trigger. We have to keep a low profile."

"Intelligence reports that the Company's already putting out tenders for scab labor, it might be possible to nip this one in the bud by picketing in the major towns and cities, B.J. Smuggle out some agitators." Ari Osnan, chief of intelligence, folded his fat arms and sat back.

"Production down sixty percent," said Harper Tew. "Within three days all current steel stock will be expended and they'll have to shut down at least three furnaces. In a week there won't be a pin's worth of steel coming out of Steeltown."

"Action Group; nothing to report."

Rael Mandella, Jr., stared long and hard at Winston Karamatzov.

"What do you mean, nothing to report?"

"Nothing to report: yet. If the scabs come, maybe then I'll have something to report."

"Explain please." Winston Karamatzov just shrugged and Rael Mandella, Jr., closed the meeting feeling faintly troubled in his heart.

Next morning all electricity, gas, and water was cut off to the homes of striking steelworkers.

"The Company strikes back," said Rael Mandella, Jr., to his strike committee. Santa Ekatrina flitted about her kitchen, happy and singing, baking little ricecakes.

"You're not going to let them get away with that," she twittered.

The local Concordat cadres within Steeltown responded magnificently.

"We shall steal power from the Company to cook our meals, we shall run water from Desolation Road, by bucket-chain if we must, and we shall go to bed at dusk and rise at dawn as our grandfathers did," they said. Midnight engineers ran plastic pipes under the wire and pumped water from the buried ocean out of street-corner stand-pipes into buckets. Armed security guards passed warily by, unwilling to provoke any incident. Santa Ekatrina turned the Mandella hacienda into a soup kitchen and persuaded Eva away from her tapestry history of Desolation Road to stir vast kettles of stew and rice.

"You've been weaving history for long enough; now you can actually be in it," she told her mother-in-law. A ghostly film of white rice-starch settled over the room and quite surprised Limaal Mandella on one of his increasingly rare returns from his hermitage at the top of Dr. Alimantando's house.

"What is going on?"

"A strike is going on," sang Santa Ekatrina, never so happy as when ladling out bowls of lentil curry to a long line of strikers. The curry-eating steelworkers pointed at Limaal Mandella and muttered in recognition.

"Child of Grace, not even my own house is sacred!" he exclaimed, and shut himself up in Dr. Alimantando's house to delve deeper into the mysteries of time and temporality.

Rael, Jr., and his strike committee watched the first of the food consignments arrive at Desolation Road. On the far side of the railroad tracks Gallacelli/Mandella Land Developments had marked off several hectares with orange plastic tape preparatory to construction of a big new housing complex for the town's projected population mushroom. The orange grid squares made a perfect landing field for the three chartered relief 'lighters to set down and offload thirty tons of assorted comestibles.

"Sign here," said the pilot, proffering a bill of receipt and a pencil to Rael Mandella, Jr. The supplies were passed by human chain to the storehouse of the new Mandella and Das Hot Snacks and Savories Emporium. The crates and boxes bore the stenciled names of their donors: the Little Sisters of Tharsis, Great Southern Railroads, the Argyre Separatists, the Friends of the Earth, the Poor Madeleines.

"What does this do to the strike fund?" asked Rael, Jr., counting off crates of cabbages, lentils, soap, and tea.

"Not having to expend so much on food, and with the successful introduction of the ration coupon scheme against cash payments, I'd say five months."

When the last sack was inside Rajandra Das and Kaan Mandella's warehouse, the doors were double-locked and a guard posted. The Company was not beyond acts of petty arson.

"Production figures?" asked Rael, Jr. It was growing increasingly difficult to maintain order in strike committee meetings now that his mother had turned the family home into a cantina.

"As I estimated." Harper Tew smiled with self-satisfaction. Before the strike he had been a subassistant production manager; somehow the Company had failed to purge the humanity out of him. "Steel production is down to a trickle, less than eight percent of total capacity. I estimate the Company should be approaching economic make-or-break point in about ten days."

At five o'clock in the morning of the sixteenth day of the strike Mr. E. T. Dharamjitsingh, a striking train engineer, his wife, Misa, and eight children were woken from hungry sleep by the unmistakable sound of rifle butts breaking down the front door. Four armed securitymen burst into the bedroom, MRCW muzzle first.

"Up dressed out," they ordered. "Five minutes."

As they fled down 12th Street clutching hastily snatched valuables, the Dharamjitsinghs saw an armored van draw up and a team of armed men start in on the buff-colored doors of every house on the street. Behind them they heard shouts, shots, and the sound of smashing furniture.

"Not this one!" a sergeant yelled to his men, eager to boot down a buff front door. "This one's loyal. Leave them be. Next door."

Two hundred striking families were evicted that morning. A further two hundred were unhomed the following dawn and the day after that two hundred more. The streets of Desolation Road were filled with unsteady ziggurats of furniture topped off with sob-eyed children. Families sheltered under improvised tents made from bed linen and plastic refuse sacks.

"This is bankrupting us," declared Mavda Arondello. "We can't afford to keep evacuating children and dependents out of Desolation Road to safe houses in the Grand Valley. The train fares are horrifying: at this rate the strike fund'll be empty in less than two months."

"Go talk to your aunt, Rael," said Santa Ekatrina, white as a ghost with rice-starch, flour, and selfless labor. Families were not just fed now, but also housed in the Mandella homestead, sleeping on the bedroom floors, fifteen to a room. "Taasmin'll help."

That same evening a sealed train steamed slowly through Desolation Road Station. From behind the counter of his trackside food bar, Rajandra Das noticed the locked doors, the shuttered windows, and the carriage plates that showed it to be made up of rolling stock from all across the northern hemisphere. The train ghosted across the switchover and into the Steeltown sidings. Securitymen cleared the freight yards and imposed a strict curfew, but Rajandra Das could see what those shut away behind window blinds could not see; the armed men in black and gold escorting grim-faced men with bags and suitcases into the newly vacated houses.

At six o'clock the sirens cried and a thousand and a half strikebreakers got out of their stolen beds and put on their working clothes and marched under heavy guard along the radial streets, along the Ring and past the mobs chanting "scab scab scab!" into the factory. Then smoke trickled from the cold chimneys and the rumble of dozing machinery shook the air.

"This is serious," Rael Mandella, Jr., told his strike committee. They had moved to the Bethlehem Ares Railroad/Hotel (recently renamed, more honestly, as had always been the intent, BAR/Hotel by painting out the periods) due to pressure of mouths in the Mandella family home.

Harper Tew estimated production would be back to sixty percent nominal within ten days.

"We'll miss economic break-point by fifty-two hours," he said. "Unless we can find a way to bust the strikebusters, Concordat is all folded up."

"We'll take care of the scabs," said Winston Karamatzov. A dark nimbus seemed to gather around him.

"At last the Action Group has something to report," said Ari Osnan.

"Quiet." Rael Mandella, Jr., locked his fingers and was suddenly terribly terribly empty. The vision, the spiritual wind, the mystic power which had driven him before it like a rail schooner, which had set a burning coal on his tongue, faltered and failed him. He was human and isolated, weak and fallible. Events had trapped him. He could not say no to the Action Group organizer and by saying yes he would become the creature of the mob. The dilemma had pinned him perfectly.

"Very well. The Action Group must do what is necessary."

That night the Economic Analogy Social Center burned down. Among the sifted ashes Dominic Frontera and his constables found the remains of eighteen strikebusters, a Company kindergarten teacher, the proprietor, his wife, and twin babies. That night a strikebuster was knifed fifteen times on the corner of Heartattack and Ring. By a miracle he survived to carry the scars to his grave. That night three of the strangers were abducted to an empty signalman's hut, where they were stripped, tied to chairs, and had their genitals snipped off with a pair of garden shears.

That night Rael Mandella, Jr., slipped home and confessed his doubts, his failings, his helplessness to his mother. Despite her absolution, he was not absolved.

Violence multiplied violence as night followed night. Atrocity piled upon atrocity. Although sympathetic to the strike, Dominic Frontera found he could no longer turn a blind eye to the madness and mayhem rocking his town. The Company had threatened direct action against the perpetrators though their securitymen held no authority beyond the wire. Dominic Frontera had promised the Company security chief immediate action though uncertain how he might deliver it. He went to visit Rael Mandella, Jr., in the bar/hotel.

Rael Mandella, Jr.'s personal bodyguard would not permit him to approach closer than three meters.

"This has to stop, Rael."

The strike leader shrugged.

"I'm sorry, but as soon as the scabs go it'll stop. It's their fault. If you want a peaceful resolution, go to the Company, not to me."

"I've just come from the Company. They said exactly the same thing but turned around. Don't play simpleton with me, Rael. I've known you since you were a boy. Now, I haven't got proof, or names, but the law is the law, whatever my sympathies, and as soon as I have the evidence, the law will be enforced."

"Are you threatening me?"

Dominic Frontera was only too aware of the futility of threatening with his handful of fat, friendly constables a man who dared the transplanetary empire of the Bethlehem Ares Corporation; nevertheless, he said, "Not threatening, Rael. Just advising."

By the end of the week all but three hundred strikebusters had left. Of those remaining, three hundred fifty-two would be remaining permanently in the town cemetery. The same weekend Concordat held its first martyr's funeral. Willy Goomeera, nine, single, separator plant operator, had been killed by a blow to the neck with a brick while attempting to close with, and knife, a scab separator plant operator from Maginot outside the Industry Is Ecstasy Infants' School. Willy was a martyr, the intended victim, turned victor, a monster. Willy was lowered into the earth in a funeral urn draped with the green and white Concordat banner while mother two sisters lover cried a river.

Rael Mandella, Jr., and his strike committee attended the funeral.

"So what about the production figures now?"

"Levelling off at about ten percent optimal. I calculate plant profitability to reach marginal in twenty-two days."

"Strike fund's only good for fifteen. Mavda, see if you can arrange cash aid from our supporters as well as the regular air drops. B.J., keep hammering at the other Transplanetaries, Bethlehem Ares's misfortune is their fortune. I think I'll have that word with my aunt to see if she can release us some free accommodation in church hostels. That should free some money from the rehousing budget."

The six conspirators bowed and went their ways and the first shovels of fine red dirt thumped down on Willy Goomeera's ceramic coffin.

49

Since becoming more than three quarters mortified, Inspiration Cadillac had grown correspondingly less tractable, thought Taasmin Mandella.

"Lady, you must not permit yourself to become involved in the Bethlehem Ares Steel dispute. You must not confuse the spiritual with the political."

Gray Lady and Iron Chamberlain were hurrying down the underground passage that led from the private rooms to the public chambers. At the word "political" Taasmin Mandella stopped and whispered into Inspiration Cadillac's ear, "Thou hypocrite. Tell me, if spirituality does not touch every aspect of life, including the political, how can it be truly spiritual? Tell me that." She strode off down the neon-lit corridor. Her prosthetic chamberlain's prostheses clicked and whirred as he bustled after her.

"Lady, with respect, you are letting yourself become emotionally clouded. Ignore the fact that Rael Mandella, Jr., is your nephew; you must make an objective decision on whether or not to permit the heretics . . . pardon, Lady, strikers, the use of our dormitory facilities. Once muddying subjectivities are removed from the issue, the decision becomes clear."

At the door to her audience chamber Taasmin Mandella halted again.

"Indeed it does, Chamberlain. I am pledging full spiritual, moral, and economic support for Concordat."

"Lady! This is madness! Consider the pilgrims, upon whose generosity we are dependent, will they not be dissuaded by this rash action? Consider the Poor Children, by siding with heret— strikers you are in effect denying their faith in the holiness of the Steeltown Shrine. You cannot abandon your faithful devotees, both pilgrims and Poor Children!"

"I know where those spurious prophecies about the factory came from, Chamberlain. I am not one third the fool you take me for."

In her audience chamber she sat enthroned, illuminated by a single shaft of sunlight caught by angled mirrors high in the dome. Around her feet were strewn flowers and tangles of metal swarf, before her a line of pilgrims with nine-pointed starbursts painted on their brows stretched into the gloom. A chilly piety leaked into the air.

"This place needs more light," Taasmin Mandella whispered to herself, picturing a Panarchic hand lifting the top off the Basilica like the lid on a jar of pickled gherkins to let the full light of day flood in.

"Pardon, madam?" asked an attendant Poor Child with a metal head.

—Poor Child, thought Taasmin Mandella. As the line of healings blessings prophecies petitions forgivenesses shuffled forward she found herself looking up at the reflections of the clouds caught in the roof mirrors and thought of her nephew fighting for the things her power had been given her to fight, out there in the desert sun, under the open sky and the eyes of the Panarch. Spirituality in action, faith in brown shoes, the knife edge of revolutionary love. She was right to pledge assistance to Concordat. For all their human sins, they upheld humanity, life, and freedom before the Company's crushing sterility, machine regimentation, and annihilation.

"Lady, the Old Women of Chernowa." A gaggle of black-shawled gap-toothed grandmothers bowed amid the flowers and swarf. They carried an ugly wooden effigy of a small child. Clumsily carved, ineptly painted, it wore an expression as if a sharp implement were being inserted into its backside. "They bring a petition, madam." The attendant bowed respectfully and gestured for the Old Women of Chernowa to approach.

"What is your petition?" Sun glinted on clear cold water, leaves cast dappled shadows in leisurely shade; Taasmin Mandella hardly heard their pleading voices.

". . . take away our sons and our sons' sons they take away our freedom, our nobility, they take all we have and give it back to us in dribs and drabs; this they call 'industrial feudalism,' and for this we are meant to thank them. . . ."

"Stop. You are from Steeltown?"

The oldest and most venerable of grandmothers cringed low in dread.

"Stand up, all of you." Sunshine and shade and clear cold water evaporated in the light of the higher sun. "You are from"—she searched her memory, cursing herself for her inattention—"Chernowa in New Merionedd?"

"That is so, madam."

"And you are oppressed by the Company . . . strikers, I take it?"

The youngest grandmother pushed to the front of the gaggle.

"Lady, they have cut off the food from our bellies and the water from our lips, the light from our eyes and the power from our fingertips, they have driven us out of our homes so that we must either leave our families, or else live like animals in rude huts of plastic and card! Gray Lady, we petition you, help us! Pray for us, intercede for us, bring the cries of the oppressed to the ears of the Panarch, let him shine his favor upon us, bless us . . ."

"Enough." The effusive woman crept back to her place, shamefaced at her outburst. "What is that you have with you?" Eldest Grandmother held up the ugly statue.

"This is our icon, the Bryghte Chylde of Chernowa, who by the intervention of the Blessed Lady saved our town from destruction by a falling space-elevator shuttle through summoning a mystic wind and blowing the danger away."

Taasmin Mandella had heard of the miracle of Chernowa. The town had been saved but shuttle and all two hundred and fifty-six aboard had been vaporized. A better class of miracle would have saved both, she thought. And it was an exceptionally ugly statue.

"Bring it here." Taasmin Mandella stretched out her left hand toward the icon. Pulses of light flowed up the circuitry in her dress and gathered around her left wrist. Her halo brightened to such an intensity that it threw shadows into the farthest recesses of the audience hall. She felt a wave of innocence break over her: the inner symphony resumed in her heart and she was free and forgiven. Metal streamers like ropes of printed circuits flowed from her hand and wrapped the Bryghte Chylde of Chernowa in a web of electronics. The congregation of the faithful watched in utter awe as the coarse wooden skin of the icon was overlain by a film of circuits. Electricity sparked along its limbs, fusion-light glowed in its eyes, and from its lips issued a stream of machine-code gibberish.

The transubstantiation of wood to machine was complete. Pilgrims fell to their knees. Some fled the basilica in fear. The Old Women of Chernowa made to bow, but Taasmin Mandella stopped them.

"Take this and show it to my nephew. It's the answer he's been waiting for. Take him my blessing too: God is on your side. You are not property." A surge of holy mischief made Taasmin Mandella raise her left fist in a clenched-fist Concordat salute. She stood so that everyone might see the Gray Lady's Solidarity, then swirled her robes and strode from the dais.

"There will be no further audiences today," she shouted to her bionic majordomo. She watched her fluster in confusion, then hurryscurry to tell Inspiration Cadillac. She did not care. God had broken through, war was declared, she had made a free act of conscience. War was declared and she was happy happy happy.

"And I am not property either," she told her reflection in the clear cold water of her garden pool.

50

Anyone presenting a Concordat card to either of the proprietors of the Mandella and Das Hot Snacks and Savories Emporium was entitled to eat freely of the wonderland of cooking sausages, grilling kebabs, chick-pea fritters frying merrily in the deep fryer and assorted bhajis, samosas, pakoras, and tiddy-hoppers. This was a gesture of filial solidarity on the part of the Mandella half of the Hot Snacks and Savories Emporium; it was having a ruinous effect on the enterprise's profitability, but the Mandella half knew the Das half had sackfuls of golden dollars salted away from his days, now sadly remembered, as town handyman, freebooter, goondah, and bum which would tide the emporium over the Concordat crisis.

The Hot Snacks and Savories Emporium was of remarkable, even unique, construction. The front half came from an aged riksha which had laid for three years behind Ed's Shed, the back half was adapted from a disused 'lighter galley augmented with fold-down bar seats, piped music, gaily colored paper lanterns, and a plethora of holy icons, medals, and paper prayer tickets. Each morning before the first light touched his window the Das half of the partnership would kick the riksha half of the emporium into asthmatic life and drive the ungainly contraption down the narrow alleys, dodging chickens, goats, llamas, children, trucks until he found a good place to park. Almost invariably this was across the street from the Pentecost Sisters' General Merchandise Store so that Rajandra Das could smile charmingly to them when they came to open the store at eight minutes of eight and they, in turn, could invite him in for mint tea at the hottest time of the day. By the time the Mandella half of the partnership arrived (the half with the needle-sharp business acumen, the genetic bequest of his rationalist father) there would be sausages frying and biggins of mint tea or coffee venting perfume into the air and a line as long as a free breakfast clutching their Concordat cards.

On the sixty-sixth day of the strike Rajandra Das was wrapping a sausage as long as his forearm to hand to a striker whose face he recognized vaguely when he froze in mid-wrap.

"R.D.," said the Mandella half. "What you seen?"

Rajandra Das automatically handed the sausage to the striker.

"It's him."

"Him?" Kaan Mandella looked but saw only a dark-haired middle-aged man watching from the end of the street.

"He had the gall to come back, after what he did. . . ." Kaan Mandella looked again but the figure was gone.

"Who was he?"

Rajandra Das did not say but he maintained a vengeful tightness all day that was most uncharacteristic. When the Hot Shacks and Savories Emporium was safely parked for the night, Rajandra Das paid a call on Mr. Jericho.

"He's back," he said, and when Mr. Jericho learned who was back, he sent Rajandra Das to gather up all the Founder Members, with the exception of Dominic Frontera, and while Rajandra Das was gathering up all the Founder Members he went to the drawer where he kept his needle-pistol and took it out of its silk wrapping.

At twenty forty-five Mikal Margolis, chief of security for the Desolation Road project, was going to have a bath in his managerial apartment. The preliminary undercover survey of Desolation Road was complete, the Company could move against Concordat at any time and crush it, it had been a hard day and a long hot bath was what he needed. He opened the door and saw the pointing end of an antique bone-handled needle-pistol.

"Don't slam the door," said a voice he had forgotten. "I can shoot you dead through it if I have to. Now, please come with me."

As Mikal Margolis was redressing, Mr. Jericho noticed the Company uniform.

"I didn't know that."

"Well, at least there's something you don't know. Chief of Project Security, no less."

Mr. Jericho said nothing but added a further crime to the charge sheet in his mind. He led his prisoner by sideways and byways to the perimeter wire. A thread of pure electric tension connected the nose of the needle-pistol to the nape of Mikal Margolis's neck.

"Under here," said Mr. Jericho, indicating an open culvert hatch Mikal Margolis had not even known existed.

"How did you find me?" asked the prisoner as the two men splashed through the sewage of Steeltown.

"Damantine disciplines, though that won't mean anything to you."

But it did, and Mikal Margolis suddenly knew a lot about Mr. Jericho. And he also knew that for all his Freelancer-trained senses, he could not escape from his captor. So he let him lead him out of Steeltown and into Desolation Road.

The kangaroo court was convened in Rajandra Das's storeroom amid crates of chick peas donated to Concordat by the Association of Meridian Street Traders. Looking around him, Mikal Margolis recognized the Mandellas, the Gallacelli brothers, the Stalins, Genevieve Tenebrae holding the globe containing her husband's ghost, even the Blue Mountains father and daughter were there. He shivered. It was like being tried by a parliament of ghosts. Then he saw Persis Tatterdemalion.

"Persis, what is this? Tell me." She looked away from him. Mr. Jericho read a formal charge. He then asked the defendant how he pleaded.

"Tell me, is Mother dead then?" the defendant asked.

"She is," said Rael Mandella, Sr.

"That's good. I would not have liked for her to see this."

"What is your plea?" asked Mr. Jericho.

"Guilty as charged."

And all the jurors agreed. All of them. Even Persis. Even the ghost.

"You know what to do then," said Mr. Jericho, and for the first time Mikal Margolis saw the rope. As he was led up to the makeshift scaffold (a pair of storestepladders), he felt neither rage nor hatred but only an overwhelming sense of disgust that the man who had taken on the Bethlehem Ares Corporation and won them to him should meet such an ignominious end. The noose was placed over his neck.

"Don't you feel any remorse at all?" asked Genevieve Tenebrae, a twisted, pale thing, a hermetic troglodyte. "Don't you feel anything for poor Gaston?"

Poor Gaston, was it? Philandering bum.

"I was a kid then," he said. "Crazy, mixed up. These things happen." He looked at Persis Tatterdemalion and held out his hands. "Look, Persis. No trembling now." The vigilantes bound those steady hands and then argued over what consignatory words to use over the condemned's soul. Mikal Margolis wavered at the top of the stepladders and felt his fury grow. He could not accept that he must die so stupidly.

"Have you quite finished?" he shouted.

"Yes, thank you," said Mr. Jericho. "Drop him."

Rajandra Das kicked the stepladder from under Mikal Margolis. Mikal Margolis felt a fist of iron try to tear his head from his body, then there was a snap (—My neck, my neck!) . . . and he thumped onto the straw.

"Goddamn cheap rope!" someone shouted. Mikal Margolis rolled into a stand and charged head down at the lightswitch. The room was plunged into blackness and shouting just as one of Mr. Jericho's needles took the skin off his cheek. Mikal Margolis blundered out into the street and zigzagged chicken-fashion toward the wire gates of Steeltown.

"Help, help, murder!" he roared. Securitymen piled out of their portable cabins and menaced the street with their gun muzzles. Mr. Jericho, taking careful aim with his needle-pistol, put his weapon up.

"Out of range. Sorry. Too much cover."

"The bastard got away!" wept Genevieve Tenebrae.

"Second time!" said Rajandra Das, watching the guards swing wide the gates to admit the escapee.

"There won't be a third either," said Mr. Jericho. No one was quite sure what he meant.

51

The meaning of Mr. Jericho's comment became clear on Tuesday 12th November, when the Bethlehem Ares Corporation crushed Concordat.

It was a very efficient operation, no less than would be expected of the Bethlehem Ares Corporation. They knew exactly where to go and whom to take. They entered houses, smashed through barricaded rooms, raided hotels, bars, offices. The wire could not contain them, they slammed through the streets of Desolation Road in their black and gold armored vans. Bursts of MRCW fire ripped the air. Dominic Frontera and his policemen were helpless before them. They were disarmed by the black and gold raiders and locked in their own town jail. Others who tried to obstruct them were treated less gently. Some were shot in kneecap or elbow. The fortunate few had only their fingers mashed under MRCW butts. Men were dragged from hotels and safehouses and made to crouch against slogan-clad walls, hands behind heads, while junior managers who drank idiotic drinks made from bananas and tapioca picked out line organizers and section reps. Some were taken away in the black and gold vans. Some were released. Some particular troublemakers were simply taken behind those walls and shot through the eye. The daughters wives lovers mothers who had chosen to remain howled in impotent fury. Company security smashed its way into the Tatterdemalion Bar/Hotel Annex and arrested three of the five strike committee members and two innocent pilgrims just to make up the numbers. The prisoners were taken into the back of the bar and shot among the beer barrels and crates. The securitymen sprinkled kerosene on the floor and burned the hotel annex behind them.

In the shantytown of Concorde that had sprung up beside the wire to house the evicted from Steeltown, black and gold securitymen sloshed riksha fuel over the plastic and cardboard shacks and ignited them. Fire swept through the township faster than the citizens could run from it. Within minutes the community of Concorde had been reduced to ashes.

Security respected neither boundary nor conscience. Sweeping protesting Poor Children aside, they emptied the Faith City dormitories and searched the lines of faces for the features on their arrest sheets. The sanctuary of the Basilica of the Gray Lady was desecrated by a charge of gun-toting securitymen, but by the time Taasmin Mandella arrived from her meditations the Bethlehem Ares Corporation had swept through and passed like a typhoon, leaving a trail of devastation and mayhem.

The Company rampaged through Desolation Road, indulging any petty whim that took it. The civil authorities were powerless to assist. It became evident that there was a secondary, more sinister aspect to the violence. The homes and businesses of the founder members of Desolation Road were singled out for attack. As the smoke went up from the bar/hotel annex, the offices of Gallacelli & Mandella developments were destroyed by a colossal explosion. Just around the bend in the alley the Mandella and Das Hot Snacks and Savories Emporium was broken into pieces before the proprietors' eyes.

"Hope you're satisfied!" shouted the Das half of the partnership. "I hope you're goddamn satisfied!" Both partners gave clenched-fist Concordat salutes to the guards' retreating backs.

"We is not property!" cried Rajandra Das. The securitymen came back and beat both of them to the ground with their weapons.

Five guards burst into the Mandella hacienda on the pretext of searching for Rael, Jr., and turned the place upside down.

"Where is he?" they demanded of the saintly Santa Ekatrina, MRCW muzzle to her temple.

"Not at home," she said. Out of frustration and petty

vengeance they slaughtered every animal in the farmyard. They smashed every stick of furniture, overturned the pots of lentils and stew in the kitchen, destroyed the house solar collector lozenge, and made to break apart Eva Mandella's tapestry loom.

"I wouldn't touch that if I were you," said Rael Mandella, Sr., with the deadly calm a hunting rifle in the hand affords. The securitymen shrugged (old fool, old stupid man) and raised their MRCW butts. Rael Mandella let out a howl of slaughtered animals overturned pots smashed solar collector and threw himself between the guards and the loom. An MRCW missile blew his chest away and threw him across the tapestry frame, where his blood stained the half-done history melodramatic red.

In the smoke and blood and stench of burning flesh the small polite cough almost went unheard, but it was just enough to make the murderers turn around. Before them stood Limaal Mandella. In his hand Mr. Jericho's needle-pistol. On his face a terrible terrible smile. Before fingers could touch firing studs they were all dead, a needle square between every pair of eyes, fired with the matchless speed and accuracy of the Greatest Snooker Player the Universe Had Ever Known.

Even as his grandfather lay sprawled and dead across his grandmother's loom and his father stood terrible and triumphant by his weeping mother with an Exalted Family needle-pistol cradled in his hand: even as all this came to pass, Rael Mandella, Jr., in the company of Ed, Severiano and Batisto Gallacelli were stealing a Bethlehem Ares Steel cargo 'lighter from the field behind Steeltown.

Preflight checks completed, Severiano and Batisto brought the fans up to speed and readied to dump ballast.

"Child of Grace," muttered Ed Gallacelli. Battle armored securitymen advanced across the field toward the Wild Geese. Anxious glances were exchanged across the command board. Something must be done, but what and by whom was uncertain. Ed Gallacelli looked from face to face.

"All right," he said. "I'll get rid of them." Before any word of protest could be voiced he had slipped out of the crew door onto the concrete.

"By the way," he shouted, voice barely audible over the growing roar of the engines, "it was me all along! Me! I was your father!" Then with a grin to the control cabin he waved farewell and ran toward the approaching guards. He fished his commodious pockets.

"Here, catch this!" He threw a mechanical dove into the air and it soared toward the Company men, singing its subsonic song. When he saw the securitymen double up vomiting and migraine-ridden he cock-a-doodle-dooed his inventiveness, threw up his arms, and released a swarm of robot bees into the air. Armed with laser stings, his tiny inventions swarmed over the crippled securitymen until one of their number with greater presence of mind than his comrades downed both sonic dove and killer bees with hypersonic bursts from his MRCW.

"Try this on for size," shouted Ed Gallacelli. He heard the 'lighter engines roar into takeoff and he felt suddenly happy for no reason that he could discern. From his sleeves issued a stream of dense black smoke. Before the cloud enveloped him he glanced over his shoulder to see the airship bank up and away from Steeltown, heading north.

They were gone.

He was glad.

Slipping heat-goggles over his eyes, Ed Gallacelli closed with the securitymen and ran around, kicking asses and balls in utter invisibility until an unscheduled wind blew and blew his smokescreen over the horizon.

"Oh, dear," said Ed Gallacelli sheepishly. "I surrender." He raised his arms. Instantly fingers were seen to tighten on MRCW firing studs. "Oops. Sorry." He gave a clenched fist salute. "Long live Concordat. Amen!" He began to laugh and laugh and laugh and laugh because the smart securityman had taken off his helmet and it was Mikal Margolis and he should have known all along and wasn't it the best joke of all, better than the tricks he'd kept hidden up his sleeve and then the squad commander gave an order and twelve laser beams spat out and bathed him in flames and did not stop firing until the ashes began to blow away on the treacherous wind.

52

After the battle of Yellow Ford, Arnie Tenebrae built a pyramid of heads outside her command tent. The Parliamentarians had been routed, fleeing across rice paddies shedding weapons, helmets, uniforms, wounded in their panic to escape the tiger-painted demons loping tirelessly in pursuit. She had ordered her death's head commandos to decapitate any dead or wounded and bring the heads to her. The pyramid was as tall as Arnie Tenebrae. She looked at the grinning heads of plowboys, riksha mechanics, 'lighter pilots, tin miners, college students, insurance salespersons, and a certain unclean madfire blazed up in her. That night she painted her face in the semblance of the deathbird and as she injected herself with morphine from the medical supplies the deathbird of the dark places rose before her, summoning, and told her in shrieks like those of a tortured man that she was the Avatar, the embodiment of the Cosmic Principle; Vastator, the Destroyer, Leveler of Worlds, Slayer of Gods, she who cannot be Predicted.

Yellow Ford, Hill 27, Elahanua's Ferry, Harper's Barn: the wings of the deathbird scattered the Parliamentarians like chaff.

"Boys against men," she told her commanders. "Hundreds to one they outnumber us, yet we reap them like rice!"

She knew her captains feared her. They were right to do so. She was mad, she sought bodies to throw on the altar of destruction, she thought she was a god, a demon, a dark angel. They were right to think these things about her. They were true. Victory followed victory.

"Our field inducer weapon systems makes us invincible," she declared to her staff after the Battle of Sakamoto Junction. Her captains and lieutenants knew that she meant that it was Arnie Tenebrae, Vastator, that made them invincible. They began to fear that she was right about that too.

Then at the battle of Tetsenok the Parliamentarians somehow turned the Whole Earth Army Tactical Group advance into a retreat. Arnie Tenebrae was not surprised. She had smelled defeat on the wind that morning.

"There is someone out there who wants me," she said. Doubt began to infest her command, doubt and the wavering of commitment. Arnie Tenebrae did not accept this doubt. How could there be doubt in the living presence of the personification of the Power Cosmic?

Yet at the next staff meeting Lieutenant Lim Chung asked, "Why are we fighting if we don't gain anything?"

Arnie Tenebrae did not feel the need to answer. Later she had Lieutenant Lim Chung taken far out into the forest, stripped, spreadeagled between two trees, and left to the elements and time.

After the battle of Hill 66, when the Parliamentarians overran the Whole Earth Army's entrenched positions despite the latters' invincible field-inducer weapon systems and invisibility fields, a whey-faced farmboy with a truce flag on his back came blundering into the Tactical Group rearguard command headquarters. Arnie Tenebrae listened patiently to the Parliamentarian's terms of surrender. Then she asked two questions.

"What is your name?"

"Trooper MacNaughton Bellewe, No. 703286543."

"Who is your chief of staff?"

"Marshall Quinsana, ma'am. Marshall Marya Quinsana."

Marya Quinsana. Well well well.

Arnie Tenebrae did not have her rejection terms sent back on Trooper MacNaughton Bellewe's flayed skin as she had intended. The boy was released alive and whole at the edge of the battle zone with a salutation from general to general in his hand and a string of shrunken heads tied to his belt.

After Hill 66 Arnie Tenebrae was quiet and dangerous. So another Cosmic Principle had entered the drama. The Avatar of the Avenger. Marvelous how all human strife and conflict was a symbolic enactment of loftier struggles between the Powers Cosmic so that every moment of the present was merely a fragment of the past repeating itself over and over again. Now the stage was set, the Götterdämmerung could fall, the Last Trump Blow and it would be her against Marya Quinsana: Vastator and Avenger as it always had been and always would be.

Donohue's Ridge, Dharmstadt, Red Bridge: three crushing defeats in as many months. Arnie Tenebrae spent much time alone in her tent cross-legged on the floor meditating upon herself. Lieutenants and captains hurried about, little mice busy with reports of surrender, massacre, annihilation. They meant nothing. Human puppets must jig to the drums of the gods. Arnie Tenebrae's hands fluttered on the dirt floor—drumdrumdrumdrum. She and Marya Quinsana, they were the drummer girls, drumdrumdrum.

She called all her remaining forces to her, less than two regular divisions, and withdrew them to the heart of the haunted Forest of Chryse to prepare for the final conflict.

53

There was a wall. Built of old gray stone, mortarless, high as a man's waist, it did not look very important. But it was important. As with all walls, it was what was on either side of it that gave the wall meaning; whether it was a wall that shut out or a wall that shut in or a wall that merely separated. On one side of the wall was a field of potatoes, morning misty, gray, and cold as an old potato. In this field stood Bethlehem Ares Steel Transport Dirigible BA 3627S *Eastern Enlighten-*

ment, powered down, empty, hatches open, cold fog swirling around its landing pods and into its open hatches. On the other side of the wall stood the Forest of Chryse, the Ladywood, oldest of all the world's young places, where St. Catherine herself planted the Tree of World's Beginning with her steel manipulators. The trees pressed close to the wall, leaning over the perimeter, dense and dark as the stones. Their branches reached toward the open potato field, in certain places their roots had tumbled sections of the old dry stone wall, yet the boundary persisted, for the boundary between forest and field was older than the wall that commemorated it. It was an exclusive wall, built to keep the world out of the forest rather than the forest out of the world.

That was to prove to be important to the three men with backpacks threading through the outmost fringe of trees. Their first footfalls on the tree side of the wall made them men without state or station; exiles. They heard their explosive devices destroy the lighter, the blast oddly muffled by the trees, and they were glad, for now they could not go home again. The smoke of the burning rose from the potato field like an indictment of guilt.

In their first hours they found many signs of the passing hand of man: small heaps of gray wood-ash, animal skins half gone to rot and leather, an unsightly litter of tin cans rusting to forest brown, but as their course drew them away from the wall toward the heartwoods the touches of humanity grew fewer. Here the mist seemed to defy the sun, lingering in damp dells and hollows, and even the sun itself seemed remote and impotent beyond the ceiling of leaves. The forest clung to itself, absorbed in a great root-dreaming, and the three men walked warily between the world-old trees. Here no bird sang, no vixen yelped, no jaguar mauled, no wombat grunted: not even the voices of the men disturbed the dreaming.

The exiles camped that night under huge beech trees older than the memories of any man. The moonring glittered incredibly high and remote in the leaf-patterned sky, and the campfire seemed very small and foolhardy; drawing the dark things out of the woods to hover around the edge of the darkness. Rael Mandella, Jr., sat watch and held the darkness at fire-length by reading extracts from the books his father had given him before the escape.

"Take them," he'd said. "They're for you, do with them what you will. Read them, sell them, burn then, wipe your ass with them, they're for you. For all useless years. I give them back to you."

Page after page was filled with arcane mathematical propositions written in his father's beautiful hand. They were his transpositions of Dr. Alimantando's workbooks, his life's labor. They meant nothing to Rael, Jr. He stowed them in his pack and sat staring into the dark until Sevriano Gallacelli relieved him.

That night the exiles dreamed an un-dream, an anti-dream of emptying in which the symbols and allegories of the dreaming mind were drained away, leaving only exhausting vacant blackness, like empty eye sockets.

The next morning the three men marched through a pavilion of light held aloft by pillars of oak. Shafts of green sunlight shone through the canopy of leaves, rippling and dappling like green river water as the branches moved in the wind, but not one rustle of the great arboreal commotion reached the forest floor. Even the exiles' trudging footfalls were swallowed up by the thick soft leafmold. In the afternoon Sevriano Gallacelli discovered a crashed reconnaissance helicopter impaled on a tree. Its crew lolled from open hatches, dead so long their eyes had been picked out by silent magpies and green moss had grown on their tongues. A small hole, thin and straight as a pencil, had been melted through canopy, pilot, and main engine.

"Lasers," said Sevriano Gallacelli. Sufficient epitaph pronounced upon the old tragedy, the three men pushed on toward the heartwoods. Until then no word had been spoken that day. In the successive hours they came upon many memories of war and outrage: streamers of ripped parachute silk waving gently from the branches of a stand of elms; a combat-fatigued skeleton with a fern growing out of its grin; charred circles in the trampled leafmold of deepwood clearings; bodies perched in the forks of branches, peculiar weapons propped at the ready. Toward evening they came upon the grimmest *momento mori*: at a path's crossing, the forked limb of a tree thrust into the earth, impaled upon its tines, human heads, eyesockets empty, lips torn away by weasels, skin peeled into shreds and tatters.

In the night the trees drew close around the campfire and again drained the exiles dry of dreams.

All the next morning they traveled through a landscape shattered by war. A great battle had been fought here. Trees were blasted into white splinters, the earth was torn and ripped into craters and foxholes. The land was heavy with fresh memories of atrocity: a burned-out one-man airbike, no sign of the one man, a framed photograph of a handsome woman with "All my love, Jeanelle" written in the bottom left corner, a cleared swath of forest where a two-man fighter had crashed, plowing up a furrow of muck and greenery. Rael Mandella, Jr., picked up the photograph of the handsome woman and placed it in his breast pocket. He felt that he needed a friend.

Yet even in the middle of destruction the Ladywood was still strong. As if trying to exorcise evil remembrances, ropes of woodbine and clematis were reaching to cover the derelict war machines, and fresh bracken had sprung up to conceal the fallen beneath a green coiled shroud. Batisto Gallacelli found an operable military radio beside a dead radio operator. The boy was no more than nine years old. The three men ate their lunch to the accompaniment of the Jimmy Wong show. The sun shone down, the late dew pinpricked the grass, and an enormous peace flowed out of the east across the deserted battlefield.

Rael Mandella, Jr., left the photograph of the handsome woman with the dead radio operator. He looked as if he needed a friend the more.

Early in the afternoon they passed from the battle-stained lands into the secret heartwoods of Chryse. Here stupendous redwoods rose one hundred two hundred three hundred meters into the sky, a city of soft red towers and wide needle-strewn boulevards. The three travelers should have been joyful so close to the heartwood and the legendary Tree of World's Beginning, so far from the war of the Powers, but a brooding sense of horror mounted minute upon minute, step upon step. Among the grandeur of the heartwoods it felt like a poison, a poison that had been drawn out of the air into the soil and the trees and communicated through the dream-draining nights into the exiles. They began to tread cautiously, eyes and ears alert, mistrustful as cats. They could not have said why. The pulse of an aircraft engine passing far to the east had them running shrieking for shelter amid the root buttresses of the redwoods. Drop by drop their humanity was being drained from them, drop by drop the forest was filling them up with its spirit, its horrifying, poisoned, blasted, inhuman spirit. They broke into a trot, a run, they did not know why they ran, or where, there was no pursuing enemy save the darkness of their hearts inside them. They ran from the fear, they ran from the horror, plunging heedless through bramble and thorn, stream and dike, running running running to be free from the horror, but they could not escape it for they were the horror.

Plunging through an enclosing ring of stupendous, redwoods, they entered a circular clearing at the center of which stood the mightiest tree of all, the FatherTree, head and shoulders taller than its strongest children. Branches swayed and swished in the wind cloud-high above them, beams of stained-glass light reached down through needles and lit the forest floor. The three men stood beneath the Tree of World's Beginning and looked up into the moving branches with unalloyed awe and joy. The holiness of that place had touched their buried humanity and released them from the horror. The branches moved and passed blessing over them.

A figure in white stood among the roots of the tree, face lifted to the sun, a figure turning slowly, ecstatically, illuminated in a column of light. In its holy revolving the figure glimpsed the three spell-caught men.

"Oh, hello," said the figure in white, stepping out of the light to greet them, no longer a mystical angel but a middle-aged man in soiled samite. "What the hell kept you?"

54

His name was Jean-Michel Gastineau, "also known as the Amazing Scorn, Mutant Master of Scintillating Sarcasm and Rapid Repartee, one-time Most Sarcastic Man in the World," and he loved to talk. The three exiles were content for him to do so as he busied himself with frying eggs and mushrooms in his small lean-to amid the root buttresses.

"Used to be something of a celebrity, years back, when the world was younger, was in a traveling show; you know, 'Wonders of Earth and Heaven,' 'The Greatest Show on Earth,' all that; there was me (The Amazing Scorn), Leopold Lenz, the dwarf sword-swallower, one meter ten tall, given to swallowing one meter fifty swords; Tanqueray Bob the were-wolf, a couple of others whose names I can't remember, the usual stuff anyway. Used to demonstrate how my sarcasm could kill cockroaches and peel paint off walls, pretty trivial stuff, till one day this poet fellow, big big guy, big as a beer tun, with a red beard, he comes and says he is the Greatest Satirist the World's Ever Known, and I says, no way, son, I was born with the gift of sarcasm: you ever hear of some folks are born with the power of command in their voices so no one can resist them? Well, I had like the power of sarcasm and satire; why, did you know that at age two, the age kids say things to make each other blub, when I said things they made little cuts on them? Thought not. Anyway, there was to be this big duel of sarcasm in a fine and fancy hotel . . . half the district turned out and well, to cut a long story short, which has always been my problem, I got a teeny bit carried away. Soon as I started on this poet guy these big long rips opened up all over his skin and the blood came pouring out, I shoulda stopped then, I shoulda, but I couldn't, the sarcasm had hold of me, I kept going and everyone in the audience starts bleeding and crying and tearing their hair out and the big guy, well, he just had one big coronary and dropped dead, right there. Well, that was the end of that, but what I didn't know was that this guy was some kind of local hero, a pretty big man in more than the obvious sense, and shoot, they came after me with guns and dogs and hawks and hunting pumas and, well, I was pretty shook up, I just ran and ran and ran and ended up here.

"I said to myself, Jean-Michel Gastineau, you're too dangerous to live among folks, if that tongue of yours ever gets out of control again folks are going to die, so I vowed there would be no more Amazing Scorn, Mutant Master of Scintillating Sarcasm and Rapid Repartee; I would see out my days as a lonely hermit, harming no one, shunning the company of my fellow humans. You see, the trees here they can't feel sarcasm. Their perceptions is too deep to be hurt by mere words. Anyhows, like youse I was drawn here to the heartwood, the Tree of World's Beginning. Those days the Ladywood was a friendly place, there was birds and wallabies and butterflies and all, not like now, not since the soldiers come: who'da thought it, pitched battles in Chryse Wood? Not Jean-Michel Gastineau: tell you this, since theyse come, the place has got dark. You know what I mean, youse seen it closer than I; the forest has this kind of like . . . mind, all those roots and branches intertwining and all that, connections and connectivity, so I was told, each tree is like an element in the network; that big scrap over Bellweather way last month ripped up a lot of higher cognitive levels: things is back to the deep dreamtime again. Anyhows, I'm getting off the subject."

The little man served mushroom omelette and maté.

"Make the tea myself from herbs and roots. Gets you going like a goat, it does. Anyhows . . . now, you eat, I'll talk. . . . I was brought here to the Tree of World's Beginning and the Blessed Lady came to me . . . word of honor, St. Catherine herself, beautiful she was, shimmering white and her face . . . like I don't know what it was. Better than an angel. Anyhows, she says to me, 'Jean-Michel Gastineau, I've a job for you. You mind my forest for me and I'll forgive you what happened in that town. The forest needs someone to be looking after it, mind it, tend it, care for it, love it even.

You'll have the power of knowing everything that happens in Chryse (that's how I knew you guys were coming; shame about that 'lighter) and you'll have command of all the Genesis zones, the hatcheries; that's where the angels are born from, under the roots of the trees; and the machines too . . . there are still a lot of them left about from the manforming days; until such a time as you're called to a higher mission, which you will be someday.' So, here Jean-Michel Gastineau is and here Jean-Michel Gastineau stays. It's a good life if you like fresh air and the like; I haven't breathed a word of sarcasm in five years. Imagine that. But these days, well, the place is going dark. I'll explain that now."

He kicked his fire of redwood cones. Sparks fled up the chimney into the gathering darkness.

"This here tree" (he patted the root ridge on which he sat) "he's called *Sequoia Sempervirens*—means 'Everliving' in old old language, and that's what he is . . . he was planted here first day of the manforming by St. Catherine herself and the forest grew up around him. But Great Father Tree, he's the oldest and the wisest. Oh, yes, wise and with a very long memory. Trees are alive, and aware, they know, you know, they feel, they think. You have any non-dreams out there? Sure you did; that's the forest learning about you, absorbing your memories to add to the great memory of Father Tree here. But they've also been absorbing all the fear and hate and shit and spunk that's been going on out there and it's made the forest dark and scary and not a little dangerous. What worries me is that it's poisoning the trees—not like slopping weedkiller on the roots, anything like that, but poisoning the soul of the place. Me and the machines can do only so much and there's whole areas of woodland dying and new growth coming up stunted and deformed. That's bad. That scares me, because if it keeps happening, the world's soul's gone.

"Sorry to go on so long. Don't get the chance to talk much. So, old Jean-Michel Gastineau make your head spin? Too much philosophy? Sure you'd like some sleep now; usually turn in about this time myself. By the by, you might have some funny dreams tonight, don't worry, it's only the Big Tree up there feeling you out, trying to communicate with you."

They slept around a charcoal brazier that night. The red glow pushed back the night and the exiles' eyes rolled and

flickered with the rapid movements of human dreaming. Rael
Mandella, Jr., dreamed he woke and the waking dream carried
him out of the little wooden house among the roots into the
night. A sense of holiness overcame him and he stood for a
long time with his face lifted to the sky, turning round and
round and round. When he grew dizzy with his turning-
turningturning so that the stars spun and the boles of the redwoods seemed to tumble upon him like matchsticks, Rael
Mandella, Jr., sank to the ground and pressed his cheek to the
cold damp soil. For a long time he remained thus and then he
dreamed he heard a voice humming a tune. He raised his head
and saw Santa Ekatrina standing in a shaft of skylight.

"Are you a ghost?" he asked, and in his dream his mother
replied, "A ghost, yes, but not dead. There are living ghosts as
well as dead ones." Then his father stepped out of the
darkness.

"What do you think you're doing here?" Limaal Mandella
asked irritably.

Rael Mandella, Jr., opened his mouth to speak but his
words had been stolen by night birds.

"Answer your father," said Santa Ekatrina.

"You're running away, aren't you?" accused Limaal Mandella. "Don't try and bluff me, son. I know what it's all about.
You can't face up to failure and you're running away."

Rael, Jr., readied to shout back that hadn't he, Limaal
Mandella, the Greatest Snooker Player the Universe Had Ever
Known, acted no better when he fled to Desolation Road,
when one by one familiar figures emerged from the moonring
shadows and joined his parents. They wore the faces of his life:
his workmates from Shift C at the foundry, the girls he had
danced with at the Saturday night socials, friends from school,
faces of Belladonna; sharks, hustlers, whores, agents, Glen
Miller with his trombone under his arm; they looked down at
him kneeling on the soft brown needle duff with infinite pity.

"What are you going to do," they said. "What are you
going to do?"

"You brought it all down on yourself," said his own
brother, covered in blue bruises. "Are you Mandella enough to
hold it?"

"You were responsible," said his mother.

"You still are responsible," said his father, failure, exile, coward.

"If only I hadn't run out of tricks!" said Ed Gallacelli, resurrected from ashes, his tongue glowing like embers.

"Stop stop stop stop!" cried Rael Mandella, Jr. "Stop the dream! I want to wake up!"

And he did wake up and found himself alone in the holy place among the trees. The moonring twinkled on high, wind whispered in the branches, and the air was still, sweet, and godly. In a shaft of starshine the light curdled, thickened, and took on solid human form. A tall, moustachioed man in a long gray coat sat himself down on the tree root next to Rael, Jr.

"Fine night," he said, searching through his multitudinous pockets for his pipe. "Fine night." He located the pipe, charged it, lit it, and took a few meditative puffs.

"You've got to go back, you know."

"No more dreams," whispered Rael, Jr. "No more ghosts."

"Dreams? The Xanthic mystagogues believe that existence ended on the third day and that our world is only the dream of the second night," said the gray stranger. "Ghosts? Pah. We are the most substantial things in the world, the foundations of the present. We are memories." His pipe made a little red glow-worm dot on the night. "Mnemologues. We are the things that make up a life; only here, in this one place, do we have body and substance. We are the dreams of the trees. Do you know what this tree is? Of course you do, it's the Tree of World's Beginning. But it is also the Tree of World's End, for every beginning must have an end. You've unfinished business in my town, Rael, and until you make an end of what you have begun, your memories won't give you peace."

"Who are you?"

"You know me but you've never met me. Your father knew me when he was a boy, your grandfather, too, and you've been carrying me around on your back these past days. I'm Desolation Road's oldest memory. I'm Dr. Alimantando."

"But they say you're traveling in time, chasing some kind of legendary creature."

"And so I am, but the memories remain. Listen; though it pains me, a gentleman of science, to have to say this; you have the magic in you. If the land here is strong enough to give body to your memories and fears, might it not also be strong enough to give body to your hopes and desires? And if that is the case, maybe then that strength is within you, as I was, and not tied to any one place, no matter how special. Think about that." Dr. Alimantando rose and placed his pipe in his mouth. He took a long look at the sky, the stars, the trees. "Fine night," he said. "Fine fine night. Well, so long, Rael. It was nice meeting you. You are a Mandella, no mistake. You'll get by." Then he folded his arms and walked into the starlight shadows.

The sound of Jean-Michel Gastineau's radio woke Rael Mandella, Jr. Like it, he was poorly tuned, somewhere between a program about the edge of the universe and a popular early-morning music show. Light streamed through the ill-fitting planks that made up the walls. There was a smell and chuckle of eggs frying on the brazier.

"Good morning good morning good morning," said Jean-Michel Gastineau. "Up and at it, we've a long way to go today and you can't be going anywhere without a decent breakfast."

Rael, Jr., knuckled sleep from his eyes, not quite comprehending.

"Uh?"

"Going. Today. Got the call. Last night. While you were busy with your mnemologue, I was busy with mine, the Blessed Lady, well, at least her memory; anyhows, she told me this was the time, that I was to go with you. Apparently you'll have need of my special talents. Might even be why you were brought here in the first place. These things have hidden connections."

"Aren't . . ."

"Aren't I the least little bit upset to be leaving all this? Well . . . only a little. It's temporary, soon as I've finished the Holy Will I can have my old job back. Anyhows, she told me if I didn't go, there wouldn't be no forest to mind. What they call a Event Cusp; there's a lot of futures hanging on a few individuals, and that includes the future of the Forest of Chryse."

"But . . ."

"But who's going to look after the Ladywood while I'm away saving it? Shouldn't be telling you this, but a whole new order of angels is being constructed right now, right under your feet in the hatcheries: the Mark Six, the Amschastrias, specially designed for environmental maintenance. The old place'll be all right for a while without me. Old Father Tree'll keep an eye on them. Well, come on. Get up, wash up, eat up! We've a long way to go before we get to the forest wall and I've to pack and say good-bye to the chickens. Don't look so surprised! Where do you think those eggs came from? Air?"

55

One of Arnie Tenebrae's Jaguar patrols captured the four men on the inside of passive defense zone 6. Standing orders called for all prisoners to be terminated immediately but Sub-lieutenant Sergio Estramadura's curiosity had been piqued by their ability to traverse ten kilometers of booby traps, pitfalls, noose wires, and shit-tipped pungi stakes without injury. Despite Parliamentarian air patrols he broke radio silence to ask advice of his commander.

"Who are they?" Arnie Tenebrae asked.

"Four men. One of them's the Old Man of the Woods guy, the sarcastic one, the others look normal. No identity, but some B.A.C. gear on them."

"Interesting. Gastineau's never formally aligned himself before. He must have brought them through the defense zone. I'd quite like to see them."

She watched her guerrillas bring the captives in. The soldiers had them bound and blindfolded and led them on leashes. Three of them stumbled and faltered over the rough ground at the end of the valley; the fourth walked straight and tall, leading, not led, as if he were seeing with senses other than sight. That would be Gastineau. Though Arnie Tenebrae had met him only twice previously, his name was legend among the veterans of the Chryse campaign, both Whole Earth Army and Parliamentarian.

—What a guerrilla he'd make. He is part of the forest, animally aware. She looked at her guerrillas, boy-soldiers clumsy in chameleon suits and heavy battle packs, faces scrolled with tattoos or painted like tigers or demons or insects; spotted, striped, paisley-patterned. Silly boys pretending silly boys' games. Runaways tearaways castaways blowaways tomboys schizoids, homosexuals and visionaries. Actors in the theater of war. Give her a thousand men like Gastineau and she'd grind Quinsana fine as sand.

The faces of two of the prisoners looked familiar. She kept trying to place them in her memory as Sub-lieutenant Estramadura stripped them of their packs, clothes, and dignity and tied them to the bamboo holding pen. Estramadura's debriefing was farcical. Had the boy no eyes, no ears? His information amounted to "all of a sudden, there they were." A man without eyes and ears will not live long in forest fighting. She searched the prisoners' clothing. Gastineau's worn whites produced nothing, the others were Company stuff, tough, well made. The pockets were empty of anything save paper tissues, fluff, and a small ball of silver paper.

Before she examined the packs she asked Lieutenant Estramadura, "Their names."

"Ah. I forgot to ask."

"Go and ask them."

He bounded down the hill to the holding pens, face red and humiliated beneath the bold blue and yellow tiger stripes.

—He will not live long. He has no intelligence.

He returned one minute later.

"Ma'am, their names are . . ."

"Mandella." She pointed to the leather-bound book on the ground beside her. "The youngest is the son of Limaal Mandella."

"Rael, Jr., ma'am."

"So."

"The other two are . . ."

"Gallacelli. Sevriano and Batisto. I knew their faces were familiar. The last time I saw them they were two years old."

"Ma'am."

"I'd like to speak with the prisoners. Have them brought

here. And give them back their clothes. Naked men are pathetic."

When Lieutenant Estramadura had left, Arnie Tenebrae stroked her fingers over her short, fur-fine hair; stroke stroke stroke, manic, compulsive stroking. Mandella. Gallacelli. Quinsana. Hidden behind the cover of the book, Alimantando. Was it divinely ordained that she could never ever never get away from them? Did the whole town of Desolation Road sail around the world like a cloud of pursuit, seeking to drag her back into stagnation and stultification? What crime had she committed that the past must visit its punishment generation upon generation; was it so vile a thing to desire a name written in the sky? She toyed with the idea of having them quickly, quietly, anonymously killed. She dismissed it. It would be impossible to do so. This meeting was Cosmically Ordained. It had happened before, was happening now, would happen again. She studied them as they knelt across the fire from her; blinking and smarting in the smoky hut. So this was her grand-nephew. She saw them peering through the smoke for her but she was invisible to them, backlit by strong sunlight streaming through the bamboo. Jean-Michel Gastineau opened his mouth to speak.

"Peace, venerable one. I know you too well. I know the name Mandella, and I know the name Gallacelli."

"Who are you?" asked Rael, Jr. He was bold. That was good.

"You know me. I'm the demon that eats up little babies, the bogeyman that scares children to bed, I'm evil incarnate, so it would seem. I am Arnie Tenebrae. I'm your great-aunt, Rael, Jr." And because it pleased her to do so, she told the tale of stolen babies, the tale that her phantom father had told her and that had brought her to this precise place and moment. The expressions of horror on her grand-nephew's face pleased her greatly. "But why so horrified, Rael? From what I hear, you're as great a criminal as I."

"That's not so. I'm fighting for justice for the oppressed against the tyrannical regime of Bethlehem Ares Steel."

"Easily said, but do me the favor of sparing me your zealous cant. I understand completely. I have been that way before you. You may go now."

When Lieutenant Estramadura returned after locking the

prisoners in their cage, once more Arnie Tenebrae was washing her hands and staring at them with rapt fascination.

"Shall I have them shot, ma'am? It is common practice."

"Common indeed. No. Return their packs to them, unmolested, and escort them to the north forest wall by New Hallsbeck. They are free to go. There are forces at work here greater than common practice."

Lieutenant Estramadura did not leave.

"Do it." She visualized him stripped and spread-eagled between two trees and left for sun, rain, starvation. When he returned, she thought. He really was too stupid to be allowed to live. She watched the Jaguar patrol escort the exiles out of the valley into the woods. A Parliamentarian reconaissance aircraft droned over toward the Tethys Hills in the east. Camouflage squads scurried about in a frenzy of nets, bushes, and tarpaulins.

—Pretty pretty airbirds, Quinsana. Call them down, call down fire from heaven, call down the world-cracking RO-TECH space weapons, call heaven to fall on me, call the Panarch Himself to annihilate me, but I can go one better. I have the key to the Ultimate Weapon! The melodrama pleased her. She remembered Rael Mandella, Jr.'s leatherbound books. She remembered the walls of Dr. Alimantando's home, all covered in the arcana of chronodynamics. Had she but paid more heed to it then. She smiled a thin smile to herself.

—I can have mastery of time.

She called her general staff to her. They squatted in a semi-circle on the dirt floor of her hut.

"Prepare all divisions and sections to move out."

"But ma'am, the defenses, the preparations for the final battle."

She looked long and dangerous at Sub-major Jonathon Bi. He talked far too much. He needed to learn the value of silence.

"The final battle will just have to be fought somewhere else."

56

Since Johnny Stalin replaced all his immediate staff with robots, the efficiency ratings had trebled. Such was the brillance of his scheme that he spent many a long afternoon in his private massage studio under the fingers of Tai Manzanera; meditating upon the brilliance of his scheme. As robots never tired, never slept, never consumed or excreted, they never needed paying. The wages of their tireless labors went to support their fleshly originals desporting themselves on permanent vacation at the polar ski resorts, the island paradises of the Tysus Sea, or in the vice dungeons of Belladonna and Kershaw's Rubber Alley. As long as the substitutions went undiscovered, the scheme would continue to be all things to all men.

"Brilliant," Johnny Stalin told himself, gazing out of his 526th floor wall-window at the deformed landscapes around Kershaw. He remembered the dread that poisoned land had provoked in an eight-and-three-quarter-year-old boy arriving at the great cube. Now he loved the sludge pools and oil gushers. He had taken his many beloveds to promenade by Sepia Bay and whispered love's sweet syllables through his respirator into the receptive ears. Profit, Empire, Industry. What was a dead lake, a few poisoned rivers, a few slagged hillsides? Priorities, that was what it was about. Priorities and Progress.

Knock on the door, "Enter," bow, and Carter Housemann; rather, Carter Housemann's robot double, was beside him.

"Postcards from China Mountain, St. Maud Station, and New Brazil Jungleworld, the usual thanks and praises." The last three replacees seemed content. And as long as the credit in their accounts continued to amass month by month they would continue to be content. "Also, the latest reports from the Desolation Road project."

Johnny Stalin's genial humor fled him.

"Tell me the worst." He rolled onto his back for Tai Manzanera to pummel his stomach. Still firm, thank God. Can't afford the least sign of weakness in upper management.

"Good news and bad news, sir. Production levels are back to normal and resistance to industrial-feudal principles has been largely eradicated. Still some black-marketeering hitting the Company commissaries and a lack of support among the citizenry of Desolation Road, but the Concordat Organization has been effectively dispersed in the wake of the destruction of its managerial echelons."

"You can lay off the Company-speak with me. If that's the good news, what's the bad?" Transplant surgery kept the ulcers tolerable but three replacement stomachs and small intestines in as many years was more than the worth of the Desolation Road project.

"We have information that Rael Mandella, Jr., plans to return to Desolation Road to avenge his grandfather's death. Also, we know that he has been in contact with the Whole Earth Army Tactical Group in South Chryse."

"Child of grace. There, on the thighs, love. That family. Bad about the old man though. I knew him well when I was a kid. Shouldn't have done that."

"There was a certain revanchist element at work under the lead of the security director. However, there is an expression about omelettes and eggs, sir. I also have information that Taasmin Mandella is organizing a protest march to coincide with your visit to the works next month. I have heard that children all over the world have been receiving visions from the Blessed Lady herself: there have been two cases reported here in Kershaw, both children stole rides on transport dirigibles."

"Damnation. Recommendation?"

"I would advise against your visiting the Desolation Road project at the planned time."

"I agree. Unfortunately, there are three board members accompanying me to make sure that I've done a good job in quelling dissent, and their diaries are very full."

At times the robot proxies were so human it unnerved

Johnny Stalin. The double's shift of weight onto one leg as an indication that it wished to suggest something reminded him so greatly of Carter Housemann it made him shudder.

"Might I inquire, as a related point, what is sir's favorite pursuit?"

For an instant Johnny Stalin feared mass program failure in all his robot doubles.

"Tilapia fishing on the Caluma River up in the Sinn Highlands. Why ask?"

"Well, maybe sir would like to spend more time at such pleasurable pursuits and less on the dreary mundanities of the Desolation Road project."

So this was how it happened. He had been expecting this for a long time, that one day his robots would ask him if he would like to take a protracted holiday and slip a machine double into his shoes and behind his desk.

"How long have you been working on the proxy?" He lay back and looked at the ceiling. Strange that it was not as fearful as he had anticipated. It wasn't like dying in the least.

"The double had been ready for almost eighteen months."

"But up until now you lacked the opportunity."

"Precisely, sir."

In his mind's eye Johnny Stalin watched fly lines plopping into the crashing dashing Caluma River. It was an attractive idea, shiny slippery and bright as a Caluma tilapia.

"I suppose with the amount of evidence against me I have no other option."

The robot gave a fair impression of being scandalized.

"By no means, sir! This is in your own best interest."

The leaves would be turning brown and amber up by Caluma Falls. There would be snow on the highlands and cold nights and warm fires in the Caluma lodge.

"Well, Tai darling, I'm afraid you're out of a job. Robots don't have much call for masseuses." He looked Tai Manzanera up and down. She was a good girl really. "I can't really leave you here either, not after this conversation. How'd you like to come with me? The fishing's great up in the Sinn this time of year."

57

On learning of her father's death, Taasmin Mandella imposed a vow of silence upon herself. Her final communication before her lips were sealed under a cumbersome metal mask fashioned for her by the Poor Children was that she would speak again only when justice was visited upon those criminals who had perpetrated these acts. Justice, she said, not vengeance.

That same night she set off alone along the bluffs, away from the furnaceous hell-mouth glow of Steeltown, following her feet down the path of mortification she had walked those years before. She found again the little cave with its water drip. There were mummified beans and carrots on the floor. They made her smile behind her mask. She stood at the mouth of the cave and looked out at the Great Desert all scabbed and leprous under the hand of industrial man. She threw back her head and released all her power in a psalm of energy.

Asleep in a thousand beds in a thousand homes a thousand children dreamed the same dream. They dreamed of ugly metal insects descending upon a desert plain and building a nest for themselves of towering chimneys and belching smoke and ringing metal. Pulpy white worker drones served the insects with pieces of red earth they had torn from the skin of the desert. Then a hole opened in the sky and out of the hole came St. Catherine of Tharsis dressed in a multicolored ballet leotard. She held up her arms to show the oil oozing from her wounds and said, "Save my people, the people of Desolation Road." Then the steel insects, who had been building an unsteady pyramid out of their interlocked metal bodies, reached the Blessed Lady with their manipulators and pulled her, shrieking and gasping, into the metal mill of their jaws.

Kaan Mandella called them the Lost Generation.

"Town's full of these kids," he explained to his clients over the bar. Since Persis Tatterdemalion's grief-stricken flight into the sunset after Ed's murder, proprietorship of the bar/hotel had passed to him and Rajandra Das. "You trip over them going down to the store, you can't move near the station for kids sleeping on the platforms. I tell you, I don't know what that aunt of mine thinks she's going to achieve. Is a children's crusade going to impress . . . you know?" The name of the Bethlehem Ares Corporation was never to be mentioned in the hotel that had once borne its title. "The lost generation, that's what they are. Frightening; you look at those kids and poof! Nothing there. Empty eyes."

The empty eyes also unsettled Inspiration Cadillac. His arsenal of cautions, advices, admonitions, and veiled threats was exhausted. All that remained was a bewildered awe at the capricious acts of the Gray Lady. He could not understand why the Divine Energy had chosen to manifest itself in such a weak and flawed vessel.

PLGRMG SAT 12 NOVODEC 12OF12 Taasmin Mandella proclaimed in a crayoned notice on the basilica wall. ALL CLRCS, PR CHLDRN, PLGRMS, CTZNS. MRCH STLTWN: MK B.A.C. LSTN. THN WLL SPK.

Pilgrims? The steel mask had clearly blinded the Gray Lady's statistical sense as effectively as it had gagged her. Since the dawn of Concordat the flow of pilgrims had steadily dwindled to a fanatical few fingers worth. God and politics, oil and vinegar. No good will come of this, Inspiration Cadillac told himself.

Just before siesta time Mrs. Arbotinski from the mail office came round to Mr. Jericho with a letter for him from Halloway. Mr. Jericho had never received a letter in his life. Nobody knew where he was to send him a letter, and if those who were interested found out, they would have sent assassins rather than letters. The letter informed him that his nephews Rael, Sevriano, and Batisto and their Cousin Jean-Michel would be arriving on the 14:14 Ares express the next day. Mr.

Jericho loved intrigue and disguise, so when the appointed time came he tidied himself up, bought lunch at one of Mandella and Das's concession franchises on the platform, and when the 14:14 Ares express *Catherine of Tharsis* pulled up in a great billow of steam and vapor, he warmly welcomed the four bearded and sidelocked gentlemen with properly familial embraces. Beards and sidelocks went down Mr. Jericho's plughole. The Gallacelli brothers paid their respects to their father and found out from their presumptive fathers of their mother's anguished flight. This upset them bitterly. Mr. Jericho spent a pleasant and stimulating afternoon in conversation with the Amazing Scorn, Mutant Master of Scintillating Sarcasm and Rapid Repartee, and Rael, Jr., returned to the Mandella family manor.

"Ah, Rael, you have returned," said Santa Ekatrina, surprisingly unsurprised. "We knew you would be back. Your father would like to see you. He is over in the Alimantando house."

Limaal Mandella greeted his son amid the four panoramas of the weather-room.

"You know your grandfather's dead."

"No!"

"The Company raided the house, you might have seen some of the damage. Rael was killed trying to protect his property."

"No."

"The grave is down in the town cemetery if you want to visit it. Also, I think you should go and see your grandmother. She very much holds you responsible for the death of her husband." Limaal Mandella left to give his son the privacy of mourning, but before he closed the door he said, "Incidentally, your aunt would like to see you."

"How does she know I'm back?"

"She knows everything."

New posters appeared on gable ends: PILGRIMAGE OF GRACE: 12 NOVODECEMBER 12 OF 12. RAEL MANDELLA JR WILL SPEAK.

Mikal Margolis was in a quandary. The Pilgrimage of Grace coincided with the visit of Johnny Stalin and the three board members. But for the presence of Rael Mandella, Jr., he would have been inclined to turn a blind eye to the march, it was futile; great popular appeal, doubtless, but ineffectual. He did not much want to risk another foray into Desolation Road to arrest the troublemakers: Dominic Frontera had obtained a district court injunction against the Company with promise of military assistance should the injunction be flagrantly violated. An undercover operation might be a good idea, but with the town filling up with media hawks, drawn by the children, who had started appearing from every which where, the slightest incident would have the public relations department breathing fire. He'd done enough damage to the Corporate chromework with his heavy-handed police tactics in crushing Concordat. Child of grace, what did they want, a Company or a mishmash of squabbling trade unions? Quandaries quandaries quandaries. Sometimes he wished he had dropped the roll of geological reports down an airshaft and remained a Freelancer. As director of security of the Desolation Road project, he had fulfilled all his adolescent fancies yet still he was not free from gravity. He looked at himself in the mirror and saw that black and gold did not really suit him.

Twelfth Novodecember 12 of 12 was beautiful for a pilgrimage. It should have been. Taasmin Mandella had been subtly tinkering with the orbital weather-control stations for a month previous to ensure not a drop of rain would spoil the Pilgrimage of Grace. A large crowd had gathered outside the Basilica of the Gray Lady. Out in the siesta heat the thousand children, arrayed in virginal white, fretted and grumbled and felt sick and threw up and fainted, like any other collection of sinners waiting in the afternoon swelter. At the appointed moment the gongs chimed and the cymbals crashed in the belfries and the great bronze gates of the Basilica swung open on unused mechanisms, and Taasmin Mandella, the Gray Lady of Silence, walked out. It was not even a very dignified walk. It was the tired walk of a woman who behind her machine mask has felt time breaking over her. A respectful distance behind her walked Rael Mandella, Jr.; her brother, his father, Limaal, Mavda Arondello, and Harper Tew, the two surviving strike committee members, Sevriano and Batisto Gallacelli, and Jean-Michel Gastineau in his guise as the Amazing Scorn, Mutant Master of Scintillating Sarcasm and

Rapid Repartee. The halo around Taasmin Mandella's left wrist burned so deep a blue it was almost black.

The pilgrimage formed up around her: Children of grace, Children of the Immaculate Contraption (Poor), various Steeltown sodalities carrying votaries, icons, relics, and holy statues, among which was the Celestial Patron of Concordat, the Bryghte Chylde of Chernowa. Behind the ecclesiastes processed the artisans, the representatives of the trades and professions of Steeltown gathering under banners that had lain hidden in cellars and attics since the Company destroyed Concordat and yes, even a few defiant Concordat banners, small but unmistakable with their bold green Circles of Life. Behind the artisans came the populace, the wives, husbands, children, parents of the workers, and among them the smaller populace of Desolation Road, its farmers, lawyers, storekeepers, mechanics, whores, and policemen. And after them came the goondahs, bums, wastrels and pie dogs, and after them the newspaper, wireless, cinema, and television reporters with their attendant cameramen, sound men, photographers, and apoplectic directors.

With Taasmin Mandella at its head the procession moved off. As it passed the Mandella residence the hymnsingers and psalm chanters fell silent in respect. The gates of Steeltown were barred against the Pilgrimage of Grace. Taasmin Mandella applied the tiniest glimmer of God-power and the locks burst and the gates swung back on their hinges. The back-tracking guards aimed the MRCWs more in fear than anger and dropped them with howls of pain as under the Gray Lady's command they glowed red hot. The crowd whooped and cheered. Driving the Bethlehem Ares securitymen before it the procession advanced toward Corporation Plaza.

Upon a balcony on the glass-fronted Company offices Johnny Stalin's robot double and three members of the board of directors watched in increasing stupefaction.

"What is the meaning of this?" asked Fat Director.

"I was under the impression that these untoward disturbances had ended," said Thin Director.

"Indeed, if this Concordat nonsense has been crushed, as you led us to believe, what were those green banners doing there?" asked Middling Muscular Director.

"Impolitic though it is for such a march to be taking place within the project," said the North West Quartersphere Projects and Developments Manager/Director's robot double, "it would have been vastly more embarrassing to have taken action against it with the film crews of nine continents watching. I suggest we just swallow the indignity, gentlemen."

"Harumph," said Fat Director.

"Intolerable," said Thin Director.

"Quite uneconomic," said Middling Muscular Director.

"Mikal Margolis will take care to things," said Robot Stalin. "Concordat will not rise again."

The speeches began.

First Sevriano and Batisto Gallacelli spoke of the murder of their father by the lasers of the Bethlehem Ares Corporation. Then Limaal Mandella spoke of the murder of his father by the missiles of the Bethlehem Ares Corporation. Taasmin Mandella nodded for Rael Mandella, Jr., to come forward and speak. He looked at the sea of faces and felt a great weariness. He had seen enough platforms, podiums, and lecterns for a lifetime. He sighed and stepped forward for the people to see.

From his position on the catwalk of Number 5 converter Mikal Margolis took full benefit of the short step into the public eye to focus his telescopic sight.

One bullet. All it needed. One bullet jacketed in and silenced by Bethlehem Ares Steel. Then there would be no more quandaries.

Limaal Mandella watched his son step forward and the people's adulation warmed him. He had done well by his sons. They were all his father would have wished grandsons to be. Then he saw a glitter of light in the pipework overhanging Corporation Plaza. He had lived too many years in the wickedest place in the world not to know what it was.

He brought his son down in a crunching tackle as his matchroom-attuned ears heard the silenced shot clear and sharp as the clarion of the Archangelsk above the voice of the masses. Something huge and black exploded out of his back, something he had not suspected had laid hidden there. He felt surprise, anger, pain, tasted brass money in his mouth and said, "Good God, I'm hit." He said it in such a matter-of-fact manner that he was still being surprised by it when the darkness came over his shoulder and took him away with it.

The crowd swayed and screamed. Two thousand index fingers pointed to where the guilty one was scrambling down a flight of ladders that led into the heart of the industrial labyrinth. Rael Mandella, Jr., was huddled over his father's body; Taasmin Mandella pulverized by the death of her twin. At the last instant of his life the mystic link between Limaal and his sister had been restored and she had tasted the blood in his mouth and felt the pain and the fear and the blackness swallow him. Though she still lived, she had died with her brother.

Then the Gray Lady rose before the people, and, removing her mask, they saw that her face was dark and terrible so that they cried out in fear.

"This is between my family and Mikal Margolis!" she cried out, breaking her silence. She raised her holy left hand and thunder rocked Corporation Plaza. At her summoning every loose piece of machinery in Steeltown leaped into the air: pipes, welding torches, garden rakes, radios, electro-trikes, pumps, voltmeters, even the Bryghte Chylde of Chernowa left its pole and flew to her call. The junk formed a wheeling flock above Corporation Plaza. It drew closer, closer still, and the terrified masses saw metal running and fusing and reforming into two steel angels, grim and vengeful, swooping above their heads. One sported airfoils and jet engines, the other twin sets of rotor blades.

"Find him!" cried Taasmin Mandella, and the angels howled off along the steel canyons of Steeltown to comply. Taasmin Mandella's halo flashed again and it seemed to the watching eyes that her cumbersome dress melted and changed shape, clinging close to her thin form, and that as she leaped from the platform to give chase herself, her mask flew to her hands and transmuted into a potent weapon.

Pandemonium reigned in Corporation Plaza. Leaderless, the demonstration surged and panicked. The Pilgrimage of Grace was a rabble. Its fury and terror had defeated it. Armed securitymen appeared on rooftops and walkways and drew a hail of stones. They readied their weapons but did not open fire. Rael Mandella, Jr., made to stand and calm the boiling crowd but Jean-Michel Gastineau pushed past him.

"They'll shoot you like a dog," he said. "This is my

moment. This is what I was commanded to do." He took a deep breath and released all his mutant sarcasm in one searing satire.

Though not directed at them, the people nevertheless felt the edge of his tongue. Some screamed, some wept, some fainted, some vomited, some bled from guilty wounds the sarcasm had opened up. He swept the beam of his satire across the security positions and there were moans and cries as the armed men realized what they were, what they had done. Some could not bear the shame and threw themselves off their high watch-places. Others turned their own weapons on themselves or their comrades; others broke down into hysterical weeping at the words of the Amazing Scorn. Some shrieked, some gibbered, some vomited as if by vomiting they could spew out all the self-hate the little man on the steps made them feel, some voided their bowels and their bladders, some fled screaming from Steeltown into the desert and were never seen again, some collapsed in blood and broken bones as the sarcasm ripped them open and shattered their limbs.

Having humbled the armed might of the Bethlehem Ares Corporation, the Amazing Scorn turned his tongue toward the high balcony, where the directors of the Company hid themselves away. In an instant Fat Director, Thin Director, and Middling Muscular Director were reduced to shuddering blobs of remorse.

"Oh stop stop stop," they pleaded, choking on their own bile and vomit, but the satire went on and on and on, slashing and cutting at every dark and shameful deed they had ever done. The satire ripped clothes to shreds, slit bodies open in long deep bleeding gashes, and the mighty Directors screamed and howled but the words cut cut cut at them, cut and slashed until there was nothing but dead, slashed meat and blubber on the horribly expensive carpet.

Johnny Stalin's robot proxy watched the quivering heaps of meat with contempt mingled with puzzlement. He could not understand what had happened save that the Directors had been weak and found wanting in some incomprehensible way. He was not weak, he was not wanting, for being a robot, he was immune to sarcasm. It was intolerable that the Directors of the Company could be so weak when he and his kind were so strong. He put out a neutrino-pulse call to his machine comrades to call them together at their earliest convenience for an emergency meeting to save the Company from itself.

On the steps Jean-Michel Gastineau fell silent. His mutant sarcasm had humbled the Bethlehem Ares Corporation. The people rose from their crouches, shaken, stunned, uncomprehending. He looked at the children dressed in virginal white, the poor, idiotic Dumbletonians, the shaken artisans and shopkeepers, the reporters and cameramen whose lenses had been cracked and microphones shattered when he released his full mutant power; he looked at the bums and the goondahs, and the poor foolish people, and he felt pity.

"Go home," he said. "Just go home."

Then by a prearranged signal five transport 'lighters that had been hovering unseen over the drama dropped their invisibility fields and the invasion of Desolation Road began.

58

Taasmin Mandella, the digital huntress, pursued her prey deeper into labyrinthine Steeltown. She felt alive as she had felt only once before in her life, when the Blessed Catherine had visited her upon her dry desert pinnacle. This time the nature of the feeling was altogether different. The miracle-gun felt hot and hungry in her hand and her transformed garment clung silky and sensuous to her body. She was enjoying herself. Mikal Margolis had fired at her twice with an MRCW he had obtained from somewhere: that had felt exciting and dangerous.

Anael Sikorsky helicoptered in over the Section 2 separator plant and reported.

"Target holding position on Level seventeen."

She dispatched a holy command to Anael Luftwaffe and was rewarded by the immediate screams of jets and the savage hammer of his wing-mounted 35mm cannons over to her right.

"Come tools come toys come steel come iron," she enchanted, and from the pieces of machine junk she called by name she fashioned a small gravity-sled. The wind streamed back her hair as she rode the surf of industry, agile between pipes and girders and ducts. This was what she was made for, the wind in her hair and a weapon in her hand, zigzagging down Henry Ford Street between the blasts of Mikal Margolis's missiles. She laughed and drove him from cover with a blast from her portable tachyon beamer.

"Take him, Luftwaffe." The jet-powered angel swooped over her head and strafed the separator plant with its finger cannons. Explosions ripped the roof off the plant and peppered Taasmin Mandella with shrapnel but she did not care; she laughed astride her air-board and transmuted the hail of metal into further attachments to her arcane weaponry. Anael Luftwaffe climbed for a roll into another attack. At the apex of his climb a wedge of three MRCW heatseekers streaked out of concealment. Anael Luftwaffe exploded into smoking ruin and rained down on Steeltown.

There. Taasmin Mandella's tachyon beam struck mere moments after the black and gold figure danced down a narrow gully between two airshafts. The Gray Lady gave a whoop and a cheer and a chase. She sniped at Mikal Margolis's heels. She could have evaporated him at any moment of her choosing, but she wanted him in the open, in the desert, where it would be middle-aged man to middle-aged saint.

Anael Sikorsky hovered close, harrying the prey. It was a very tight alley . . . Taasmin Mandella's concentration was focused to its utmost point maneuvering her sled around the valves and pipework.

"Sikorsky, get back." A fan of laser fire raked the air. Anael Sikorsky swerved to avoid the ruby beams, glanced against a settling tank, bounced wall to wall to wall, and crashed in a blossom of flame.

So it was to be man to saint after all. She was pleased. In the distance the voice of holy conscience niggled her, but only in the distance. Her twin's death was closer and more intimate. She could taste the darkness still. Mikal Margolis broke from the tangle of industrial plumbing and sprinted across the 'lighter field. Taasmin Mandella whipped him with a swarm of robot bees from one of the multitudinous muzzles of her God-gun. She willed her sled high into the sky so that she might dramatically swoop down upon her prey and cut him off.

Mikal Margolis released an arc of missiles from his MRCW. A pulse of power flowed along the printed circuits in her costume and transformed them into birds. Taasmin Mandella shrieked in delight. Her power had never been so great. Her halo glowed collapsar-black, twinkling with the swallowed white stars of conscience. She drew a ring of fire around Mikal Margolis with her flamethrower and slid the sled to a halt before him. She put up her weapon before her face and willed the flames into extinction. Mikal Margolis responded in cautious kind. Behind him the smoke of Sikorsky's burning went up into the sky together with the sound of a great despairing wail from Steeltown.

"Let me see your face," said the Gray Lady. "I want to see how you've changed."

Mikal Margolis removed his helmet. Taasmin Mandella was surprised at how little he had changed. Aged, wearied, tanned, grayed, but unchanged. Still the victim of circumstance.

"Please spare me any melodrama," said Mikal Margolis. He dropped his MRCW. "I don't suppose this would have worked against you anyway. And please don't go on about your father and your brother. It's pointless. I don't feel any especial remorse; I'm not that kind of person, and anyway, I was just doing my job. Now, get on with it."

The dust blew in little eddies around his feet. Taasmin Mandella slowly channeled all her power into one God-bolt that would transform Mikal Margolis to carbon steel. She raised her left hand to strike and was suddenly, stunningly, embedded in a shaft of solid light.

A figure walked across the landing field toward her. Where it had come from, Taasmin could not see, but the figure was that of a small, slim, crop-haired woman wearing a suit of glowing picture-cloth.

"No!" wailed Taasmin Mandella, the Gray Lady. "No! Not now! Not you, not now, of all times!"

"You may recall that part of the conditions of your prophethood was that you would be called to give an account of your stewardship of your power," said Catherine of Tharsis. Mikal Margolis made to recover his weapon and leave. St. Catherine froze him into immobility with a gesture.

"Tight-focus timeloop," she explained with a smile. "Soon as we're gone he'll snap out of it."

"You have a lousy sense of timing," said Taasmin Mandella, frozen in white radiance.

"Like the outfit," said the Blessed Lady. "Like it a lot. Very becoming to you. We servants of the Panarch, incidentally, do not have to justify our comings and goings to you mortals. This is the appointed time, you must come with me and give an account of how you have used your privileges."

The column of light began to spin about Taasmin Mandella, and she felt herself being stretched, pulled like festival taffy, transformed into something other than human. She felt the earth slip away from her. She was light; light. . . . She gave a final spit of disgust, then the Catherine-power enfolded her and, as she had once fantasized naked on the burning bluffs, she was transformed into a creature of purest light, white, shining light eternal, purest information, and foutained into the sky.

The small skinny woman which was the biological construct of the Blessed Lady of Tharsis's incarnation moved her hand in the special way that manipulates space and time and vanished.

59

Disguised as a Penitential Mendicant, Arnie Tenebrae spent five days wallowing in mud, flagellation, prostrate prayer, and kneeling upon sharp stones submerged in sewage before she slipped away from the main pilgrimage by the Steeltown gates, concealed herself behind a domestic methane tank, and spoke the five words into her thumb-communicator that gave the order for invasion. At her command the five transport dirigibles that had slipped with muffled fans into position over Steeltown shed their invisibility fields and began to broadcast messages of reassurance and liberation to the stunned faces beneath them. From their belly hatches Whole Earth Army shock-troops dropped suspended by LTA harnesses, field-inducers at the ready to pound the enemy into the red jam at the slightest display of resistance. The enemy were past resistance.

"Do not be afraid," boomed the taped messages. "Desolation Road is being liberated from the tyranny of the Bethlehem Ares Corporation by the Whole Earth Army Tactical Group: do not be alarmed. We repeat, you are being liberated. Please remain calm and render all assistance to the liberation forces. Thank you."

Behind the methane tank Arnie Tenebrae slipped off the excrement-smeared burnoose that had for five days concealed her battle suit and combat pack. She painted her face in the semblance of the Deathbird and slipped on her microphone set.

"Group nineteen, to me," she whispered. "All other battle groups as ordered." In their prearranged positions around the

perimeter of Corporation Plaza, a dozen similarly attired
Penitential Mendicants threw off their disguises and moved
through the crowd toward the Company offices. Even as the
airborne troops touched down, released their harnesses, and
moved to their planned positions controlling the power plant,
the landing field, the station, the truck depot, the mayor's
office, the police barracks, the microwave link, the solar power
plant, the banks, the law offices, and transport depots, Arnie
Tenebrae rendezvoused with her battle group and stormed the
sanctum of Bethlehem Ares Steel.

As old Mrs. Kanderambelow, who operated the telephone
exchange, made tea for the six polite if rather frighteningly
decorated young men in battle dress, and Dominic Frontera
found himself staring down the emission heads of four field
inducers, Group 19 rode up to the executive levels in the
executive elevator. Miss Fanshaw, Company secretary of the
year, rose from her desk to protest the unwarranted invasion
and was smeared all over the wall by a ram of gravito-strong
force. Arnie Tenebrae blew in the black and gold door with its
black and gold crest and strolled in.

"Good afternoon," she said to the tear-stained, blood-
stained, humiliated section managers, plant supervisors, financial directors, marketing chiefs, and personnel consultants.
"Where's the North West Quartersphere Projects and Developments Manager/Director?" A sudden shrill of energy answered her and stabbed a crater in Sub-lieutenant Henry
Chan's stomach. He goggled at the unfamiliar sight of his
spine and then collapsed in two halves. "Shields, boys, he's got
an F.I." Defense canopies rang like temple gongs under the
field-inducer sledgehammers. The be-sarcasmed executives
fled, shrieking, past the red crushed patch that had been the
Model Secretary of the Year.

"Where the hell is he?" someone shouted.

"He has a light-scatter field up around him," said Arnie
Tenebrae, relishing the tight tactical situation. "Everybody
out. We'll only get in each other's way. I'll take him myself."
She had a personal private interest in doing so. The troops
withdrew to the elevator head to guard the executive prisoners.

"Hey, Johnny, where did you get the F.I.?" A howl of
power blew a stuffed antelope's head to duff and sawdust.

Johnny Stalin became visible for an instant, crouching behind the Manager/Director's chair. He vanished the instant Arnie Tenebrae blasted the end of the board table to flinders with a beam of hypersound. "Invisibility screen too. Not bad." She circled the room, fully visible, defense canopy up, senses pricked like a cat's ears. "Johnny," she sang, "I had to come see you when I found out it was you. Remember me? The sweet little girl you kissed behind Rael Mandella's methane digester?" Her pulse of power screeched and howled off Johnny Stalin's defense canopy. He flickered into momentary translucency. "Come on, Johnny, make a decent flight of it. You know the kind of weapon you're using, you know you can't use it offensively and defensively at the same time, and I know that invisibility field's draining your power. How say you show yourself and make a decent fight of it?" A patch of air shimmered and Johnny Stalin shivered into visibility. Arnie Tenebrae was surprised at how he had changed: gone was the chubby, scared little boy, whining and obstreperous; the figure before her could almost have been the masculine counterpart of herself.

"You're looking well, Johnny." She checked her wrist gauges: eighty-five percent charge. Good. She circled to her left. Johnny Stalin circled to her right. Both watched for the telltale moment when the other's canopy went down in the instant before firing. Arnie Tenebrae circled, waited. The air grew stale within her defense canopy.

"Oh, Johnny," she said again, "remember, there's a dozen of them waiting for you if you get past me." She fired, plunged for cover. Stalin's return fire was slow slow slow. Arnie Tenebrae had all the time in the world to turn, aim, and punch a force-field fist through his lowered canopy that smashed him apart like an egg.

Commander Tenebrae had her men search through the smoke and the rubble for some souvenir of Johnny Stalin that she might add to her collection of trophies, but they found only pieces of charred machinery. Then trooper Jensenn brought Arnie Tenebrae Johnny Stalin's head and she sat for a long time laughing at the wires and the complex articulated aluminum joints that served for cervical vertebrae.

"A robot," she laughed. "An olly-o, jolly-o robot." She tossed the head away and laughed and laughed and laughed so long and so hard that it began to scare the soldiers of Group nineteen.

60

Dominic Frontera was first to learn that the liberation of Desolation Road was actually an occupation and that all the rejoicing citizens who had carried the Whole Earth Army guerrillas shoulder high through the alleys were hostages to Arnie Tenebrae's dream of Götterdämmerung. He learned this at six minutes of six in the morning when five armed men took him from the cellar of Pentecost's General Merchandise Store, where he had been held incommunicado and stood him against the brilliant white wall. The soldiers drew a line in the dust and stood him behind it.

"Any last requests?" said Captain Peres Estoban.

"What do you mean, last requests?" said Dominic Frontera.

"It's customary for a man facing a firing squad to be granted a last request.

"Oh," said Dominic Frontera, and voided his bowels into his nice white ROTECH uniform. "Um, can I clean up this mess?" The firing squad smoked a pipe or two while the mayor of Desolation Road dropped his pants and made himself presentable. Then they blindfolded him and put him back in front of his wall.

"Firing party, shoulder arms, firing party, aim, firing party . . . firing party . . . Child of grace, what now?"

While feeding the chickens, loyal but unintelligent Ruthie had seen the soldiers take her husband and stand him against a wall and point weapons at him. She emitted a cry like a little astonished bird and chased pell-mell, helter-skelter all the way across to the mayor's office to arrive just as Peres Estoban was mouthing the order to fire.

"Don't kill my husband," she shrieked, throwing herself between executioners and executionee in a welter of flying arms and skirts.

"Ruthie?" whispered Dominic Frontera.

"Madam, out of my way," ordered Peres Estoban. Ruthie Frontera stood solid, a drab Valkyrie with fat legs. "Madam, this is a legally constituted Revolutionary Firing Party executing its legally constituted sentence. Please move out of the line of fire. Or," he added, "I will have you arrested."

"Huh!" said Ruthie. "Huh huh huh. You're pigs you are. Let him go."

"Madam, he is an enemy of the people."

"Sir, he is my husband and I love him." There was a flash of light that even Dominic Frontera could see through his blindfold as Ruthie Frontera née Blue Mountain discharged in one intense moment twelve years of accumulated beauty. She swept her charisma beam across the firing party and each soldier in turn gibbered as the full potency of her loveliness came to focus on him and they dropped, eyes wide open, mouths trickling froth. Ruthie Frontera freed her husband and that same morning escaped with aged father and as much of a household as they could fit into the back of a purloined Bethlehem Ares Steel truck. They smashed through the Steeltown perimeter wire and drove out into the land of Crystal Ferroids and were never seen again in Desolation Road. It was commonly suspected that they perished in the Great Desert from madness caused by drinking radiator water. This was far from so. Dominic Frontera and his family reached Meridian and were posted to pleasant and peaceful Pine Rapids in the Sinn Highlands, where there were tall trees and clean air and gently plashing waters. He lived there very happily as mayor until one day a visitor for the winter season recognized his wife and his father-in-law from another place and another time and told him how his wife had been mixed together like a cocktail in a Genesisory by a crazy man who hated wives but loved children. After that Ruthie Frontera no longer seemed so beautiful to the mayor of Pine Rapids, but that may not have been the fault of the gossip so much as her father, who in designing her had cursed her that she might only exercise her power of beauty three times and then it would be gone forever. So in saving Dominic Frontera from the firing squad, Ruthie had lost his love and that is an old old story.

The executive directors of the Steeltown project alas did not have a Ruthie to save them by love. Over a period of ten days they were taken in batches of five and blasted to pieces by the field inducers of Arnie Tenebrae's Army of Liberation. The representatives of the media were brought at gunpoint to witness and record the glorious executions of the despots, but they had all of them long before reached the conclusion that Desolation Road and its people were hostages to Arnie Tenebrae's improvisations with Marya Quinsana.

Curfew was imposed and strickly enforced. Pass cards were issued for walking in the street and rationing introduced. Goods trains were stopped up the line at the edge of the Crystal Zone, driven into Desolation Road, and systematically looted. All food was the property of the Revolutionary Directorship and theoretically pooled to be shared equally among all, but Desolation Road was hungrier than it had ever been even in the hungriest days of the strike. The lion's share went into the mouths of the two thousand troops occupying the town and citizens, steel workers, pilgrims, Poor Children, reporters, goondahs, and bums subsisted on lentils and rice. Mr. Peter Iposhlu, a market gardener, under the Mandella/Gallacelli land agency, refused to surrender his crop to the Whole Earth Army and was hanged from a cottonwood tree. Alba Askenazy, a harmless and well-regarded beggar, tried to steal a salami from the Revolutionary Commissary and received identical treatment. Rajandra Das had to beg for ration vouchers from his clientele to continue the Hot Snack and Savouries end of the business while the bar/hotel, under Kaan Mandella's caretakership, was forced to post "Closed Until Further Notice" signs in the window for the first time in popular memory. After curfew, however, its cellars were bright with the candles of counterrevolutionary mice.

"Just what does she want from us?" asked Umberto Gallacelli.

"She says she wants to draw the Parliamentarians in after her for a final big battle," said Mr. Jericho.

"Child of grace!" said Louie Gallacelli. "How do you know that?"

"Talking to the soldiers," said Mr. Jericho unconvincingly.

"I think she wants to get her own back on us all," said Rajandra Das. "She thinks we ran her out of town, so now she's going to make us pay. Gold-digging bitch."

"Revenge then?" suggested Umberto Gallacelli.

"I think there's something here she wants," said the Amazing Scorn, voice a hushed whisper, throaty and cancerous. He had burned his throat out on the day of deliverance in Corporation Plaza, his power had overreached itself. He could never be sarcastic again. "When she captured us in Chryse, she seemed as if she wanted us alive for some reason, something to do with this place."

Mr. Jericho pounded a fist into the palm of his other hand in the supposed fashion of one in deep thought. He was consulting with his Exalted Ancestors, rifling their stored personas for ancient insights.

"Blessed Lady! I know! Child of Grace, the time machine! The mark two Alimantando time winder. Holy God, the final weapon . . ."

Bootsteps crunched on the dirt outside. Shhing and hushing, the curfew breakers extinguished their candles and crept away through the web of tunnels and caves to their fearful beds.

On the twelfth day of the occupation Arnie Tenebrae set about her preparations for battle. Loudspeaker vans liberated from the Company announced that all citizens above the age of three were conscripted into the universal labor force and gave times and places of muster. Under the field-inducers of the 14th and 22nd Engineering Corps, the people were set to digging revetments into the cliffs, laying a circular minefield all around Desolation Road at the inner edge of the Crystal Lands, and constructing a maze of trenches, bunkers, dugouts, and foxholes from which defenders could command fields of fire along Desolation Road's eccentric street plan. The sun rose to siesta height, but the universal labor force worked on, for the liberation had freed the day from the tyrannical siesta. There were faintings, there were collapsings, there was sluggish dragging and dropping of tools. A fat sweaty hotel owner called Marshall Cree set down his shovel and refused to work anymore. Two guards from the Corps of Engineers came and led him away. Half an hour later his severed hands were displayed on a sharpened tree branch and taken around the workings for all to see. If he would not use his hands for the Army of Liberation, he would not use them at all. At thirteen minutes of thirteen, when even in winter the sun tipped its crucible of molten heat over Desolation Road, the two guards from the Corps of Engineers came for Genevieve Tenebrae.

"Oh no no no no no, not me, please!" she screamed, flailing and kicking so hard it seemed her ancient cardboard bones must snap. The guards took her not to the amputation block, but to her own house, where her daughter awaited her.

"Hello, Mother," said Arnie Tenebrae. "Are you well? Good. Just called to say hello." Genevieve had always been slightly afraid of her stolen daughter. Whenever she heard her daughter's name on the radio, in connection with some new atrocity, she had told herself that Arnie was a Mandella, yes, not her flesh and blood at all, because of the fear. Now the sight of her battle-armored and demon-painted daughter terrified her.

"I really wanted to give my regards to my mother and father, but they're dead, and so is my brother, and so is my nephew. And no one thought to tell me."

"What do you want?" asked Genevieve Tenebrae.

Arnie let her gaze roam judgmentally over the sordid room, untidy with neglected bric-a-brac and the little forget-fulnesses of an old crazy woman. Her eyes came to rest upon the blue bubble on the filthy mantelpiece. It was suspended above something that looked like a sewing machine tangled up in spider silk. Inside the iso-informational field her adoptive father still turned blue somersaults. He no longer spoke. After twelve years of solitary confinement there was nothing for him to say. Arnie Tenebrae's lips brushed the blue bubble.

"Hello, Daddy. I've come to set you free, like you set me free." The controls of the time winder were similar to the wrist sets of the field-inducers; not surprisingly, for the Whole Earth Army weapons had been modeled on Dr. Alimantando's designs. She smiled as she set the verniers to zero.

"Good-bye, Daddy."

The blue bubble popped, an implosion of air. Her father's ghost was gone.

She gave the time winder to Major Dhavram Mantones of the elite 55th Strategic Engineering Group.

"Make it work for me, Dhav," she said, then went to watch the progress of the construction. She liked to walk along the trenches and revetments and play heroes and demons in her head.

Dhavram Mantones was back first thing next morning.

"It can't be done," he declared. "The best I can achieve is a localized temporal stability field."

"If Dr. Alimantando can do it, you can do it, Dhav," said Arnie Tenebrae, glancing out of the window of her Steeltown headquarters as if to emphasize the fleetingness of time. "If you need help, get Mr. Jericho, Rajandra Das, and Ed Gallacelli. They worked on the original time winder. We should be able to persuade them."

The instrument of persuasion was a device called Charley Horse. It was nothing more than a triangular billet of metal, apex upward, suspended a meter and a half above the floor. It was equally simple in operation. The person to be persuaded was stripped, hands bound to a beam above the head to encourage secure seating, and placed astride the metal billet. A few hours of Charley Horse was enough to persuade the most recalcitrant of riders. Mr. Jericho and Rajandra Das did not even require a minute's persuasion.

"We don't know anything more than you do."

"What about Ed Gallacelli?"

"He's dead."

"Might he have told his dear wife?"

"Might have, but she's left. Flown away."

"Then who might know?"

"Limaal Mandella."

"Don't be clever. He's dead too."

"Maybe Rael, then. Limaal passed a lot of Dr. Alimantando's secrets to Rael, Jr."

"We know. We didn't find anything in the notebooks. Or in the house."

"Maybe you should ask him personally. Limaal might have told him something not in the books."

"Indeed he might."

To Rael Mandella, Jr., virtual recluse since the murder of his father and the disappearance of his aunt and his Pyrrhic victory over the Company, came the surprise invitation for a ride on Charley Horse. He was not appreciative of the treat; after only four hours he was removed in a near comatose state by which time Arnie Tenebrae was convinced anyway that he knew nothing of the inner arcana of Dr. Alimantando's chronokinetic arts. She did obtain one piece of information from him that earned him his reprieve: that all Dr. Alimantando's secrets, including the mystic Temporal Inversion that made chronodynamism possible, were somewhere on the walls of his house. Dhavram Mantones was dispatched to take a closer look at the frescoes on pain of a permanent visit to Charley Horse. Rael Mandella, Jr., was cut down and taken back to his family home. A pity. Arnie Tenebrae would quite have enjoyed leaving him there to see if he could beat the current thirty-hour record for horseback riding.

Rael Mandella, Jr., was taken delirious into his grandmother's kitchen, where she and his own mother tended him and put him to bed. There he hallucinated that he had once had a father made from maple and a mother made from flowers and bean cans. He lay thus for three days and a neighbor's daughter, a shy girl called Kwai Chen Pak who had assisted Santa Ekatrina in the soup kitchen days, brought him flowers and pretty stones and from the scanty rations made him candy kangaroos and raisin-bread men. At the end of this time he awoke to learn two important things. The first was that he desperately loved Kwai Chen Pak. The second was that in the night the host of the Parliamentarians had settled around Desolation Road in readiness for the last battle.

61

"**M**ust be well on eight thousand of them," said Mr. Jericho, straining his disciplined eyesight to make sense of the shifting heat-shimmer out among the crystalloids. Sevriano Gallacelli shifted his shovel and pretended to be working while the guard was watching.

"So, what are those things then?" He nodded toward the enormous three-legged machines that had been stalking arrogantly around the crystal landscape vaporizing chunks of ferrotrope with vicious blue-white beams.

"I don't rightly know," said Mr. Jericho. "They're something like the scout walkers ROTECH used to use years back. Tell you one thing, when the action starts, it's going to get mighty hot around here. Those things are toting tachyon beams."

The two men swung their shovels and pretended to dig while they watched the ungainly contraptions march around the desert without the slightest attempt at concealment, and they formed the mutual and inescapable conclusion that the end was nigh for Desolation Road.

In forward observation post five Arnie Tenebrae was reaching similar conclusions.

"Evaluation?" she asked her aide, Sub-colonel Lennard Hecke.

"Fighting machines, ideally suited to the terrain. I hate to say such things, ma'am, but they could step right over our mine defenses."

"That's what I thought. Weaponry?"

"Ma'am, I hate to say this too, but . . ."

"But those tachyon beams could timeslip past our field-

inducer defenses and punch holes right through our canopies." She left Lennard to inspect the invincible fighting
machines and went in search of Dhavram Mantones. She
wished to ascertain the state of her own invincible fighting
machine. As she climbed the bluffs she passed the bodies of
the two SRBC newsmen who had tried to fly a flag of
surrender. Spreadeagled upside down on wooden frames, their
bodies were beginning to turn to leather after three days in the
sun and smelled abominably. Surrender was not just imper-
missible, it was inconceivable.

In forward command station Zebra Marya Quinsana
observed the mummifying bodies through field glasses. It was
not the barbarism of the execution that shocked her; it was the
familiarity of many of the stooped figures at work upon the
terraces and fortifications. Even the town of Desolation Road
itself, that part of it sandwiched between the ugly concrete
carbuncle of the basilica and the towering pipeworks of the
factory, was unchanged, a messy conglomerate of wind-
pumps, flashing solar lozenges, and red tile roofs. She
wondered what Morton was doing. She had not seen him at
work upon the bluffs, but there were other constructions under
progress within the town. She had not thought of him in
twelve years. She thought, too, of Mikal Margolis; poor stupid
boy who let the wind blow him where it would. She wondered
what had become of him after she had left him at the soba bar
in Ishiwara Junction.

There would be time enough for reverie afterward. The
Whole Earth Army defenses looked strong but not so strong,
she thought, as to defy her tachyon-beaming fighting machines. She had spent a lot of political capital in obtaining the
specifications for ROTECH's scout walkers from the wise ones
of China Mountain and she was confident that the investment
would be well spent. Her ground forces outnumbered the
opposition three or four to one, her tachyonic weapons systems
gave her the edge over the Whole Earth Army field-inducers.
. . . It was tempting to toy with notions of victory and
ambition. She needed a clear head and a calm constitution. As
she left command post Zebra she became aware of a faraway
insect drone.

The same sound infringed upon the lunatic perceptions of
Arnie Tenebrae while she sat at her desk toying with string.

Her mind latched onto the insect drone and forgot to listen to Dhavram Mantones's report on the progress in deciphering Dr. Alimantando's hieroglyphics. Drone, buzzz, lazzzy beee in the bonnet of winter—she remembered flower-filled mornings splashing in the irrigation canals, days filled with sun and bee buzz.

"Pardon?"

"We've something you might like to take a look at."

"Show me."

The drone sat in her ear all the way to Dr. Alimantando's house and up in the weather-room, thick with dust and littered with half-empty teacups left by Limaal Mandella, her attention kept wandering out of the four windows in airborne pursuit of the drone.

"This is it, ma'am." Dhavram Mantones pointed to a patch of faded red scrawling at the precise apex of the ceiling. Arnie Tenebrae stood on the stone table and peered with a hand lens.

"What is it then?"

"We believe it is the Temporal Inversion formula which will render the time winder and anything within its sphere of influence timeloose and chronokinetic. We're going to try it out this evening."

"I want to be there."

Where was that droning coming from? Arnie Tenebrae was beginning to fear it originated from within her own head.

The sound even filtered down to the sub-basement of the bar/hotel, where a clandestine resistance meeting was in session. Five souls gathered around a brown wooden box: a radio transmitter built into a packing crate.

"Pray they don't intercept us," said Rajandra Das, mindful of crucified television news reporters.

"Have you got them yet?" asked Santa Ekatrina Mandella, dedicated anti-authoritarian. Batisto Gallacelli thumbed the transmit switch again.

"Hello, Parliamentarian forces; hello, Parliamentarian forces; this is Desolation Road, can you hear me, this is Desolation Road." He repeated his incantation several times and was rewarded by a crackle of voice. The anti-liberationists pressed close around the hand-set.

"Hello, this is Free Desolation Road, we warn you,

exercise extreme caution, Whole Earth Army in control of Temporal Displacement weapon: I repeat, be alert for time displacement weapon. Urgent you attack soon as possible to save history. Repeat, urgent you save the future: over . . ."

The voice crackled an answer. Alone of the five, Mr. Jericho was not concentrating on the static syllables. His attention was fixed on some point beyond the roof.

"Shh." He palm-downed for hush. "There's something up there."

"Over and out," whispered Batisto Gallacelli, and cut transmission.

"Do you hear it?" Mr. Jericho turned slowly, as if trying to maximize a little lost memory. "I know that sound, I know that sound." No one else could even hear it through tile, brick, and rock. "Engines, air engines . . . wait a moment, Maybach/Wurtel engines, push/pull configuration! She's come back!"

Heedless of pass laws and illegal congregations, the counterrevolutionaries boiled up out of the sub-basement into the street.

"There!" Mr. Jericho pointed to the sky. "There she is!" Three pinpricks of light winked in midbank and swelled with a breathtaking shout of power into three shark-nosed propeller airplanes. In arrowhead formation the three airplanes pounded over Desolation Road, and as they passed the lead plane snowed leaflets. The streets were instantly full of running guerrillas. They separated the five counterrevolutionaries and drove them into shelter. Mr. Jericho glance-read a leaflet blowing past him in a cloud of dust and prop-wash.

"Tatterdemalion's Flying Circus Has Come to Town," it read. "Bethlehem Ares, Beware!" The innocence made him smile. Thirty years old and she still hadn't learned worldly wisdom, God bless her. The flying circus looped over Desolation Road and came in at roof height. Six ripping explosions tore across the town. Mr. Jericho saw blue-white beams flash from the airplanes' wingtips and he whistled in blatant admiration.

"Tachyonics! Where in the world did she get tachyonics from?" Then he was hurried into the bar/hotel and the soldiers took up rooftop positions to return fire.

As she led her formation in across the railroad lines for a

strike at Steeltown, Persis Tatterdemalion realized she was having the time of her life.

"Angels green and blue," she sang, "commence second attack run."

There had been no escaping. Ed was gone and gone was Ed, but she could fly over the edge of the universe and never be far enough away to forget about him. Even in Wollamurra Station there had been no escaping. There had been a filling with craziness instead, a craziness that found her two crop-spraying punks out of jobs to fly the two stunters she'd bought from Yamaguchi and Jones, equip them with the very latest in military technology, and make a crazy, name-of-love attack first on a Bethlehem Ares Steel train chuffing across the High Plains and then on the slag-black heart of the dream-grinding Company itself, fortress Steeltown. She waggled her wings and the flying circus closed in behind her.

She loved the way the soldiers ran like chickens from the snap snap snap of her tachyon blasters. She loved the purity of the blue-white beams and the bright flowers of the explosions as she destroyed offices, storage tanks, trucks, bunkers, draglines, solar-collectors. She'd loved it from the instant she'd pressed the firing buttons and sent two Class 88 haulers, fifty wagons, and two engineers up in a blaze of subquantal fusion.

"Boom!" she sang, and pressed the firing studs. Behind her three parked cargo 'lighters exploded in gouts of fire.

"Whee!" she cried, and banked the Yamaguchi and Jones for another pass. Her radio crackled and a familiar voice hissed in her ear.

"Persssiss, dear, it'ssss me. Jimmmm Jericho, you know?"

"Yah, I know," she shouted. Her tachyon blasters cut long smoking gashes through Steeltown. Chimneys collapsed, pipework tumbled.

"Immmmportant inffformation. Desssolattttion Road isss under occupattttion, repeat, under occupattttion, by the Whole Earthhhh Army Tactical Group, repeat, Whole Earthhhh Army Tactical Group. Company isss defffeated, repeat, defeated." A fan of missiles broke from ground and homed in on her.

"Kaboom!" she said and vaporized them. "Defeated?"

"Yesss. An sssspeaking to you ffffrom the bar/hhhotel on

illegal rrradio sssett. Sssuggessst you attack military targetsss, repeat, military targetssss. Arnie Tenebrae in command."

She passed low over Desolation Road again and saw the trenches and dugouts. She flew over the bluffs and saw there the crucified bodies and the sunshiny helmets of the soldiers in their cliffside positions. Arnie Tenebrae? Here?

"Angel Group, reform," she ordered.

"Good girl," hissed Mr. Jericho, and broke transmission. Angels green and blue fell into arrowhead formation behind her. Good kids. She briefed them on the new situation.

"Check," said Callan Lefteremides.

"Check," said her brother Venn.

Angel flight turned as one and closed on the Whole Earth Army positions. They flew scant meters above the desert. Wingtip tachyon-blasters snipped at the defenses, missiles burst from the revetments toward them.

"Angel green angel green, missile on you . . ." A Long Brothers Type 337 "Phoenix" surface-to-air missile, fired in panic by one Private Cassandra O. Miccini, caught Venn Lefteremides, and blew the tail clean off his Yamaguchi and Jones. Angel Green rolled into a death spiral and crashed in the middle of the abandoned new housing complex beyond the railroad lines.

Persis Tatterdemalion thought she had seen the flutter of a parachute. So, Arnie Tenebrae, this is for you. She turned the nose of her airplane Steeltown-wards and thumbed the firing studs.

Arnie Tenebrae watched the air strike from her window with curious admiration.

"They're good. Awfully good," she mused as the two survivors of Tatterdemalion's Flying Circus skipped in at rooftop height to launch another tachyon strike into Steeltown.

"Ma'am, don't you think you should move away from such an exposed position?" suggested Lennard Hecke.

"Certainly not," said Arnie Tenebrae. "They can't harm me. Only the Avenger can harm me."

Out in the Land of Crystal Ferrotropes the Avenger Marya Quinsana watched the dogfight.

"Whoever they are, they're very good. Get a check on the registration numbers. I want to know who's flying them."

"Certainly. Marshall, a communication from the town, from the hostages." Albie Vessarian, a fauning sycophant destined never to stop a bullet, handed her a memo from telecommunications and hurried to comply with her order to identify the pirate aircraft.

She scanned the communique. Temporal weapons? She threw the flimsy away and returned to the air attack in time to see Venn Lefteremides roll, crash, and burn.

"So," she breathed. "This is it. Order the attack!" Fifteen seconds later the second attacker was shot down and crashed into the Basilica of the Gray Lady.

"Order the attack!" shouted General Emiliano Murphy.

"Order the attack!" shouted Majors Lee and Wo.

"Order the attack!" shouted assorted captains, lieutenants, and sub-lieutenants.

"Attack!" shouted the sergeants and group leaders, and forty-eight long-legged fighting machines took their ponderous first step toward Desolation Road.

"Ma'am, the Parliamentarians are attacking."

Arnie Tenebrae received the news with such phlegm that Lennard Hecke thought she had not heard.

"Ma'am, the Parliamentarians are attacking."

Arnie Tenebrae received the news with such phlegm that Leonard Hecke thought she had not heard.

"Ma'am, the Parliamentarians . . ."

"I heard you, soldier." She continued shaving her scalp, scything away great meadows of hair until her head gleamed naked beneath the sun. She regarded herself in a mirror. The result pleased her. Now she was the personification of war, the Vastator. Avenger beware. She spoke unhurriedly into her whisper-mike.

"This is the commander. The enemy is attacking with unconventional armored forces employing tachyonic weaponry: all units exercise extreme caution in engaging. Major Dhavram Mantones, I want the time winder running."

Dhavram Mantones came on the thimble-phone, crackling and distressed.

"Ma'am, the Temporal Inversion is untested: we're still doubtful about one of the operands in the equation; it could be plus or minus."

"I'll be there in three minutes." To her forces at large she said, "Well, this is it, boys and girls. This is war!" As she gave the order to attack, the first explosions came from the perimeter positions.

62

Gunner Johnston M'bote was one of those inevitable people whose lives are like steam trains, capable only of forward motion in a limited direction. Personifications of predestination, such people are doubly cursed with an utter ignorance of the inevitability of their lives and thunder past those countless other lives that stand by the side of the track and wave to the express train. Yet those standers by the track know exactly where it is that the train is going. They know where the tracks lead. The train lives merely hurtle onward, uncaring, unenlightened. Thus Mrs. January M'bote knew the instant the district midwife presented her with her ugly, nasty little seventh son that no matter what he made or did not make of his life he was destined to be a number two belly-gunner in a Parliamentarian fighting machine in the battle of Desolation Road. She saw where the tracks led.

As a child Johnston M'bote was small, and he remained small as an adolescent, just the perfect size to be rolled up into the belly turret slung beneath the insect body of the fighting machine like a misplaced testicle. His head was round and flat on top, just the perfect shape for an army helmet; his disposition darting and nervous (labeled "hair-trigger" by the army psychologists), ten out of ten for suitability; his hands long and slender, almost feminine, and quite the best shape for the admittedly tricky firing controls of the new Mark 27 Tachyon equipment. And he possessed an I.Q. of such fence-post density that he was unemployable in any profession that demanded the slightest glimmer of creativity. One of Creation's natural belly-turret gunners, Johnston M'bote was doomed to begin with.

Little enough Johnston M'bote knew of this. He was having too much fun. Curled like a fetus in the clanking, swaying, oil-smelly metal blister, he peered down through the gun slits at the lurching desert beneath him and sent streamers of heavy machine-gun fire arcing across the leprous sand. The effect pleased him greatly. He could not wait to see what it looked like when he used it on people. He squinted up at the views in the eye-level television monitors. A lot of a lot of red desert. Legs swung, the fighting machine heaved. Gunner Johnston M'bote spun round and round in his steel testicle and fought with the urge to press the little red trigger in front of him. That was the fire control for the big tachyon blaster. He had been warned against its indiscriminate use: it wasted energy, and the commander did not entirely trust him not to shoot the legs off the fighting machine by mistake. Stamp stamp, sway sway. His Uncle Asda had once owned a camel and the one ride he had taken on the bad-tempered thing had felt very much like the rolling gait of the fighting machine. Johnston M'bote strode to war in twenty-meter boots with the Big Swing Sound of Glen Miller and his orchestra blowing soul in both earphones. He rolled his shoulders and poked alternate forefingers into the air, up down, up down; the only kind of dancing possible in the belly turret of a Mark Four Fighting Machine. If this was war, thought Johnston M'bote, war was terrific.

A military issue boot, made by Hammond and Tew of New Merionedd, pounding heavily on the ceiling hatch three times; thump thump thump, accompanied by a muffled half-heard stream of abuse. Gunner Johnston M'bote thumbed at his radio channel selector. ". . . to Baby Bear, Daddy Bear to Baby Bear, what'n'hellyouplayingatdowntheredon't you know there'sawaryoudumbstupidsonofa . . . target bearing zero point four degrees declination, fifteen degrees." Tongue protruding in unprecedented concentration, Gunner M'bote spun little brass wheels and verniers and aligned the big tachyon blaster on the unremarkable section of red cliff face.

"Baby Bear to Daddy Bear, I have the target all set; now what you want me should do?"

"Daddy Bear to Baby Bear, fire when ready. Holy God, how dumb . . ."

"Okay, Daddy Bear." Johnston M'bote gleefully pressed both thumbs to the much anticipated little red button.

"Zap!" he shouted. "Zap, you bastards!"

Sub-lieutenant Shannon Ysangani was withdrawing her combat group as per orders from Arnie Tenebrae from the perimeter positions (which smelled oppressively of urine and electricity) to the Blue Alley revetments, when the Parliamentarians vaporized the entire New Glasgow Brigade. She and her fifteen combat troops constituted the sole two percent that survived. Shannon Ysangani had been leading her section past the front of the Jolly Presbyter Pilgrim Hostel, when an unusual brilliant light from an unusual angle threw an unusually black shadow against the adobe walls. She had just time to marvel at the shadow, and the way the red and blue neon Jolly Presbyter suddenly lit up (a hitherto-undiscovered electromagnetic pulse side effect of the tachyon devices), when the blast picked her up body and soul and smashed her into the facade of the Pilgrim Hostel and, by means of a finale, brought walls, ceiling, and fat neon Presbyter himself down on top of her.

But for her defense canopy Shannon Ysangani would have been smeared like potted meat. As it was, she was englobed within a black bubble of collapsed masonry. She explored the smooth perimeter of her prison with blind fingertips. The air smelled of energy and stale sweat. Two choices. She could remain under the Jolly Presbyter until she was rescued or her air ran out. She could drop her defense canopy (possibly all that was keeping multitons of Jolly Presbyter from crushing her, like a boorish lover) and punch her way out with field-inducers on offensive. Those were the choices. She had fought enough battles to know that they were not as simple as they appeared. The ground shuddered as if one of the ineffable footsteps of the Panarch had fallen on Desolation Road; there was another, and another, and another. The fighting machines were moving.

She could not believe the ease with which the Parliamentarians had broken through the perimeter defenses. She could not believe so much death and annihilation could have been contained in such a short flash of light. The earth shook to a sustained concussion. Another flare of light, another annihilation. She found she could not believe in this new death either. War was too much like the Sunday night thriller on the radio to be credible for what it was. Another blast. The Jolly Presbyter settled with a heavy grunt on top of Shannon Ysangani. Someone must carry the news of the destruction back to headquarters. A voice she barely recognized as duty nagged at her. Do your duty . . . do your duty . . . do your duty . . . Shock. Explosion, close by. Thud thud thud, the metal boots of a fighting machine close by, what if one comes down on top of me, will my defense canopy hold up? Duty, do your . . .

"All right! All right!" She knelt in the darkness beneath the smothering corpulence of the Jolly Presbyter, checking her fire controls by touch. She wanted to be sure, sure, and sure again. She would get only the one shot. Shannon Ysangani sighed a short, resigned puff of a sigh and collapsed her defense canopy. The debris groaned and settled. Creaking, crashing . . . she brought the field-inducer up and punched a pull power burst through to the sunlight.

It might have been a different world she stepped out into. The entire southeast end of Desolation Road lay in tumbled smoking ruins. Glowing glass craters, nine-rayed like St. Catherine's starburst, gave testimony to the punishing effectiveness of the Parliamentarians' new weapon. They had passed this way in force, their behemoth fighting machines, creatures of childhood iron nightmares, stood astride streets and buildings, hissing steam from their joints and trading ponderous artillery barrages with crannies of Whole Earth Army resistance entrenched along First Street. The Parliamentarians' passage through the outer defenses had flattened the town like a rice field before a whirlwind. Yet their advance had not gone totally unopposed. Like a dead spider beneath a boot, the command turret of a fighting machine lay smashed open in a tangle of metal legs. Shannon Ysangani flicked for her defense canopy, then paused. In this kind of war, perhaps invisibility would be a better tactic, operating on the principle of what can't be seen can't be shot at. She thumbed open her section's radio channel and called the survivors to her. The few were fewer. Twelve out of fifteen, crawling from the chaos in the wake of the battle. Sub-lieutenant Ysangani then thumbed the command channel and made a brief report of losses to Commander Tenebrae.

Arnie Tenebrae sat amid her war staff, fingertips touched together in the attitude of meditative serenity. Ninety-eight percent casualties in the initial engagement and now the Parliamentarians were kicking at the skirting boards of Steeltown. Once ninety-eight percent casualties would have outraged her military sense and sent her shouting brilliant, inspiring orders to her troops. Now she merely sat, fingertips touched together, nodding.

"Orders are revised," she said when the Sub-lieutenant had finished. "Under no circumstances are troops to use defense canopies. Employ light-scatter and high mobility. You are guerrillas. Be guerrillas." She cut communications with the defenders and turned her whole self to the complex machine-thing humming on the tile floor. "How much longer?"

"Ten, twenty more minutes before we get the power hooked up," said Dhavram Mantones. "And we'll have to defend the power source."

"Order it done." Arnie Tenebrae suddenly stood up and went to her room. She regarded her painted face in the mirror on the wall. Foolish vanity, she was Deathbird no longer, she was Timebird, the Chronal Phoenix. As she wiped the foolish paint from her face she reflected on the ninety-eight percent casualties on the perimeter dugouts. Meaningless. Plastic soldiers. The defense of the time winder was paramount now, and for it she would gladly embrace hundred-percent casualties. Hundred-percent casualties. Universal death. The concept began to appeal to her.

In best guerrilla fashion Shannon Ysangani's squad tippy-toed through the alleys of Desolation Road. Occasional glass craters commemorated those who had trusted too much in their defense canopies. On the corner of Blue Lane a fighting machine came smashing its way through Singh Singh Singh and MacIvor's Law Offices. As her troops faded into invisibili-

ty, Shannon Ysangani found she and Trooper Murtagh
Melintzakis separated from their comrades. Shannon Ysangani hid her invisible self in the porch of New Paradise Tea
Rooms and watched the turrets swing left and right, left and
right, searching out lives to extinguish. Evil machines. She
thought she could even discern the helmeted crews at their
battle stations. Her terror of the metal thing had paralyzed her
military sense, she was no more capable of attacking it than of
attacking a childhood iron nightmare. Not so trooper Murtagh
Melintzakis. His childhood sleep must have been untroubled,
for he slipped out of invisibility, raised his field inducer to
attack, and the turret muzzle which by sheer misfortune
happened to be pointing at him spat point-blank sub-quantal
fury over him. The novalight bleached every centimeter of
exposed paintwork on the corner of Blue and Chrysanthemum. The neons on the empty hotels spasmed with brief
luminescent remembrance and, light-scatter circuits tem-
porarily overloaded, the remnants of Group Green appeared as
vague translucent ghosts. Shannon Ysangani screamed a
panicked order to split up and escaped down Blue Alley.

"Hey, nice shooting, Baby Bear! Like, nice shooting!"

Gunner Johnston M'bote grinned and spat simultaneously,
a fear uniquely his by dint of no one wishing to duplicate it.

"Nothing really. Just pointing it the right way at the right
time. Hey!" Wandering eyeballs registered movement on one
of the tiny monochrome televisions. "Hey, there's a bogie
getting away!"

"Oh, let her go . . ."

"But she's an enemy! I want to shoot her."

"You go easy with the T.B., Baby Bear, you'll shoot one of
our legs off if you're not careful."

"The hell I will!" said Johnston M'bote huffily. He vented
his ill feelings on the facade of the New Paradise Tea Rooms
with a handful of rounds from his 88mm cannon before Daddy
Bear (in reality Sub-commander Gabriel O'Byrne) jawed him
over the waste of ammunition. So he treated himself to a good
scratch deep inside his fetid underwear and Fighting Machine
T27, *Eastern Enlightenment*, lurched off to support the big
firefight around the gates of Steeltown, in the process acciden-
tally and without malice cleaving away half the Stalin

household and the whole of the Stalin wife with one careless swing of its two o'clock foot.

"Hey, there's a guy down there!" Johnston M'bote could see him through the gunslits in the belly-turret, a curiously foreshortened Mr. Stalin waving fists of impotent fury at the fighting machine that had just killed his wife of twenty years.

"A what?"

"A guy down there, Daddy Bear."

"Looks like he owned the house you just smashed through, Daddy Bear," chirped Mummy Bear from the glamour of the top turret. Johnston M'bote only knew Mummy Bear by his querulous voice on the interphone. He had never seen him, but he suspected some kind of rivalry between number one bombardier and commander. Come to think of it, he'd never seen the commander either.

"A what?" said Daddy Bear again.

"A guy, down there, in a big big patch of beans," said Johnston M'bote, ideally poised to witness what happened next. "You know, I think we should be kind of like . . . careful, you know, like you're always warning me to be. . . . Oh. Well."

"What, Baby Bear?"

"Nothing Daddy Bear."

T27, *Eastern Enlightenment*, Daddy Bear, Mummy Bear, and Baby Bear hot-legged it over Green Street with Mr. Stalin an unfortunate red smear on the two o'clock leg.

"Holy Catherine! Do you know what you just did?" shrieked Mummy Bear, and proceeded to tell his commander at such length and in such detail that Johnston M'bote patched out the recriminatory bickering and danced his little jigajig finger dance to "Tombolova Street Serenade" by Hamilton Bohannon and his Rhythm Aces. War was fun again.

Fun pounding at the sand-bagged emplacement with his cannon, fun straddling fleeing guerrillas and incinerating them with a "zap!" from his TBs, fun even when it was scary, when we heard the crew on T32, *Absalom's Peach*, all die live on his earphones in a pother of confusion over targets.

"I tell you there's no one there!"

"There's got to be!"

"The computer says . . ."

"Stuff the computer!"

"Stuff you! Look, see! I was right, there isssqrzhggmm-stphughzzsss . . ." And T32, *Absalom's Peach*, took a full field inducer burst from a Whole Earth Army boy soldier that spattered its Daddy Bear and Mummy Bear and Little Baby Bear up into the air in a fountain of metal shards and red rain.

Watching the death of *Absalom's Peach*, Johnston M'bote felt an unaccustomed sensation in his head. It was an original thought, an insight, and a clear sign that his preordained existence was approaching the end of the tracks. It took him so by surprise, this original thought, that it was almost a full minute before he thumbed for Daddy Bear.

"Oh, Big Bear," he sang, "I think we are dealing with an invisible enemy." Daddy Bear sputtered and gurgled on the interphone, a commander promoted beyond the level of his competence.

"Well, has anyone got heat goggles?" Mummy Bear had left his with his stick of insect repellent in his tent. A bitter argument ensued. Johnston M'bote slipped his pair on and assumed the semblance of a dyspeptic owl. The fuzzy monochrome haze which he perceived paid an almost immediate dividend.

"Hey! Daddy Bear! Daddy Bear! I've got a bogie! A real live bogie!"

"Where?"

"Port side, one hostile . . ." He liked using military expressions.

The name of the bogie was Shannon Ysangani.

"Come on, let's get her, there she goes. . . ." Dangling from the belly hatch twenty meters up in the smoke-filled air, Gunner Johnston M'bote steered the fighting machine with directions bawled into his helmet interphone. Faithful and obedient, the fighting machine stomped through the abandoned west wing of the Mandella hacienda, popping open like a peapod that most secret room which Grandfather Haran had locked and cursed never to be opened again.

Dust sifted down onto the heads of the Mandella dynasty hiding in the deepest sub-cellar. The rocks shuddered and groaned. Half-delirious from his ride with Charley Horse, Rael Mandella, Jr., hallucinated his days of leadership in the Great

Strike and Kwai Chen Pak hurried to soothe his rantings with herb tea. Eva, working blithely at her loom, selected a pick of flame red yarn from her combs and declared, "All this will have to go into the tapestry."

Fighting machine T27, *Eastern Enlightenment*, stood at attention in the Mandella's central courtyard, spraying steam from its pressure valves. Smoke blew around the turret and endowed it with an otherworldly, malign intelligence.

"You see anything down there, M'bote?"

Gunner M'bote hung out of his belly-blister, probing with his goggles the great steam and smoke thrown up from the edge of Steeltown, where Parliamentarians and Whole Earth Army defenders had broken upon each other like clashing waves. A shimmering vagueness moved through the monochrome murk.

"Yep! There she is! Shoot her someone!" Mummy Bear swung creakingly around to comply; Daddy Bear raised the murderous two o'clock foot to stomp.

The nature of Shannon Ysangani's belief in God had changed fundamentally in the past few minutes from Benign Big Softie who apportioned to some slightly more luck than justice demanded, to a Mean and Vengeful Old Fisherman who would not let a victim off his line. It had been luck when Murtagh Melintzakis was burned in place of her. It was vengeance now that she could not shake the agent of that burning off her. The fighting machine was playing with her. There was even some punk of a crewman hanging out of his turret tracking her every twitch with heat goggles. And her brilliant invisibility was as useless as her defense canopy. All that remained was for her to fight as Murtagh Melintzakis had.

"God damn you, God!" she cried solipsistically as she scrambled toward Fortress Steeltown with the fighting machine smashing a path of relentless pursuit. "God damn you God damn you God damn you!"

The big guns were swinging, the ugly little monkey-man pointing, the foot was rising, and she did not, categorically not, never no way not, want to end in fire the way that ten-year-old boy-soldier had ended, a shriek of agonized plasma. As she raised her field-inducer to fight, she realized how weary she was of killing things. Tired, sick, disillusioned. Stupid monkey-man was gibbering from his hatchway and she did not want to kill him.

"I don't even know you," she whispered. Yet to do anything else would be to end in fire. The contact closed. The instant before her defense canopy dropped for attack a pulverizing steel kick drove her against the llama-shed wall. The shot shied wide, the defense bubble popped, and Shannon Ysangani smashed into the all-too-solid adobe masonry. Body-things cracked and crunched inside her; she tasted steel and brass. In a vague miasma of semi-awareness she saw that her shot had not missed altogether. She had blasted away the upper gun turret, gunner, and gun. Steam and oil fountained from the metal wound like heart-blood. She giggled a rib-grating giggle and went dark.

"Shit shit shit shit shit shit shit shit . . ."

Curled up for safety in his comfortable fun belly-turret, Johnston M'bote scarcely heard his commander's execrations.

"I got you, oh, I got you, I got you you bitch bastard whore, I got you I got you . . ." Johnston M'bote's tongue poked beneath his teeth as he whispered furious glee to himself and spun his little brass wheels and verniers. "Oh, I got you, lady!" He pointed his big weapon at the woman lying in a cracked pile of adobe bricks. "I got you . . ." What was Daddy Bear shouting? Didn't he know how hard it was to shoot with the damn fighting machine swaying and heaving like a Saturday night drunk? Warning? What the hell about? Crosshairs glowed, perfect target. Gunner Johnston pressed the little red button.

"Zap!" he shouted, and in a dazzling flash blasted the ten o'clock leg clean off.

"Damn it," he said.

"You stupid bastard!" shrieked Daddy Bear. "I warned you, I said be careful. . . ." T27, *Eastern Enlightenment*, tottered like a tree on the edge of a precipice. Metal shrieked and clanged, gyro stabilizers howled as they fought to hold the fighting machine upright, then failed, catastrophically, unequal to the test. With majestic, balletic grace, the fighting machine toppled, tachyon blasters firing wildly in all directions, steam exploding from the wrecked joints, and smashed itself open on the adamant earth of Desolation Road. In the closing seconds of his plummet Johnston M'bote was permitted to see that his whole life had been directed toward this moment of glorious annihilation. In the instant before the belly-turret popped and he was crushed beneath the weight of falling metal like a ripe plum, Johnston M'bote saw back to the moment of his birth and realized as he saw his perfectly shaped head emerging from between his mother's thighs that he had always been doomed to begin with. He felt a sense of deep deep disgust. Then he felt nothing ever again.

Oscillating across the boundary between pain and consciousness, Sub-lieutenant Shannon Ysangani saw the behemoth fall, brought low by its own weapon. She felt a great, agonizing, flesh-tearing fit of giggling boil up inside her.

Buried five levels deep beneath Steeltown in her time-transport center, Arnie Tenebrae, too, saw the behemoth fall. To her it was a more colorful fragment from the mosaic of war. Her wall of television monitors presented her with war in all its many colors, and Arnie Tenebrae savored each, eyes flicking from monitor to monitor to monitor; quick, brief encounters with war, jealous of losing so much as an instant of the War Between the Powers.

The Vastator turned her attention from the televised massacre to the time winder in the middle of the floor.

"How long now?"

"Two minutes. We're hooking up the field generators to the fusion tokamak now."

A cry came from the observers monitoring the monitors.

"Ground troops! They're sending in ground troops!" Arnie Tenebrae spun her attention back to the picture wall. A thin white skirmish line was slipping effortlessly through the trenchways toward Steeltown. The fighting machines' artillery provided withering cover. She thumbed up the magnification and saw familiar bulky packs on white Parliamentarian shoulders.

"Clever clever clever Marya Quinsana," she whispered, so that no one would hear and think her insane. "You've the measure of me pretty close, but not quite neat enough." Weapons-fire reached her ears like the sound of childhood pop guns as skirmishers fell upon defenders. A pop-gun war, a lie-down-for-twenty-seconds-you're-dead war, and when it was all

over everyone would get up and go home for their dinners.
Field-inducers hammered at field-inducers until the tachyon
equipment on board the fighting machines spoke and declared
game over for today and always.

"Ready to go!" shouted Dhavram Mantones.

"Then we'll do it, shall we?" said Arnie Tenebrae,
Vastator. She shouldered her battle pack. Dhavram Mantones
threw the handswitch that diverted all the power from the
Steeltown tokamak into the time winder. The eons opened up
before Arnie Tenebrae like a mouth, and she threw herself into
the chasm in a cascade of afterimages.

Then reality ended.

The first that Mr. Jericho and the refugees in the bar/hotel
knew of the end of reality was when they found themselves
bobbing against the ceiling. Though separated at the time
of the air strike, they had all come together by means of the
tunnels and caves that honeycombed the rocks beneath
Desolation Road: no sooner had worried greetings been
exchanged than they found tables, cups, carpets, bottles, and
chairs floating around their ears. Kaan Mandella chased after
the beer-crate radio transmitter in a kind of unsteady breast-
stroke beneath the roof beams. Rajandra Das anchored himself
to the pelmet and peered upside down out of the window.
Attackers, defenders, life-careless camera teams, llamas, pigs,
and pie dogs were floating around the eaves of the houses.
Halfway down the street, gravity seemed to have reversed

completely, houses, trees, animals, soldiers, earth, and rocks were falling into the sky. In the other direction three empty hotels and the Excelsior Curry House were submerged in a huge red sand dune. A dark shadow fell across the free-fall street; something big as a barn, blocky and dirty orange, was flying over Desolation Road.

"What is going on?"

Mr. Jericho's Exalted Ancestors had been arguing deep in his hypothalamus as he bobbed against the candle brackets. Their final conclusion was appalling.

"They must have got the time winder to work."

"It wasn't like this when Dr. A used it."

Half the room could not understand what Rajandra Das and Mr. Jericho were talking about.

"Alimantando kept his Temporal Inversion Formula a secret: Tenebrae's engineers must have guessed wrong. Instead of creating fluidity through time, they've created a zone of temporal fluidity here, now, and reality is breaking down. The laws of space-time are bending, and I think pieces of alternative universes are being superimposed onto this one."

"What does that mean?" asked Santa Ekatrina Mandella, who had been married to the laws of space-time for eleven years.

"It means the end of consensus causal reality." The first earth tremors shook the bar/hotel. Freed from gravity, the very rocks beneath the street were shifting and stirring. "Unless."

"Unless?" asked Sevriano and Batisto Gallacelli simultaneously. The Exalted Ancestors had already answered this question, too, and their answer was no less appalling than their first one.

"Unless we can shut down the power supply to the time winder."

"You mean close down the Steeltown tokamak?"

"I do. And I need you with me, Rajandra Das. I need your charm over machines."

"You'll never do it, old man," said Kaan Mandella. "Let me."

Mr. Jericho already had the door open. A glowing wind filled with ghostly faces swept along the street, driving all unanchored free-fallers out into the desert.

"I'm afraid only I can do it. Can you keep a secret? Ever heard of the Damantine Disciplines?"

"Only the Exalted Families . . ." started Kaan Mandella, but Mr. Jericho said "Precisely" and dived out into the street. Rajandra Das plunged after him after a moment's hesitation. "Try Persis on the radio again," he called in parting. "We may need her to run interference for us." He did not add, "if she's still alive."

At the Junction of Bread Alley gravity was restored but a downpour of boiling rain drove Mr. Jericho and Rajandra Das into shelter. Under a windowledge they found a parboiled guerrilla. Mr. Jericho stripped him of his battle armor and dressed Rajandra Das in helmet, power pack, and weapons pack.

"You might need it," Mr. Jericho said. It did not take Damantine-disciplined hearing to make out the booms of small-arms fire close by. The two men dashed through the tailing drops of scalding rain into Mosman's court, where the hands of the municipal clock were spinning around at a rate that compressed hours into seconds. Aging visibly as they ran, refugees from the accelerated time zone fled up the street into a jungle of green lianas and vines which had snagged around the smoking skeletons of two fighting machines. Mr. Jericho detoured around the relativistic zone, passed through a region of inexplicable night into Alimantando Street. The shocking concussion of a close-by field-inducer charge knocked him and Rajandra Das off their feet. Rajandra Das followed Mr. Jericho to cover as a volley of shots from the roof of the mayoral office shattered the facades of the houses on Alimantando Street. One second later a time quake ripped away the mayoral office into anywhen and replaced it with a quarter hectare of green pasture, white picket fence, and three and a half black and white cows.

"Child of grace!" whispered Rajandra Das. Mr. Jericho found a dead Parliamentarian boy-soldier in the doorway of a burned-out house and looted him of his clean white combat gear. Purple lightning flickered fitfully at one end of the street.

The two men scrambled through a world fallen into insanity. Here gravity had shifted ninety degrees to change streets into cliff faces, there bubbles of weightlessness bounced

down the lanes waiting to trap the foolhardy who ventured out
from their cellars; here half a house ran backward, there
garden plants grew to shady trees in seconds. Green figures like
long, thin men were seen capering on rooftops and drew the
fire of those soldiers capable of fighting. Phantoms of children
yet unborn danced hand in hand under trees that were yet
seeds.

"How far do you think it reaches?" asked Rajandra Das. A
powerful wind had sprung up, driving them inward toward
Steeltown, where the heart of the madness was spinning faster
faster faster, reaching deeper into the Panplasmic Omniverse.

"Local as of yet," replied Mr. Jericho. The steel wind
whipped at him. "But the longer the time winder runs, the
greater the zone of interference."

"Suppose I shouldn't say this, but my feet don't want to go
on. I'm terrified."

Mr. Jericho looked on the spinning curtain of lightning-
streaked smoke that shrouded Steeltown.

"So am I," he said. As Mr. Jericho and Rajandra Das raced
for the timewall, reality shuddered and shook. A whale swam
into Desolation Road station. An Archangelsk urinated in a
cabbage patch. A ghostly figure, tall as a tree, stood astride the
community solar plant and ripped searing solos from his red
guitar. Lightning flew from his fingertips and gathered into
tiny balls which blew like tumbleweeds around the two men's
feet. Mr. Jericho and Rajandra Das plunged into the whirlwind of smoke.

"What the . . . ?" A battle of statues was being fought
here: slugs and snails engaging each other with tachyon beams
slow as drunkards' punches.

"Time distortion," explained Mr. Jericho. "Let's go."

"You mean through?"

"They can't see us. Watch." Mr. Jericho danced across the
battle ground, ducking under sluggardly tachyon beams,
dodging sessile field-inducer bursts. "Come on." Rajandra Das
crept through the Einsteinian battlefield. He tried to imagine
how his passage seemed to the time-frozen combatants: was he
a whirlwind, a flash of light, a blur of multiple images, like
Captain Quick in the old comics his mother had used to buy
him? He followed Mr. Jericho down a corridor between two

steel converters into an unexpected free-fall zone. Rajandra Das's momentum took him straight up in an elegant reverse dive.

Mr. Jericho was shouting something, something about his field-inducers? He hadn't even thought about the device he was wearing. Defense canopy up? He didn't know how to do it. He fiddled with his wrist control and was rewarded with a prickle of static electricity across his face in the same instant as a sudden smashing blow sent him spinning through space. As he ricocheted off the side of Number 16 smokestack, he caught a glimpse of Mr. Jericho being bounced from wall to wall like a ball in a pachinko parlor. The central fusion tokamak was clearly well defended.

A second field-inducer blast sent Mr. Jericho zigzagging from steel furnace to ground to conveyor to converter. Only his looted defense canopy saved him from pulverizing death.

—Too old for this, he told his Exalted Ancestors. They reminded him of duty, and honor, and courage. Well they might, free as they were from the tyranny of time-bound flesh. —They can bounce us around like rubber balls all day if they want to. He saw Rajandra Das loom up before him; the two men smashed together and rebounded. As Mr. Jericho cartwheeled through the Anarchic Zone, his Exalted Ancestors reminded him that every second the world was oscillating farther from consensus reality.

In mid-bounce Rajandra Das realized that he had passed from the stage of being too terrified to be scared into the sublime state of hysteric comedy. What could be more ridiculous than being bounced around a steel works in the middle of a time storm by a gang of terrorists defending a fusion tokamak powering an out-of-control time machine? He knew that if he laughed at the joke, he would not be able to stop.

A crackle came over his ear-thimble.

"Hello, boys. Having fun?"

Mr. Jericho heard the voice on his earphone and answered.

"Persis! Darling! Jim Jericho. Request you launch an immediate attack on the forces entrenched around the Steeltown fusion plant."

"Check."

"Persis, I suggest you beware of severe reality displacements."

"You don't need to tell me."

"And Persis . . ."

"Yes?"

"If all else fails, and only if all else fails, if we can't get through, destroy the tokamak."

"There'll be . . ."

"A fusion explosion. Yes."

"Check. Here . . . we . . . go. . . ."

A rally of shots from the tokamak positions volleyed Jim Jericho like a handball as the Yamaguchi and Jones Stunter howled in over the smokestacks. Wing-mounted tachyon blasters kicked out, there was an explosion that made Mr. Jericho fear that maybe she had destroyed the tokamak, then Persis Tatterdemalion was climbing into the sky away from winged figures pursuing her with scimitars. Mr. Jericho dropped his canopy and caught hold of a stanchion. Rajandra Das did likewise, and as he drifted past, Mr. Jericho caught hold of his collar.

Not so much as a scrap of flesh or cloth remained of the defenders. The generator hall was empty of everything save the song of the tokamak.

"Spooky things," said Rajandra Das, laying rude hands on the controls.

"I thought you knew about these things."

"Locomotive tokamaks. This is different."

"Now you tell me."

"Well, Mr. Damantine-disciplines, you shut it down."

"Wouldn't have the first idea."

Distant explosions rent the air. Metal creaked and groaned and the iron tread of a fighting machine shook the generator hall. Rajandra Das's fingers moved over the control lamps, then hesitated.

"What happens when the power goes off?"

"I'm not certain."

"Not certain? Not certain?" Rajandra Das's exclamation rang from the steel walls.

"Theoretically, reality should snap back to consensus reality."

"Theoretically."

"Theoretically."

"Hell of a time for theoretically." Rajandra Das's fingers danced over the controls. Nothing happened. Again the fingers played. Nothing happened. A third time Rajandra Das played the control board like a chapel harmonium and a third time nothing happened.

"What's wrong?"

"I can't do it! It's been too long. I've lost the touch."

"Let me see . . ."

Rajandra Das waved Mr. Jericho away from the control lights with the muzzle of his field-inducer. He whispered some consignatory mumbles and emptied a full power burst into the control board. The two men staggered back from the explosion, blinded by sparks and flying circuitry. The fusion tokamak's usual serene hum rose to a shriek, a howl, a roar of outrage. Rajandra Das fell on his knees for divine forgiveness for a wastrel's life when the all-destroying fusion scream was silenced. And in the same instant the men felt themselves, the power hall, Steeltown, the whole world turn inside out and inside out again. With a thunderclap of inrushing reality the time winder imploded and drew Arnie Tenebrae's five-level-deep time-control center and all its staff into neverwhenness.

The timewall exploded outward. Free-fallers dropped out of the air; whales, archangels, and guitar players vanished, and the boiling rain blew away on the glowing wind. Every clock stopped in the time burst and stayed stopped forever, despite the attempts of subsequent generations many kilometers removed from the day of the time storm to restart them.

64

In the aftermath of the time storm Mr. Jericho emerged from the hall of the dead tokamak to find that theoretically, he had only been partly correct, theoretically. A full quarter of Steeltown had been sheared away as if by a knife of marvelous sharpness and in place of the pipes and girders red rock stretched to the horizon. The encirclement of Crystal Ferrotropes was broken by incongruous expanses of virgin dunes, green oases of banana trees, and a pockmarking of fused glass craters. As Rajandra Das joined his friend and the two men returned to Desolation Road, they passed through a fantastical landscape of the bizarre and curious. Streets ended in empty desert or were buried in huge sif dunes; locomotives stood in the middle of market gardens, houses in lakes. One track of the railroad line ended abruptly in a small but luxuriant patch of jungle, and the whole of the new development beyond the railroad was returned to bare High Plain.

Faces began to fill the streets. Dumbfounded by the alchemy that had engulfed Desolation Road, they searched for time-lost houses and families. They did not know, nor could they, that when the reality-warping power of the time winder was shut off, all those phantom geographies of Desolation Roads that might have been were fixed, fused, and made permanent the moment Mr. Jericho and Rajandra Das closed the door to the Panplasmic Omniverse.

The break was sealed; the battle was over. The survivors assessed degrees of victory. A full third of Marya Quinsana's Parliamentary Legion had been decreated when the time storm struck, returned to whatever tasks, occupations, or lives they might have led had not the beat of the recruiter's drum seduced them. Those who had not been swept into other-when-ness had sustained only slight casualties. The defending Whole Earth Army had been largely annihilated. Seventy-percent casualities, her entire command structure beheaded in whatever had taken place within the heavily guarded redoubt under Steeltown: Shannon Ysangani surrendered her remnant army to General Emiliano Murphy and cried tears of joyous laughter as her comrades were taken to the desert-edge detention camps.

"We lost!" she laughed, tears streaming down her face. "We lost! We lost!"

The Whole Earth Army was no more.

Two hours before nightfall the Yamaguchi and Jones twin-prop stunter GF666Z came in for landing beyond the railroad tracks. The last survivor of Tatterdemalion's Flying Circus was carried shoulder-high through the streets by the friends who loved her most, and Angel Red was brought in triumph and humility to the bar/hotel, where all hearts and hands saluted her.

That same evening Marya Quinsana made a torchlight triumph through Desolation Road. The Steeltown Ring was lined with fighting machines for her, the citizens cheered for her but she was unsatisfied. She had not won a clean victory. Tinkering with time and history offended her political sensibilities. History was written in the stones. It was not a numinous thing to be tossed sparkling in the air to lie where it fell. She did not like to think of her life and world as a mere mutability of potentials. She did not like to think about where all her decreated boy-soldiers had gone.

After the service of thanksgiving in the Basilica of the Gray Lady she demanded that Arnie Tenebrae be brought to her. She wanted very much to vent her dissatisfaction in mutilation and torment, but the subsequent search of Desolation Road and Steeltown did not turn up so much as her corpse. So after five days of triumph and victory before the cameras of the nine continents, Marya Quinsana returned to the hills of Wisdom to take the First Ministerial ring of office from the finger of the Honorable Vangelis Karolaitis only to find that that fine old gentleman was neither fine, gentlemanly, nor ultimately honorable, for he had enough accounts of his security minister's atrocities and outrages in quashing the Whole Earth Army Tactical Group to be very very sure that she would never take the ring from him while he lived. As for Little Arnie Tenebrae, Deathbird, Vastator, she was never heard of again, though there was no shortage of explanations, rumors, and idle gossip which in time became the fabric of folk story, which in time became legend, which in time became myth, and so Little Arnie Tenebrae's name came to be written in the sky which was only what she always ever wanted.

65

Inspiration Cadillac awoke in a steel shriek from an iron dream. Memory and awareness defied him—what were these bright lights, this high roof, these green-robed servants bowing awe-struck from his presence? He sat up to require an explanation and was answered with cries of alarm and religious dread.

"Master, master, oh, it's true, it's true! Oh, master, bless me."

A young postulant with a half-metal face fell to the floor in blatant adoration. Inspiration Cadillac stepped from the bed (an operating table?), caught sight of himself reflected in the white wall tiles, and remembered everything.

—Total mortification! Manmade steel . . . He looked down at his body, his hands, his limbs. Metal; smooth, hard metal untainted by corrupt flesh, unstained by red blood, all pure, holy metal. He threw up his steel arms in thanksgiving.

"Total mortification! Successful total mortification!" Glory-alleluiaing, the technical staff prostrated themselves. Inspiration Cadillac beheld his own glory in the wall tiles and remembered . . .

. . . the voice of the Great Engineer, calling him to prophethood

. . . army poised against army and the Poor Children, between them helpless, leaderless

. . . bright lights, humming, luminous machines, cold cold tiles, flashing steel, darkness.

"How long has it been?" he demanded of a female cybernetician.

"Eight days, holy one. The world has gone mad, holy father: the dome of the basilica has been destroyed, the sanctuary defiled by the fleshlies in their thanksgiving for victory; a war has been fought, lost, and won in these very streets, hundreds have died and . . . and forgive me, but time and space itself went mad. Everything is changed: madness has run loose in the universe."

"Peace, little one. It is then time that order and harmony were restored," said Inspiration Cadillac. In a flicker of concentration a black halo appeared around his right wrist. The technicians gasped and allelluiaed. "What the Gray Lady was, I now am, and more. She was base flesh, I am sanctified steel. I am the chosen of the Great Engineer, the Future Man; in my circuits burns the power . . ." And he opened his right hand and darkness flowed over all the technicians save those two who had spoken with Inspiration Cadillac, and it transformed them into black smoking somethings so hideous and obscene they defied the imagination. Inspiration Cadillac laughed a metal laugh. He had the addiction for power, and each successive abuse must be richer, deeper, fuller. Before his cowering acolytes he transformed himself, sprouting wings, rotor blades, buzz saws, tachyon blasters, radio antennae, portable table-harmoniums, wheels, tracks, jets, rockets, washing machines in a blur of alchemy.

"Come with me," he commanded the cyberneticist and the technician who had hailed him master. "I am tired of transformation." To the cyberneticist he said, "You shall be my chamberlain," to the technician, "you my chief engineer.

Don't fear me . . . you must love me. I command it. Now, I wish to receive the adulation of my people."

"Ah," said the chamberlain.

"Eh," said the chief technician.

"Where are the faithful?" demanded Inspiration Cadillac.

"Alas, they were not faithful as we were faithful," said the chamberlain.

"They believed you'd died when the airplane crashed into the dome and it collapsed," said the chief engineer.

"You were, of course, safe underground," said the chamberlain.

"But they weren't to know that," said the chief engineer.

"So they, ah, turned their devotions elsewhere."

"They've found something else to worship."

"It's, ah, a train."

"It came out of Steeltown after the time storm and offered to take all the Poor Children to safety."

"You see the parallel, holy father: the prophecies you circulated about the Steel Messiah coming out of Steeltown to save the faithful from war and devastation."

"They, eh, went with it."

"What?" roared Inspiration Cadillac. Growing rotor blades, he leaped into the air.

"Go west," advised the chamberlain.

From the air Inspiration Cadillac could see how some calamity worse than mere war had struck Faith City. The dome of the Basilica of the Gray Lady (now, he noted, the Basilica of the Total Mortification) lay in shards and slabs on the tiled floor of the audience chamber. The entire east wing together with a dozen hectares of Faith City had been swept away and replaced with a similar area of planted and irrigated maize. The Gray Lady's private quarters were a fused cracked crater in the rock, and beside it stood the tangled remains of some kind of clumsy three-legged device.

—What has been happening? War, dread, outrage, apostasy; with a locomotive!

It was not even a particularly good example of locomotive building skills, Inspiration Cadillac decided, spying it from afar as a line of white steam on the western horizon. A Great Southern Class 27 fusion hauler; tokamaks due a good overhaul. Paintwork blistered and peeled, what was that it read Adam Black's Traveling Chautauqua and Educational 'Stravaganza? Pathetic. Shining silver-bright in the desert sun, Inspiration Cadillac patched in his public address system and chastized his people.

"O ye of little faith!" Faces at the windows of the ramshackle carriages. They looked frightened. That was good. "O faithless and perverse generations! I promised that I would return to you as the Total Mortification, yet not one of you would wait the eight days for the promise to be fulfilled! Covenant-breakers! Idolators! You worship this . . . Golden Calf rather than the physical manifestation of the Cosmic Engineer! See how I shatter all false idols!" He helicoptered in over the speeding train and raised his hand to hurl a thunderbolt of cybernetic command.

"We'd all much rather you didn't do that," said the train quite unexpectedly. The power evaporated from Inspiration Cadillac's fingertips.

"What?"

The train repeated its statement word for word.

"A talking train! My my my."

"Something more than that," said the Great Southern Class 27. "I am the Total Mortification."

"Nonsense! Blasphemy! I am the Total Mortification, the one, the only."

"You are a manmade machine. I am a machinemade man. At heart, you are flesh, for you still wear the outward form of a man, but I have gone beyond such anthropomorphic chauvinism. I am machine in the form of machine."

Poor Children's heads poked out of the windows, evidently enjoying the theosophical wranglings. Inspiration Cadillac found his curiosity roused despite his fury and asked, "What manner of creature are you?"

"Take a look in my liveried carriage," the train replied. Inspiration Cadillac retracted his rotors and made a jet-power landing on the paint-peeling roof. He extended a telescopic camera eye over the edge to peer in. The windows were thick with cobwebs and dirt, as was the carriage itself; dust, cobwebs, age, and neglect. In the center of the carriage sat a cracked leather armchair and in the armchair sat a mummified corpse. Upon the corpse's head was a metal diadem of peculiar and intricate design.

"Adam Black that was," said the train. "When his soul passed into me, I sealed the carriage, never to be opened again. All that carriage represents is past me now, I am a machine/man, the true future man, the Total Mortification if you wish. For many years I traveled the railroads of the world searching for some purpose for my spiritual identity, then I heard of the Dumbletonians of Desolation Road, a place I knew well in my fleshly incarnation, and my heart told me that here was the reason for my being. So I came, and they hailed me the Steel Messiah, and so they came with me in their tattered caravan of old carriages and wagons. And as there can be only one Steel Messiah, alas we must now do battle."

Inspiration Cadillac sprang away from the speeding train with a pulse of pure jet power as Adam Black sent a circuit-fusing cybernetic command crackling along his superstructure. Inspiration Cadillac climbed to a safe altitude, then unleashed a bolt of purest God-power that severed the Poor Children's shanty-coaches from the Traveling Chautauqua and Educational 'Stravaganza. By the time the blasphemous train had applied emergency braking and ground to a halt, Inspiration Cadillac had spun a diamond-filament cable out of his feet and was towing his faithful back to Desolation Road. Adam Black blew white steam, reversed direction, and accelerated after the Poor Children.

Inspiration Cadillac dropped his cargo and turned to meet the aggressor. Adam Black braked and stood pulsing with fusion power on the track.

"Not here," he said. "You will agree that the safety of the Poor Children is paramount?"

"Agreed."

"Very well then." Adam Black throttled up and accelerated along the westbound line. Inspiration Cadillac loosed a blistering command for his rival's fusion engines to explode. Adam Black's computerized defenses effortlessly nullified the spell. Rocketman and trainman battled with commands and countercommands for fifty kilometers into the desert without success. For the next twenty kilometers they employed physical weaponry. Sonic clashed with sonic, missiles were met with swarms of robot killer bees, machine guns with roof-mounted laser turrets, limpet mines with robomonkeys, lightning with lightning, claws with water cannon, servo-assisted punches with polymer foam, blasts of superheated steam with microwave bursts: the Total Mortifications battled until Desolation Road was no more than a memory over the eastern horizon.

Then Inspiration Cadillac saw a dazzlesome flash far off on the edge of the world. It was followed by another flash, then another, then another, and in the blinking of a blinded eye he was embedded in a cone of white-hot light. Even as the realization of what Adam Black had done came to him, his chromed skin began to glow cherry red, then scarlet, then yellow, and his circuits fused and ran like tar.

—Most ingenious, redirecting ROTECH sky mirrors to focus on me. I didn't think enemy mine was so resourceful. Brave thoughts but empty. He was now shining white hot. Though they repaired themselves as rapidly as the heat destroyed them, his transmogrification circuits would hold only a matter of minutes before they dissolved. He tried to reach out and break Adam Black's control of the Vanas but the locomotive will was too entrenched.

He could feel his yet-human brain boiling in its metal skull.

Then he had it.

—One better, he cried to his fiery systems. One better. He summoned all his failing strength and reached into the sky, up, up, past the sky-mirrors and the orphs and the blitches and the habitats, to the world-busting partacs. He slipped in, possessed the guidance and firing systems and aimed fifteen orbital sub-quarkal particle accelerators at Adam Black, a tiny hurtling flea on the skin of the round earth.

In the instant before Inspiration Cadillac gave the command to fire, Adam Black guessed his strategy.

"Stupid stupid stupid, the blast will destroy us both! No! Don't!"

"Yes yes yes!" cried Inspiration Cadillac as his sanity melted and his brain dissolved and he fired the partacs.

In Desolation Road the people said it was like a second dawn: it was beautiful, they said. They had seen fifteen violet beams strike down from the sky like the justice of the Panarch and then the white blast, pure as virtue, had filled the western horizon for a whole two seconds. Beautiful, they said, beautiful . . . the afterblast had dyed the western lip of the world pink and blue and the insubstantial veils of auroral discharges had wavered like ghosts over the scene of the explosion. For a month after, Desolation Road was treated to stunningly beautiful sunsets.

When the Poor Children returned, towing a rickety train of old carriages and rolling stock made from reprocessed favelas behind them, they brought with them the true story of the end of Adam Black's Traveling Chautauqua and Educational 'Stravaganza and Inspiration Cadillac, Chamberlain of the Gray Lady, Total Mortification.

"The world was not ready for Total Mortification," they said. Chamberlain and chief engineer, cyberneticist and technician deliberated over the significance of what had happened at the western edge of the world, then gave the long-awaited and half-forgotten order that sent the Poor Children of the Immaculate Contraption into Steeltown by dead of night to steal one of the abandoned and forgotten Class 88 steel haulers that had lain gathering rust and spiders since the days of the Great Strike. Under the leadership of the chamberlain and chief engineer, whose names were Plymouth Glyde and Spirit Dynamo, the Poor Children of the Immaculate Contraption departed Desolation Road to pursue the still unresolved issue of machine rights. They steamed out of Desolation Road in the opposite direction to that from which they had come so many years before, because to go that way would have led them to a yawning hole in the desert, a crater of green glass where Adam Black's aged tokamaks had exploded under the shriek of superaccelerated sub-quarkal beams from heaven and dispersed the atoms of man, machine, and mortification into the beautiful sunset.

66

On dusty evenings when the summer lightning brought ephemeral life to the cracked neon tubes of the closed-up hotels and diners, Mr. Jericho and Rajandra Das would sit on the porch to drink beer and remember.

"Hey, remember Persis Tatterdemalion," Rajandra Das would say.

"She was a fine lady," Mr. Jericho would reply, watching the lightning crackle along the horizon. "A fine fine lady," and they would call to mind the colorful thread of history she had woven into the tale of Desolation Road until it reached an end with her flying off into the sunset after being lauded savior of the town with her two sons on either wing in the cargo 'lighters bought at crash-out prices from the Bethlehem Ares Corporation. The money from the sale of the bar/hotel had enabled her to hire two additional pilots: Callan and Venn Lefteremides, war-scarred but intact after the attack on Desolation Road.

"Wonder what she's up to these days?" Rajandra Das would say, and Mr. Jericho would reply, "Flying still. Last thing I heard she had set up the Flying Circus over Transpolaris way, New Glasgow, I think, and she was making it pretty big."

Then Rajandra Das would say, "Wonder what Umberto and Louie are doing?"

After the final battle, while the ROTECH time-security teams were tooth-combing Desolation Road for whatever it was that had so rudely shattered their comptemplative peace, Persis Tatterdemalion had made it clear to the Gallacelli brothers that she had not returned for them but to gather her

sons to her and sell the bar/hotel. The brothers' one-and-only
love for her had never been reciprocated. It was possible for
three men to love the same ideal woman, but not for that one
woman to love three men. So they packed all the years into
cardboard suitcases along with their underpants, their documents, their cash boxes, and Umberto's collection of porno-
graphic photographs. In the absence of trains (the Company
was being tardy about repairing the gap in the line seventy
kilometers due west due to disputes over the danger money
payable on account of the radiation) an overland truck convoy
took Umberto and Louie on to Meridian, where Umberto had
established a real estate business, selling plots of land in the
Ecclesiastes Mountains and Louie leased an office from which
to practice the business of lawyering, some years later
obtaining a famous acquittal in the case of the Butcher of
Llandridnodd Wells.

"The old place was never the same after the war," Rajandra
Das would always say. This was a conversation he and Mr.
Jericho had held so many times that it had passed through the
meaningless mumbles of prayers and responses into renewed
meaningfulness. "When the folks went, the place just died."

First the pilgrims and the Holy Children, then the
gentlemen of the media. Next, the hoteliers, hostel keepers,
and restauranteurs who had sheltered, fed, and watered them.
Then, blown away in a day and a night, the Bethlehem Ares
Corporation, blown away in a hurricane of tumbling profit
margins and drawn knives up in the lofty troposphere of the
executive levels as the scandal of the robot duplicates was
gradually unearthed, like buried excrement. All its labor units,
its managers and section overseers, all were dispersed like so
much red dust across the face of the planet. Finally, the Poor
Children of the Immaculate Contraption, after the Battle of
the Prophets blew a ten-megaton hole in the Meridian-
Pandemonium mainline. And last of all, Jean-Michel Gastineau, the Most Sarcastic Man in the World, sarcasm forever
blunted, went home to his woods and glens in haunted
Chryse.

"And what did it all achieve?" Rajandra Das would finally
ask. By time-honored tradition Mr. Jericho refrained from
reply though he perhaps knew better than anyone else left in

Desolation Road. "Nothing," Rajandra Das would self-answer. "I tell you, all that praying and marching and striking, all that fighting and bloodshed and days and nights of fear, what did it get them? Nothing. Nothing at all. Waste of time, energy, and lives."

Mr. Jericho did not speak of words like "principles" or "absolutes" when Rajandra Das vilified Concordat's failure to win a true victory over Bethlehem Ares Steel, for he was no longer sure he believed in absolutes or principles. To him the collapse of the Company and thus of Desolation Road was of little consequence so long as the sun kept shining, the crops kept growing, and the occasional rains kept falling from heaven. His belief in Desolation Road was more selfish than Rajandra Das's. He liked to think it was also more realistic. He remembered the first day it had ever rained. Fifteen years had gone past since then. Time passed by so soon. There was an irrational fear wandering around inside him that Desolation Road might vanish entirely from existence and he would not notice the difference. The people had gone, the shops had closed, the banks transferred their credit back to the big cities of the Grand Valley, the lawyers, hairdressers, mechanics, counsellors, doctors had left the same day the railroad was repaired; all that remained were the farms and the solar panels and the creaking wind-pumps and the empty empty streets. These days the trains called only once a week, if even that. Everything was as it had been at the beginning. History had stopped for Desolation Road and Desolation Road was thankful for it.

One day as the two men sat in their leather chairs watching the desert dust whip along the street, Rajandra Das said, "You know, I suppose I mustn't have been the marriageable type."

Mr. Jericho did not know what he meant.

"I always thought one of those Pentecost sisters would lay ahold of me, but they never did. Funny thing. I always reckoned they would. Well, now they're away God knows where, and here I am, without a wife, without a farm, with only a token half-share in the porch I'm sitting on. Haven't even got my charm over machines, that got took back; what I am is a bum again. Maybe that's what I always was, that's why they never married me."

"You thinking of leaving?" asked Mr. Jericho. He had known Rajandra Das long enough to read his heart like a railroad timetable.

"There's nothing holding me here, least of all this place. You see, I always wanted to see Wisdom, those sparklin' towers beside the Syrtic Sea."

"Should have asked Miss Quinsana to take you back with her."

Rajandra Das spat at the moonring.

"She wouldn't give me a wipe of her ass now and she ain't worth one of mine. No, if I go, I want to go on my own. I've got time enough to learn to be a bum again and I'm old enough to enjoy that time. No future to worry about."

Mr. Jericho looked into the heavens. The stars seemed close enough to touch that night.

"Maybe I should go with you," he mused. "I always said I was just passing through." But he stayed and Rajandra Das found himself running up on the blindside of a slow early-morning ore train. As he swung onto the wagon-plate and scrambled up the ladder onto the top of the car, he felt the years fall away. This was what he had been meant to do all his life. He was the Bum Eternal, the archetype of the Traveling Man. He had just taken a long wait between trains.

For a year and a day he roamed the world's interesting places, sending back picture postcards of himself standing by the Chasm of Lyx or in the floating flower market of Llangonnedd or squatting outside the legendary Glen Miller's Jazz Bar on Belladonna's Sorrowful Street. Kaan Mandella pinned the postcards up around the back-bar mirror for all citizens to see and wonder upon. Then one Thursday Rajandra Das succumbed to the urge that he had successfully resisted for the year and the day and went to Wisdom, the most beautiful city in the world. He had resisted the temptation for so long because he feared he might be disappointed, but as he walked the shining boulevards and gazed on mighty bridges and towers and took his siesta (agreeable habits dying hard) in a café beneath the shade of the bo trees lining Nevsky Prospect and dined in the waterside seafood restaurants and rode a tram to the top of each of the forty hills, it was all as he had imagined, glorious in every detail. He wrote card after card of glowing praise to Mr. Jericho.

"This is the most wonderful place in the world," he wrote in his final card from Wisdom, "but I can't stay here forever. There's other places to see and there's always Widsom to come back to. It's not going anywhere. If I'm passing through, I'll pay you a call."

It was Rajandra Das's final card from anywhere. Riding back to Llangonnedd and wondering where he might go that would satisfy him after the fulfillment of a lifetime's ambition, a tickle of dust prickled his nose. A sudden fit of sneezing seized him and he sneezed out his last little drop of power over machinery. He lost his grip on the bogie, fell with a small cry under the wheels of the Wisdom-Llangonnedd Syrtis Express, and died.

On the day that Mr. Jericho received his final postcard, a train arrived in Desolation Road. Since the town died, this was a sufficiently unusual event for the entire citizenry to turn out to welcome it. Most trains thundered through at 400 km/hr., leaving dust and flying pebbles as souvenirs. Even more unusual than the train's stopping, two passengers stepped off. Apart from traveling salesmen and gullible tourists whom Kaan Mandella lured to the bar/hotel with the promise of trips to the geological curiosities of the Crystal Land, the rule was that people always got *on* trains at Desolation Road. These passengers did not look like salesmen or tourists. They wore knee-length silk jackets of the kind that had recently become fashionable in the Big Cities. They wore high-heeled hand-tooled leather gaucho boots and upon their heads were wide-brimmed round cardinal hats. They looked like killers.

One side-of-eye glimpse was enough to convince Mr. Jericho. He slipped away from the gawking crowd and went to his bedroom. In the bottom drawer of his tallboy was the manbone-handled needle-pistol wrapped in the red paisley scarf. Mr. Jericho knew who the visitors were. They were assassins of the Exalted Families, come to kill him.

At last.

Their names were AlphaJohn and BetaJohn. Since being decanted from Paternoster Damien's Genesis-bottle, they had spent their lives searching the world for Paternoster Jericho.

For the first five years of their lives (passed in the two-in-one mutuality unique to twin-clones) they had searched the cities and the towns. They had found nothing. Then for a year and a half they went back over the territory that had been covered by their predecessors before they had been in-vitroed. Killer-clones bred for their gift of pair-empathy, they knew themselves infallible and scorned the skill of those predecessors. But that search, too, found nothing. Then for another year and a half they studied old records and data nets for some thread they might follow; some scent, some spoor, some fingerprint that might lead them to Paternoster Jericho. They were dogged, they were determined, they were zealous. They could not be other. But the scent was cold, the spoor rained away, the fingerprints smudged. So they called up an Exalted Families' computer, and with its help compiled a list of places where Paternoster Jericho was not or had not been and by a process of elimination reduced the planet's teeming millions in all its towns, cities, and metropolises down to fifteen locations. Last on that list was Desolation Road. It was the last place in the world they thought of looking for him.

Therefore AlphaJohn and BetaJohn were confident when they asked Rael Mandella, Jr., if there was a man named Jericho in town and when in all innocence he answered yes and told them where they might find him, they felt something close to joy that the investment made in creating them had paid its due dividend. AlphaJohn and BetaJohn counted twelve canals down and five canals in and found Mr. Jericho pollinating a stand of hybrid maize with a feather.

—Should have kept on passing through, he said to himself, and went forward to greet his assassins. Polite bows, names, pleasantries about the weather were exchanged.

"From Damien?" asked Mr. Jericho after a time. Cart-wheel-brimmed hats tipped simultaneously.

"World searched," said AlphaJohn.

"Last place," said BetaJohn. They rested their hands above the pockets Mr. Jericho knew must hold their needle-pistols.

"Took your time," said Mr. Jericho, rifling his Exalted Ancestors for something that might save him from the indignity of dying in a maize field. "Tell me, you boys good?" The Johns nodded. "The best?" Again the slow tilt of the wide-brimmed hats. "How do you know?" Hats halted in mid-tilt. Little black currant eyes looked out from the shade. "All you've ever done is hunt people. If you're good, you've got to prove it. To me. Against me." He let them cogitate on that for a few seconds, then whipped them again. "I reckon this old man could take you both. What do you say?" By their reactions to his words Mr. Jericho reckoned they must be clones, perhaps even pseudo-simultaneous clones, for their eyes sparkled pseudo-simultaneously at the challenge.

"Accepted," said AlphaJohn.

"Designate," said BetaJohn.

Mr. Jericho suppressed a little grin of triumph. He had them, and knowing that, he knew he could beat them. A true professional would have stitched him crotch to forehead immediately after wishing "good morning." These clone twins were vain and if they possessed the fault of vanity there would be other faults to exploit.

"Outside the bar," said Mr. Jericho. "Whole town free-fire zone." Their telegraphic mode of speaking was infectious. "No civilians, no hostages, no poisons, formal rules. Needle-pistols only. Take it you boys have them? Good. Be there . . . high noon." No, that was siesta time. Siesta time was traditionally inviolable. Nothing must be permitted to disturb the dying town's rest in the heat heat heat of the noontime. "Sorry, old custom, have to be fifteen o'clock." When the second advent of the Pantochrist was heralded by the hosts of the Five Heavens, even that would have to wait until after siesta time in Desolation Road.

67

Mr. Jericho stood in the fifteen o'clock dust beneath the time-stormed bar clock and remembered kneeling. Kneeling in the Hall of Ten Thousand Candles (no misnomer, he had been set to count them once as punishment for a boyhood misdemeanor: 10,027) trying to ascribe meaning to Paternoster Augustine's riddlesome roans. Unvastened as he was then, bereft of the souls of his ancestors, Paternoster Augustine's quandaries had seemed pointless; now he treasured their little wisdoms.

"Use your senses," Paternoster Augustine had told him and told him again. "Use all your senses. Consider the rabbit." Ah, but he had been down his burrow for five years now and he was old, and though he had of late taken up the Damantine Disciplines to ward off tightening sinews and grating bones, he was not the man he had once been. Ah, but then he would have drubbed these two vain striplings in a trice. Then. Now it was his trained senses against identity-telepathy. Witch-magic. He spat into the wind three times and crossed fingers and toes.

No one was more surprised than he when the little automaton gentleman dressed in Deuteronomy green who had sounded the time for Desolation Road defied his time-frozen mechanics to waltz out and strike the bronze bell with his little mallet. On the last note of the fifteen the little man seized arthritically forever and two pairs of high-heeled hand-tooled leather gaucho boots kicked up the dust and turned toes toward Mr. Jericho's battered brogues.

"Formal rules?"

"Formal rules."

"No poisons?"

"No poisons."

"Might as well begin then." And two steel needles kicked puffs of dried whitewash out of the wall at the end of the street.

—My but they're quick! Mr. Jericho crawled out of the far side of the veranda under which he had rolled and looked for cover. A needle grazed his left earlobe and buried itself in the warped wooden planking of the veranda. —Fast, very fast, too fast for an old man? Mr. Jericho jumped behind a low wall and squeezed his first needle off at the snake-quick figure in black silk that had fired on him. —Run run run! the Exalted Ancestors shouted, and he ran ran ran just as a string of needles pitted and cracked the white plasterwork where he had been crouching. —Always remember there are two of them, the limbosouls told him.

—I'm not about to forget it, he told them, and rolled and fired all in one cat-graceful action. The needle howled wide of the black-hatted figure diving down from the roof.

—One in the street, one in the alley. They've got you running. You get them running. You built this town with your own hands, you know it. Use that knowledge. The Ancestors were dogmatic. Mr. Jericho zigzagged down Alimantando Street toward the timelost patch of jungle vinery and drew a stitching of needles closer and closer to his twinkling heels. He leaped for the veranda of the Pentecost Sisters' General Merchandise Store and the last needle embedded itself in his footprint.

—They are good. A perfect team. What one sees, the other sees, what one knows the other knows. He consciously brought his breathing under discipline in the Harmonic Mode and let his Ancestors kick him into the sensory state of the Damantine Praxis. Mr. Jericho closed his eyes and heard dust motes fall in the street. He took a deep breath through his nostrils, tagged a stench of hot tense sweat, popped up at a window, and pumped off two needles.

—Knowledge. An unbidden memory, demanding as unbidden memories always are, bubbled to the front of his head: Paternoster Augustine's garden; a pergola amid trees and singing birds, velvet-smooth grass beneath feet, the scent of hyme and jasmine in the air, above head the mottled opal of Motherworld.

"Learn all you can," said Paternoster Augustine seated in a epidoptiary of rare fritilliaries. "Knowledge is power. This is no riddle, but a true saying and much to be trusted. Knowledge is power."

—Knowledge is power, repeated the massed choir of all souls. What do you know about your enemies that will give you power over them? They are identical clones. They have been reared in identical environments so that they have developed the same responses to the same stimuli and thus can be considered to be one person in two bodies.

That was the sum total of his knowledge of AlphaJohn and BetaJohn. And now Mr. Jericho knew how to beat them.

A shadow squeezed off a needle from behind a pump gantry. Mr. Jericho shifted his head the moment he sensed the metal latticework cool in the man's shadow. He slipped from the General Merchandise Store veranda, crept tigerman through the jungle vines, and made a low fast run through the maize fields for his destination. The solar power plant. Mr. Jericho crawled soily-bellied through the geometrical domain of reflections and held his antique needle-pistol pressed close to his chest. He smiled a thin smile. Let the smart boys come hunting him here. He waited as an old, dry black spider waits for flies. And they came, cautiously advancing through the field of angled mirrors, starting at reflections and flibbertygibbets of the light. Mr. Jericho closed his eyes and let his ears and nose guide. He could hear the heliotropic motors shifting the lozenges to track the sun; he could hear water gurgling through black plastic pipes; he could hear the sounds and smell the smells of confusion as the clones in the mirror-maze found themselves cloned. Mr. Jericho heard AlphaJohn wheel and fire at the looming shape rearing up behind him. He heard the glass crack into a spiderweb of fissures, the reflection shot through the heart. There was quiet for a while and he knew that the Johns were conferring, ascertaining each other's position so they would not fire on each other. Telepathic conference done, the hunt resumed. Mr. Jericho rose to the crouch and listened.

He heard footfalls on soft red dust, footfalls approaching.

He could tell that the target's back was momentarily turned by the sound his heels made on the earth. Mr. Jericho smelled human sweat. A clone was entering the row of mirrors. Mr. Jericho squeezed his eyes tight shut, stood up, and fired two-handed. The needle took AlphaJohn (or maybe BetaJohn, the distinction was trivial) clean between the eyes. A tiny red caste mark appeared on his brow. The clone emitted a curious squawk and slipped to the ground. An echoing, answering wail came up from the depths of the mirror-maze and Mr. Jericho felt a glow of satisfaction as he loped through the rows of reflectors toward the cry. The twin had shared his clone-brother's death. He had felt the needle slip into his forebrain and rive away light life love, for they were one person in two bodies. As Mr. Jericho and his Exalted Ancestors had surmised. Mr. Jericho found the brother gasping on the ground, eyes gazing at the high arch of heaven. A little stigmata of expressed blood sat on his forehead.

"Shouldn't have given me the chance," said Mr. Jericho, and he shot him through the left eye. "Punks."

Then he returned to the bar/hotel, where the little man in Deuteronomy green had frozen in commemoration of the last gunfight. He went up to the bar and told Kaan Mandella to drop whatever he was doing, pack all his worldly possessions, and come with him that very hour to the important places of the world, where together they would regain all the power and prestige and transplanetary might that had been Paternoster Jericho's.

"If that was their best, they are no match for this old man, none of them. They have gone soft over the years, while the desert has made me old and hard, like a tree root."

"Why me?" asked Kaan Mandella, head swirling whirling with the unexpectedness of it all.

"Because you are your father's son," said Mr. Jericho. "You are marked with the family curse of rationalism as Limaal was before you, I can see it, smell it, down there beneath the dollars-and-centavos business nose, deep down there you want order and power and an answer to every question and in the place where we are going that is going to be a very useful skill. So, are you coming with me?"

"Sure. Why not?" said Kaan Mandella with a grin, and

that very afternoon the two of them, armed only with an antique manbone-handled needle-pistol, successfully held up and hijacked the 14:14 Ares express and rode it into Belladonna's Bram Tchaikovsky Station and a destiny as glorious as it was terrible.

68

Now that the final summer had come, Eva Mandella liked to work outdoors under the shade of an umbrella tree by the front door of her rambling home. She liked to smile and talk to strangers, but she was now so incredibly ancient that she no longer dwelled in the Desolation Road of the 14th Decade but rather in a Desolation Road peopled with and largely constructed from the memories of every decade since the world was invented. Many of the strangers she smiled and talked to were therefore memories, as were the pilgrims and tourists for whom she still laid out every morning her hand-woven hangings worked with the traditional (traditional in that she had invented it and it was curious to her times and place) designs of condors, llamas, and little men and women holding hands. Sometimes, increasingly rarely, there would be the clunk of dollars and centavos in her money box, and Eva Mandella would look up from her tapestry loom and remember the day, month, year, and decade. Out of gratitude for having drawn her back to the 14th Decade, or possibly out of denial of it, she would always refund the money to the curiosity-seeking tourists who bought her weavings. Then she would resume her conversation with the unseen guests. One afternoon in early August a stranger came and asked her, "This is the Mandella house, is it not?"

"It is," said Eva Mandella, at work upon her tapestry history of Desolation Road. She could not tell if this stranger was memory or reality. He was a tall leather-brown man in a long gray desert coat. On his back was a large pack of great complexity sprouting coils of cable and antennae. He was too much a memory to be real but too rank with dust and sweat to be wholly memory. Eva Mandella could not remember his name.

"Is Rael in?" asked the stranger.

"My husband is dead," said Eva Mandella. The tragedy was so old and cold and stale, it was no longer tragic.

"Is Limaal in?"

"Limaal is dead too." But often the memories of both son and husband whiled away long afternoons in remembrance of other days. "My grandson, Rael, Jr., is in the fields at the moment, if you want to talk to him."

"Rael, Jr., is a name I don't know," said the stranger. "So I will talk with you, Eva. Could you tell me what year it is?"

"One thirty-nine," said Eva Mandella, drawn back from the desert of ghosts to the dying summer, and in doing so passing through the place of recognition and so knowing name and face of the stranger.

"That early," said Dr. Alimantando. He took a pipe from his coat pocket, filled it, and lit up. "Or rather, that late? I was trying for either eighteen months from now, or about three years back, to try to find out what happened, or rather is going to happen to the town. Accuracy's a bit tricky with the really long jumps: ten minutes ago I was eight million years away."

What was wonderful to Eva Mandella was not how far or how fast Dr. Alimandando had come, but that he had come at all; for even she who had known him personally in the early days of the settlement had almost come to believe those who said Dr. Alimantando was as legendary as the greenperson he had gone to hunt.

"So you didn't find the greenperson then?" she asked, setting up a new pick of desert-coat gray thread.

"I didn't find the greenpeople," agreed Dr. Alimantando, drawing long and leisurely on his pipe. "But I did save the town, which was my chief concern. That much I have achieved and I'm quite content though I'll never get a word of thanks or praise for it because no one'll ever know. Even I forget sometimes: I think living across two time-lines is blurring my memories of what is history and what isn't."

"What are you talking about, silly man?" scolded Eva Mandella.

"Time and paradox, reality-shaping, history-shaping. Do you know how long it's been since I stepped into time that night?" He held up one long digit. "That long. One year. For me. For you . . . Eva, I hardly knew you! Everything's changed so much. In that one year I traveled up and down the time lines, up and down, forward and back." Dr. Alimantando watched Eva Mandella's fingers weaving threads together, twisting, twining, warping, wefting. "Time traveling is like your weaving," he said. "There is no single thread running from past to future, there are many threads, and like your warps and wefts, they cross and mingle to form the fabric of time. And I've seen the fabric, and guessed at its width, and I have seen so many things, strange and wonderful things, that I should be here until nightfall if I were to tell you them all."

But he did, and he was. By the time he had finished chronicling his adventures in plastic forests billennia dead, sketching down in his notebooks the bizarre polymer flora and fauna, and his sightseeing trips around the future achievements of mankind, colossal feats of science, and learning that rendered the jewel in this age's crown, the manforming of the world, trivial and petty by comparison; by the time he had related his travels in the planetary jungle of flower-ripe trees in search of men no longer human, so transformed were they by their own hands that they wore the form of pulpy red melanges of organs, bulbous arboreal creatures with hard shells and gripping tentacles casting their reality-shaping intelligences into the chasms of the Multiverse so to commune with the lofty interdimensional wills that presided there, by the time he had told all this *and* how he had seen the sun glaze over with ice and walked on the lava-warm rock of the newborn earth with the lightnings of Genesis forking all around him; and how he had seen St. Catherine plant the Tree of World's Beginning in the bare red rock of Chryse and also stood upon the summit of Olympica, loftiest of mountains, to see the sky lase violet with glowing partac beams as ROTECH battled the otherwordly invaders known as the Celestials on the very first day of the 22nd Decade, *and* how that very morning, this very morning, he had sipped his breakfast mint tea upon the planetary ice cap as the horizon filled with the bloated, moribund sun while around his tent under the surface of the ice crawled the peculiar geometrical patterns that he reasoned must be the remnants of the humanity of that time of ending: by the time he had told all this the shadows *were* growing long beneath the umbrella tree and the air held an edge of evening crispness and the moonring was beginning to sparkle overhead and Eva Mandella had woven Dr. Alimantando and all his tales of wonder and horror into her tapestry in a colorful knot of jungle greens and battle violets and morbid reds and ice blues through which ran the gray thread of the time traveler.

"But," said Dr. Alimantando, "nowhere in all my ramblings across the ages of the world did I find the age of the greenpersons. Yet all history is patterned with their footprints." He gazed at the silver bracelet moonring. "Even this place. This place more than most, I think. It was a greenperson who led me here to found Desolation Road."

"Silly man," said Eva Mandella. "Everybody knows that Desolation Road was founded by charter from ROTECH."

"There are histories and histories," said Dr. Alimantando. "Since going timefree I've caught glimpses of so many other histories running parallel to this one that I'm no longer certain which is true and real. Desolation Road had other beginnings, and other endings."

For the first time Dr. Alimantando saw what it was that Eva Mandella was working upon.

"What's this?" he exclaimed with greater surprise than any tapestry should elicit.

Eva Mandella, who had been slowly, gently, sinking down toward the desert of ghosts again, was startled into the present by her guest's outburst.

"That's my history," she said. "The history of Desolation Road. Everything that happens is woven onto the frame. Even you. See? History is like weaving; every character a thread that moves in and out of the weft of events. See?"

Dr. Alimantando unbuttoned his long duster coat and withdrew a roll of fabric. He spread it out before Eva Mandella. She peered in the moonring silvery twilight.

"This is my tapestry. How did you get my tapestry?"

"From farther up in time. This is not my first visit to Desolation Road." He did not tell her where he had found it, fixed to its frame in the dust-choked ruins of the very house before which he sat in a future Desolation Road, dead, deserted, swallowed by dust. He did not want to frighten her. Eva Mandella tapped the cloth with a forefinger.

"See? Those threads I have not woven yet. Look, a green thread, and a dust brown one and . . . " She grew unexpectedly frightened and angry. "Take it away, I don't want to see it! I don't want to read what the future will be, because my death is woven in there somewhere, my death and the end of Desolation Road."

Then Rael, Jr., came from the maize fields to take his grandmother in for her dinner, because she often wandered so far into the desert of memories that she would forget to come inside when the chill night fell. He feared for her frailty though she was stronger than he would have guessed; he feared her turning to ice in the night.

In these latter days of history many of the old traditions of the first days were reestablished in their honored places. Among them was the tradition of open-door hospitality to strangers. Dr. Alimantando was set in the honored place at the table and between forkfuls of Kwai Chen Pak's lamb pilaf learned the reasons for the empty seats around the planed desert oak board. In the course of this old tragedy much that had appeared strange to him when he stepped out of time was explained and his year of traveling through such history had lent him a certain detachment from events, even events among the friends in a town he had invented himself. Though the folk history raised more questions than it answered, the timestorm clarified a puzzlement in Dr. Alimantando's mind. He now understood why he had been unable to reach the central period events that had led to the ultimate destruction of Desolation Road: the rogue timewinder (plus rather than minus, he surmised) had generated a zone of chronokinetic repulsion about itself that increased in strength the closer he approached the three-year distant heart of the mystery. He contemplated traveling back before the battle of Desolation Road, perhaps living through it incognito. The idea sorely tempted him, but he knew that to do so would rewrite all the history he had just learned.

But the bright illusion of traveling onward, upward, forward hung before him like a glowing Paschal candle. As the meal progressed he felt the death gathering around the table, the death and the ghosts of the dead and the bone-deep tiredness of Desolation Road, and he knew that his town no longer held any future for him. Ruins, a patchwork mishmash of impossibilities, dust, decay, sleep. Desolation Road was dying. His eccentric notion of a place where all would be welcome had seen its day. The world had grown too cynical for such innocence.

Light-years beyond the window of the bedroom Kwai Chen Pak had given Dr. Alimantando the stars shone. He remembered a time when they had seemed close and warm, caught on the branches of the cottonwood trees the night of the first party in the world. He remembered innocence, and naivete, and suddenly the burden of his dream seemed too weighty to bear.

Time was vast. There was a whole eternity for the greenpersons to hide their shining cities. While he still searched he could never be disillusioned. The desert wind smelled green tonight and the lights of the moonring tinkled like wind chimes. He turned away from the window to sleep on his disillusionment and the greenperson was there, clinging upside down to the ceiling like a green house-gecko.

"Greetings of the decreated," it said. "We, the impossible, salute you, the all-too-probable."

Dr. Alimantando sat down on the bed with a start.

"Oh," he said.

"Is that all you can say?" The greenperson pitterpattered around the ceiling on little green feet.

"In that case, how is it, then, that I've searched from world's beginning to world's end for you and have been unable to find you?"

"Because I have come out of nonexistence to greet you."

"So you are a figment of my imagination after all." Kwai

Chen Pak had placed dried herbs under the pillow to aid beneficial dreams; their green fragrance suddenly filled the room.

"No more than you are of mine." The greenperson fixed Dr. Alimantando with its green green eyes. "Remember we talked of destiny? Only it was density, not destiny. You see, this was not your destiny, and because it was not your destiny to which I was leading you disguised as a sprig of broccoli, we have been uncreated."

"Explain, riddlesome creature."

The greenperson dropped from the ceiling, turned cat-agile in midair and squatted on the floor like a green toad. As toad it seemed more man than in its lizard guise but so close Dr. Alimantando shivered at its alienness.

"Desolation Road was never meant to be. We failed once when you were stranded here and founded the settlement, but no matter, we thought, the comet was on its way, destiny was assured. But we failed a second time, a catastrophic time when the comet came. It should have smithereened you into a diaspora to the nethermost parts of the globe; instead, you toyed with history and saved your town at the price-ticket of consensus reality: taking for granted, that is, that both those words are numinous and illusory."

The greenperson drew little moist-finger railroad tracks on the floor tiles and shunted finger-trains across complex sets of points.

"Reality, railroads, and weaving. Eva is close with her tapestry but she does not have enough yarn to weave the other histories of Desolation Road. I am one of those unwoven husk-histories: I would have no existence save for the great time storm that parted momentarily the veils between our realities and permitted me to enter from my unreality, my alternative weaving, and travel at will."

"How could you . . ."

Five green-bean digits raised in a sign of peace and hush.

"Our time-science is greater than yours. Bear me out, my tale will last only a little while. In another time you crossed the Great Desert and on attaining the farther green edge, settled in the small community of Frenchman, a town not unlike that you fled in Deuteronomy, save that its people did not brand you a demon, wizard, or eater of children."

"That's refreshing to know."

The wind was rising outside the window; ghosts and dust were blowing through the alleys around the Mandella home.

"Our shepherding of you—that was not me, incidentally—sparked a fascination with the odd shades of our pelts. 'Green people,' you thought, 'how might that be?' You delved, you experimented, you probed; in short, and I must be short, for I tend to run to verbosity, you developed a strain of symbiotic vegeplasms which, in conjunction with the human bloodstream, rendered it capable of photosynthesizing food from water, sunlight, and trace minerals in the fashion of our sessile rooted cousins." The greenperson upturned its apple-green backside for Dr. Alimantando's inspection. "Observe: no asshole. One of the modifications we made to your original design, together with hermaphroditism—though I doubt you noticed that—psychological polymorphism, which is how you see me as many different things, and Intimate Consciousness, by means of which we perceive, in common with your sessile cousins, the plants, the Universe directly rather than through the analogies and analogues of human perception, and thus we are able to directly manipulate space and time."

Perhaps by a trick of the silvery moonring, perhaps by dint of temporal probability and paradox, the greenperson's features were growing more recognizably human, less greenly alien.

"But none of this came to pass," complained Dr. Alimantando. "I never crossed the Great Desert, so you never came to be."

"Let us rather say that the probabilities were radically altered. The one who guided you across the Great Desert, his probability was significantly decreased, while mine was significantly increased. Time lines converge, remember? You see, the comet was on its way, hooray, hooray, for a year and a year and a year and a day. The history after you abandoned Desolation Road would be slightly different: places, times, characters, but worldlines converge." Finger-expresses collided head on on the spittle-drawn mainline. "The greenpeople would again spring Aphrodite-shelled from your brow, Dr. A, and leap off through time in search of an age and civilization friendly to them. They were persecuted, you know. Brown, yellow, red, black, even dirty white skin—that the world can accept, but green? Green?"

"But you yourself gave me the secret of the Temporal Inversion that was the key to chronodynamism; through it I saved Desolation Road from the comet . . . and destroyed you."

"Well reasoned, my good doctor, but not quite correct. You did not annihilate me, you gave me life. I am the product of the stream of events you set in motion."

"Your riddling grows wearisome."

"Patience, patience, my good doctor. You see, I am not the greenperson who guided you across the Great Desert. You uncreated him, poor child, though I think that maybe he will come to be again, and maybe again guide you across the desert of grit and the desert of stone and the desert of sand. Time lines converge. No, I am another greenperson entirely. Maybe you have seen me before?" Dr. Alimantando studied the viridian features and they seemed to him somehow familiar, a memory, an unplaced recognition cast in jade.

"Now, the totally unacceptable part of the evening," announced the greenperson. "Though I should not exist, I do. There must therefore be an extra-scientific reason for me; a miraculous cause." The greenperson balanced on one leg. "One leg, ten legs, a thousand legs, a million legs: all the legs of science will never stand balanced unless the one leg of the miraculous supports them." It set its leg down, bent, stretched. "The science which doesn't include that which it can't explain is no science at all."

"Superstitious nonsense."

"Those tree-dwelling arboreals you visited, they have a science, too, the study of the unstudiable. The things we call mystical and magical, the sciences of the higher orders of organization which distills like sweet nectar down the coils of Helix of Consciousness: this is their study. They study the unstudiable to know the unknowable: what is so great about knowing only what can be known?"

"You riddle and rhyme as readily as ever," said Dr. Alimantando, temper prickling.

"Alliteration! I love alliteration! You want a riddle? Here's a riddle: what is my name?"

Dr. Alimantando harrumphed in annoyance and folded his arms.

"My name, good doctor. Know my name and you know everything. A clue: it's a proper name, not a jumble of letters or numbers, and it's a man's name."

And for the same reason that people, however reluctant, are unable to resist a game of I Spy with My Little Eye, Dr. Alimantando began to guess names. He guessed and guessed and guessed into the dark and the cold of the night, but the greenperson, squatting amid sticky train tracks and growing more unplacably familiar with the passing hours, just shook its green head and said no no no no no. Dr. Alimantando guessed until his voice was hoarse and the first glow of dawn began to light the edge of the world but the greenperson still said no no no no no.

"Give me another clue," croaked Dr. Alimantando.

"A clue, a clue," sang the greenperson. "A clue then. It's a common name from your old home country, friend. I am a man of green Deuteronomy." So Dr. Alimantando listed every family name he could remember from his youthful days in Deuteronomy.

". . . Argumangansendo, Amaganda, Jinganseng, Sanu-sangendo, Ichiganseng . . ." and still the greenperson shook his head (growing increasingly familiar with every syllable of the tongue-rolling Deuteronomy names) and said no no no no no. As the world tipped its rim beneath the edge of the sun, Dr. Alimantando's imagination was empty and he said, "I give up."

"Done them all?"

"All of them."

"Not quite true, good doctor. You've left one name out."

"Yes, I know."

"Tell me that name."

"Alimantando." And the greenperson reached out his hand and touched his finger to Dr. Alimantando's and the hand was his own and he penetrated in a sparkle of green light to the heart of the mystery. The Ring of Time, the great Annulus within which all things circled, must heal itself of the wounds his toying with history had opened. Beyond the outer edge of the ring and at its hub flowed the miraculous which had broken into time to ensure that the greenpeople would come to be by making him his own creation. From eons hence one of the sons of the future would lead him by his bootstraps across the Great Desert: that greenperson was not the greenperson who now confronted him, for that greenperson was his future self. He now knew from whence the red chalk scrawl on his ceiling had come. He had given himself his own greatest desire and in doing so had embarked himself upon the green chronodynamic merry-go-round, which had at first taken him away from his destiny to be father of the greenpeople, but had in time brought him to this miraculous moment of genesis. The Great Annulus was healed and whole. The future was assured, the past immutable.

"Let it be," said Dr. Alimantando.

Miraculous greenness flowed from the greenperson's fingers into Dr. Alimantando. His hand turned green, his wrist, his arm. Dr. Alimantando cried out in alarm.

"There will be some pain," said the greenperson. "There always is at a birth."

Dr. Alimantando tore at his clothing with ripe green fingers and it came away to reveal the green tide sweeping across his body. He fell to the ground with a wail, for even as the last trace of brown was washed from his outer form, the inner man was beginning to transform. Green blood surged through his veins, displacing the crude meat-red fluid. Hormonal glands squeezed and swelled into new shapes, organs twisted or shriveled to the dictates of the alien functions of the green lycanthropy. Juices trickled, glands stirred, empty spaces collapsed inside him. Dr. Alimantando rolled and writhed on the floor tiles for time out of mind and then it was complete. The dawn light streamed through the window and by its sustaining light Dr. Alimantando explored his new body.

"You to me, me to you, we to we," sang the greenperson. "Behold thy future self." Greenperson stood before greenperson, twin statues of jade. "The future must preserve itself, the greenpeople must come to be, therefore the miraculous broke through and made you me. Now, are you coming with me? There's an awful lot to do."

"An awful lot," agreed the greenperson.

"Indeed," said the greenperson, and there was a sudden aroma of new-mown hay and ancient redwood forest and fresh-turned soil after rain and wild garlic in the hedgerows of

Deuteronomy, and in a single step the green men walked a million million years into the dreamtime.

At six minutes of six heavily pregnant Kwai Chen Pak Mandella (wife in name and not law, for there was no longer any law in Desolation Road capable of recognizing marriages) came knock knock knocking on the guestroom door with a tray of breakfast. Knock knock knock no answer knock knock knock no answer so she said to herself, he must still be asleep, and entered quietly to leave the tray by the bedside. The room was empty, the window open. Dust had blown onto the bed, which did not seem to have been slept in. On the floor the stranger's clothes lay strewn and ripped, and among them the curious Kwai Chen Pak found a curious thing; a paper-thin silvery skin in the shape of a man, dry and scaly, flaking in her fingers, as if some strange desert snake had shed its skin and departed in the cold of the night.

69

It was raining the day they broke into the sealed house, the man and the two women; a weighty, penetrating rain, falling heavily from heaven, punishing the earth. Prior to that Tuesday it had not rained for three years. There was a dreadful smell in the sealed house, the smell of something that had begun to die years before but was not yet done dying. Thus Rael Mandella, Jr., was prepared when he found the body in the chair by the fire though the shriveled skin and bared teeth and staring, mummified eyes drove a little cry of fear from him. Hearing the small cry, Santa Ekatrina at once took Kwai Chen Pak back to the house, for if a corpse were to pass a pregnant woman, the child would assuredly be stillborn. So Rael Mandella, Jr., carried the paper-light corpse from the sealed house on his own and all alone he dug a shallow grave in the puddingy soil of the town cemetery. The rain ran down his face and his neck and his bare arms and filled up the grave, and because there was no mayor and no priest to say the proper words he bent his head and said the consignatory sentences himself, in the pouring, drenching rain. When the grave was covered with puddingy soil, he hammered in a wooden headboard and painted on it the words "Genevieve Tenebrae: founder citizen of Desolation Road," and because he did not know dates or places, he wrote the simple epitaph: "Dead by a broken heart." Then he splashed back through the red mud to his hearth and wife and his soul was heavy because now there were only the Mandellas left.

Weaving by gaslight in her loomroom, Eva Mandella saw the end of time stretched across her tapestry frame. She tied off Genevieve Tenebrae's life-threads and wove them back into the ground. So few threads remained.

"Where do they lead, what is their future?" she asked the hissing gas jets. They knew and she knew, for both the gas jets and she had worked upon the tapestry of time too long for them not to know the shape of it, the cut of it, and that the form of what had been woven demanded the form the unwoven must take. The end of all things was approaching; all the threads led into the red dust and beyond that she could not see, for the future was not the future of Desolation Road. She wove fearful of that future under the hissing gas lamps and all the while the thread ran down to nothing through her fingers and the rain rained down.

For three days the rain rained as no rain had ever rained before, not even when The Hand sang one hundred and fifty thousand years of rain out of the dry, mocking sky. Rael Mandella watched the rain from each of the hacienda's windows in turn. From those windows he saw the dashing rivers of rainwater swirl away the next season's crops and it seemed to him that he heard the laughter of the Panarch in the heavy drops: divine syllables telling him that the future was not for Desolation Road. For three days it was so, then the gray clouds curdled, the sun broke through the intestinal moilings, and a great wind from the south drove the rain before it and left the world steaming and vaporing in the fifteen-minutes-of-fifteen sun. That night, cries broke the meditative desert quiet: terrible, racking cries filled with fear and anguish, the cries of a woman in labor.

"Whish whish whish, easy there, little chicken-bones, little piece-of-the-moon, let it come, let it come, come on. . . ." Santa Ekatrina pleaded and Kwai Chen Pak, little chicken-bones, little piece-of-the-moon, squeezed and huffed and let out another racking cry which sent Rael, Jr., fretting in the parlor with his mystical grandmother, leaping up from his chair and reaching for the door handle. Toward dawn Santa Ekatrina turned that door handle and summoned her son into the birth room.

"It's near now, but she's very weak, poor child. Take her hand and give her all the strength you can."

As the sky began to lighten scarlet and gold, Kwai Chen Pak's eyes opened wide wide wide and her mouth stretched ohahoh big enough to swallow a world and she squeezed squeezed squeezed squeezed squeezed.

"Come on come on come on come on come on," whispered Santa Ekatrina, and Rael, Jr., closed his eyes because he could not bear to see what was happening to his wife but he gripped her hand as if he would never let it go again. "Come on come on come on come on come on," then there was a gasping cry and Rael, Jr., opened his eyes to see the ugly red squawling thing in his wife's arms and the sheet was stained red and black with vile, evil female things.

"A son," said Santa Ekatrina, "a son." Rael, Jr., took the tiny red squirming thing from his wife and carried it out into the morning, where the sun cast giant shadows across the land. Gently, passionately, Rael, Jr., carried his son through the ruined fields and laneways to the edge of the bluffs and there held the boychild up to the sky and whispered his name to the desert.

"Haran Mandella."

Lightning answered along the horizon. Rael Mandella, Jr., looked into his son's empty black eyes and saw the lightning crackle beyond the open pupils. Though those eyes could not yet focus on his face, it seemed to him that they saw into a greater, wider world than that bounded by the circle of the horizon. The dim rumble of the thunder disturbed Desolation Road's weary ruins, and Rael Mandella, Jr., trembled, not by dint of the rolling thunder but because he knew from the eyes that he held in his arms the long-awaited complete one who ended the curse of the Mandella generations, the child in whom mystical and rational were harmoniously reconciled.

The thunder shivered the red rocks of the sub-cellar where Eva Mandella's thread of time wound itself onto the tapestry frame and the gas jets trembled in anticipation and whispered "red dust red dust red dust." History was closing its wolf-jaws behind Eva Mandella: she was now weaving events only minutes old into the history of Desolation Road. The birth of a son, the thunder; her fingers warped the threads with a hasty dexterity that frightened her. It was as if Desolation Road were impatient to be rid of itself. Her fingers wove through the present moment and on into the future, the end times she remembered from the tapestry Dr. Alimantando had shown her. Dust red, red dust, it was the only thread that remained, it was the only color that would finish the tapestry and make it whole. She wrapped a long pick of dust red onto her shuttle and completed the history of Desolation Road. As the thread ran down to a nubbin end and history ended, Eva Mandella saw the gas jets shudder and felt an alien breeze stroke the backs of her hands.

Finished. The tapestry was finished. The history was complete. Desolation Road, its beginnings, its endings, were written here. She traced with her fingers the four threads that led onward, outward, through the end times into the future. One thread had been started only minutes before, its ending she could not see in the gathering gloom though she sensed with a sudden mystical shock that it led out through the rocks and stone into a place beyond her understanding.

Of the thread of her own life she could not find where it ended. She could trace it from its starting place in far New Merionedd along the silvery line to the green place within the storm; she saw the twin threads of mysticism and rationality issue from her womb, she followed herself down the years of tranquility and tragedy until she reached the place where the thread joined the annihilating dust, and there it was lost. It did not end, it was not snapped or cut, it was simply lost. Yet hints of its color spread throughout the tapestry. Perplexed, Eva Mandella placed her finger on the point of junction and a strange thrill ran through her. She felt light-headed, girlish, lost in innocence. She felt herself floating, attenuating, dissolving, all her hopes, dreams, fears, loves, and loathings turned to glittering dust and fell into the tapestry. Eva Mandella's body grew insubstantial and transparent. She passed body and soul into the latticework of threads that was the history of Desolation Road. For her part in the history was to record, and through recording become that history. The time-tapestry sparkled with the silvery love of Eva Mandella, then a gust of the alien wind reached into the room and snuffed out the hissing gas jets.

The wind was rising, gusting, and buffeting maliciously, a forewarning of the brown dust-rollers combing in across the Great Desert. The dust storm broke across the wasteland in a hurricane of flying needles and a fury of lightning. Drawn to the earth by the Crystal Ferrotropes, the lightning bolts crashed and blasted them to black wind-whipped powder. The Great Dust Storm was coming, growing greater, stronger, more hungry with every meter it advanced across the dune fields. Rael Mandella, Jr., pressed his son to his breast and ran before it. Needles of dust whipped at him as he squeezed through his door into his home.

"Quickly, quickly, the Big Dust is coming," he cried. Son and mother wrapped themselves in headcloths and mittens and braved the searing sandscour to stable the animals and shutter the windows. The Big Dust crashed upon Desolation Road in a screaming and howling of demons. In an instant the air was opaque, abrasive, deadly. With a shrill of windblown sand every centimeter of proud paintwork was stripped, sanded, blasted down to bare wood and metal. Trees were planed, then whittled, to matchsticks, the metal gantries of the wind-pumps shined to silver brightness. The black lozenges of the solar-collectors were pitted and cracked; before the afternoon was done their black glass faces lay ground to wind-rounded pebbles.

The dust storm blew on into the night. Kwai Chen Pak, lying on her bed of birth, baby Haran hunting blindly for the nipple, listened to the wind shrieking round the rooftiles and cried out in fear, for suddenly it seemed to her that every demon from Desolation Road's demon-haunted past was howling for her flesh. Santa Ekatrina and Rael, Jr., did not hear the cries of irrational panic. They searched by candlelight the wind-gusty rooms and cellars for Eva, who had vanished as the storm broke upon the Mandella house. Rael, Jr., feared her dead and blasted to polished bone but Santa Ekatrina had glimpsed the glowing tapestry and a strange and terrible fear had gripped her. She felt as if the wind had swept into the house and shivered her bones to sand. She suspected, but never said, for she was not sure herself that she believed Eva Mandella had passed into the tapestry and thus returned to the beginning of the history of Desolation Road.

For five days the dust storm scourged Desolation Road. The wind capered around the abandoned hotels and luncheonettes, it swept over the cracked egg-dome of the Basilica of the Total Mortification, it eddied around the humming steel chimneys of Steeltown, and played upon the intestinal pipeworks like a harmonium. It heaped dust upon the skeletons, tumbled walls, filled fields with dunes, wore homes to sand. It split open the stump of Dr. Alimantando's rock house and scattered books, tools, rugs, kitchen implements, bathroom fittings, eschatometers, thanatoscopes, to the end of the earth. The wind blew and blew and blew and stone by stone, brick by brick, grain by grain, speck by speck, it carried Desolation Road away with it. It tried to carry away the Mandella household; it gibbered and clawed, it ripped tiles from the roof and threw them into the air, it shrieked fear and fury at the refugees who daily and nightly dreaded the gust that would whirl away their roof and walls and expose them soft and naked to the knives of the storm.

For five days it was so, then on the sixth morning Rael Mandella, Jr., heard a noise over the screaming wind. He heard the sound of a locomotive whistle. It was not very loud, or very different from the whistling of the wind, but once he had heard it he could not mistake it again.

"A train, a train!" he cried, bustling mother, wife, son into a flurry of cardboard-suitcase packing. "We can escape!" The wind had abated sufficiently for them to wrap themselves in headcloths and heavy burnooses and brave the dust storm. Rael, Jr., released the animals from the stables. Llamas, goats, pigs, chickens, galloped into the dust and vanished. He wondered what might become of them. Then blindly, dust-bound, the Mandella family groped along the suffocated streets of the disintegrated town to the railroad track. There they squatted and listened to the singing of the sand on the polished rails.

Desolation Road was no more. The wind had blown everything away. The houses were gone, the streets were gone, the fields were gone, the hotels and inns were gone, God and Mammon were gone; everything was as it had been in the beginning: bare rock and steel. The refugees waited and waited and waited. Twice Rael, Jr., thought he heard the whistle of a locomotive, twice he leaped to his feet in anticipation, twice he was disappointed. The wind slackened, the orange opacity grew less impenetrable. Baby Haran Mandella warbled and moaned. Kwai Chen Pak pressed him close to her and suckled him beneath the safety of her windproof robes.

"Listen!" cried Rael, Jr., mad-eyed from five days of dust-devils. "There! Did you hear it? I heard it. Listen!" Santa Ekatrina and Kwai Chen Pak listened as bidden and this time, yes, they did hear it, a locomotive whistle, far off down the line. Then a light glowed through the blowing dust and there it was again, the call of the whistle and the last train in history ground into Desolation Road and took the refugees aboard.

As the train pulled away, Rael Mandella, Jr., took his tiny son into his arms and kissed him. The Great Dust passed over toward the north and the sun came out from behind the clouds of dust and shone down on the desolation.

Desolation Road was gone. There was no need for it now. It had served its purpose and could return thankfully to the dust; its time over, its name forgotten.

But its name could not be forgotten, for the things that had happened there in the twenty-three years it bore that name were too wonderful to be forgotten and in the Pelnam's Park district of Meridian its last child grew into manhood: kind, respected, and beloved by all. One summer's day that man's father called his son into the bee-busy garden and said to him,

"Son, in three weeks you will be ten years old and a man: what will you do with your life then?"

And the son said, "Father, I am going to write a book about all the things you have told me, all the wonders and miracles, all the joys and sadnesses, the victories and the failures."

"And how do you intend to write this book? There is more to the story than I have told you."

"I know," said the son, "for I've seen it all written in this." He showed his father a strange, glowing tapestry, of intricate, brilliant craftsmanship, marvelous and magical.

"How did you come by this?" the father asked his son. And the son laughed and said, "Father, do you believe in little green men?"

So he wrote that book, the son, and it was called *Desolation Road*: the story of a little town in the middle of the Great Desert of the North West Quartersphere of the planet Mars, and this is the end of it.

Read the extraordinary short fiction
of the author of **DESOLATION ROAD**

EMPIRE DREAMS

by Ian McDonald

Collected here for the first time are Ian McDonald's
startling short stories. Fresh and vivid, it was
these stories that garnered the author a nomination
for the John W. Campbell Award for Best New
Writer.

Buy **EMPIRE DREAMS** on sale now wherever
Bantam Spectra books are sold, or use the handy
coupon below for ordering:

"PROFOUND AND BEAUTIFUL ...
A TENSE THRILLER."
—Orson Scott Card

MEMORY
WIRE

BY ROBERT CHARLES WILSON,
AUTHOR OF A *HIDDEN PLACE*

Seeking escape from his tragic past, Raymond Keller volunteered to become an Eye—an all-seeing, unfeeling human video recorder. For a long while, this detachment works for Keller—until he meets Teresa, a beautiful and haunted young artist. She's addicted to oneiroliths, the extraterrestrial dreaming jewels which affect their users in a manner unthinkable to Keller ... they make you remember. Now, as he and Teresa become swept up in an international smuggling plot, Keller must struggle to overcome not just his fears and his training, but his wiring as well.

A tense thriller and a moving love story, *Memory Wire* is a dazzling tour-de-force from one of science fiction's most extraordinary new talents.

Buy Memory Wire, *on sale in December wherever Bantam Spectra Books are sold, or use the handy coupon below for ordering:*

Special Offer
Buy a Bantam Book
for only 50¢.

Now you can have Bantam's catalog filled with hundreds of titles plus take advantage of our unique and exciting bonus book offer. A special offer which gives you the opportunity to purchase a Bantam book for only 50¢. Here's how!

By ordering any five books at the regular price per order, you can also choose any other single book listed (up to a $5.95 value) for just 50¢. Some restrictions do apply, but for further details why not send for Bantam's catalog of titles today!

Just send us your name and address and we will send you a catalog!